KATIE ASHLEY

Strings of the Heart

Copyright © 2014 by Katie Ashley

Formatting by Cris Soriaga | BookMarked! Designs

Edited by Marrion Archer | Making Manuscripts

Marilyn Medina | Eagle Eye Reads

Cover Designed by Letitia Hasser | RBA Designs

Sometimes I have the strangest feeling about you. Especially when you are near me as you are now. It feels as though I had a string tied here under my left rib where my heart is, tightly knotted to you in a similar fashion—
Charlotte Bronte, *Jane Eyre*

Never let anyone pull at your heart strings unless they plan on permanently tying them to their own—
Anonymous

There are strings in the human heart that had better not be vibrated.—**Charles Dickens**

To my readers, thanks for the Runaway Train

love.

You rock my socks!

Prologue: ALLISON

"**G**o on, Allison," Mallory urged.

"Yeah, do it now!" Kim chimed in, as she nudged me forward.

I tore my gaze from staring out the ballroom's glass doors back to my two best friends. Their bright eyes danced with a mixture of excitement coupled with the champagne we'd been sneaking when the adults weren't looking. I'd downed two flutes myself, and it was strictly the bubbly fueling my courage at the moment to give in to their dares.

"He's alone for the first time all night. It's the perfect time," Mallory said.

Gnawing my bottom lip between my teeth, I shuffled indecisively on my heels while wringing my hands. Turmoil raged within me about my potential course of action. "I know, but…"

"But what?" Kim pressed.

"What if he laughs at me?" My eyes widened in fear at the wild thoughts galloping through my head. "What if he won't do it, and then he tells Jake what I asked him?"

Mallory rolled her green eyes. "Quit stalling, and just do it!"

Kim nodded. "You'll always regret it if you don't."

I threw both of my hands up in defeat. "Fine, fine. I'll do it." I wagged a finger at them. "But if it goes horribly wrong, I'm never speaking to either of you again."

With a laugh, Mallory said, "Yeah, right."

Glancing over my shoulder, I searched through the crowded room teaming with party guests for my parents. Relief flooded me at the sight of them completely occupied. Although intrigued by why my older brother, Jake, stood before them soaked to the bone in his dress suit with a sheepish grin on his face, I managed not to let my curiosity get the better of me for once. Instead, I focused on the task at hand.

Just the thought of what I was about to do sent my spray tanned legs shaking beneath the yards of satin on my Sweet Sixteen gown. I took a few deep breaths to try and calm my nerves. The last thing I needed was to pass out and have my dress around my head for all my friends from school to see. I'd picked the lavender perfection a few weeks before. It was exactly like what I had envisioned when I'd made sketches of my dream dress. The bodice was encrusted with silver sequins and beading while the bottom of the gown flowed out, making me look and feel like a Disney Princess.

I tried my best to tune the voices of doubt out of my head. On my trembling legs that reminded me of the new colt at Jake's farm, I pushed myself forward and headed out the door into the courtyard. Standing in front of the sparkling fountain was the man I'd been in love with for the past three years. Rhys McGowan—the bassist for the world famous band, Runaway Train, and my older brother's best friend. The man who had no idea how I truly felt about him because all he saw me as was Jake's kid-sister. But that was all going to change. Tonight I was going to make him see me as more.

For a moment, I could only stare at his broad back, watching his movements as he smoked his cigarette. In an instant, I was transported back in time to the first time I'd met him. My older sister Andrea and I had gone up for a weeklong campout at Jake's farm. I didn't know at the time that he had invited his new bandmates to come along. The guys were just starting out, playing weekends at Eastman's Pub in downtown Atlanta. I knew AJ because he was our next-door neighbor when I was little, but the two other guys, Brayden and Rhys, I'd never seen before.

The moment Rhys stood up from his lawn chair and held out his hand to me, I was a goner. I liked every single thing about him, from his bygone era manners to his wavy dark hair and chocolate brown eyes. He was younger than the other guys, and somehow that made him seem more accessible to my teenage self.

But my love for him was sealed the next day—the day he became my true knight in shining armor. During a swim at the waterfalls on Jake's land, I was deep underwater when I swam by a downed tree and became entangled in the branches. Panicking, I flailed left and right, but I couldn't seem to get loose. And then out of nowhere, Rhys's strong arms pulled me free. When I reached the surface, I was coughing and sputtering between fearful tears. "Hey now, don't cry. You're okay," he had said, pulling me against his bare chest.

I'd melted against him. Even after I could breathe again and knew my life was no longer in danger, I couldn't bring myself to tear away from him. Instead, I kept trembling all over from my growing feelings, which Rhys mistook as me still being shaky from almost drowning. When he started rubbing wide circles over my back, I sighed with contentment.

I jumped at the sound of a voice behind us. "What the fuck do you think you're doing?" Jake demanded.

A chuckle rumbled through Rhys's chest. "Easy man. I'm not putting the moves on your baby sister."

"Yeah, well, that's what it looks like to me."

A whimper escaped my lips as Rhys gently took my arms and extracted me from his embrace. He then turned back to Jake. "She got tangled in that downed tree and almost drowned, you ass." He shook his head. "I don't like to think what would've happened if I hadn't seen her."

A shudder rippled through Jake as he processed Rhys's words. "I-I didn't know. I'm sorry," he replied, as he took long strides in the water to come to my side. He wrapped his arms around me. "Oh, Allie-Bean, thank God you're all right. I don't even want to fucking think of anything bad happening to you." Once again, a shudder rippled through him.

He placed a tender kiss on the top of my soaked head. "It's all right. I'm okay," I said, never taking my eyes off Rhys.

When Rhys winked at me, my heart fluttered, and once again, I found myself fighting for breath. "Yeah, she's fine. She's tougher than she looks," he said.

"Come on. Let's get you inside," Jake said.

"No, I want to stay," I insisted, unable to bear the thought of being deprived one second with Rhys, my savior.

"Are you sure?" Jake asked, concern etched on his dark brows.

"Hell, Jake, quit babying her. She said she's fine," Rhys countered.

"Fine. But just be careful, okay?" Jake replied.

I bobbed my head. "I will. I promise."

With a final glance at me, Jake swam back over to where the others were. As Rhys turned to me, the sunlight hit the water droplets on his face, causing him to have an almost angelic glow. He gave me a beaming smile. "Stick close to me, and you'll be fine. I won't let anything happen to you."

"Thanks," I murmured.

Now three years later, I still loved Rhys with all my heart and soul. Of course, he didn't actually know how I felt about him. And there was no time like the present to let those feelings become known.

"Hi Rhys," I said.

At the sound of my voice, he whirled around. "Hiya Allie-Bean," he said, tossing his cigarette to the ground. As he stomped out the glowing embers with his shoe, I wrinkled my nose both at the smell of the smoke and at him using Jake's old nickname for me. "What are you doing out here?"

I shrugged. "I could ask you the same thing."

"Well, I decided to have a smoke after finding your brother and Abby swimming in the fountain."

I widened my eyes in surprise. "Is that why he's all wet?"

Rhys laughed. "Yeah, it is. Not quite sure how they both ended up soaking wet, but I'm sure there's a pretty good story about how it happened." He winked at me. "Maybe even a naughty one."

A warm flush filled my cheeks at his words and gesture. From the smoldering looks Jake had been giving his new girlfriend all night, I could imagine there was *definitely* something naughty behind why they ended up in the fountain. But I had also been glad to see the way he looked at her with love in his eyes, too. Since I was a romantic at heart, I hoped he had found someone to settle down with.

Shifting on my heels, I cleared my throat. "I just wanted to say thanks again for playing at my party. It was amazing."

Rhys grinned as he reached in his pocket. After he dug out a tin of mints, he popped a couple in his mouth. When he offered me one, I shook my head. "You're welcome," he said.

Taking a few tentative steps closer to him, I said, "You always seem to be doing nice things for me. I mean, you saved me all those years ago and now you're making my Sweet Sixteen something that everyone will be talking about at school on Monday."

"Regardless of the fact that Jake would've whipped my ass if I had said no to your party, I was glad to do it." He cupped my chin. "Anything for you, Allie-Bean."

His simple touch sent my heartbeat thrumming wildly in my chest. Since it seemed so loud in my ears, I hoped that he wouldn't be able to hear it over the roar of the fountain. "I'm glad to hear that," I whispered breathlessly.

"I have something for you."

"Y-You do?"

He cocked his dark brows at me. "Do you think I'd come play at your birthday party without getting you a gift?"

"The fact you came and played is more than enough of a present," I countered.

He reached in his suit pocket again. This time he brought out a small jewelry box with a pink bow. He thrust it at me. "Happy Birthday, Allie-Bean."

Oh. My. God. He'd gotten me jewelry? With shaky hands, I reached forward and took the box from him. I don't know how my trembling fingers managed to undo the bow, but when I did, I slid it off and opened the lid. Peeling away the tissue paper, I found a round pendant on a silver chain. A hand-painted white magnolia with glittering leaves of vibrant green filled the pendant. "Oh, it's so beautiful," I gasped, as I took it into my hand.

"You really like it?" he questioned, his voice lacking the confidence it usually had.

"Yes. Yes, of course I do," I quickly replied, never taking my eyes off the necklace.

"When I saw it, I thought of you. A magnolia is a delicate and pretty Southern symbol, and you're a pretty Southern girl."

"I've always loved magnolias. Wherever did you find it?"

"My sister makes them. Well, she paints them."

I jerked my gaze up to meet his. "Your sister?" In the three years I'd known Rhys, he'd rarely talked about his family, least of all mentioning a sister. I had assumed that he was an only child.

His expression saddened as he rubbed his neck furiously with one of his hands. "Yeah, my younger sister, Ellie. She's really talented when it comes to painting."

"We have something in common then," I said, thinking about how I loved to draw and sketch. My dream was to one day become a fashion designer and have my own clothing line.

"Yes, you're both artistic," he murmured softly.

Sensing that was all I was going to get out of him, I smiled and replied, "Please thank her for me, and tell her what beautiful work she does."

Gratitude replaced the sadness on his face. "I will."

I held out the chain. "Will you put it on me?"

He frowned. "But it doesn't match your dress."

"I don't care. I want to wear it."

"You seriously want to wear it now?" he asked incredulously.

There was something so endearing about how much he wanted the necklace to please me. It made me want to throw my arms around his neck and smother his face with grateful kisses. "Of course I do. I think it's my most favorite gift I've received tonight."

As he took the chain from me, his lips quirked up, as if he was smirking at me. "I think you're just humoring me."

Furiously, I shook my head from side to side, trying to show him my sincerity. "No, I'm telling the truth—I promise." I turned around and lifted up my mass of loose curls so he could put the necklace on me. Once I heard the clasp fasten closed with a snap, I turned around. "Thank you, Rhys. I'll always think of you when I wear it."

He gave me a genuine smile that melted my heart. "You do that." As I absently ran my fingers over the magnolia, Rhys asked, "Now was there a reason why you came out here to see me, Allie-Bean?"

My fingers froze as I felt a warm flush fill my cheeks. "Oh, um, never mind. It wasn't important."

"Sure it was."

I nibbled on my bottom lip. "I just wondered if you would…" I swallowed hard, trying to muster my strength.

"If I would what?" Rhys prodded.

"Give me a birthday kiss," I whispered.

When a beaming smile lit up his face, I felt like I might combust. "Well, I'm happy to oblige your request, young lady." He leaned in and bestowed a tender kiss on my cheek. I couldn't hide my disappointment, and I guess he noticed when he pulled back. "What's wrong? Don't tell me I did it wrong," he teased.

"No, you didn't. It's just…" While my heart beat out-of-control, the voice in my mind was strong as it goaded me. *Go on, Allison. You can do it.* "I wanted a real kiss from you."

Rhys's smile instantly faded. His brows shot up into his hairline as his chocolate brown eyes widened in disbelief. "You want a *kiss* from *me?*"

I couldn't believe I was still standing in front of him, least of all bobbing my head. "I want you to be my first kiss," I blurted before I could stop myself.

"Sweet Sixteen and *never* been kissed?" he questioned almost incredulously.

His surprise caused embarrassment to flood my face. "Not properly really—not by someone I *really* wanted to kiss."

"And you want to kiss me?"

"Yes. Very much," I whispered.

A strangled noise came from the back of his throat. "I can't believe this," he murmured.

I glanced down at my silver heels peeking out from my hemline. "I'm sorry."

Rhys's fingers gripped my chin and lifted my gaze to his. "Don't be sorry, Allie-Bean. It's just, you're jailbait for me," he protested.

"But it's not like that really."

"Oh, I'm sure Jake and your parents would certainly disagree."

Although part of me wanted to turn and run, I stood my ground. I'd come too far to give up now. "It's just a kiss. No one will ever have to know but you and me."

With a wry look, he said, "And your two friends who practically have their noses pressed to the glass right now watching us."

I whirled around to glare at Mallory and Kim. With a hasty flick of my wrist, they instantly backed away from the window and then disappeared. "Sorry about that," I mumbled.

When I dared myself to glance at Rhys, he appeared to be raging war on himself. I took a tentative step forward, closing the small gap between us. In a voice I almost didn't recognize, I said, "Make this the happiest night of my life by kissing me."

"But if Jake caught us or found out—" Rhys cast a glance around the patio as if searching for Jake's wrathful gaze.

"Please, Rhys."

"Okay, fine." When he was assured we were truly alone, he cupped my face in his hands. I sucked in a breath, my already frantic heartbeat accelerated into a wild gallop. In a dizzy flurry, the patio began to spin around me. As his mouth hovered over mine, Rhys whispered, "Happy Birthday, Allison."

The instant his mouth touched mine, I trembled from head to toe. His lips were everything I dreamed they would be—warm, soft, commanding, consuming. I could have stayed in that moment with Rhys's hands on my face and lips on mine for the rest of my life. While I would have preferred the slick feel of his tongue against mine, Rhys kept the kiss incredibly chaste.

When he pulled away, I blinked my eyes several times before they would focus. Surprise flooded me to see Rhys staring down at me with an almost dumbfounded expression on his face. His brows creased in confusion, and he appeared to be unable to speak. His reaction was nothing like I had expected.

"I...I have to go," he murmured, before he started backing away from me.

"Thank you," I said.

He didn't respond. Instead, he just kept staring at me like he was seeing me for the first time in his life. I'd never seen him look so lost and confused. "Rhys?"

He got to the door of the ballroom before he finally turned around. With his back to me, he reached for the door handle. His hand hovered there for a moment before he glanced at me over his shoulder. His eyes still held the wild, confused look he had earlier. "You're welcome, Allison."

Before I could say anything else to him, he ducked back inside the ballroom. Alone, I tried to sort through the out-of-control emotions careening through me.

Long after Rhys had disappeared back inside, I still remained by the fountain. I knew the instant I returned to my party, the moment would be over—I'd be Cinderella after the clock struck twelve. So I stayed outside, running my fingers over my lips that Rhys had kissed.

As I thought about his reaction, I could only hope that he had felt more than he had imagined. That in that moment, he had seen me as more than Jake's little sister—as someone he could one day be with. Deep down, I believed that someday we would be together. All the things that kept us apart for now—my age, what my parents and Jake would think, his celebrity status—they wouldn't matter.

Regardless of the heartache to come, one day he would really be mine.

1: RHYS

Four and a half years later

The tour bus jostled over a patch of uneven pavement, yanking the delicious, illicit dream of a beautiful, yet faceless brunette out of my mind. Although the dream faded into foggy wisps of images, I didn't even have to shift my hips to realize I had sprung a massive morning boner. With my eyes still closed, I craned my ear to take in the sounds around me. Normally, a morning jerk-off session wouldn't have been an issue when I rode along with Eli and Gabe on the Jacob's Ladder bus—the reigning bachelor's oasis that harbored scantily clad women and free-flowing booze. But they had stayed back the night before in Nashville instead of following us on to Louisville, so I had to bum a ride on AJ and Mia's family friendly bus, which meant I could be interrupted at any moment by a toddler or screaming infant.

Just when I thought it was safe enough to let my hand trail over my bare chest and under the covers, a tiny voice shouted, "Unca Weese!" I had only a millisecond to react before the curtain to my roost was jerked away, and my drowsy world was invaded by AJ's precocious three-year-old daughter, Bella. Somehow in my hazy state, I had the presence of mind to bunch the covers around my waist to shield her innocent eyes from my unfortunate morning wood.

When I reluctantly popped open my eyes, Bella pounced on me. "Oomph, easy, Bells," I grunted.

"Wake up time," she ordered. She propped her elbows on the mattress while swinging her legs back and forth.

I groaned. My idea of when it was time to get up and hers was much, much different. Of course, there was no way in hell I would be able to get up in front of her. Boxers or no boxers, there would be too much explaining to do, and she was just the kind of inquisitive kid to want to know what was going on below my waist. Shifting my hand under the covers, I winced as I cupped myself to keep the sheet from tenting.

Cocking her head, Bella's dark eyes curiously surmised me. "Do you have a boo-boo on your pee-pee?"

Fuck me, was this seriously happening? How the hell was I supposed to answer that question without it resulting in AJ kicking my ass? Pausing for a moment, I tried to find a way to work her question to my advantage. "Um, yeah, I do. Hurts pretty bad, too. So I better lie here a little while longer and let it get better." When she started to crawl onto my bunk, I shook my head. "No, don't wait for me. You go on and get some breakfast."

After a moment's contemplation, Bella asked, "Want Mommy to come kiss it and make it better?"

"Oh, hell no!" I cried, jerking my arm over my eyes to try to bleach out the mental image of Mia anywhere near my dick. Sure, Mia was fine as hell, but she was AJ's wife and a mother. You just don't fantasize about a chick once you've accidentally walked in on her breastfeeding.

Since both her father and mother had mouths like sailors, Bella didn't even bother chastising me for cursing like Jude and Melody would have. Instead, she frowned. "Why not? When I have boo-boos, Mommy makes it feel better when she kisses it."

"AJ!" I bellowed at the top of my lungs. At this point, I didn't care if I woke up baby Gaby. I needed him to get Bella out of here ASAP.

Thankfully, he appeared almost instantaneously to put me out of my misery. "What's wrong?" he asked.

I opened my mouth to explain, but Bella beat me to it. "Unca Weese feels bad because he has a boo-boo on his pee-pee. Why don't you kiss it and make it better, Daddy?"

AJ's dark eyes widened to the size of dinner plates. His mouth opened and closed a few times, but he didn't manage to get any words out. Finally, he sputtered, "N-No I will not be kissing his...*pee-pee*!" He then turned his wrath on me. "What the hell are you doing talking about *your* pee-pee with *my* daughter?" he demanded.

I held up my hands defensively, but then quickly dropped one when I realized I needed to keep one hand on the blanket. "I didn't bring it up; she did. Right after she busted in on me trying to hide my morning wood."

Scrunching up his nose, AJ's expression morphed into one of disgust and anger. "Jesus, dude, would you tone it down? You're on the bus with my kids."

Rolling my eyes, I snapped, "Like I have any control over that shit."

While AJ opened his mouth to argue with me, Bella tugged his hand. Her lips had pulled down in a frown. "But why won't you kiss his pee-pee, Daddy?"

"Because you just don't kiss pee-pees! *Ever!*" He gave her a serious look. "You certainly shouldn't now and especially not even when you're older."

I couldn't help the snort that escaped my lips. "Yeah, right, like you would want Mia to adopt that mantra," I muttered under my breath.

He shot me a death glare while Bella threw up her little hands dramatically, looking a lot like her mother when she was frustrated. "Fine. I's only twying to help." When she started to stomp away, AJ snatched her up and started tickling her, causing her to dissolve into giggles. "Stop, Daddy."

"Not so fast, mija. What have Mommy and I said to you about respecting other people's privacy when we're on the road?"

Squirming in AJ's arms, she replied, "That I's sposed to call for them or knock and then wait for someone to come out. Not budge in thewe."

"Barge in," AJ corrected.

"Wight," Bella replied solemnly.

"But did you wait for Uncle Rhys to come out of his roost?" Doing her best to avoid the question, Bella stared down at the floor like it was the most fascinating thing she had ever seen. That caused AJ to put on what I liked to joke was his stern "Daddy Face." "Isabella Sofia, answer me."

"No," she replied softly. Her gaze went from the floor to mine. "I just wanted to see Unca Weese," she replied, her bottom lip trembling.

Almost instantaneously that often dormant soft spot within me ached at her sad little face. Out of all the Runaway Train guys, I was probably the least kid friendly. But then there were times when my bandmates' kids totally got to me. And this was one of those moments.

Dangling my legs over the side of the roost, I pulled myself into a sitting position. Once I was sure the sheet was still covering me adequately, I said, "It's okay, Bella. Don't cry."

When she started the sniffling, I grimaced. Dammit, there was nothing I hated more than when chicks resorted to crying. Seeing Bella cry was pure agony. "I sowwy, Unca Weese. Don't be mad at me," Bella said, grinding the tears from her eyes.

Leaning forward, I patted her leg. "Aw, I'm not mad at you, sweetheart. Just don't do it again, okay?"

"I pwomise."

AJ glanced between me and his daughter, and then his expression softened. He kissed the top of Bella's head. "All right, go on and get your breakfast."

Bella placed a smacking kiss on AJ's cheek before he let her down. As she went tearing down the hallway, she questioned at the top of her lungs, "Mommy, what's mowning wood?"

At the sound of Mia's shriek of horror, AJ groaned and rubbed his hand over his face. "Maybe having Mia and the girls out on tour wasn't the best idea in the world."

I laughed. "I think it was going fine until Bella achieved mastery in comprehension and talking."

He nodded glumly. "And there's no speaking over her head. She picks up everything that is said. I'm surprised she's not asking Mia if she kisses my pee-pee."

"Give her time."

"Ugh."

"AJ!" Mia called.

"Guess it's time to face the music," he muttered.

"I'll be there in a few minutes to give Mia my apologies. I'm going to go ahead and grab a shower. We're first up for rehearsal, right?"

"Yeah, that's right."

As AJ trudged down the hall to try to explain to Mia why their daughter needed clarification on morning wood, I ducked into the bathroom for a quick shower and shave. Once I finished, I threw on a pair of ratty jeans and a T-shirt. I escaped the confines of the steamy bathroom to find AJ seated at the table with Bella. Mia stood at the stove with Gaby on her hip. As I surveyed them, they looked every bit the picture-perfect family. It was hard to believe they were on a tour bus living a nomadic life for nine months out of the year. Mia hadn't been convinced that she could do a tour with two children, but the other Runaway Train wives, Abby and Lily, had convinced her and promised that with Jake's little sister, Allison, along, there would be plenty of help.

Just the thought of Allison sent a raging burn tearing through my chest like an out-of-control wildfire. Shaking my head, I tried to shake myself of the feelings I was experiencing. Masking my emotions with a smile, I called, "Morning."

"Morning," Mia echoed. After I eased into the kitchen for some much needed coffee, I leaned over and gave eleven-month-old, Gaby, a kiss on one of her chubby cheeks. She grinned and kicked her legs, looking more and more like Bella's mini-me.

In a low voice, I said to Mia, "Sorry about Bella hearing me say morning wood."

She rolled her eyes. "It's okay. I'm becoming resigned to the fact that my daughters will have the foulest mouths in school." Tilting her head, she added, "Maybe I should think about homeschooling, like Lily does."

"There are worse things in life than foul-mouthed daughters, I suppose," I mused.

"I guess so." After I poured a steaming cup of coffee, Mia asked, "Want some pancakes?"

"Sure, I'd love some if you don't mind."

She smiled. "Of course I don't."

Leaning back against the counter, I returned her smile. "I just know that like me, you're not a morning person."

Mia laughed. "That's so true. Trust me, if you had told me three years ago, I'd enjoy cooking breakfast, of all meals, in a cramped tour bus kitchen, I would've thought you were crazy as hell. But here I am."

"Love makes you do crazy things, huh?" I asked.

A dreamy expression came over her face as she gazed past me to where Bella had climbed into AJ's lap as they colored a picture together. "Yeah, it does."

After I grunted disdainfully, I said, "That's exactly why I plan on never being in love."

Shifting Gaby to her other hip, Mia wagged a finger at me. "Oh Rhys, I can't wait to see what happens to you when that special lady finally gets her hooks in you."

A funny feeling rippled through my chest, causing me to rub my pec. It was almost the very same place where I'd had the chest burn earlier. "Whatever," I mumbled, turning to head to the table.

"Wait, could you do me a huge favor?"

"Depends," I replied, after taking a scalding swig of coffee.

She smacked me playfully on the arm before she picked up a bottle off the counter. "Can you run these eardrops over to Jake and Abby's bus? Jules has had a nasty earache, and they ran out this morning."

"Will you have me some extra crispy bacon to go with my pancakes when I get back?" I asked, giving her my best pleading expression.

Mia laughed. "Yes, I will."

"See, there's another reason why I never plan to fall in love. Between you, Abby, and Lily I get perfectly spoiled without any of the commitment hassles of a relationship."

Waving her spatula at me, Mia said, "Watch it, mister, or you'll come back to a bacon-less plate."

I grinned at her before trotting down the aisle. As I pounded down the bus stairs, I couldn't help thinking how much had changed in the last few years for my bandmates. Once upon a time, Jake would have needed more condoms or lube, not baby ear drops. But that had all changed once he and AJ had gotten married and had kids. Lately I felt more and more isolated around my brothers. They were all husbands and family men now, and that was the *last* thing I wanted.

While my bandmates had been very lucky in love, they were the only positive married relationships I'd ever seen. The cynical part of me thought that both Jake and AJ were still in the honeymoon phases, having only been married for a couple of years. Through my own parents and their friends, I'd grown up seeing the emotional wastelands left behind from unhappy marriages. I'd watched my own father shuffle a mistress or two while he and my mother stayed locked in a relationship without mutual respect or affection. In their world, divorce was still somewhat of a social stigma, not to mention a way to disperse with family fortunes.

In the end, I guess I felt like I wasn't a candidate for love. Unlike my bandmates, I hadn't grown up in a loving home with parents who hugged and kissed me. I'd been shuffled to boarding schools and raised by my nanny, Trudie. While I had been in a relationship or two and said the dreaded "L" word, I had never truly felt it. Just being around the relationships of my bandmates showed me I had no fucking clue what romantic love was or how to express it.

So here I was somewhat floundering in the new world I found myself in. Sure, Runaway Train still toured the country to sold-out arenas while playing kick-ass tunes, but it just wasn't the same as it once had been. Unless I went back to Jacob's Ladder's bus after a show, I didn't get to binge drink or potentially get some groupie action like I used to on the Runaway Train bus. We were blessed that our fame and celebrity had grown to where we could all afford our own buses now. Of course, I didn't quite feel like flying solo. Instead, I left the solo buses to my bandmates and their families.

The worst was the fact that AJ, Brayden, and Jake were all on my ass to settle down. Like I couldn't be the swinging bachelor the rest of my life? I guess at twenty-seven I should have been thinking of getting married, but it was really the last thing on my mind. Well, it had been up until a few months ago when my life got shot all to hell.

As I cut through the alleyway past Brayden's bus, I saw one of our bodyguards leaned up against the door to Jake's bus. "Morning, Dustin," I said.

He eyed me with a drowsy expression. "You're up awfully early this morning," he mused.

"I have an alarm clock named Bella."

He laughed as he unlocked Jake's bus. "Those are the worst kind. They don't have a snooze button."

"You got that right."

The musical sound of a cartoon greeted me as I shuffled up the bus steps. Angel, Jake and Abby's Golden Retriever, came to greet me on the stairs with a lick on my hand and a wag of her tail. Baby jabber came from the kitchen table. As I reached the top, I could see five-month-olds, Jax and Jules, seated in their highchairs. "Hey, Abby, I have those eardrops you needed."

But it wasn't Abby who rose from a chair at the table. Instead, she was the living and breathing embodiment of the newest hell I found myself in. To put it mildly, she was the forbidden fruit I had dared to taste. Just her memory conjured the same raging wildfire in my chest as I had earlier.

"Oh, uh, hello, Allison." I don't know why I hadn't anticipated this. When we had pulled out for the new tour, she had been on board Jake and Abby's bus. Since Abby insisted on being a full-time mother, Allison was going to be a part-time nanny for the twins. She was also using the summer break from college to fulfill a prestigious internship at the design school she attended. I couldn't imagine how awkward it was going to be once she started working with our head stylist to get us ready for shows.

Allison gave me a shy, yet guarded smile. "Hi, Rhys. Abby's in the shower, and Jake's still asleep. It's just me and the twins this morning."

I bobbed my head as the realization dawned on me that we were truly alone for the first time since everything had gone so horribly wrong. Since that day in

Savannah when I had broken her heart, we'd always been surrounded by Jake and Abby or my other bandmates. For a moment, all I could do was take in every aspect of her appearance—her waist-length dark hair that was pulled back into a ponytail, her warm brown eyes that stared questioningly at me, her tall, lean figure that I happened to be very well acquainted with. Any man with eyes and a working dick would have found her beautiful and sexy as hell. But I wasn't supposed to look or even touch, and because I had, everything was strained between us.

Finally, I came back to myself to dumbly wave the box in my hand. "Mia said Abby needed these."

Allison took a tentative step forward. When she reached for the drops, our hands touched, and as cliché as it sounds, I felt a zing from my fingers straight to my chest. Quickly, I jerked away from her grasp. Allison's expression saddened at my reaction. "Thank you. Jules really needs these."

"You're welcome," I replied. I glanced over at the twins who were staring me down between gumming their fists. "Well, I better go, so you can get back to feeding them." I forced a smile. "I wouldn't want them to eat their hands or anything."

A tiny giggle escaped Allison's lips at my statement. It felt like music to my ears to hear her laughing at me again. During the three weeks we'd shared in Savannah, there had been a lot of laughter between us. I'd certainly missed it. If I was honest with myself, I'd missed her.

I pushed the thought from my mind as I turned and started back down the aisle. I didn't get far before I skidded to a stop. Frozen, my mind whirled with thoughts. I had to do something or say something. It wasn't going to be long before someone noticed us acting awkwardly around each other. Slowly, I turned around. Allison's gaze was fixed on me as she nervously chewed her bottom lip.

I shook my head. "Listen, things can't keep going on like this between us."

"I know," she murmured.

"The past is the past, and we can't keep letting it cripple us in the present." I literally grimaced after the words left my lips. Not only were they a horrible cliché, but my words made it all seem so simple—as if all that had been said and done between us could be swept easily under the proverbial rug. "I know things were left pretty bad between us when I left Savannah. I am sorry for that. I hope you know I would never intentionally hurt you."

Allison appeared unable to speak. Her chest rose and fell in harsh pants, but she finally bobbed her head. After drawing in a ragged breath, I continued on. "I think the best thing would be for us to forget what happened and try to move on."

"If you think that's best," Allison replied, her voice devoid of emotion.

"I do. Really, it's the *only* thing we can do." When Allison closed her eyes as if she were in pain, I took a few tentative steps toward her. When I got closer, her eyes snapped open, and she jerked away from me.

Rubbing the hair at the base of my neck, I sighed in frustration. "We were friends before. Can't we be friends again?"

"Of course we can," she answered a little too quickly. The wounded look in her dark eyes betrayed her uncertainty.

But I didn't intend to argue with her if she was even partially agreeing. Instead, I threw out my hand. "So, friends again?"

I tried ignoring how her hand trembled as she slipped it into mine. "Yes, friends."

At that moment, the bathroom door flung open. I jerked my hand back from Allison as Abby stepped out in a robe with a towel around her head. Her eyes widened at the sight of me before she gave me a beaming smile. "Hi, Rhys. What are you doing up so early?"

"Bella woke me up."

Abby giggled. "She's a mess, isn't she?"

"Oh yeah."

Crossing her arms over her chest, Abby asked, "So did you come over here hoping I was up cooking?"

I laughed. "No, no. Mia asked me to bring the drops over for Jules."

"Oh, thank you, thank you. We were going to be in big trouble when the last dose I gave her wears off."

"You're welcome." I flicked my gaze over to Allison who was now busying herself with feeding the twins some sort of rice cereal. "So I'll see you guys later."

"Bye, Rhys," Abby said, as she went over to bestow kisses on the twins' cheeks.

I caught Allison's mournful gaze one last time before I started off the bus. It told me all I needed to know; that the words she'd just said were a total lie. Deep down, I knew they were for me as well. But what the fuck else were we supposed to do?

Three months ago a perfect storm had destroyed everything we had once been to each other. A homesick girl all alone in Savannah, my parents' loveless world of perfection and excess, and a bottle of silver tequila became the ingredients that fed the storm that forever changed our lives. And now like the strings on a once finely tuned instrument that had bowed under the tension, we were broken, if not ruined.

2: ALLISON

Three months earlier

As I lounged on the wooden railing of the wraparound front porch, I fought the urge to cry for the millionth time today. Nibbling on my bottom lip, I brought my legs up to rest my chin on my knees. In my hand I held the item that had set off my emotions yet again—my phone. Just as I was trying to delve into my assigned reading of a tome on the life of Coco Chanel, my phone had dinged, alerting me of a text. For most people, a picture of twins sporting matching onesies wouldn't necessarily cue the waterworks. But in my case, it was just a tangible symbol of the homesickness that cloaked itself around me like a heavy coat.

At her baby shower, I had gotten my sister-in-law, Abby, a joke gift to go along with the other presents I'd bought my soon-to-be niece and nephew. They were a pink and blue onesie with the words: *Watch your language, asshole. I'm a baby*! I had done the embroidery myself. Considering the mouth Jake had on him, coupled with his bandmates, I knew the twins were going to be exposed to a plethora of four letter words. Abby had squealed over the onesies, and even Jake had found them funny.

I'd forgotten all about the onesies until the picture had come through via text of my almost one-month-old niece and nephew sporting them with Jake giving a double thumbs-up over their heads. Immediately an agonizing burn tore through my chest, and I wanted so much to be back home where I could hold them in my arms. Although my older sister, Andrea, had married two years ago, she hadn't had kids yet, so Jax and Jules were my first niece and nephew. It wasn't just the fact that I loved babies and children that made me want to be around them. It was more the fact that I was so very close to my family, especially Jake, that I needed to be with them.

So it didn't help that I found myself almost three hundred miles away in Savannah. Not only was I so far from the twins, but the rest of my family, my friends, and everything I held dear in the world. I'd decided that instead of attending the satellite campus for the Savannah

College of Art and Design in Atlanta, I needed to go four hours away from home to gain freedom and independence. With ten and twelve years between me and both my half-siblings, I'd grown up pretty spoiled, not only by my parents, but by Jake and Andrea as well. I'd lived in an almost cocooned world of safety and comfort for almost twenty-one years. There was a part of me that felt to truly mature and grow as a person, I needed to clip the strings that were tied so tightly to my parents. I needed life experiences outside of the comfortable suburb I'd grown up in. Looking back now, I had been utterly delusional.

Practically the moment my parents' SUV, coupled with a U-Haul, left the driveway of my new home, I realized I'd made a *huge* mistake. Now two months later, my misery still hadn't dissipated. Of course, it also didn't help I was licking my wounds from a breakup with my boyfriend of six months right before leaving home. So now I was in a strange city without my friends, family, and a boyfriend. More than anything in the world, I wanted to be back home where everything was familiar and comfortable. In the end, I guess you could say I wasn't a big fan of change.

A lot of people in my situation would have just accepted defeat, thrown in the towel, and gone back home with their tail between their legs. But I wasn't that kind of person. Tenacity resided in my DNA, and I was determined to see at least this semester through. Then, and only then, would I allow myself to pack it up, move myself home, and transfer to SCAD-Atlanta.

Although seeing the picture of Jax and Jules had tested my resolve on seeing things through. They were already growing so fast. I'd flown up the weekend after they were born, but since Jules was in the NICU, I didn't get to see that much of her. Now that they had been released from the hospital, I wanted a chance to snuggle them both.

Knowing that Abby was waiting on a reply, I quickly texted *OMG, J & J look so cute. Would give anything to be holding them.*

Her reply came right back. *Next weekend that u can get free, Jake & I want to fly u up 2 see them.*

A strangled cry came from deep within my throat when I read the text. With shaky hands, I started texting back my thanks. I was wishing I didn't have to work the next day, and I could actually get away. Abby promised to FaceTime with me and the twins soon. I was so thankful that Jake had married such a sweet and caring woman. She had embraced me as the sister she'd never had, and it meant so much.

Long after Abby had texted a final *See u soon*! I remained unable to focus on my assigned reading. Instead, I sat with my head in my hands fighting the urge to cry. Just when I thought things couldn't get any worse, three little words caused my entire world to tilt and spin on its axis.

"Hey, Allie-Bean."

Jerking my head up, I peered down the porch to the top of the stairs where he stood. "R-Rhys?" I stuttered.

He grinned. "Yes, it's me."

"But what are you—" In a rush to see him, I tried sliding off the railing. Instead, I made a total ass out of myself by getting my legs tangled together and falling off the side. Thankfully I only fell into the shrubs that ran the length of the porch. "Oomph," I muttered, as I tried clawing my way out of the greenery that was scratching my bare arms.

"Hang on. Let me help," Rhys said, leaning over the banister.

The last thing on earth I wanted was for him to help me out of the mortifying situation I found myself in, but when I realized I was getting nowhere fast, I relented. I grasped his hands and let his strength pull me back over the railing. Once my feet were back on solid ground, I went to readjusting my top and jeans.

When I thought I was thoroughly put back together, I finally looked at Rhys. "Thank you."

"You're more than welcome. It's not every day I get to save a damsel in distress."

I laughed. "You seem to be saving me more times than I would like to admit."

A genuine smile stretched across Rhys's face. I knew, that like me, he was thinking back to that first weekend we had ever spent together. "At least these shrubs seem a little less dangerous than that downed tree."

"That is true." Rhys snickered for a moment, which caused me to throw him a puzzled look. "I'm sorry. I'm just having a shrubbery moment from *Monty Python*."

"*Monty Python*?"

His eyes widened as he held up a hand. "Don't tell me you've never seen *Monty Python and the Holy Grail*?" When I shook my head, he tsked at me. "We'll just have to remedy that one ASAP. You can't go through life without the cheeky, sarcastic humor that is I."

I smiled at his enthusiasm. "Sounds good to me."

Sweeping his hands to his hips, he asked, "So how are you, Allie-Bean?"

My response to his very general question was to burst into tears. I detested my out-of-control emotions, but the very fact he was standing before me today, not to mention partially rescued me, was just too much. Regardless of other boyfriends over the years, I had never stopped loving Rhys. He was the ideal man that no other guy could ever live up to. He was the dream I hoped to one day come true.

Even though his reflection was wavy, I could make out his concerned expression. Good lord, was it possible for me to do anything else mortifying in front of him? Swiping the tears from my eyes, I said, "I'm so sorry."

"Do I need to go?"

"No!" I shouted a little too quickly. At his raised brows, I tried backpedaling. "I'm sorry for flaking out on you. It's just been a hard day." After a mirthless laugh, I added, "Actually, make that a hard two months."

"Jake mentioned you were a little homesick."

"He did?" Immediately my heart plummeted into my stomach. Of course Rhys hadn't come to see me of his own volition. That would have been far too much to hope for. He had been coerced by my well-meaning brother, which crushed my hopes and dreams.

"Yeah, he asked me to check in on you when I got to Savannah."

"When did you get in to town?"

"Just this morning."

"And you came so soon?" I couldn't help asking while trying not to let my traitorous heart get too excited.

Rhys smiled. "Of course I did. Jake's my family, and that means you're my family, too." He patted my cheek. "Truth be told, I couldn't bear the thought of you homesick and miserable."

"That's so sweet," I murmured.

Cocking his head, Rhys said, "Well, it would be pretty unchivalrous of me to say that you're a good excuse to get out of the house and away from my fucked-up family, right?"

"Just a little."

"So I guess the crying jag there tells me all I need to know about how you're holding up?"

I sighed. "Yeah, pretty much."

Fiddling with his collar, Rhys said, "Jake also said you'd just been through a break-up."

I swept my hands to my hips. "Was there anything Jake didn't tell you?"

"He just said you were homesick on top of the fact your boyfriend broke up with you because he didn't want to do the long distance thing."

With a laugh, I replied, "The long distance thing is just what I told my parents and Jake. There was more to the story."

"Oh?"

"Since you're Mr. Inquisitive today, I'll give you the full scoop. Then you can decide if you'll report in all the details to Jake."

Rhys chuckled. "All right, Miss Sassy, hit me with it."

"Mitchell didn't think our sex life was adventurous enough, so he wanted me to start going to this private sex club his father belonged to."

Rhys's usually tan skin paled, and he staggered back. "Fuck me, I didn't need to know that."

"Well, that's the truth about what happened. We actually broke up a few weeks before I left, but I figured my parents could handle that story better. I mean, if Jake found out, Mitchell probably wouldn't need to worry about his sex life because Jake would render him dickless."

After staring in disbelief at me for a moment, Rhys finally threw his head back and howled with laughter. "Yeah, you got that one right. Of course, I'm tempted to find this asshole myself. Who the hell does he think he is trying to corrupt you like that? He should be happy some beautiful girl wanted to waste her time with him at all."

My heart beat wildly like a jackhammer in my chest at his words. "Thank you. He really was a decent guy. I just didn't know there was all that seedy stuff below the surface."

"Don't let a jerkoff like that bring you down. You're better than that."

"That's sweet, Rhys. Thanks."

"And now I think it's time for a conversation change. Somehow I feel like I fell into the *Twilight Zone* by standing here talking about sex with you."

With a scowl, I countered, "I'm almost twenty-one, Rhys. I'm not a baby anymore." I'm sure my petulant tone did nothing to prove my point. All I needed was to stomp my foot, and I would look like I was throwing a tantrum like a toddler.

"Okay, okay, you're not a baby. That has been fully illustrated to me today," he replied, with a grin.

"Good. Now we can officially change the subject."

Rhys glanced around the porch. "So this is a really nice place. I expected you to be in some of those converted hotel room dorms or any of the other shitty housing for college students."

I laughed. "I lucked out on finding this place in a Craigslist ad of all things."

"You're shitting me?"

Shaking my head, I replied, "Totally serious. Of course, after I met the owner, Cassie, I wasn't too surprised that she listed the room like she did."

Cocking his brows, Rhys inquired, "Is she an eccentric old woman with a house full of cats?"

I grinned. "Actually, she's twenty-five. She rents out four of the five bedrooms."

"Nice."

"My parents were much more sold on me living here than in some of the SCAD dorms, especially since I lived at home the past two years commuting to Georgia State."

With a wink that got my poor heart stuttering and sputtering again, he said, "They wanted to keep their little angel out of temptation and trouble once she went away from home for the first time."

"Something like that."

As Rhys leaned in closer, an impish look twinkled in his eyes. "Tell me, Allie-Bean, how much trouble have you been up to? I promise it'll just stay between you and me."

"Ha, like I'd fall for that one," I countered.

"Scout's Honor," he replied, holding up the three finger salute.

With a sigh, I leaned back against the banister. "The truth is actually worse than anything I could lie about."

"Seriously?"

I nodded. "I don't go anywhere besides school and work."

"Ah, but you could be holding back the truth about what *kind* of work you do. Art students get into all kinds of seedy and salacious jobs. Like nude modeling, for instance."

"I-I don't t-think so!" I sputtered, my face flooding with warmth.

Rhys laughed at my embarrassment. "Then what is your innocent place of work?"

"The same place I worked at back in Atlanta—the Mellow Mushroom. They just gave me a hook-up for the one down on Liberty," I replied.

"You work at Penis Pizza?" he asked, his voice laced with amusement.

"Excuse me?"

He grinned. "Sorry. That's just what the guys and I used to call it when we lived in Atlanta."

I rolled my eyes. "Why am I not surprised by that?"

"Come on. Anyone would call it that with the smiling mushroom head décor."

Holding up my hand, I said, "No need to explain. I get the comparison—I promise."

As a smile continued to play on his lips, he said, "You know, the one thing I love about you, Allison, is that I don't feel like I need to censor myself. Even though you're Jake's little sister and I probably should watch myself, I can be exactly who I am."

"I'm not sure if that's such a good thing or not."

"It's good. I'm sure of it. It's quite a novelty when I'm here in Savannah, that's for sure."

"I'll take your word for it."

"So why don't we get out of here for a little while?"

"Really?"

He nodded. "You said yourself that you haven't been able to see much of Savannah."

"That's the truth."

Opening his arms wide, he said, "Then let me show you all that my beautiful hometown has to offer."

"Okay. Sure, why not? Just let me throw my book inside and get my keys."

Always the gentleman, Rhys bent over and picked up the Chanel biography that had gotten knocked to the floor during my fall. "Thanks for getting that," I said, when he handed it to me.

"You're welcome, Allie-Bean." When I started in the house, he grabbed my arm. "Mind if I see inside?"

"Of course not. I guess it was rude of me not to ask you inside."

"Don't worry about standing on ceremony with me, Allison."

I smiled and held the door open for him. I could tell he was impressed when he stepped inside the foyer. I'm sure it paled in comparison to the mansion he'd been raised in, but it was quite an impressive older home—the kind that Savannah was famous for.

"This place is huge when you get inside," he remarked.

"Yeah, my bedroom even has a sitting area in it. The one way that it's just like the dorms is I have to share a bathroom with one of the other girls." After tossing my book down on one of the marble top tables in the living room, I grabbed my purse and slid it on my shoulder. "Ready."

Rhys turned from craning his head up the staircase to eye me curiously. "Don't I get to see your bedroom?" he asked, causing my stomach to do a flip-flop at the potential innuendo.

Ducking my head, I replied, "Oh, I, uh, well, it's kind of messy."

"That's okay. You can clean it before I come over next time."

"Next time?" I questioned lamely, jerking my chin up to meet his gaze. So this wasn't just going to be a one-time deal of checking in on me just for Jake? He actually wanted to spend time with me? That was a major newsflash.

"Yeah, I thought you could host our movie night of *Monty Python*."

Like an overeager puppy, I quickly replied, "Oh yeah, of course I will."

He smiled. "Good. It's all settled then."

"Ready?" I repeated again.

"Let's go."

After locking the front door, I followed Rhys down the porch steps and onto the sidewalk that ran along Oglethorpe Avenue. "You really haven't been able to explore the city while you've been here?"

I shook my head. "Between work and school, I usually spend my downtime being emo and staying locked in my room." A laugh bubbled from my lips at Rhys's almost horrified expression. "I'm just teasing about staying locked in my room."

"I would hope so."

"The truth is I have been staying pretty busy. I'm applying for a summer internship in fashion design."

"Good for you. What does it entail?"

Giggling, I said, "*Entail*? I don't think I've ever heard you talk so proper than I have in the last ten minutes."

Rhys scowled. "It's a hazard of being back home around pompous sounding assholes. It usually takes me a few weeks of being back on the road with the guys to get it out of my system."

"I like it. There's nothing wrong with an expansive vocabulary."

Cocking his brows at me, he asked, "Are you trying to say using big words is sexy?"

"Mmm, hmm. Totally."

"Then I'll just have to keep giving you an illustrious repertoire of wording, eh?"

"Ooh, I like it very much." Those words were certainly an understatement. I mean, Rhys wanted me to think he was sexy? He didn't say he wondered if other girls found it sexy. Just *me*. Call me crazy that I was probably reading too much into it, but I couldn't help it. I would take anything I could get.

Rhys grinned and shook his head at me. "So what's this internship about?"

Part of me was reluctant to talk about it because I didn't want to jinx it. Getting full college credit for what I wanted to do was almost too good to be true. But Rhys's interested expression made me forget my resolve. "It would be designing and implementing a collection of my own."

"That sounds intense."

"It is. I would receive credit not just for this summer, but it would also take the place of several other fashion design classes."

"Who would you be working for?"

Here was the kicker of revealing everything. After nibbling on my bottom lip for a moment, I replied, "Runaway Train."

"Huh?" he asked, his expression waxing confusion.

"I would be designing and making some of the wardrobe for Runaway Train and Jacob's Ladder. I would also be doing hands-on work with the current stylist."

"Does that mean you'd be touring with us?"

"Yeah, it would."

Rhys's expression was hard to read. It seemed like many different emotions filtered through him. When he smiled, I exhaled a breath of relief. "That sounds like an amazing opportunity, Allison."

"Really?"

"Hell, yes. I mean, it's one thing getting to come out on tour and work firsthand with a tried and true designer and stylist, but then there's the fact that you would be creating your own collection at your age. That's very impressive."

"You sound as if it's a done deal, and I've already gotten it. I won't know for a few more weeks if I'm accepted or not. There are a ton of applicants, too."

Shaking his head, Rhys said, "There's no doubt in my mind you'll get it."

"But how do you know how good I am at fashion design?"

"I don't have to know how good you are at it. I know *you*, and that's plenty enough to tell me that you're one of the candidates at the top of the list."

I couldn't help feeling extremely flattered by his high praise of me and my abilities. "Thank you for believing in me."

"No need to thank me, Allie-Bean." He cocked his head at me. "Now are you ready for our tour?"

"As ready as I'll ever be," I replied, with a smile.

After taking a left, Rhys motioned at an imposing mansion. "Do you know what that is?"

I nodded. "The Juliette Gordon Low House—the founder of the Girl Scouts lived there."

He smiled. "See, you're not totally lost about Savannah culture and landmarks."

"I've never got to go inside it though." Tilting my head, I asked, "Want to be my tour guide there?"

"I would love to." After peering at the sign giving tour hours, he then glanced down at his expensive-looking watch and grimaced. "Unfortunately, it's four and just closing." Flashing a grin, he said, "I could try to use my VIP status, but I'm not sure how many of the tour guides would actually know me."

"I'm sure a lot of the Girl Scouts would. Runaway Train's audience is pretty vast on the age scale."

"Maybe."

"Well, bummer on the tour. Guess that means you'll have to bring me back another day, huh?" I teased.

With a roll of his eyes, he replied, "You act like it would pain me to spend time with you. That is not the case."

"Really?" I asked, as my heartbeat sped up.

"Of course not. Plus, I love history."

As I dodged out of the way of some Girl Scouts leaving the museum gift shop, I eyed Rhys curiously. "Hmm, I never pegged you as a history buff."

He laughed as he shoved his hands in his jean pockets. "Actually, I'm pretty sure I was more of a history nerd."

I couldn't help laughing at the absurd thought of him being a nerd. Sure, it would seem from the way he had been speaking very formally and properly this afternoon that he could be a nerd, but at the same time, I'd spent lots of downtime with him, and he was the furthest thing from a nerd. That wasn't just my crush talking either.

"You can laugh, but seriously, I have photographic evidence of my nerdom," Rhys argued.

"I find it very hard to believe considering who you are now that you were ever even remotely in the category of a nerd."

Rhys tsked at me as he checked left and right for traffic. "I'm going to gloat pretty badly when I show you the pics and get to say 'I told you so.'"

"Ha, we'll just have to see."

We then stepped into one of Savannah's many squares—Wright Square, as Rhys was quick to inform me. He practically dragged me over to a giant rock sitting to the right hand side of the square. "This is the rock dedicated to Tomochichi. When English settlers arrived in Savannah in 1733, he was the Yamacraw Chief who gave them assistance. This stone was erected over a hundred and fifty years after his death…"

As Rhys continued rattling along about Tomochichi, I tried to feign interest when I frankly could have cared less. When he eventually finished, I cocked my head at him and grinned. "Ooh, talk nerdy to me some more," I teased.

He laughed before playfully nudging me with his shoulder. "Twerp." Patting the stone, he said, "What if I was to tell you that the stone had some mystical qualities?"

"Seriously?"

He nodded. "The legend is that if you circle the stone three times while continuously saying, 'Tomochichi,' whatever you wish will come true."

Sweeping my hand to my hip, I eyed him suspiciously. "That sounds like a load of bullshit. Like a very warped 'wish upon a star.'"

Rhys shrugged. "It may or may not be. But isn't it worth trying a chance at having a wish come true?"

I glanced between him and the rock not really believing that at twenty, I was actually going to take superstition seriously. While looking at Rhys, I could tell he was silently daring me to do it. "All right. Fine."

"You're really going to do it?" he asked, a little incredulity in his voice.

"Oh yeah, I'm doing it."

He chuckled. "Guess that internship is a wish heavy on your heart, huh?"

I fought the urge to laugh in his face if he thought that I would actually waste my wish on the internship. Sure, it was important, but there was nothing more important to me than finally being with him. Without another word to Rhys, I reached out my hand and touched the stone. "Tomochichi, Tomochichi, Tomochichi…," I began, as I started speed walking around the rock.

When I made my first lap, I found Rhys grinning at me like the Cheshire cat in *Alice in Wonderland.* Ignoring him, I kept walking and reciting "Tomochichi." Of course, while I might have been saying the dead chief's name out loud, it was Rhys's name I was saying inside my head.

Once I was finished, I took my hand off the stone and turned questioningly to him. "Now what?"

"You just wait for your wish to come true."

"Have you ever done it?"

"Nope. Not even when I was a kid here on a field trip, and the tour guides told us about it."

"Why not?"

He shrugged. "I guess I didn't have anything to wish for."

"Well, that's just sad. Life is all about having wants and desires, isn't it?"

"I suppose so. I just never gave much time and effort to thinking about them."

It was so strange that I had known him for seven years, spent hours and hours of time with him in different places, yet when it came down to it, I felt like I didn't know him at all. He was a puzzle that needed to be solved, but at the same time, I had the feeling that some of the pieces were missing. Pieces that I would somehow have to dig deep to unearth.

"Where to now, Captain Tour Guide?"

"River Street is just a few blocks down there." He motioned to the north.

"Okay, sounds good."

"I'll sweeten the tour by taking you in to River Street Sweets for a famous praline."

"Mmm, I love pralines. I don't think I've been down on River Street since our 8th grade overnight field trip."

"I think you're totally overdue for one then."

As we continued the walk down to River Street, Rhys pointed out different landmarks of interest. He didn't just keep it to a history lesson. He also told me great places to eat and hang out. Of course, I didn't care about any of the places unless he planned to bring me back to them.

When we got down to the cobblestoned pavement of River Street, Rhys and I stopped into a few shops. I especially enjoyed the ones with gag gifts and T-shirts. Once we'd laughed and dared each other to buy several obnoxious ones, Rhys steered me into the huge candy store. The moment I stepped inside, I closed my eyes and inhaled deeply. "That smell is pure heaven," I murmured.

He laughed. "I would have to agree."

After eyeballing the many delicious goodies under the glass, I decided on some chocolate covered pecan clusters along with a caramel apple dipped in nuts. I also added a famous praline. As I munched on one of the samples of chocolate bark, Rhys put in an order that caused my eyes to bulge. "What?" he asked.

"You're getting all that for you?"

"I've been known to have them ship stuff to me when I'm out on tour," he replied, getting out his wallet.

"Who knew you had such a sweet tooth?"

"It's epic. Trust me."

I couldn't help protesting when Rhys had them ring up my sweets with his. "No, let me get mine," I protested.

"It was my idea, so let me treat you."

"But only this one time since I'm a poor, struggling college student, and you're mister money bags."

Rhys laughed. "Whatever." Once he had paid, he gave them his address to ship the candy to. I had been wondering how he would possibly get it out of the store, least of all back to his house.

After that was sorted, we walked back out into sunshine. "Are you hungry?" Rhys asked.

"Maybe a little," I replied, after polishing off my second pecan cluster.

"How about some good seafood?"

"I'd love some."

"Follow me then."

When he started into Huey's, which looked like a higher-end restaurant, I grabbed his arm. "No, I'm not dressed for this place," I hissed, motioning to my jeans and T-shirt.

"It'll be fine."

"No, Rhys, please."

His brows shot up. "Does it really bother you that much? Because I could give two shits about the way you're dressed, and I'm a VIP."

A smile played on my lips at his words. "Are you sure?"

"I'd hardly call my Ralph Lauren shirt and shorts black tie. Besides, it's a tourist trap. Lots of people stumble in not realizing."

"Fine. If you say so."

"Trust me," he said, holding my gaze with his dark eyes.

"Okay," I muttered lamely.

He grinned as we walked up to the hostess stand. When the hostess glanced up from a pile of menus, she did a double take at the sight of Rhys. I think it was safe to say she totally recognized him not from being a hometown boy, but from his Runaway Train fame. "Oh, um, hi, how many?"

"Just two. Can we get a table with a river view?"

"Sure, yeah, one second." She wrote and rewrote some numbers on a whiteboard before grabbing two menus. "Right this way," she replied, with a megawatt smile that belonged on a Miss America contestant.

As she started leading us through the maze of tables, I leaned in close to Rhys. "I'm pretty sure your VIP status just jacked someone else's table for us."

Rhys chuckled. "I'm surprised she even recognized me. The bass player is never the noticed one in a band."

I fought the urge to tell him that not all bass players were as hot as he was. Instead, I replied, "Here I thought it was the drummer lost behind the kit."

"Do you think AJ could ever be lost to fans?"

I laughed. "Not really."

The hostess motioned to our table, which gave us a great view of the river past the crowds sauntering down the street. Once she sat the menus down, she swept a strand of hair behind her ear and smiled broadly at Rhys. "Have a great dinner."

"Thank you. I'm sure *we* will."

Once she was out of earshot, I couldn't help laughing. "Frankly, I don't think she even noticed I was alive. She had total Rhys tunnel vision."

"You say that like it's a bad thing," he teased, as he picked up his menu.

"Now you're starting to sound like Jake or AJ."

"That's an awfully cocky combination."

I laughed. "Exactly." Glancing at my menu, I asked, "So what's good here?"

"Since I've eaten your nana's cooking before, I know you like Southern food."

"What kind of Southern girl would I be if I didn't enjoy collard greens and fried green tomatoes?"

"Not a very good one," Rhys replied. Waving his menu, he added, "This place is fucking fabulous when it comes to Southern food. The fried green tomatoes here are kick-ass. Plus there's low country boil on the menu, so you should be able to get the greens I know you love."

My stomach rumbled in appreciation at his words. "Sounds good to me. Of course, everything looks good."

When our waiter, with the name-tag, Lance, arrived, he had a star-struck moment as well at Rhys's presence. "I know you're here to eat and I don't want to bother you, but I'm a *huge* Runaway Train fan," he said, after he got our drink and appetizer orders.

"Thank you. That means a lot," Rhys said politely. With the charm that I'm sure that had been bred into him from the time he was born, he added, "I'd be happy to sign something for you."

Lance's eyes bulged, and he momentarily fumbled with his leather envelope for taking orders. "That would be awesome. Thank you. Seriously, thank you!"

He then proceeded to back into another waiter and almost mowed him down along with a tray of alcoholic beverages. I had to bring my napkin up to my face to hide my laughter. When I recovered, I put down my napkin and asked, "Who would have thought it would have been the guy who lost his shit for you, rather than the girl?"

"Oh, I guarantee she'll manage to find a way to slip her number to me."

"You can't be serious." When he nodded, I said, "But you're here with me."

He shrugged. "You could be a friend or a sister. To some women it wouldn't matter if I was sitting here with a wedding band on."

"That's disgusting," I huffed, while reaching for my glass of water.

Rhys chuckled. "Why are you getting so incensed?"

"Because marriage is a sacred thing. A woman should see a gold band and understand that a man is off limits."

When Rhys raised his brows at me, I felt warmth flood my cheeks. With just that one action, he had made me realize the irony of my comment. After all, I wouldn't even be here if my parents hadn't had an affair. Obviously, my mother hadn't let the gold band on my father's hand stop her. With my gaze focused on the white tablecloth, I asked, "Mind if we change the subject?"

"I'm sorry."

"It isn't your fault." I glanced up to meet his gaze. "I guess I should say that I truly meant what I said. Regardless of what my parents did, I think cheating is very wrong. It's something I could never do."

Leaning forward, Rhys patted my hand tenderly. "You don't have to worry about it. I know as well as anyone that we are not our parents."

"You're right," I murmured.

"Now why don't I tell you about Jax peeing in my face when Jake made me change his diaper last weekend?"

I giggled. "Oh no, he did?"

Thankfully, the conversation then flowed just as easily between us as it had all day. While it certainly wasn't the first time we had ever been together, it was the first time it had been just the two of us. Usually we were with at least Jake and Abby, if not AJ and Brayden and their families. Rhys wanted to know about the classes I was taking. In between the appetizers of my gumbo and Rhys's fried green tomatoes, I steered the conversation away from me and to him. "So how long are you here in Savannah?"

He took a bite of crispy fried tomato. "It just depends. Two weeks, three weeks, or until my parents drive me absolutely fucking nuts, and I have to flee for my sanity."

My spoon filled with gumbo paused in midair as my heart ached for him. "Is it really that bad?"

With a shrug, Rhys replied, "Now they're more annoying than anything else. Once they realized they weren't going to be able to control my life, they eased up a bit."

"Jake told me once they had disowned you," I said, softly.

"Oh yeah, they did that after I left law school when the band got its first deal. As their firstborn son and keeper of the family name, they were not exactly thrilled I was 'throwing away my life on a foolish dream.'"

Processing his words, I took another steamy bite of gumbo. Once I had swallowed it, I asked, "Did they change their mind when you had more financial success?"

Rhys speared a piece of tomato a little more forcefully than necessary. "No, it had more to do with my grandfather's death, and the stipulations of his will."

"Oh?" I asked, but I was interrupted by the waiter bringing out dinner. Although I was already half full from chocolate and now gumbo, the platter full of fried shrimp, oysters, and scallops made my stomach rumble in appreciation. After Rhys and I both dug in, a silence hung over the table while we began devouring our dinner.

After we both made a dent in our plates, I gave Rhys a sympathetic look. "I'm sorry about your grandfather."

"Thank you. He was actually one of the most decent men I knew in spite of his wealth."

"What was it in his will that made your parents change their minds?"

"One thing my grandfather believed in was family unity and putting on a strong family front to the world. As the only surviving son, most of the business investments would be going to my father. In order to receive them, he could not have *his* only son disowned. So in a way, my grandfather's death paved the way for our reconciliation." With a mirthless laugh, Rhys added, "It wasn't so much that they cared about me. They cared about the money they would otherwise be losing."

I shook my head. "I don't believe that. Your father could have always rigged something on paper and continued ignoring you in real life. He must've wanted a reason to reconnect with you."

After dabbing his mouth with his napkin, Rhys leaned back in his chair. "Not everyone's family is like yours, Allison. They don't all have honest motives for what they do, and most don't experience or share much love. My parents have never hugged and kissed me like your parents do. I don't know if I ever even remember them telling me they loved me." When I gasped in pain for him, he shrugged, "It's just something I've come to terms with over the years, and something I've learned to accept."

"But it's so wrong."

"I don't need your pity. I'm perfectly fine with the way things are."

"No, you're not. I can tell you're putting on a front for me when truthfully, the situation with your parents is something that bothers you a lot."

"Dabbling in psychology along with fashion design, are you?" he asked sarcastically.

"I just don't like to see people I care about hurt. I hate what your parents have done to you so much." Before I could stop myself, I reached across the table for his hand. "You deserve so much more, Rhys."

Disbelief at my words and actions momentarily flickered in his eyes. "You are aware that there aren't many people in the world like you—people who are truly kind-hearted and care about their fellow man."

"Maybe not in the world you grew up in, but there is in your band world. I hope you know how much you're loved by them…by us."

"I do," he said softly.

"You're loved by all your fans, too, but I know that isn't a tangible love. You think that if they really knew you besides your persona that they might not love you. But it's still love and admiration you should appreciate. Take that and couple it with the real love of your band family. So whatever the past was, you just have to see that you have so much love surrounding you now."

"You know, you're awfully wise for just a twenty-year-old kid."

Ouch. Had he seriously just called me a kid? I so did not want to be in "kid" territory. After I recovered from my slight horror, I said, "Well, I'm different because I'm an old soul."

"Yes, you are. That's one thing we have in common. I was always old for my age. I never really fit in with the kids around me. That, plus my intelligence, made me somewhat of a misfit. I didn't exactly feel like I belonged until I met Jake, Brayden, and AJ."

"And they completed you."

Rhys snorted. "That sounds completely sappy and emasculating."

"I like the sound of it. I know Jake had a terrible hole within him that needed completing. You and the guys did that."

"And Abby."

"Yes, she did." Tapping my fork on my plate, I decided to address something that was still bothering me. "For the record, I'm not a kid, okay? I'm pretty sure that you hated for the guys to call you that back in the day."

"Back in the day? Hell, they still pull that bullshit on me."

I laughed. "Am I going to have to have you repeat after me? Allison, you are a woman."

With a scowl, he replied, "I know you're a woman."

"You called me a kid two seconds ago," I countered.

"Even if it's hard for me to believe you aren't the same thirteen-year-old I rescued all those years ago, I am aware that you are indeed a grown woman."

"Good. I'm glad to hear that."

"You're welcome, kid," he replied, with a teasing wink.

"You, sir, are impossible."

"Want some dessert?" he asked.

Tilting my head, I tried reading Rhys's watch. "Wait, what time is it?"

"Almost six thirty."

I slammed my napkin down on the table. "Oh shit, really?"

"What's the problem?" Leaning forward, he gave me an impish grin. "Don't tell me you turn into a pumpkin at eight?"

With a grin, I replied, "Ha, ha, not exactly."

After taking a sip of his wine, Rhys's expression darkened a little. "You didn't tell me you had a date tonight."

"No, it's nothing like that." Part of me debated lying to him and telling him I had to go to work. Where I needed to be was somewhere secret—something I hadn't even told my parents or Jake about. It wasn't something I was ashamed of. It was just something I wasn't sure how they were going to feel about it.

When I continued to remain evasive, Rhys said, "Are you sure? You're certainly acting like there's some mystery man you have to get to."

As he continued staring me down, I finally decided to give in. "Do you promise not to tell Jake?"

Rhys's dark eyes widened. "You're doing something Jake doesn't know about?"

"Seriously? I'm twenty years old. Jake certainly doesn't know half of what I do or don't do," I replied.

"Interesting," Rhys replied.

"You didn't answer me."

Holding up his hands, he replied, "Fine, fine. But only if it turns out not to be something dangerous or illegal."

"Okay, here it is. I have to get back home and change because at ten tonight, I'm singing at Saffie's Tea Room."

Silence permeated the table as Rhys didn't have a quick response or retort. Instead, he sat motionless, ingesting what I had just said. Finally, he replied, "Did you just allude to the fact you're singing at some club tonight?"

"Yes."

"And just how is that possible? You're only twenty."

"The owner happens to be Cassie, the woman who owns the house I live in."

"I see."

Taking my napkin back in my hands, I twisted it nervously at his response. I don't know why I was so concerned with his approval. In the end, he wasn't my parents or Jake. He was just the guy I was completely in love with.

"You see, she has this band that plays during the week. Well, when the lead singer broke up with the drummer, she left the band, and in turn, she left Cassie without entertainment."

"What's the name of this band?"

"Pink Magnolia."

Rhys's brows shot up, sending my already frayed nerves into overdrive. I couldn't help hoping that the name of the band had made him think of the magnolia charm he'd given me on my sixteenth birthday. I was probably desperately clawing at straws on that one. "I see," he once again replied.

"Anyway, so after she heard me singing in my room when I was unpacking, she totally ambushed me to take the singer's place until she could find a replacement. At first, I didn't want to because Jake is the entertainer in the family, not me. Truth be told, I'm not that great a singer. But she was desperate, so I finally agreed to do it."

"Saffie's Tea Room," he repeated in an even voice. "Am I correct in assuming this is named after Sappho, the Greek poetess?"

"Yes, it is," I replied, twisting my napkin a little farther.

"The *lesbian* Greek poetess."

"Yessss," I hissed like the sexual orientation was supposed to matter.

Leaning in on the table with his elbows, Rhys cocked his head at me. "Let me get this straight. You are underage and singing at a lesbian nightclub?"

"Mmm, hmm."

Rhys stared at me for a moment before howling with laughter. "What I wouldn't give to see Jake's face when he finds out."

"It's not funny," I huffed indignantly. "It's a perfectly respectable establishment. And the girls in the band have been nothing but sweet and helpful to me." When he snorted back his laughter into his napkin, I said, "As a matter of fact, I'm having so much fun doing it, I told Cassie not to worry about finding a replacement. I would just stay on until I went back home."

The mention of home sobered Rhys up. "You're going back to Atlanta?"

Glancing down at the table, I sighed. "I guess I'm just a big baby. I miss my parents and my friends. I even miss my dog, Toby. Most of all, it's hard not being able to see the twins whenever I want to."

"But that will change when we go out on tour."

"I know," I murmured.

Reaching across the table, Rhys took my hand. "It's okay to be homesick, Allison."

"It shows a total lack of character strength not to be able to embrace difficulties and challenges."

"Bullshit."

I couldn't help my brows shooting up at his word choice. But then I shook my head. "Oh really? I bet you're never homesick," I challenged.

Sadness flickered in his eyes, and instantly, I regretted my words. "There has never really been much of a home here for me. You don't really bond with your parents when it's your nanny who dries your tears after a nightmare or sits by your bedside when you're sick. When I was far too young, I got shuttled off to boarding schools where I only came home on the weekends. Then I moved to Atlanta for college and now I live on and off of a tour bus." Running his fingertip over the rim of his wine glass, he said, "There's really never been a home for me."

"I'm sorry."

"Don't be. It is what it is. So while it's true I don't really get homesick, there are times I long for Savannah. I get homesick for my nanny, Trudie, for the familiar landmarks, and most of all, for my sister."

Latching on to the mention of his secretive sister, I quickly said, "I hope to get to meet her while you're here."

Refusing to look at me, Rhys stared at his wineglass, lost in thought. "Maybe," he finally murmured.

I didn't have to look at his watch again to know I had to go. As if sensing my need, Rhys jerked his gaze to mine and grabbed his phone. "I'll get us a cab, so you can make it home quicker."

"Thank you," I replied, as Rhys began texting furiously.

After motioning the waiter over for the check, Rhys reached his hand in his pocket for his wallet. When he started to hand the envelope with his card in it to the waiter, I shook my head. "No, please, I can pay for my own," I protested.

Rhys shook his head. "I told you earlier I would treat you to dinner, and I meant it." With a wink, he added, "What kind of gentleman would I be if I allowed you to pay?"

"The kind who believes in women's equality and Dutch treat?"

"Not when it comes to you, my love."

That statement combined with the tender expression on Rhys's face caused a shudder to ripple through me. "Okay, fine then. But when we do movie night, I'm covering dinner. Okay?"

As Rhys rose up from his chair, he grinned. "Will it be Penis Pizza? Because I'll totally let you buy me some of that."

I laughed. "Yes, it will." Wagging my brows, I added, "I'll make sure you get an extra-large slice of sausage, too."

Rhys's eyes bulged at my comment. As we started out of the restaurant, he shook his head. "Not quite the sweet and innocent little Allison I used to know, huh?"

"Not by a long shot."

"I've missed a lot not seeing you as much in the last few years, huh?"

"You have a lot to catch up on."

"I look forward to it."

I tried not letting my mouth gape open when we stepped out onto River Street to a chauffeur driven car waiting for us. "This doesn't quite look like a cab."

Rhys's response was to open the door for me. After I slid across the seat, I glanced expectantly at him. He shrugged. "It's an app on my phone that brings a car to you."

After taking in the sleek interior of the town car, I nodded. "Nice. Very nice."

"I'm glad you like it."

We drove along the dusky streets in silence. Occasionally, when we hit a bump in the road, Rhys's leg would knock into mine. Each time, he would apologize. When the car pulled up outside my house, Rhys once again held the door open for me. He asked the driver to wait a moment, and then he started to walk me to the door. "Would I be overstepping my bounds if I asked to come see your set tonight?"

His question sent me reeling. I had never in a million years thought a Grammy winning musician like him would want to hear me sing with a nightclub band. It seemed like today was the day for wonders to never cease. At my hesitation, he held up his hands. "It's okay. I shouldn't have asked."

"No, that's not it at all."

"It isn't?"

I shook my head. "It isn't that I don't want you to see me perform. The truth is I would be honored. It's just I'm surprised someone like you would want to spend their evening listening to me sing in a lesbian bar." I shrugged. "I guess I thought you had better things to do with your time."

He barked out a laugh. "Well, the setting will certainly prove to be interesting, although it might be nice not to worry about being hit on for once."

"Yes, how troubling it must be for you to be such a handsome and desirable millionaire rocker," I teased.

Cocking his head, he asked, "You think I'm handsome?"

My chest began to rise and fall in rushed, heavy pants as I desperately tried to catch my breath. "Of course I do," I quickly replied. At Rhys's smile, I quickly added, "In your mind, doesn't everyone?"

"I'm not talking about everyone—I'm talking about *you.*"

"Yes, you're very, very handsome, okay? Now can you please get out of my way so I can get ready?"

"Excuse me. I wouldn't dare to deprive your adoring public of your presence."

"Smart ass," I mumbled, as I started digging my keys out of my purse.

As I started to unlock the door, Rhys sidestepped me. Bracing his hand on the doorway, he smiled one of the smiles that had captured my heart when I was thirteen and now made me both lovesick and horny. "My very handsome self will see you at ten tonight at Saffie's Tea Room."

"Okay," I murmured.

Just being in Rhys's presence was enough to make my libido go into overdrive, but when he started to lean in closer to me, I fought the urge to combust from both nerves and hormones. It didn't help that he smelled so amazing, or that I could feel the heat pouring off his body. Feeling lightheaded from the closeness of him, I tried not to faint.

After placing a chaste kiss on my cheek, he pulled away. "See you later."

Extreme disappointment at the simple kiss ricocheted through my body. "Bye," I replied forlornly, as he pounded down the porch steps.

Why did he have to seem so approachable and so acquirable in one moment, and then in the next seem totally and completely unattainable?

3: RHYS

When I dared to glance down at my watch, I grimaced. I was officially half an hour late for Allison's set. I should have known better than to have gone back home before heading to Saffie's Tea Room. I had been roped into joining my parents in the dining room. They were halfway through their three-course dinner with some of their friends from the Fortune 500 Club. It was a true hell on earth. The moment dessert had been brought out, I had politely excused myself. While my mother threw questioning looks my way, I purposely evaded her. Even though I was twenty-seven, I knew she would give me grief when I returned for bailing on the Mastersons and the talk of their single daughter at Vassar who was dying to meet me. Like I wanted to settle down period, but the last woman on earth would be with a former debutant who cared not about a love match but more about a status and society match.

By the time I'd gotten to shower and thrown on some new clothes, it was the time I should have been showing up, not leaving. Because I was running late, I allowed my parents' driver to drop me off, rather than driving myself. I figured I wouldn't lose time having to park. I shifted on the leather seats of the Bentley Mulsanne—one of my parents' pretentious and extravagant cars—as the driver inched through the weekday summer tourist traffic.

In so many ways, it had been a mind-fuck of a day being with Allison. Although I had seen her at Jake and Abby's wedding and other events in the last couple of years, it hadn't truly hit me until today that she really had grownup. Hearing about her sex life had been a jolt to both the head, and to the pants if I was honest, that I hadn't needed. At the same time, I wouldn't have had to hear about the sex life to see how far she'd come from the gangly teenager I'd met so many years ago. As beautiful as she was, Jake, and his dad, Mark, had a lot to worry about when it came to Allison and men.

While it might have been her who was homesick, she had truly made my first day back home enjoyable. Since leaving home, my visits back to Savannah were purely out of obligation, not of desire. Being able to be with her in the next few weeks was certainly going to make my stay a lot easier, and it sure as hell wasn't going to be out of any obligation to Jake or to her. It was because I wanted to spend time with someone who was beautiful, intelligent, and fun to be with as Allison. She sure as hell wasn't a chore, that's for sure.

Once the driver finally let me out in front of the club, I barely had time to take in the outside of Saffie's Tea Room. For Allison's sake, I was glad to see it wasn't in a seedier area of town. Jake would probably freak just a little bit less knowing that the club was in a good area. Of course, he wasn't going to be thrilled that Allison had kept something from him and her parents. It was so unlike her. She had always been such a good girl. I guess she really was spreading her wings and testing out the rebellious waters.

After I hurried down the brick steps to the club's entrance, I was surprised to see a shredded bouncer checking IDs next to a stylishly dressed woman taking payment for the cover charges. When I handed over my ID, the bouncer eyed me suspiciously. "Are you lost?" he asked.

"I'm here to see someone perform," I replied.

With a grunt, he thrust my ID back at me. Although I could hear music coming from inside, I wasn't sure it was still Allison. I hoped like hell I hadn't missed her. When I handed my money to the woman, I asked, "Is Pink Magnolia still playing?"

She nodded. "They're on for thirty more minutes."

"Thank God."

She laughed. "Honey, they aren't that good."

Ignoring her, I entered the dimly lit club. Twinkling lights crisscrossed across the ceiling and down the walls while candlelight flickered on the tables with purple, white, and black linen tablecloths. Past the tables, there was a wide dance floor in front of a stage. As my gaze flickered around the room, I heaved a relieved sigh at how the interior looked. In the end, Saffie's reminded me a lot of some of the higher-end clubs in New York and even Atlanta.

Like being zapped with a Taser, my attention was drawn away from taking in the club's scenery to the small stage. Allison sat at a baby grand piano, appearing totally poised and self-possessed. It was a quite a different demeanor from earlier, especially when she was falling over the banister. Her long brown hair cascaded in loose waves down her back, resting just above her waist. Her red dress reminded me of something out of a Roman or Greek history book, and she certainly looked every bit like a goddess perched on the piano bench. A single red orchid rested behind her ear, making her appear even more delicately feminine.

Something within me came alive at the sight of her bathed in the glowing stage lights. It was as if I was seeing her, truly seeing *her*, for the first time. She wasn't an awkward teenage girl with braces and gangly legs anymore—she was a woman. If I was truly honest with myself, I would admit that she was a gorgeous and sexy woman. At that moment, I was really glad she was performing in a lesbian bar because I didn't like the idea of any douchebags trying to hit on her.

As she turned to the crowd and smiled, she appeared such a paradox. While a beam of light gave her a glowing halo around her head, her red dress totally annihilated anything angelic about her. "For our next song, I'd like to play an old favorite of mine. It's a cover of Joan Armatrading's *The Weakness in Me*," she said, the microphone causing her voice to echo throughout the cavernous room. As she and her bandmates started up the opening chords of the song, she once again peered into the audience. She appeared to be searching for someone—searching for *me*. When her eyes locked on mine, I nodded my head and smiled.

She briefly returned my smile. While holding my gaze, she began to sing. "I'm not the sort of person who falls in and quickly out of love. But to you I gave my affection right from the start."

As her voice filled the air around me, I stood rooted in my spot, utterly transfixed by her performance. Women bumped into me as they jostled through the crowd to either slow dance or grab a table, but I barely noticed them. I couldn't seem to take my eyes off Allison. Her voice had a sensual, throaty quality to it. Allison hadn't given herself enough credit. Her voice was not as strong as Abby's, but she certainly had more talent than the woman at the door, and Allison herself had insinuated. It was easy to see that she had inherited some of Jake's musical and singing talent. Sure, the band would never make it out of this basement club, but they had a rapt audience, which meant a lot in the long run.

Taking my phone out of my pants pocket, I started filming some of her performance. Deep down, I knew that Jake would want to see this. After he got over the initial shock of his underage sister singing in a nightclub, he would be proud of Allison's accomplishments. It was easier to hold my hand steady than it was to contain my out-of-control feelings toward Allison. Brotherly affection was sure as hell not filling my mind at that moment.

When she finished playing the final chords of the song, a roar of applause erupted in the room. Allison smiled while breathlessly saying into the microphone, "Thank you. Thank you all so very much."

As she swept off the piano bench, I got a swift kick in the pants at the sight of her wiry knee boots. They looked like something out of the movie *Gladiator*, and fuck me, they were sexy as hell. What the hell was I thinking? In no way, shape, or form was I ever to put the words "sexy as hell" and "Allison" in the same sentence. I'd known her since she was thirteen. She was like my own little sister. Bringing my hand to my face, I furiously scrubbed my eyes and forehead, as if I were able to scrub the X-rated images of Allison out of my mind.

At that moment, a sultry beat came from the stage, and I instantly recognized the song as *Am I the Only One*. Allison stood in front of the tall microphone stand. "Please baby can't you see my mind's a burning hell? I got razors a rippin' and tearin' and strippin' my heart apart as well."

While I was able to hear more of Allison's vocal range on the song, I could have given a fuck less about her singing. Instead, my mind had drifted back into X-rated territory with the way Allison was rocking the microphone stand. As she slid her fingers and hands provocatively up and down the silver metal while swiveling her hips to the beat, I found myself thinking about those very same fingers pumping up and down on my dick. When she straddled the stand and her thighs replaced her hands in the rubbing, sweat broke out along my forehead. All it took was the straddling and hair tossing to have a partial erection slamming at the front of my pants.

I couldn't help glancing down at my traitorous dick. No, no, no, this couldn't possibly be happening. It was one thing to think she was sexy, but now I was leering at her like a horny bastard desperate for a fuckfest. If Jake caught one glance at my thoughts, he would have ripped my head from my shoulders, and considering how horrible I felt for fantasizing on Allison, I would have let him.

"Damn, she's hot. What I wouldn't give to be between those thighs," someone said next to me.

"I know. I bet she tastes just as sweet as she looks," another replied.

My gaze snapped from Allison to two chicks standing beside me. One caught my eye and waggled her brows suggestively. "Easy man, I know she's batting for your team. Doesn't mean I can't fantasize, right?"

Although my dick thought it was quite arousing having a woman hot for Allison, my mind thankfully overrode it. I'd gone down the threesome path once or twice, but I couldn't even imagine doing that with Allison. Not to mention, I had a feeling this chick would not be interested in me partaking with her.

Allison finished up the song to wild applause and ear-splitting whistles. Desperately in need of a drink, I hauled ass over to the bar. "Crown Royal, please," I called over the chatter to a bartender with multicolored hair.

As she sat an empty glass in front of me, she raised her pierced brows. "You must be from out of town."

With a laugh, I eased onto one of the stools. "I seem to be getting that a lot tonight."

She took the bottle of Crown from under the bar and filled my glass with the amber colored liquor. "We have mostly a local crowd, but occasionally we have a tourist stumble in by mistake."

After sucking down a burning gulp, I said, "Actually, I'm here for Allison Slater."

The bartender grinned. "Somehow it doesn't surprise me that you're hooking up with the only straight girl in the place."

Furiously, I shook my head. "Whoa, hold up. We're not hooking up. She's my best friend's little sister—she's like *my* little sister."

"Oh, is that really all she is?" The bartender winked at me. "No offense, sweetie, but you sure as hell weren't looking at her like a little sister." She tilted her head thoughtfully. "Well, maybe in Alabama," she teased.

"Whatever," I grumbled into my Crown.

After downing one glass, I asked for another. I took my fresh drink over to an empty table. Thankfully, the alcohol helped cool my libido and any more salacious thoughts about Allison. After a few more cover songs, Allison performed some of the original songs of Pink Magnolia, which from a musician's standpoint weren't that strong. I was thankful that this wasn't Allison's dream, and she had other talents to see her through. It was just before eleven when they wrapped up the set.

"Thank you all so, so much for your support. Have a great night!" Allison cried into the microphone. Craning my neck, I watched as she headed offstage. While she received kisses on the cheeks and hugs from some of the patrons, Allison kept her gaze on mine as she bobbed through the crowd toward me.

Breathless, she finally plopped down in the chair across from me. "So what did you think?" she asked, her dark eyes still dancing from the adrenaline high pumping in her veins.

I smiled. "You were amazing."

Her brows shot up. "Really?"

"Come on, stop fishing for compliments." When her brows creased slightly, I reached over to take her hand. "You're good, Allison. I wouldn't tell you that if it wasn't true."

A pink flush tinged her cheeks. "Thank you. Maybe I should invite Jake to the show."

"Oh, I'm sure he would get a *real* kick out of your pole dancing on the microphone stand." I couldn't help laughing when she squealed and then covered her face with her hands.

"I would die…just die for Jake to see me like that," came her muffled reply.

"You looked good up there."

Peeking at me through her fingers, she asked, "Really?"

"Very kick-ass and very sexy," I admitted.

When she removed her hands, she stared at me. "You really thought I was sexy?" she asked incredulously.

For reasons I didn't understand, Allison genuinely cared about my opinion. "Of course I did. I would've been blind not to appreciate your microphone groping skills." While I was being honest, she didn't need to know everything, such as how she'd managed to get me hard. "You know, I wasn't the only one either. Two chicks beside me had a lot to say about you."

"They did?"

I nodded and leaned in closer to her. Lowering my voice as best I could over the booming house music, I said, "One was speculating on how good you would taste." Allison once again squealed and covered her face. Her innocent response caused me to laugh. "There's nothing wrong with having admirers."

Pulling her hands away, she fanned her face. "I guess not, but I think it's time to change the subject."

"If you insist."

Tilting her head, she asked, "So do you think Pink Magnolia could be opening for Jacob's Ladder and Runaway Train soon?"

I laughed. "Not exactly."

She giggled. "I didn't think so. But in a way, I'm glad. It's fun just doing it during the week, letting off some steam through the music. As far as ever really performing—" She wrinkled her nose. "That's just not for me."

"You are meant for bigger and better things in the world of fashion."

"I sure hope so."

An attractive girl with cropped black hair sat a fruity looking drink with an umbrella down in front of Allison. "Drink up, Sonny. You sure as hell earned it tonight. That Etheridge cover was out of this fucking world."

"Thanks, Cassie." Allison grinned as she picked up the drink. "I am feeling a little parched after all that singing."

Glancing between the two of them, I teasingly said, "Wait a minute, she's not twenty-one yet."

Cassie's dark eyes narrowed as she leaned in closer to me. "Yeah, well, you know what, pretty boy? I don't give a fuck how old she is."

I felt like I had to stand my ground with this chick who looked like she wanted to kick my ass at daring to question her. "The owner might. I'd hate to see you lose your liquor license."

Both Cassie and Allison burst out laughing. "What's so funny?" I demanded.

"I am the owner," Cassie replied.

Nodding, Allison said, "Rhys, this is my roommate I was telling you about, Cassie Broughton."

My brows shot up in surprise. After all, Cassie didn't look like she was much older than Allison, and here she owned a club. I threw out my hand. "Rhys McGowan. Nice meeting you."

Pumping my hand, Cassie gave me a genuine smile. "Nice to see you again."

"Again?" I questioned.

She nodded. "You probably don't remember me, but our parents are friends. I think we were forced to attend some dinner parties together when we were teenagers. Knowing my mother, she probably tried desperately to get you to date me." With a dramatic flair of her hand, she said, "It's so unsettling to have your only daughter be a lesbian. One simply cannot spend every waking moment planning the society wedding of the year. Why you'd have to go up north with all those—" She lowered her voice. "undesirable liberal Yankees just to have a legal wedding." Placing the back of her hand on her forehead, she gasped. "Heaven forbid."

Suddenly, it hit me. I had met her before at party or two, and she'd been funny as hell. The much needed comic relief in the situation we found ourselves in. "Cassandra, right?"

Rolling her eyes, she huffed out a contentious breath. "Only society assholes call me that."

I laughed. "Trust me, I have no love for our parents' world."

Cassie grinned. "I knew I was going to like you. Allison talks about you all the time." She winked at me. "Nothing but good."

With a strangled cry, Allison hurriedly corrected her. "*The band.* I talk about Jake and you guys." She once again grabbed her fruity concoction and took two long pulls of it through the small straw.

An awkward silence fell over the table. Clearing her throat, Cassie leaned in on her elbows on the table. "So what do you think of my club?"

"It's great," I replied, enthusiastically. "How is it you came to own it?"

"My inheritance from my grandmother. It's her house where Allison and I live." A wistful smile graced Cassie's face. "She was kind of a society rebel herself. You know the type—she drank and smoked when it wasn't ladylike and cursed like a sailor. I like to think she would have approved of me buying an establishment that served hard drinks to people looking to engage in indecent acts."

I chuckled at her summation of Saffie's Tea Room. "Compared to a lot of clubs I've been in, this place seems pretty tame."

"Trust me, it gets crazy on the weekends."

My gaze flickered over to Allison. "Do you perform during these 'crazy weekends'?"

A flush entered her cheeks. "We've done a set on Friday nights before, but mainly, it's a DJ."

Cassie snickered. "I like to keep Allison out of here on the weekends. It never fails that some drunk chick wants to convert her to bat for the other team."

"So I've seen," I replied, winking at Allison. Once again, Allison sputtered with mortification at mine and Cassie's comments, and again I found it utterly endearing. She might've been twenty now, but in so many ways, she was still the innocent, naïve teenage girl

I'd met so many years ago. Most of the girls and women I came in contact with were so worldly and stuck on themselves. Being with Allison was definitely a nice change.

"If you don't mind, I'm going to change the subject away from my alleged allure," Allison said.

"Go right ahead, Sonny," Cassie replied.

Allison focused her attention on me. "I have tomorrow night free. Would you like to get together for movie night?"

I grimaced. "I would love to, but I have this stupid bachelor auction thing I'm emceeing."

With a teasing roll of her eyes, Allison said, "Like I haven't heard that excuse a million times."

I laughed. "I swear to you that it is the truth. More than anything in the world, I'd rather be watching *Monty Python* with you than in a monkey suit with a bunch of society assholes."

"I think I've heard about that auction. Isn't your mother heading it up?" Cassie asked.

"Unfortunately, yes. That's how I got roped into emceeing. The only time she likes to admit my fame is when it can best be used to suit her purposes. This time it appears having a celebrity emcee will get more people out to empty their pockets. I would have told her no, but it's for a cause really close to my heart."

"And which one is that?" Allison questioned softly.

"Autism research." While I kept my eyes on the table, I could feel Allison's inquisitive gaze on my cheeks. I'm sure she was trying to decipher the motives behind why someone like me would possibly be interested in the charity.

"That's so sweet that you're thinking of Lucy. I'm sure it means a lot to Brayden and Lily that you're working to raise money for research," she said.

I jerked my gaze up to meet hers. Although she had missed the mark, I replied, "I suppose they do."

"Who are Brayden and Lily?" Cassie asked, as she glanced between the two of us.

"My bandmate and his wife. Lucy, their youngest daughter, was just diagnosed as a child on the autism spectrum. Hers is more of a sensory nerve disorder that the doctors think can be helped, if not corrected, with a lot of extensive physical therapy."

"That's a rough diagnosis. At least it sounds like there are some positives in it."

Allison nodded. "There are no two sweeter and more patient parents than Brayden and Lily."

"That is the truth," I replied.

With a sweet smile, Allison said, "Well, I'll miss having movie night with you, but at least I know it's for a really good cause."

Leaning forward on the table with my elbows, I cocked my head at her. "Who says we can't spend the evening together?"

"What do you mean?"

"Why don't you come to the auction with me? It should only run about two or three hours. We could have dinner afterwards."

Gnawing her bottom lip between her teeth, Allison said, "Oh, I don't know."

Cassie nudged her playfully. "You should totally go. I mean, you'll only end up sitting at home alone with a pint of ice cream if you don't."

Allison scowled at Cassie. "Thank you so much for reminding me what a loser I am with no life," she replied sarcastically.

I laughed. "Come on. You'll get to see even more of Savannah's history and culture. The auction is being held at the Mercer Williams House."

"Is that the house from *Midnight in the Garden of Good and Evil*?"

Nodding, I replied, "It sure is."

"I thought that was more of a museum now?"

"While it is open for tours, Jim Williams's sister still lives there. That's how Mother was able to book the event. She goes way back with her."

"It really does sound like fun," Allison said, with a hesitant smile.

"Then why haven't you said yes? I don't think I've had to work this hard for a date in a long, long time." Allison dark eyes bulged at the mention of the word "date." Trying to backtrack, I said, "Well, you know what I mean."

"I just don't want this to be a pity thing."

"A pity thing?" I repeated.

"I know that Jake asked you to check in on me because I was homesick. I don't want you to feel like I have to tag along to everything or else I'll be at home sitting in a dark room all depressed."

I laughed. "This has nothing to do with pity or Jake. It's all about you and I having fun out on the town. Okay?"

"Okay."

"So does that mean you'll go?"

"Yes." But then her brow creased with worry. "It's black tie, right?"

"Yeah. Is that a problem?"

Her hands fretted anxiously with the umbrella in her drink. "It's just with me being new in town, all my nice dresses are back home."

Cassie cleared her throat. "No need to fear. I have the perfect dress you can borrow."

"You do?" Allison asked.

With a laugh, Cassie replied, "Yes, it's a little, black couture number with the tags still on it. My dear mother brought it back from Fashion Week in Paris a few years back." She winked at us. "It was one of her last ditch efforts at trying to feminize me."

"Are you sure you don't mind me borrowing it?"

Cassie rolled her eyes. "Does it look like I'm ever going to wear a dress, least of all some bullshit couture one?"

"Not really," Allison replied.

"Exactly. So it's yours as long as you're not uncomfortable wearing a dress that is a few seasons old."

Allison furiously shook her head. "No, I'd be happy to."

Cassie grinned. "Then it's all settled." She turned to me. "Now you make sure to show our girl a good time."

Fuck me that the words, "Allison" and "good time", sent my perverted mind once again in a direction it shouldn't have. Of course, it didn't help I had such a delectable vision in front of me with her fitted dress and high-heeled boots on. Shit, I was so utterly screwed.

After sucking down the rest of my Crown, I met Allison's gaze and plastered on what I hoped was a brotherly smile. "I'll try my best."

4: ALLISON

As soon as I could clock out, I peddled like lightning home. I only had an hour to shower and get ready before I was supposed to meet Rhys at the Mercer Williams House. Considering I reeked of pizza and beer, I needed some time to transform myself so that I would look and smell acceptable for him.

I tore through the front door to find Cassie lounging on the couch. "There you are. I laid the dress out for you on your bed."

"Thank you," I panted. Without another word to her, I streaked down the hall to my bedroom. When I threw open the door, I bent over at the waist, bracing my hands on my knees to try and catch my breath. Once I had regulated my breathing, I jerked my head up and eyed the dress draped across my homemade quilt. "What the…?" I murmured, taking a few shaky steps over to the bed. "Cassie!"

"What?" she called.

"Get in here!" I demanded.

Within seconds, I heard her footsteps hurrying along the creaky old floorboards. When she burst through the door, she stared quizzically at me. "What the hell is the matter?"

I couldn't find the words, so I pointed to the dress. Cassie crossed her arms over her chest. "Don't tell me you don't like it?"

Reaching my hand out, I lightly touched the silky material. "No, it's not that. The dress is gorgeous."

"Then what's the problem?"

I didn't know quite how to articulate that the little black dress was in fact an extremely tiny black dress. I took it in my hands and held it up to my body. "Don't you think it's a kinda…" I wrinkled my nose. "Slutty?"

Cassie threw her head back and laughed. "Well, duh, of course it is. After all, it came from Paris."

As I eyed the bottom of the dress, I couldn't help thinking the slits and tears in the fabric made it look like it had been caught in a paper shredder. I loved fashion, but at the moment, I was not digging the designer's approach.

"You're going to be a fucking knock-out in that dress. I predict that several guys will come in their pants at the mere sight of you."

"Eww," I muttered with a laugh.

With a knowing look, she said, "Would it be gross if it were *Rhys* blowing his load just looking at you?"

"Must you be so vulgar?" I said, mimicking the haughty tone I'd heard her mother use at Cassie's antics.

Cassie grinned. "Why yes, darling, I must. And don't try to change the subject from Rhys."

Feeling warmth flooding my cheeks, I laid the dress back down on the bed. "I need to hop in the shower."

"There you go avoiding it again. I know how you feel about him, Allison."

"But *he* doesn't know."

"*But* he should. You need to tell him. Hell, if you can't say the words, then you should show him with your actions." When I opened my mouth to protest, Cassie shook her head. "I know what I saw the other night. The man may be in denial, but he is totally and completely into you."

More than anything in the world, I wanted to believe what Cassie was saying was the truth. While I'd never had the chance to be alone much with Rhys, I couldn't help but see how differently he had treated me yesterday, not to mention that he called me sexy and beautiful. Surely someone who just considered you their little sister wouldn't say that. But at the same time, there was still far too much unsaid between us to believe that we had really turned a corner.

I shook my head at Cassie. "You don't understand. What happens between us…it has to be all or nothing. If things were to go wrong, it would affect so many others besides us."

"But you won't ever know if it's going to work or not if you don't try."

"Look, I know you're right, but I just have to take things slow, okay?"

Cassie scowled. "Just how much slower do you plan on going? You're already moving at glacial speed now."

With a sigh, I held up my hand. "Can we finish this discussion later when I'm not running horribly late?"

"Fine, fine. Go shower the tomato and beer smell off you."

I threw my arms around Cassie and squeezed tight. "Thanks for the dress, but most of all, thanks for caring about what happens between me and Rhys."

She squeezed me back. "I just want you to be happy, Sonny."

"I know."

After I pulled away, she smiled. "Now hurry up. You don't want to make Prince Charming wait too long."

"Exactly," I replied, before hustling into the bathroom.

Once I was undressed, I hopped into the steamy shower. I managed to wash my hair, shave my legs, and bathe all in record time. After I dried my hair, I wrapped a towel around me to run out to get my dress off the bed. As I came out of the bathroom, I skidded to a stop. Cassie was no longer alone on the bed with my dress. Instead, she was making out with some woman I'd never seen before. "What the hell?" I couldn't help saying.

Cassie pulled away and shot me a sheepish grin. "Sorry, Sonny. We got a little bored waiting on you to get out of the shower."

Tightening my towel around me, I mumbled, "Please don't let me interrupt you," before starting to back up into the bathroom.

"Whoa, whoa, don't go anywhere." She motioned to the blonde waifish girl next to her. "This is Shelly. She's going to do your hair and makeup."

I glanced between Cassie and Shelley. "She is?"

Shelly smiled. "I own a salon just up the street."

Cassie nodded. "She was coming over tonight anyway, so I thought she could help you out. You know, make you absolutely drop-dead gorgeous for Rhys."

"Are you sure you don't mind?" I asked Shelly.

"Of course not." With a wink, she added, "I'm happy to do anything in the name of love."

I laughed. "Okay, if you insist, I would love for you to make me beautiful."

"You've already got that in spades, love. I'm just going to enhance what you have."

Glancing down at my lacking cleavage, I asked, "Can you enhance this, too?"

Shelly grinned. "I'm not a miracle worker. I'm pretty sure that dress is going to help cinch you up and push you out. Go on and put it on, and then I'll do your hair and makeup."

I nodded. After taking the dress and the underwear I would need back into the bathroom, I slid them on. Since there was no way I could zip the dress by myself, I came back out to get Cassie to help. After I was zipped up, I was pushed down into a chair, and Shelly started working on me. Minutes ticked by as my hair was dried, curled, and teased, and then my makeup was done. "There. All done," she finally said.

Whirling out of the chair, I hurried to get a glimpse of myself. As I stood back from the tall, oval mirror that I'd brought from home, I couldn't help shaking my head in disbelief. Part of me fought the urge to reach forward and tap the glass to make sure it was really me. "Oh my God, Shelly, you're really a miracle worker."

She laughed as she fluffed and then sprayed some of the curls trailing down my back. "Once again, I only enhanced the beauty that was already there."

My gaze dipped from my long and feathery fake eyelashes to my plumped-up lips shimmering with gloss down to the tight, strapless bodice of the couture dress. Shelly had been right when she said that the dress would help enhance my cleavage. For once, my B-cup was looking like a full C as it spilled over the top of the dress.

I don't know when I had felt so beautiful—maybe my Sweet Sixteen party, if even then. I desperately needed to feel this level of desirable to boost my confidence to approach Rhys. He was used to gorgeous women brazenly throwing themselves at him. Although I could never see me throwing myself at him, I could definitely work on making him notice me. Then maybe things would really begin to change for us.

"You're going to take his breath away, Sonny," Cassie said behind me.

"Thank you. I sure hope so." My gaze flickered to the clock on my nightstand. "Oh shit, I'm already ten minutes late!"

Cassie reached out to place her hands on my shoulders. "Easy, you've got to breathe or you'll pass out."

"But—"

"No buts. There's a cab waiting on you outside, so you'll be there in less than ten minutes with traffic."

"There is?" I asked, as I hurried over to dig my slinky, black heels out of the closet.

"Yep, I called one for you while Shelly was working her magic."

After I slid on the heels, I grabbed my purse. "Thank you both so very, very much for tonight."

"You're welcome," they replied in unison.

When I got to the door, I turned around. "Oh, just one thing."

"What?" Cassie asked.

"Could you please refrain from making out on my bed? I don't even get to make out on it."

Cassie laughed. "No problem." Shooing me with her hand, she said, "Now get the hell out of here."

"I'm going, I'm going," I said, slipping out the door.

After I hurried out of the house and pounded down the steps, I slid into the seat of the cab, which in a corny way felt kind of like Cinderella's carriage. "Take me to 429 Bull Street, and please try to hurry if you can," I said to the driver.

He took my request to heart as we squealed away from the curb and started careening down Oglethorpe Avenue before making a sharp right. I gripped the leather seats while silently praying I actually made it to the Mercer Williams House in one piece. When we got to the turn to Monterey Square, we began to inch along. Peering out the window, I watched valets in white jackets run along the front of the house, handing tickets and then parking cars. "You can just let me out here," I said to the driver."

"All right."

After I dug a ten out of my wallet, I handed it to him. "Thanks."

"Have a good evening, miss."

"You too," I replied, as I put one high-heeled shoe out onto the pavement. Once I closed the door, I started walking as fast I could on my heels. I followed some of the couples through the wrought iron gate and up the front walk. When we got to the door, a man in a tux was checking invitations.

That's when I started to panic. Rhys hadn't mentioned that I would need an invitation. Just as I was about to dig my cell phone out of my purse to text Rhys, the man questioned, "Miss?"

"Oh, um, I don't have an actual invitation. I was invited by someone," I said, instantly realizing how idiotic I sounded.

Glancing down at his clipboard, he demanded, "Name?"

"Allison Slater."

His finger ran down a sheet and then he stopped. "Good then. Go on in."

I exhaled a relieved breath as I breezed past him into the black and white tiled foyer of the house. Instantly, I felt like I was stepping right into the movie *Midnight in the Garden of Good and Evil*. I half expected Kevin

Spacey to walk by, puffing on a cigar, as he played Jim Williams.

Standing on my tiptoes, I craned my neck, searching the long, crowded room for Rhys. When I didn't see him, I started into the first room on the right. It was filled with people talking and drinking champagne. I left that room and made my way across the hall. When I still didn't see him, I decided that I better start asking.

Tapping one guy on the shoulder, I said, "Excuse me."

After he whirled around, his gaze dipped slowly down my body, as if he were trying to memorize every curve I had. "And what can I do for a sweet thing like you?" he drawled.

"Do you know where I could find Rhys McGowan?"

He smiled. "Are you looking to bet on him tonight?"

I furrowed my brows in confusion. "Excuse me?"

Leaning in much closer to me than I would have preferred, the guy said, "Why waste your money on him when you could go home with me? I guarantee I'd show you a screaming good time. All. Night. Long."

"Give it a rest, Donaldson," Rhys's voice came from behind me.

At the feel of his hand on my lower back, I instantly relaxed. Tilting my head, I took in his tight smile. "I apologize for not being able to meet you sooner."

"It's okay."

Rhys glanced from me to my lecherous admirer. "I see you're making some acquaintances."

Donaldson, as Rhys had called him, held out his hand. "Where are my manners? I didn't introduce myself properly to you. I'm James Donaldson."

"Allison Slater," I replied, shaking his hand quickly. But before I could pull away, he was bringing the back of my hand to his lips.

"I'll see you later then, Miss Slater. I certainly hope you'll be betting on me tonight."

"Don't fucking count on it," Rhys growled under his breath.

James winked at me before thumping Rhys on the shoulder. "Always a pleasure seeing you, too, McGowan. Have a lovely evening."

Rhys scowled at James as he walked by us. Then he turned back to me. "I'm sorry you had to deal with that asshole."

"He wasn't that bad."

"Oh, trust me, I've known him since we were kids. Not only is he a bully, but he is a womanizing douchebag."

"Then I should have kneed him in the balls rather than allowing him to kiss my hand."

Rhys stared wide-eyed at me for a second before busting out laughing. "While I would have loved to see that, I'm not sure you would have made the best impression."

I giggled. "Me either."

"Enough about that asshole. Thanks to him I didn't even get to greet you properly."

"It's okay."

He shook his head and stepped out in front of me. Taking my hands in his, he surveyed my appearance. The heat of his stare caused my heart to break into a gallop. "You are absolutely breathtaking tonight."

"Thank you," I replied, breathlessly.

Rhys smiled. "Considering that you're putting every woman in this room to shame, I'm not surprised that jerkwad was coming on to you."

"Aren't you the flatterer tonight?" I teased, while trying to keep my careening emotions in check.

"I just call it as I see it." When his gaze dipped from my eyes down to my chest, his jovial expression momentarily faded.

In one fluid movement, Rhys closed the space between us, backing us into the corner of the drawing room. Immediately my head spun as I went into sensory overload at the nearness of him. His deep musky scent filled my nose while the heat radiating off his tux-clad body almost singed the skin exposed by my strapless couture. While I stared questioningly into his face, his dark eyes remained locked on my chest. To the average observer, one would have assumed Rhys was exhibiting typical male behavior by ogling my breasts, but I knew better. Most of all, I knew him better than that. His attention was drawn to the pendant nestled in the valley between my average-sized cleavage.

When his fingers grazed against the bare skin of my breastbone, I couldn't help the tremble that went through my body. I wanted nothing more than to feel his hands on me. If I was honest, I fantasized about them most nights, especially to get me through a dry spell without an orgasm.

Once he had grasped the pendant, Rhys weighed it in his hand, taking in every aspect of it before his gaze flicked up to mine. "I can't believe you still have this, least of all wear it."

His almost accusatory tone momentarily stung me, and I jerked back from him. His grasp remained firm on the pendant, causing the satin ribbon to slice into my neck almost like I was on a leash. "Why wouldn't I still have it?"

He shrugged. "I guess because it was so long ago when I gave it to you."

"It was at my Sweet Sixteen party," I reminded him.

"I remember," he murmured.

"You do?"

He held my gaze as he fingered the raised magnólia on the pendant. "Of course I do." One side of his lip quirked up in a half smile. "That was only four years ago, Allie-Bean. I'm not so old that I'm having memory loss."

A nervous laugh escaped my lips. "You're not old."

"Just older than you," he mused.

"Only by a few years," I countered, kicking my chin up determinedly.

In his brown eyes flecked with gold, I saw the question he would never dare to verbalize. Four and a half years had passed since that momentous night by the fountain at my party. There had been other loves and other life experiences for me. After all that time and distance, he wondered what it was about the simple necklace, hand painted by his sister, that made me continue to wear it, especially on the choker so close to my heart?

What I wanted so desperately to tell him was I wore the necklace because in spite of all the loves and other life experiences for me, I was still madly and completely in love with him. Swallowing hard, I replied, "I like to wear it because I love magnolias—I always have. Magnolias remind me of strong women—the kind I aspire to be like. But most of all, it reminds me of home."

Rhys bobbed his head, accepting my half-truths as if they were the gospel. In the end, maybe avoidance was better for both of us. At least for now, I would keep telling myself that. Now that we were on the cusp of unchartered territory, I would play the game for as long as I had to in order to win his heart.

He tenderly placed the pendant back on my breastbone and then stepped back. "I'm glad you still have it, and that it means so much to you." Just as we were about to lapse into an awkward silence, Rhys asked, "Are you hungry?"

Of course he would have to change the subject. "Maybe a little."

"Come with me." He then led me back into the hallway and down to the dining room. He grabbed me a plate and started piling on some hors d'oeuvres. "You still like all things cheese, right?"

I stared at him in shock. "Uh, yeah, I do."

He grinned. "Try the spinach and cheese canapés. They're delicious."

As he went about adding some fruit to my plate, I couldn't help asking, "How did you remember I liked cheese?"

He shot me a withering look. "Like I haven't sat beside you at a million BBQs and dinners over the years. You even eat shredded cheese on your hot dogs."

If this had been an old Southern novel or movie, I might've swooned at that very moment. Sure, it was just a detail about cheese, but he remembered it. About me. "You're right. I do. My mom claims it was because she craved it so much when she was pregnant with me. Apparently, she never liked it before." I clamped down on my lips to once again keep from blabbering like an idiot.

Rhys smiled as he handed me the plate. "There. That should take the edge off until we can go to dinner."

"Thank you, kind sir," I teased.

With a laugh, he rested his hand on the small of my back. He then led me down the hall to a beautifully decorated living room or sitting room. Motioning up the length of the room, he said, "The auction is going to be in there. Most of the people who are betting will be in there and in here."

Chewing on one of the canapés, I wrinkled my nose. "It's still so bizarre to me that they have bachelor and bachelorette auctions. It seems so outdated."

"I totally agree with you. That's one reason why you won't find me listed in the program."

"What a shame. I might've been inclined to bet on you."

Rhys gave me a sexy smirk that outrivaled any of AJ's. "Yes, but you're the lucky girl who gets to have me for free," he challenged.

I swallowed hard. Trying to save face, I quickly said, "That's true. I wouldn't want to waste my money."

Rhys laughed heartily. He opened his mouth to say something else when we were interrupted by a woman in a glittering blue gown. "There you are," she said.

Rhys instantly tensed. After appearing to force a smile, he replied, "Hello, Mother."

Although I tried not to stare, I couldn't help taking in every aspect of his mother. They both had the same dark hair and eyes. Her hair was swept back into a tight chignon at the base of her neck. Although she had to be in her fifties, she appeared very fit and youthful. She had a face devoid of wrinkles, which was either good genes or a good plastic surgeon. I was betting on the latter.

"It's almost time to start." She glanced from him to me. Her red lips pursed curiously while her eyes narrowed shrewdly. "And who is this young lady?"

"This is Allison Slater. You know my bandmate, Jake?"

Disdain flooded her face at the mention of the band. "Yes, I do."

"This is his younger sister. She's attending SCAD."

"How lovely," Rhys's mother replied, with as much enthusiasm as if Rhys had said I was in Savannah for a prostitution convention. Instantly, I was assaulted by the line from *Pretty Woman* when Julia Roberts's character, Vivian, says about Edward's friend that you could freeze ice on his snotty wife's ass. That was the epitome of Rhys's mother.

Ignoring her tone, Rhys said to me, "This is my mother, Margaret."

"It's nice to meet you," I said, extending my hand.

After she gave my hand a quick shake, she turned her attention back to Rhys. "I hope that you'll fetch a good price tonight at the auction."

"I think we're going to raise a good deal."

"You misunderstood me. I meant, I hope *you* bring in a lot of money."

Rhys dark brows knitted in confusion. "I don't think I understand."

"You're the final bachelor of the evening."

I couldn't help gasping in surprise, especially after the conversation we'd just had. Rhys also appeared floored, but then his face reddened with anger. "I don't recall agreeing to be paraded around tonight, Mother. In fact, I'm pretty sure you know how I feel about auctions."

She gave a dismissive wave of her diamond encrusted hand. "It's all for a good cause, isn't it?"

"I don't like being played like this. I think I will have to graciously bow out."

Margaret narrowed her eyes at him. "With your name already in the program? I don't think so, Rhys." When Rhys started to protest further, Margaret shook her head. "I will not have my event ruined by your petty demands."

As an antique clock struck the hour, Margaret jerked her chin up at Rhys. "It's time to start the auction." Without another word, she turned and stalked away from us.

Rhys's jaw clenched and unclenched. Reaching out, I tentatively touched his arm. When he didn't flinch away, I patted him. "I'm so sorry."

He momentarily closed his eyes. "It's okay. I don't know why I'm even surprised. She does bullshit like this all the time."

"I know earlier I was teasing, but if I had any money, I'd totally bet on you."

Rhys's eyes popped open and a smile curved on his lips. "I think that's a great idea."

"But—" I started to protest.

He shook his head. "To ensure that I don't have to be someone's plaything for an evening, I'll give you the money to bet on me."

"Seriously?"

"Sure. Why not?"

"But how will I know when to stop?"

"That's the thing. You *won't* stop. You *will* be the winner. Okay?"

I nodded. "Okay."

Rhys leaned in and kissed my cheek. "Thanks, Allison. You're a lifesaver."

I enjoyed the nearness of him for a fleeting moment before he whirled around and made his way to the front of the study. Picking up a microphone off a marble-topped table, he stood behind a small wooden podium that had been brought in. "Good evening, ladies and gentlemen. I hope you've come here ready to dig deeply into your pockets for this wonderful cause because it's now time to start the auction for autism research."

Applause rippled through the room. "I am your host this evening, Rhys McGowan—" He was interrupted by shrieking whistles and cheers. He smiled good-naturedly. "Thank you, I appreciate your enthusiasm. I hope you're paying attention to your programs this evening for which bachelors are available and in what order. So let's get this started by calling up our first bachelor of the evening, Walt Harrison."

I stood back, watching Rhys go through the motions. He was actually quite good at emceeing. He kept the crowd laughing and the bachelors moving through.

I was momentarily distracted when a girl my age bumped into me. "Nice dress."

"Oh, thank you. I actually borrowed it from a friend."

A sickeningly sweet smile appeared on her face. "No doubt from the back of her closet considering it's so old. I can't even count how many seasons ago that dress was fashionable."

Her friends encircling her giggled behind their hands. While there were a million and one things I wanted to say to her, I found it incapable to verbalize any one of them. Gripping my champagne flute tighter, I merely edged away from the group of stereotypical society bitches.

I had just taken a sip of bubbly to calm my nerves when a voice behind me caused me to choke. "Don't worry about my niece, honey. She's a second generation cunt."

Whirling around, I took in an elegantly woman in an emerald dress. Her salt and pepper hair was swept back from her face with glittering combs. She gave me a genuine smile—the first one I had witnessed all night besides Rhys's. "Thank you…I think."

She laughed. Extending a white gloved hand, she said, "I'm Vivian Percy."

"Allison Slater."

"I don't think I've seen you around these shark-infested waters before."

"No, thankfully, this is my first time and hopefully my last."

"I don't blame you on that one. Who are you here with?"

"Rhys McGowan." When her blue eyes widened, I quickly said, "He and my brother are bandmates."

"Ah, yes, Rhys McGowan. He grew up to be such a cutie pie, didn't he?"

With warmth flooding my cheeks, I replied, "Yes, he did."

"Thinking of betting on him this evening?"

"Um, well…" I wasn't sure if Rhys wanted me to make our plans known.

"He's a hot ticket, honey. If it were me, I wouldn't have to think twice."

"Yes, I am planning to bet on him."

Vivian smiled. "Good for you. Now hold my spot a minute while I run and grab a bite to eat. I'm famished."

"Sure."

Two more bachelors were auctioned by the time Vivian returned. "Who is next?"

I glanced down at the program. "A Jackson Marshall."

Shifting her plate to her left hand, she said, "Oh, thank God, I didn't miss him."

"Is he your boyfriend?" I asked casually.

Vivian hooted with laughter. "Oh honey, maybe forty years ago I would've tried to get my hooks into him, but he's young enough to be my grandson."

"I'm sorry."

She waved her hand that held a canapé. "Don't be. There is a reason why I want to bet on him."

Rhys interrupted my thoughts by saying, "Going once, going twice, sold for one thousand dollars."

As applause erupted around us, Vivian leaned in to whisper in my ear. "Jackson's father was arrested awhile back for absconding with investors' money—total white-collar criminal, if you get my drift. The one thing that people in Savannah society prides themselves on are being close-minded, unforgiving assholes. It doesn't matter that Jackson is an upstanding young man with a 4.0 GPA at Vanderbilt. Most people here would love to see him ostracized, even though he couldn't help, nor was responsible for, what his daddy did."

At that moment, Rhys called Jackson's name. When he strode up to the podium, my eyes bulged in surprise. It was as if Chace Crawford had entered the room. Jackson's blue eyes sparkled as he glanced into the crowd. "Oh my," I murmured.

Vivian chuckled. "I forgot to mention how handsome he was, didn't I?"

"Just a little."

Taking the microphone, Rhys read off a biography about Jackson that of course made him sound entirely too good to be true. When he finished, Rhys said, "Now let's start the bidding at five hundred."

Silence reverberated around the room. As Jackson's beaming smile receded a bit, Rhys cleared his throat. "Do I have five hundred?"

As Vivian drew in a breath, I shot in front of her. "Five hundred!" I blurted before I could stop myself. It didn't matter that I didn't have five hundred dollars or that I didn't even want to begin to explain to my parents why the charge on my "emergency" credit card was actually for a bachelor auction.

A gasp went up in the crowd, and Rhys blinked at me a few times like he wasn't sure he could believe what he was seeing. Jackson, meanwhile, broadened his smile and winked at me. I ducked my head as my cheeks flushed.

"Well, well, look at you," Vivian whispered.

Cutting my eyes over to hers, I replied, "I couldn't help it. I felt so bad for him up there."

"Never fear, honey. I'm about to put all these narrow-minded assholes in their place." She grinned. "I just hope you don't mind if I outbid you."

"Oh no, please do. My bid was simply a moment of impulsive stupidity."

I then shifted my gaze back to Rhys who appeared to have finally recovered from my outburst. It seemed that I had gotten the ball rolling on some bets for Jackson. "We have nine hundred. Do I hear a thousand?"

With a wave of her hand, Vivian said, "*Ten* thousand dollars."

My mouth gaped open in shock while chatter buzzed around us. Jackson grinned and shook his head at Vivian. Rhys coughed. "I believe that was for ten thousand dollars?"

"That's right, sugar," Vivian drawled.

"So we have ten thousand for Jackson Marshall. Do I have eleven?" He then had the audacity to look at me and raise his brows. When I scowled back at him, he laughed. "That's ten going once, twice, and sold to Mrs. Vivian Percy."

As faint applause echoed around us, Jackson came striding toward us. He pulled Vivian into a bear hug. "Thank you, Miss Vivian. You once again have managed to be far too generous when it comes to me."

She gave his cheek a smacking kiss. Rubbing her lipstick off him, she said, "I think it was just enough." She winked at me. "I'm sure that'll have their tongues wagging all night, especially when Jackson here goes for the highest price all evening."

"I do appreciate it. And I hope you'll let you me take you out for dinner and drinks—all on me, of course," Jackson said.

"I would be honored. I'd love to catch up with you about how college is going." Vivian snapped her fingers. "Oh my, I just remembered that Jules will be here for a visit in a few weeks."

Jackson smiled. "I'd love to see her."

"Then it's all settled."

After he gave Vivian another hug, Jackson turned to me. "Thanks for betting on me, even if you didn't win, Miss...?"

"Slater. Allison Slater."

"Nice to meet you, Miss Slater."

"And you're welcome. You know, for my bid."

Leaning in closer to me, he gave me a smile that would've normally caused my panties to get wet. "I'd love to take you out for dinner sometime, too."

"Really?"

He nodded. "What are you doing after this?"

Glancing away from his hypnotic blue eyes, I stared over to where Rhys stood at the podium. He was auctioning another bachelor, but his attention was focused on me and Jackson. I couldn't help getting a sense of a pleasure from the fact he looked like he wanted to punch Jackson for daring to talk to me. "You seem like a really wonderful guy, but I have plans."

"Meaning there's someone else you care about?"

I nodded. "Yes, there is."

"Ah, all the good ones are always taken."

I couldn't help blushing with his compliments. "Thank you."

"See you around."

Waving, I watched him disappear through the crowd. The sound of Rhys's gavel coming down caused me to jump. "And now we come to our final bachelor of the evening." He paused and smiled. "Which appears to be me."

Whistling pierced my eardrums. Turning to Vivian, I said, "I'm going to get closer."

"You do that, doll."

When I was almost right in front of Rhys, he asked, "Shall we start the bidding at five hundred?"

I opened my mouth, but a voice behind me cut me off. "Five hundred."

Glancing over my shoulder, I saw it was Vivian's niece—the bitch who had insulted my dress. Oh, she was going down all right. "I have five hundred. Do I have six?"

I thrust my hand into the hair and said, "Six."

Rhys grinned. "I have six. Do I have seven?"

For the second time that night, the bitch knocked into me. "One thousand."

Amused chatter filled the air that Miss Bitch had upped the ante. Rhys bobbed his head. "Well, then, it appears we have a thousand. Do I have fifteen hundred?"

"Two thousand," I spat.

"Okay, that's two thousand. Do I have—"

"Three thousand," Miss Bitch interrupted Rhys.

I glared at her. "Four thousand."

Stepping between us, Margaret said, "Ladies, you need to follow protocol."

Lowering her voice, Miss Bitch hissed, "You are not going home with him. I *am*."

Feeling like I was back in high school rather than a grown woman, I snapped, "Wanna bet?"

Rhys cleared his throat into the microphone. "So that's four thousand, do I have forty-five hundred?"

"Five thousand," Miss Bitch said, never taking her eyes off mine.

At this rate, we could go on all night. Something had to be done. Drawing my shoulders back, I punched my hand into the air. "Ten thousand."

Miss Bitch's eyes widened. "Did I hear you just bet ten thousand dollars?"

Cocking my brows, I countered, "Did I stutter?" When she didn't respond, I said, "Yep, I thought you heard me correctly."

I flicked my gaze from hers to Rhys. He grinned and shook his head. "Looks like we have a bid of ten thousand. Do I hear eleven?"

I shot Miss Bitch a look that dared her to try eleven. She then huffed out a frustrated breath before crossing her arms over her chest. I took that as she was conceding. When no one else bid, Rhys banged the gavel down on the podium. "Looks like Mr. Marshall and I will be tying for the highest bids tonight of ten thousand dollars." Once again applause and whistling assaulted my ears. "Thanks to everyone who came to help make tonight such a success. Thanks also to all the bachelors who have offered their time and services. Most of all, thanks to my mother, Margaret McGowan, for planning and executing this evening's festivities."

When the applause started to die down, Rhys bypassed anyone else waiting to talk to him and came straight for me. I couldn't help the beaming smile that lit up my face when he pulled me into his arms.

"I think I just won a date with you with your money," I said against his ear.

He chuckled, causing my body to vibrate with his. When he pulled away, he was still smiling. "I believe you have. And where do you intend to take me on your date?"

Since I had had enough high class for one night, I knew it had to be somewhere low-key. "How about a B&D burger and some fries?"

"Ah, I see how it is. You're planning to go cheap on me now that you've spent a lot of my money."

I grinned. "Yep, sounds good to me."

"You're in luck, cheapskate. I happen to love B&D burgers."

"I'm glad to hear that," I replied, a little breathlessly since Rhys still had his arms around me.

Someone cleared her throat behind us. It was Margaret with her "I've been sucking on lemons" expression. "Rhys, darling—" she began.

He held up a hand. "Mother, I'm sorry, but this young lady just bought my time fair and square."

"The newspaper wants to get a picture of us."

When Rhys scowled, I nudged him forward. "Go on. Your adoring public awaits you."

"I would happily like to tell my adoring public to get bent," he said, in a low voice.

I couldn't help giggling. "Why don't you give me your keys, and I'll wait at the car."

He cocked his brows questioningly at me. "I think you're just trying to abscond with my car."

"Could be. Guess you'll have to wait and see."

Rhys laughed as he dug a ticket out of his pants pocket. "Go ahead and have the valet bring it around. I'll be there as soon as I can."

"No problem."

As I started out of the study, I ran into Vivian in the hallway. "Leaving, dear?"

"Yeah, Rhys and I are going to get some dinner."

She grinned. "Have fun. Oh, and do something I would do."

I couldn't help laughing at her audacity. The truth was I would be happy to do all the wicked and naughty things Vivian could possibly do if only Rhys was willing. Being in his arms earlier, if only momentarily, felt so damn good. I couldn't help but wonder if he had any idea what he did to me. Ugh, I hated feeling this mixed up and neurotic. I had to remember that I was strong, beautiful, confident, and that there was no reason why Rhys shouldn't want to be with me.

As I handed over the ticket to the valet, I silently said a wish for strength so I could get my man.

5: RHYS

Out the entire evening, the highlight for me was sitting in a tux at B&D's, stuffing my face with a burger and fries, with a beautiful girl across from me. Once we devoured our food and had gotten enough odd looks from the other patrons because of our formal wear, we headed back to Allison's place. I stopped off and picked up a six-pack on the way.

After I parked the car, I turned to Allison who hadn't made a move to get out yet. "What's wrong?"

"I'm a little scared to go inside."

Twisting in my seat to see her better, I asked, "What do you mean?"

She giggled. "I have a feeling that Cassie and her date might be banging on the couch. They were already making out on my bed earlier tonight."

"Damn," I muttered, trying to rid myself of any thoughts of Cassie having sex.

After Allison got out of the car, she glanced up at the clear sky filled with stars. "It's such a pretty night. Why don't we have our drinks out on the veranda?"

"Sounds good to me, Scarlett," I teased.

"Oh, shut up. Like you don't have a veranda yourself," she said, as we started around the side of the house.

"Why of course we have a veranda. I just like to be uncouth and call it a back porch."

Allison laughed, causing my chest to have an odd clenching feeling. I'm not sure why I cared so much that she found me amusing. But more than hearing her laugh, I loved making her laugh. "What is it about being in Savannah that makes me want to talk and act like a proper Southerner?" she asked.

"I'm not sure. But the city certainly has some kind of pull on you," I replied, as I uncapped a beer and handed it to her.

"Think it's the voodoo?"

I snorted. "Could be." I then raised my beer up to the full moon. "Here's to all the voodoo and hoodoo that makes Savannah what it is."

Thrusting up her longneck, Allison said, "To the hoodoo and voodoo." Then she took a long swig of the beer.

I sat the six-pack on the table, and then we eased down onto the porch swing. For a while we sat in silence, merely listening to the heave and sigh of the swing. Turning my head, I eyed her profile in the moonlight. "You know, I just keep learning more and more about you, Allie-Bean."

"And precisely what did you learn about me tonight?"

I swallowed a large gulp of beer. Then I grinned at her. "First of all, you become a tough little cookie when provoked."

Allison threw back her shoulders and huffed out a breath. "She was a bitch. No, actually, she was a cunt," she replied.

Beer spewed out of my mouth onto the tiled floor. "Holy shit, did you just say *cunt*?"

Giggling, she ducked her head. "Yeah, maybe."

"Okay, chalk that up as something else I've learned tonight. You can have a real potty mouth when you want to."

She smirked at me. "Like I didn't learn it from my big brother?"

"Well, that's probably true," I conceded.

"So what else did you learn about me?" Allison prompted.

"Well, besides the fact you can go from genteel to raging bitch in a few seconds, I found out that you can handle your own in a tough social situation like that. And you certainly know how to dress to impress."

"Thank you," she murmured softly.

"Most of all, I've learned you are a woman of many complexities, and it's very intriguing."

Her mouth made a perfect little "O" at my declaration. Everything I said was the truth. In the last thirty-six hours, I truly had come to see Allison in an entirely different light. It was hard imagining that I'd known her seven years and not realized it at all. Not only was she a woman now, but she was a very interesting one. I wasn't even sure Jake was aware of all the many facets that made up her character.

"You've learned so much about me, but I'm still missing some things on you," she said.

"I'm sure all you would have to do is Google me, and a lot of shit would come up."

She wrinkled her nose. "I don't want impersonal information like that about you. I want it straight from the horse's mouth."

"Fine. I have nothing to hide, so fire away." I cocked my brows at her. "But be forewarned that turnabout is fair play."

"I don't mind."

"So shoot."

Tilting her head, Allison asked, "How old were you when you lost your virginity?"

The audacious question, coupled with her interested expression, caused me to spew out the sip of beer I'd just taken. Swiping my hand across my mouth, I said, "Damn. Going straight for the jugular on that one, aren't you?"

She giggled. "Would you rather me have asked the last time you cried?"

I shook my head furiously. I wasn't one of those emotionally stunted men who thought it was weak to cry. It was more the fact that I didn't want to have to acknowledge that it had been three days ago after I saw my sister. I wasn't ready to go there with her yet.

"So answer the question," she pressed.

"Actually, I was a late bloomer. I was nineteen."

Her brows rose in surprise. "Seriously?"

I laughed. "You sound so shocked."

With a shrug, she said, "I just imagined you being young. Like fifteen."

"I was finishing up high school at fifteen. Trust me, for most of my teenage years, I wore glasses, had acne, and weighed one thirty soaking wet." I shook my head as I was assaulted by a barrage of painful teenage memories of being bullied and being made fun of. It was just another reason that I hated living in the past—it was too fucking painful.

Trying to lighten the dark mood pervading me, I motioned to myself. "I was not always the stud you see before you today," I teased.

My efforts were rewarded by a laugh from Allison. "I find that hard to believe."

I couldn't help shuddering. "Oh trust me, there's photographic *and* video evidence."

She shook her head. "Nope, I'm sorry, but I can't imagine a time when you weren't a hottie."

"As fucking misguided as you are, I gotta say thanks for the compliment."

With a grin, she took another sip of her beer. "So who was she?"

Shifting in my chair, I couldn't help feeling a little uncomfortable with her questioning. I mean, where the hell was she going with this? And now because she had brought it up, I couldn't help wanting to know the same shit about her...or did I?

"You want me to elaborate about losing my virginity?"

"Of course. After all, elaboration is the key element of Southern storytelling, and we are in the most Southern city in the South."

"True, very true." I took a long pull from my longneck. For reasons I couldn't even fathom, I felt the need to defend myself to Allison. "The thing is, I had gotten some action, but I still hadn't sealed the deal, so to speak."

"Lovely," Allison said, wrinkling her nose.

"Hey, you're the one who wanted me to elaborate."

She laughed. "You're right. Please continue."

"By the time I'd turned nineteen, things finally were looking up for me. I'd just met Jake and the other guys, and we were starting to play at Eastman's. After being sick, I got put on steroids and started beefing up. I got Lasik surgery, and my mother actually gave me a year's supply of chemical peels for my acne as a birthday present."

"But you digress," Allison said, with a grin.

"I'm trying to save face here about why I was so old when I lost my virginity."

"Pray continue."

I laughed. "Anyway, her name was Melanie. She was in some of my law classes at Emory. Since I was feeling more confident, I got up the nerve to ask her out. Thankfully, she said yes, and we started dating."

Surprise filled Allison's face. "Oh, so you have been in a relationship."

"A few, yeah. None really lasted a long time. I did have my heart broken when I was twenty-one."

"Interesting. And where was the deed done?"

With a wink, I replied, "In a pretty posh suite at the Ritz in Atlanta."

Her eyes bulged. "Really?"

"Hey, give me some credit here. I'm not the type of guy to lose it in the backseat of a car."

She giggled. "No, I can't see you doing that." Leaning her elbows on the table, she added with a teasing lilt to her voice, "Of course, you had to pick somewhere high-end. Couldn't lose the V-Card at the Holiday Inn, could you?"

"Hey now. I can't help how I was raised, even if I try to escape it as often as I can."

"So we know you had a posh first experience. But what about the relationship itself? How long did it last between the two of you?"

Tilting my head, I delved into my past. "Six months. She was a few years older than me." At Allison's continued questioning expression, I said, "She wanted more—a whole lot more than I was ready or willing to give at nineteen."

"I see," she murmured.

"And what about you?" When her usual red flush tinged Allison's cheeks, I shook my head. "Oh no, don't think you're getting out of this one."

"I'm not," she huffed.

"Then spill it."

"Fine," she muttered. I turned a laugh into a cough when she squared her shoulders determinedly while downing the rest of her beer. "I was seventeen."

"Man, you beat me by two years, huh?"

"Sex is never a competition."

"Sometimes it is to see who will finish first," I mused, which caused her to blush. "Anyway, please continue with the sordid details."

"Like you, I was in a relationship. Dylan and I started dating when I was sixteen."

Holding up my hand, I asked, "Just how old was he?"

"Eighteen."

"Older man, huh?"

With a slight shrug, she replied, "I was a junior, and he was a senior."

"Cradle robber," I teased.

"I would hardly call that age difference cradle robbing."

"Was he like the typical older guy who dated younger girls to get one thing?"

"Not exactly. I mean, our six month anniversary fell right after my seventeenth birthday, and he hadn't really been pressuring me or demanding anything of me."

"So where did you do the deed?"

A shy smile pulled at the corners of her lips. "Jake's farm."

Her declaration caused me to bolt upright in my chair. "Excuse me?"

"You guys were out on tour, and no one was there. It was the perfect place where we could be alone. I told my mom I was spending the weekend with my best friend, Kim. We didn't go in the house—we stayed in the loft."

I shook my head in disbelief at her. "Jake would blow a fucking gasket if he knew you lost your virginity in *his* loft."

Allison merely rolled her eyes at my declaration. "Like he hadn't defiled that place in a million different ways before Abby came along."

"Actually, he never brought chicks to the farm. I'm pretty sure the only woman he's ever had sex there with is Abby."

"Really?" Allison asked, her brows rising in surprise.

"It's the truth. I'd tell you to ask him, but that would be totally inappropriate."

She giggled. "I agree."

We sat in silence for a few moments. After I popped the tops on another beer for the two of us, my curiosity got the better of me. I detoured to a questioning path I had no fucking business going down. "Besides this Dylan, has there been a lot of other guys?"

Allison cocked her brows at me. "Are you actually asking me for my number?"

Grimacing, I guzzled down half the beer I'd just opened. After I swallowed, I shook my head. "Sorry. That was wrong of me."

As her fingers played with the label on the beer bottle, Allison stared straight ahead. Finally, she murmured, "Three."

"Excuse me?"

Her gaze flicked to mine, and she gave me a mischievous smile. "My number is three."

I sucked in a breath like I'd been sucker punched in the gut. I wasn't sure why her number mattered to me. I didn't know whether to be relieved or slightly shocked. Not that in the vast scheme of things, three was that big a number. I knew Jake would be horrified she had been with one guy. "I see."

Raising her beer bottle to her lips, Allison snorted. After taking a sip, she eyed me. "That's all you have to say. 'I see'?"

"Congratulations?" I suggested.

She laughed and shook her head. "Not quite the reaction I expected."

"And what did you think I would do?"

Tilting her chin in thought, Allison replied, "Go all apeshit and tell me that three was entirely too many partners for a girl my age."

"Oh please, you make me sound like some uptight Neanderthal man. Your life, including the sexual aspect of it, is entirely your business and yours alone. Fuck anyone else who tries to tell you anything different."

"Thank you for your candor."

"You're welcome," I replied, with a smile.

"As much as I would like to think I was liberated sexually, I'm still pretty old school."

"You mean like not wanting to partake in that asshole's sex games?"

"No, I meant my attitude about who I will be with." Cutting her eyes over at me, she shook her head. "I can't believe we're having this conversation. It seems the alcohol is freeing my tongue more than I would like. The truth is that two were relationships, Dylan and then the douchebag of late, and then one was pure lust."

"Seriously?"

"Now you're getting judgey?"

I laughed. "No, it's just hard to believe that after how you've described yourself that you actually just succumbed to lust."

A giggle burst out of Allison lips. "Did you just say *succumbed?*" This time she snorted. "Oh Rhys, you sound positively blue blood when you're down here and away from the guys. They would so call your ass out if they heard you."

"Whatever," I grumbled.

Nudging my shoulder with hers, she said, "Your turn."

"I don't think that's a good idea."

"And why not?"

"I don't want you to think badly of me."

She rolled her eyes. "Like I don't already know you're a slut."

"Y-You think I'm a slut?" I sputtered indignantly.

"Yeah, I do."

"I'll have you know my number isn't over a hundred."

"How comforting," she mused.

Rising to my feet, I stalked over to the trashcan and tossed my beer bottle. "You know, the fact that I'm now a famous musician and have that low a number is pretty impressive. Your brother's was off the charts."

"Not surprising that Jake surpassed slut to reside into dirty whore territory."

My anger dissipated, and I found myself laughing at the summation of her brother. After popping the top of my third beer, I sighed. "I think it's time for a conversation change."

"More questions?"

"Sure. Just ones that don't have anything to do with sex."

"Sounds fair to me." With a grin, she added, "Fire away."

I thought about a safe question to ask her. "Okay, how old were you when you drank for the first time?"

"Sixteen—it was the champagne at my party."

"Ah, I see."

"And you?"

"Twelve."

Allison's eyes bulged. "Twelve? That's just a baby."

"It was just one drink. I didn't start down an alcoholic path at that age."

She giggled. "I'd hope not." Taking another sip of her beer, she asked, "So where was it?"

"It was during a society party of my parents. I wanted to be like the older guys who were there. We've already established that I was a socially awkward misfit, so it should make total sense that I was being a dick to try and fit in. So when they dared me to drink a glass of Scotch, I downed it in one gulp." I shuddered as the memory flickered through my mind. "I thought I was going to die. I think I ended up puking most of the night, and lying to my nanny that it was some stomach bug."

Allison frowned. "You poor thing."

I chuckled. "Nah, I deserved it. But it did teach me a lesson about trying to fit in with the older kids. From that point on, I didn't give a shit about what they thought—I was really my own person."

"Such a wise revelation to have for such a young person," Allison mused.

Shaking my head, I replied, "Kids in my world grow up fast. When you're shuttled away to boarding school practically as a baby, you learn to only rely on yourself. In the end, that's all you have."

When I looked up at Allison, tears shimmered like diamonds in her dark eyes. Trying to ease the tension of the moment, I laughed. "Okay, no more beers for you."

"Sometimes you remind me so much of Jake."

"I do?"

She nodded. "He tried for so long to close himself off to other people—not to let them see his weaknesses." A lone tear streaked down her face. "His pain."

"Allison—"

"I see you, Rhys," she whispered.

My heartbeat thrummed wildly in fear at her statement, causing me to feel like an utter pansy. Christ, what had I done to make it so easy for her to be able to see through all my bullshit? The better question was why she was still sitting beside me after seeing the real me?

As if reading my mind, Allison said, "I see all of you, and I'm not disgusted."

Not liking the direction the conversation was taking, I rose out of the swing. I needed to put distance between Allison and myself. Things were getting too personal and deep too quickly. I couldn't remember the last time I'd opened up to anyone like I had with her. It wasn't enough that she was so compassionate and caring. At the same time, she distracted me by being so fucking hot. At one moment, I wanted to hug her to me for the comfort she could provide. Then at the next, I wanted to peel her sexy-as-hell black dress off that could make a guy spring wood at fifty paces and stroke every inch of her creamy white skin.

"Yeah, well, I think that's enough for tonight. You have class in the morning, and I need my beauty sleep to gird up strength to deal with my parents."

After wiping her tear-stained cheeks, Allison bent over and picked up her sexy heels that she had discarded when we sat down. Her eyes held so much emotion that I could tell she was fighting hard to hold it back. "Thank you for inviting me tonight."

"It's me that should be thanking you. I might've been auctioned off to a cunt, as you called it, if it hadn't been for you."

A shadow of a smile played on her lips. "I'm glad I could save the day."

Without second guessing myself, I leaned in and gave her a hug. As we swayed back and forth, Allison's hands came up to grip the back of my shirt. Having my arms around her stirred me on both an emotional and physical level. But with her sexy curves pressed against me, I was certainly focusing more on the physical side.

She was so delicate, just like the magnolia on the pendant I'd given her. With her scent and softness overwhelming me, my mind railed at me to pull away. All right, asshole, you have about two seconds to pull away before she *feels* just how much you're enjoying copping a feel.

When I finally pried myself away, I smiled at Allison. "I'll text you about doing movie night soon."

"I'll look forward to it."

After placing a tender kiss on her cheek, I turned and walked away. But even as I put distance between us, I couldn't shake the feeling of that hug. Even when I lay down that night, I could almost still feel her in my arms.

And that made me scared as hell.

6: ALLISON

The following two and a half weeks flew by in a whirlwind of school, work, and most importantly, Rhys. We hadn't spent a day apart since he arrived in Savannah. True to his word, he came to my house the night after the auction for *Monty Python* and Penis Pizza. He ended up sleeping on the couch because we kept talking and drinking beer long after the movie was over. The second best thing besides Rhys dressed to the nines in a tux was Rhys tangled in blankets with tousled hair while asleep on the couch.

Of course, that night I also experienced a level of mortification I hadn't known existed. I'd fallen asleep snuggled next to Rhys with the strains of Hugh Jackman singing as Jean Valjean in *Les Misérables*. The closeness of him, coupled with his smell, had done a number on me as I slipped further and further into dreamland. Amid the foggy wisps of my sub consciousness, I began to dream. As I lay on my bed, Rhys loomed over me, his eyes hungry with lust. I found that not only was he very naked, but I was naked as well. Rhys's mouth captured mine with his own. At the feel of his warm lips on my own, I reached up to wrap my arms around his neck, drawing him closer to me. My fingers ran through the silky strands of his hair, as he thrust his tongue into my mouth.

As we continued to kiss, he brought one of his hands up to cup and knead my breast, tweaking the nipple into a hardened peak. I moaned into his mouth, scissoring my legs to get the friction I desperately wanted. Sensing my need, Rhys's other hand slipped between my thighs. His fingers slid long strokes up and down my wet slit before one finger plunged inside me. "Rhys," I panted, as one finger became two.

"Allison," Rhys murmured, as he stared into my eyes with a combative mixture of love and lust.

I cupped his cheeks in my hands, feeling the stubble along his skin. I wanted nothing more to feel that stubble grazing the inside of my thighs as he went down on me. As his fingers pumped in and out of me, I arched my hips in time. "Please, please," I begged.

"Allison," Rhys repeated, his free hand shaking my shoulder. When his fingers disappeared from inside me, I cried out in frustration.

"No, don't stop!"

He started shaking me harder and harder until my eyes snapped open. Rhys stared down at me, not with lust, but with concern. "Allison, wake up. You're having a nightmare."

"Oh…my…God," I muttered, as my hands came up to cover my cheeks that blazed with humiliation. How was it possible I had just been having a sex dream about Rhys as he lay right next to me? I wanted to bolt from the couch and lock myself in my room, but I remained paralyzed on the couch.

"Are you okay?" Rhys asked.

"Fine. Just fine," I muttered behind my hands.

"That must've been some hell of a dream the way you were moaning and thrashing about. I'll know now not to watch any horror movies late at night with you."

When I continued to keep my face hidden, Rhys hand came to gently pull mine away. "Hey, what's the matter?"

I bit my lip to keep from blurting that my panties were soaked from having a literal wet dream about him. I sure as hell hoped he couldn't smell my arousal. Instead, I sighed. "Just embarrassed, that's all."

Rhys gave me a genuine smile. "You've got nothing to be embarrassed about. Want me to lie here with you until you can go back to sleep?"

I couldn't believe he was willing to do that. "Please."

"First order of business is to put on something less depressing to watch than Les Mis. I think a comedy is in order to chase away the nightmares."

"Me, too."

And then he had dug out *Robin Hood: Men in Tights* from my roommates and my communal DVD collection. He had wrapped me in his arms, and we both fell asleep again. It had been heaven on earth, minus being woken up from the naughty sex dream.

As the days went on, we continued spending more and more time together. When we were together, everything was good—the conversation, the food we ate, the places we went to see. Rhys was the quintessential Renaissance man. He was someone who could be doubled over with laughter at inane comedies like *Anchorman and DodgeBall* one night and then the very next be thoroughly enraptured at a poetry reading or art gallery opening. You could talk to him about anything—

philosophy, history, or literature. He was always well versed and could bring the most interesting aspects to a discussion. He'd won over two of my roommates by being able to help them with their Design Law class. Being with Rhys was like getting to see the very best of both worlds—the society intellectual he had been born as and then the down and dirty, beer-drinking rocker he had become. Rhys's complexities just made me love him all the more.

In each and every way, we seemed like the perfect loving couple. But we weren't—there still managed to be a wall between us, preventing us from taking it to the next level. As much as I hated it, Rhys kept things strictly platonic. He never sat too close to me on the couch or held my hand when we were out exploring the city. I was trying to be patient and go with the flow, hoping that things would change, but my patience was starting to wear thin the more time went by.

But tonight was the change I desperately was hoping for. Earlier in the week, I had accepted an invitation to a party at his parents' house. So far, Rhys had never taken me there. We had hung out strictly at my house. While I had met his mother at the bachelor auction, I couldn't help thinking that the invitation truly meant something more.

So once again, I found myself living a Cinderella-esque lifestyle where I dashed in from work to get ready for the ball with my handsome prince. After the bitch had made snide comments about my dress last time, I was determined not to face that again this time. While I was completely ready to spend far too much out of my savings on something posh, Cassie once again came through for me. Through her family connections, I was able to borrow a dress from an upscale store. The only catch was I would have to model for them in their fall collection show, which I guess wasn't so bad. With my height, barely there boobs, and small frame, I had been courted to model before. But just like performing, it wasn't for me. I was much too shy for the limelight, and I much preferred staying behind the scenes with fashion design.

As I slid the gold tube of lipstick over my lips, I put the final touches on my appearance. With my reflection staring back at me in the full-length mirror, I couldn't help feeling just like Cinderella. The store had really come through in the most perfect dress imaginable. It was satin and strapless in a deep red, almost wine color. From the bust to the waist, the crisscrossing design fit me like a second skin before flowing out around my hips. Rather than the magnolia necklace, I was wearing the pearls Jake and Abby had given me for my high school graduation. And on my feet were the sexiest strappy heels that matched the color of the dress.

Glancing at the clock on my nightstand, I realized it was almost time for Rhys to pick me up. I grabbed the glittery clutch purse I would be carrying and then hurried down the hall. In the kitchen, I could hear Cassie chattering away with two of our other roommates, Kelly and Tammy. When I appeared in the doorway, I received several whistles. I couldn't help grinning. "Thank you."

"You're going to knock 'em dead tonight," Cassie said.

Sticking my foot out from beneath the dress, I asked, "Are you sure these heels aren't too much?"

"No, they're sexy as hell," Cassie replied, to which Kelly and Tammy nodded.

"They just don't feel like me." Running my hand over the satin, I sighed. "I guess that none of it feels like me."

Cassie shook her head. "You look absolutely sensational, heels and all. You're dressing the part that's expected for you tonight. Be thankful that Rhys seems to appreciate you just as much when you're in jeans and smelling of tomato sauce after work."

I laughed. "I guess you're right." The sound of a car pulling up interrupted anymore of my self-deprecating tirade.

"Is that him?" Tammy asked.

"I hope so," I replied.

"Daaaamn, Rhys has one sweet-ass ride!" Cassie exclaimed. When I turned around, she was at the window, peeking outside through the blinds.

"Would you please stop that? It makes you look totally creepy spying on him like that."

"I'm not spying. I'm being a concerned homeowner. A strange car pulled into the drive, so I am checking it out."

Rolling my eyes, I muttered, "You're impossible."

"What kind of car does he have?" Tammy asked, joining Cassie at the window.

"You know I don't know anything about cars."

Cassie flipped the blinds again. "Hmm, it's definitely a classic. Maybe a '60's Ferrari or Porsche."

"Yeah, it's old. It was left to him in his grandfather's will."

"Sweet," Tammy said.

At the ring of the doorbell, I skidded across the floor in my uber-high stilettos. "Once again, I'm thinking these shoes were a mistake."

Just as I threw open the door, Cassie called over her shoulder in a not discreet voice, "Would you stop already? Seriously, those are the sexiest 'come-fuck-me-heels' I've ever seen you wear. They sure as hell give me a lady boner, so I can't imagine Rhys not springing some wood at the sight of them."

Mortification rocketed through my body as Rhys stood before me, hearing every. Single. Word. Of course, the first thing he did was eye my shoes, which were on display a little more than usual since I'd been holding up the hem of my dress to run to the door. Once he'd had his fill, he glanced back up at me. A sexy smirk curved on his lips. "Nice heels."

"T-Thank you." Not only did my heartbeat accelerate at his smirk, but moisture dampened my panties.

"I'd say I agreed with Cassie on the 'come fuck me' status, but that would probably be inappropriate."

No, it wouldn't. In fact we should ditch the party so you could 'come fuck me' right now. Tuning the inappropriate thoughts from my mind, I said, "Uh, yeah, I guess so."

I'd been so distracted by the shoes comment that it took me a moment to process what Rhys had on. Blinking several times, I fought the urge to brace a hand on the doorjamb, so I wouldn't slide into a puddle of lust on the floor. "You're wearing a kilt?" I questioned lamely.

His cocky smirk faded and was replaced by a sheepish look as he glanced down at himself. "I guess I forgot to mention that my parents' party recognizes Tartan Day." At what I imagined was still my deer-in – the-headlights expression, he continued on. "It's when people with Scottish heritage celebrate the Declaration of Arbroath."

"I didn't realize you had such strong Scottish roots. I mean, I kinda gathered your family origin from your last name."

"Yeah, my great-great grandfather was a lord with a pretty expansive estate."

My brows shot up at his declaration. "Does that mean I should start addressing you as 'my lord'?"

He laughed. "Not quite. My great-grandfather was the fifth son, so he didn't get to inherit the title."

"I see."

Cassie came to join me at my side. She gave a low whistle at the sight of Rhys. "Look at you, stylin' and profilin' in a skirt. Didn't take you for a cross-dresser."

With a good-natured chuckle, Rhys replied, "It's a kilt, not a skirt."

Cassie motioned to his crotch. "You free ballin' under there?"

Although my mind had certainly gone there, I still let out a horrified gasp at Cassie's question. Rhys wagged a finger at Cassie. "A gentleman never tells."

"Whatever," Cassie replied.

Wanting to escape before the conversation got any crazier, I said, "We should go. We don't want to be late."

Rhys nodded and then opened the door for me. After saying goodbye to Cassie and the others, we headed out onto the porch and then down the stairs. As he held open the car door for me, Rhys gave me a genuine smile. "I meant to tell you earlier, but I was a distracted. You look very beautiful tonight, Allison."

The sincerity with which he said the words, coupled with the way he was looking at me, caused my cheeks to warm while a delighted shiver ran down my spine. "Thank you."

After I sank down on the leather seat, Rhys leaned in rather than closing the door. "And I'm really glad you're wearing a long dress to cover those heels. They're awfully distracting."

My stomach flip-flopped at his words. It didn't help matters that he gave me a teasing wink as he shut the door. While he went around the front of the car, I tried smoothing down my dress—anything to try to get a hold of my raging hormones.

When he got into the car, I couldn't help cutting my eyes over to see how he maneuvered himself in the kilt. He must've had practice because he managed, unfortunately, not to flash more than the tops of his knees. We drove along the streets with the radio playing softly in the background. I was anxious to see where Rhys lived. I imagined it was somewhere in the Historic District—some pre-Civil War home that had been in his family for generations.

As we neared Forsyth Park, Rhys turned off on a street I'm not familiar with. It doesn't take me long to spot his house, or I should say, mansion. It's the one where expensive cars are lining up to the valet stand. It's pretty much everything I envisioned in my mind. Instead of waiting for the valet, Rhys pulled into the driveway that wound around to the back of the house.

After turning off the car, he glanced over at me. "Pretentious, isn't it?"

"It's magnificent. I love antebellum homes."

"Well, it's from the 1830s."

"I can't wait to see inside."

"Then let's go." Rhys then climbed out of the car and came around for me. Once he opened the door, I slid out, careful not to stumble on my heels.

When we continued up the pathway to the back of the house, I couldn't help asking, "We aren't going in the front?"

Rhys rolled his eyes. "And have to pass through the doorman and all that bullshit? I don't want any part of that."

"Oh," I murmured.

"What do you mean 'oh'?" he questioned, as he walked ahead of me.

"I just thought you might be embarrassed of me," I murmured.

Skidding to a stop on the brick walkway, Rhys stared at me with an incredulous expression. "You are not serious?"

I shrugged. "It's not like I fit into this world."

"Neither do I," he countered.

"But you were born into it. You're a blue blood for God's sake. Besides, your mother made it very clear a few weeks ago that I wasn't the type of girl that you should be interested in." Realizing I had said too much, I quickly tried backtracking. "I mean, the type of girl you should be hanging out with," I hurriedly added.

"I don't give two fucks what kind of girl my parents think I should be hanging out with. I like being with you. I can't remember a time when I've had more fun or been more at peace than I have with you. You're the only thing that has made this visit tolerable. All those reasons? They're what matters, not my parents."

Between his words and the intensity of his stare, I had to focus on breathing. *In and out, in and out,* I recited in my head as my chest rose and fell in harsh pants. Finally, when I felt like I wasn't going to pass out, I murmured very ineloquently, "Okay then."

He smiled. "Good. I'm glad we have that settled." He held out his arm for me to take just like a gentleman of years past would. "Now come on. It's time we jumped into the shark tank."

I slipped my arm through his and let him lead me up the walkway. When we got to the backdoor, Rhys didn't even bother knocking. Instead, he barreled right on inside. A flurry of activity was going on in the massive kitchen with its marble tiled floor and granite countertops. The caterers and wait-staff buzzed around like busy worker bees. I'm sure Rhys's mother would have considered them more as drones. They didn't acknowledge our presence. Only one elderly, African-American woman's face lit up at the sight of Rhys.

"Why hello there, stranger!" she cried.

Rhys's face broke into a smile for the first time since we'd pulled into the driveway. "Ozella, my most favorite cook in the whole wide world."

She wagged a finger at him. "I'm the only cook you've ever had."

He laughed. "You're still the best."

His compliment sent a beaming smile across her face. "Well, since you're a world traveler and famous musician, I'll take your word for it."

After they exchanged a hug, Rhys turned back to me. "Allison, this is Mrs. Ozella Princeton. She was our family's personal cook from before I was born up until a few years ago."

She smiled. "If I hadn't had to retire for health reasons, I'd still be here. But I always come supervise Mrs. McGowan's major parties."

I held out my hand. "It's nice meeting you."

"Likewise." Once she released my hand, she smacked Rhys playfully on the shoulder. "Now why didn't you call and tell me you had settled down?"

Both Rhys and my eyes bulged at her mistake. "No, no, we're not together like that," Rhys quickly corrected.

Ozella's brows creased in confusion. "Then how *are* you together?"

"He's my brother's best friend," I replied, at the same time Rhys said, "She's my bandmate's little sister."

"Uh-huh," Ozella replied, a knowing look flickering in her eyes. I couldn't help wondering why she had jumped to such a conclusion. Had Rhys never brought girls around before? Or was it more in the way we interacted with each other?

Her comment left us all in an awkward silence with me gnawing my lip, and Rhys fidgeting with the lapels and then the cuffs on his tux top.

"Zell, we need you," someone called from across the room.

"Be right there," Ozella called. Leaning in, she gave Rhys another hug. "Sorry, honey. I've got work to do."

"It was so good seeing you," Rhys said, as he squeezed her tight.

"You too. Don't be a stranger when you're in town. Come to see me anytime."

Rhys nodded. "I will."

Ozella winked at me. "You're welcome, too, Allison."

"Thank you," I murmured, not daring to look at Rhys's expression.

After Ozella had hurried off, Rhys turned to me. "Come," he said, holding out his hand to me. "Let's go find my parents so I can properly introduce you."

Although I nodded in agreement, I fought the urge to stay in the kitchen or anywhere that was far, far away from his parents. It had been bad enough spending any time with his mother. I couldn't imagine his father would be any better.

Tucked close to his side, I followed him out of the kitchen and into a long hallway. It reminded me a lot of the entrance hallway at the Mercer Williams House. My heels clacked along the marble floor beneath my feet while two glittering, crystal chandeliers lit our way. From ahead of us, I could hear the sound of a string quartet playing. A classical repertoire floated through the air, and for a moment, the relaxing music calmed me.

Pointing up the hallway, Rhys said, "The first room on the right is the ballroom. That's where the music is coming from and where most of the party guests are. The doors open to a veranda."

I widened my eyes. "You have a ballroom?"

He shrugged as if it was the most normal thing in the world to have a ballroom. "We also have a study, library, and a billiard room, just like in *Clue*."

A nervous giggle escaped my lips. "You do?"

"It was fun growing up with such a big house to explore, but now it seems a bit pretentious."

Inwardly, I agreed with him. I'd never been comfortable with over-the-top expressions of wealth. While my parents made good money, we lived rather modestly compared to a lot of their friends. I was thankful that when Runaway Train took off, Jake stayed very true to his roots, which meant staying at the farm he grew up on. "I never knew you were this rich."

Rhys shook his head. "Just remember, this is my parents' world—it isn't mine. It never has been, nor will it ever be."

"I'll try," I murmured, as Rhys swept me into a room to the left. This must have been the formal living room. It was heavy on the formal part with chandeliers, Persian rugs, and ornate furniture. It certainly wasn't the type of living room where you kicked off your shoes and watched TV.

"Rhys darling, there you are," Margaret called from the corner of the room. She, and who I assumed was Rhys's father, was talking with another couple. As we approached, the couple excused themselves, and then it was just the four of us.

"Mother, I believe you have had the pleasure, but Father, please allow me to introduce to you, Allison Slater."

Rhys's father's dark eyes narrowed slightly at me as he took a puff of a foul-smelling cigar. "It's a pleasure to meet you, Miss Slater. I'm Elliot McGowan," he said, extending a hand. Just like Rhys, he was outfitted in a blue and green checked kilt.

As I shook his hand, I quickly replied, "It's a pleasure meeting you too, sir."

"I understand you're here in Savannah for school."

"Yes, sir. I attend the Savannah College of Art and Design."

"And what exactly do you plan to do with your degree?"

"Fashion design."

At his father's obvious lack of enthusiasm for my major, Rhys cleared his throat. "Allison's just been accepted for a very prestigious internship."

I smiled. "Rhys flatters me, but I will be fulfilling my internship while out on tour with his band."

Margaret made a strangled noise beside me. When I turned to her, she asked, "So you and Rhys will be spending a lot of time together?"

With a nod, I replied, "Yes, just for the summer. I'll pick up classes again in the fall."

"I see," she said, not bothering to hide her disdain.

Craning his neck around the room, Rhys asked, "Where's Ellie?"

Margaret immediately stiffened before exchanging a glance with Elliot. "Tonight just isn't the place for Eleanor," Elliot replied.

Rhys's pleasant expression instantly darkened. "What the hell is that supposed to mean?"

A nervous titter escaped Margaret's lips as she gave a flippant wave of her hand. "You know your sister's limitations. A crowded party full of strange people isn't the place for her."

"What you mean to say is, it's the perfect place for you to be embarrassed by your own daughter?"

"Rhys, you may be a grown adult, but I will not have you speak to your mother with that tone," Elliot warned.

Shaking his head, Rhys questioned bitterly, "I don't know why I'm even surprised. Is she even here, or did you keep her as far away as possible by having her stay at the Brandewine Institute?"

"She is here, just like she is every weekend. She just will not be attending the party."

"You two really disgust me sometimes," Rhys bellowed, before he turned and strode determinedly out of the room.

I exchanged a horrified glance with Rhys's parents. "Excuse me," I said, before hightailing after him. When I got back into the foyer, I glanced left and right to see where Rhys had gone. I heard a door slam in the back, so I raced as best I could in my heels and dress to catch up with him.

As I got outside, I saw him stalking across the garden area. "Rhys, wait!" I called.

He froze. He still hadn't turned around by the time I got to him. Instead, his broad shoulders were drawn, his head tucked into his chest. Tentatively, I reached my hand out to touch his arm. Words seemed to escape me. There was obviously a sordid history about Rhys's younger sister that I wasn't privy to—one that hurt him very deeply. "I'm so sorry. Are you okay?"

Rhys turned his head to look at me. "There's nothing you need to apologize for. It's my fucking parents and their bullshit way of thinking."

My hand rubbed up and down his arm. "I'm still sorry they upset you. It's obvious that you love your sister, and that you don't want to see her mistreated."

"I do love her." Rhys's shoulders slumped farther. "Sometimes I think I'm the only one who does."

"Then let's go see her. I'm sure she wants to spend time with you."

With a slight nod of his head, Rhys started toward the front door of the carriage house. His hand hovered over the ornate door knocker before he pulled it back. "Allison, before you meet her, I guess I need to explain about Ellie."

"Okay," I replied cautiously. At that moment, I didn't know what to expect behind that door. Between what Elliot and Margaret had said, coupled with Rhys acting so mysteriously, I didn't know if Ellie was just your typical rebellious daughter that her uptight parents were ashamed of or if there was something else— something much more serious.

"Ellie is different."

"Different how?" I pressed.

He grimaced. "I hate even saying that about her. The truth is she's severely autistic. She isn't anything like Lucy." He shook his head. "It's a horrible thing to do, but I guess to prepare you in the best way, she's an autistic savant, like Rain Man, except she's nonverbal."

My heart ached for the pain I could feel coming from Rhys. "Why don't your parents want her coming to the party?" I questioned softly.

Rhys ran a hand over his face that wore an agonized expression. "Although my mother may head up charity campaigns for autism research, she prefers to keep Ellie out of sight. Most of the time, Ellie does fine in crowds— loud noise or music doesn't bother her like some autistic people. She even seems to thrive on being with people, or at least she has at her group home. But my mother would never risk having Ellie at one of her parties. To her, Ellie will always be an embarrassment—like a crack in a beautiful piece of Waterford crystal. You would think after twenty-three years, she would have accepted the imperfection, but she hasn't. During the week, Ellie lives at the Brandewine Institute, which is a group home for adults with disabilities. Basically, it's a place where a lot of wealthy society families from Georgia and South Carolina, stick their mentally challenged adult children."

"That's so sad."

"I wouldn't stand for it if Ellie wasn't happy there. She fits in well, and she spends hours painting." He stared pointedly at me. "That's where she painted your necklace. She really enjoys painting intricate details like that on small objects."

"She truly has a gift."

Rhys gave me a sad smile. "She's good at so many things, but unfortunately, my parents refuse to see it. They only focus on what she can't do, rather than what she can. She never got to be a debutante and have a coming out party, and she'll never be in the papers for a society wedding."

Reaching out, I once again touched his arm. "I still want to meet her."

"Okay," Rhys replied, with an edge of caution in his voice.

A few seconds after Rhys tapped on the brass knocker, the door flew open. A silver-haired woman with a warm, friendly smile appeared before us. "Rhys McGowan, aren't you looking dapper this evening?" she exclaimed.

Rhys bounded forward to hug the woman. "Thank you, Trudie. I do clean up well, don't I?"

Squeezing him tight, Trudie patted Rhys's back. "Yes, you do. Why I almost wouldn't have recognized you out of your ratty jeans and T-shirts."

With a chuckle, Rhys argued, "Hey now, you act as if I look like some homeless person. I may wear that around the house, but I always dress up at the Brandewine Institute when I come to see Ellie."

I couldn't help raising my brows at Rhys's admission of how he had been sneaking around the past two weeks. Truthfully, it was none of my business what he had done during the times he wasn't with me. But it was surprising that I was just now learning about Ellie.

"Yes, that's true. It doesn't matter what you have on. You'd be as good-looking as any movie star, even in a potato sack."

"Thank you, Trudie. You always flatter me."

Trudie grinned. "I bet Ellie is going to be excited to see you again. She lights up whenever you are around."

Rhys grimaced. "I know. I've been down to the Brandewine Institute every day since I've been back. But it isn't enough. I've got to start coming home more when I'm on break, if only for Ellie's sake."

Patting Rhys's arm reassuringly, Trudie replied, "In her own way, she understands. And she loves to do those camera talks with you on the computer."

Rhys smiled. "The Skype chats."

Trudie snapped her fingers. "That's it." She then turned her attention to me as if realizing for the first time Rhys wasn't alone. "Well, who do we have here?"

"This is my friend, Allison. She's my bandmate, Jake's, little sister."

A knowing look came over Trudie's face. "I see." When I stuck out my hand for her to shake, she drew me into her embrace instead. "It's lovely meeting you, Allison."

"Thank you. It's nice meeting you, too."

As she pulled away, she tenderly cupped my cheek as if we were lifelong acquaintances. "What a beautiful young woman you are," she remarked.

Warmth rushed to my face at her compliments. "Thank you."

She glanced from me to Rhys. "How fortunate you are that your bandmate has such a pretty sister."

Rhys cleared his throat, and I could tell he was uncomfortable with the attention that Trudie was giving me. "Yes, I am. Although I'm pretty sure Jake wouldn't appreciate me saying that."

"Did you make the trip down with Rhys?" Trudie asked.

I shook my head wildly at her assumption. "No, no, I'm from Atlanta, but I'm here in Savannah for college at SCAD."

"Oh, how interesting. What's your major?"

"Fashion design."

Glancing at my dress, she nodded. "I can see that—you have impeccable taste."

"Thank you very much."

After clearing his throat, Rhys asked, "Where's Ellie?"

Trudie's bright expression dimmed a little. "She's at the front window. She's been glued to watching all the catering trucks coming and going." Trudie shook her head. "Even though she's in her own world most of the time, she does seem to love a party."

Rhys clenched his jaw. "I know." After nodding to Trudie, he once again reached for my hand, and I took it. He led me through an arched doorway into a room filled with floor-to-ceiling windows. At the far end of the room, I saw Ellie—or at least her back. Each of her hands gripped the sides of the lace curtains as if they were the lifeline to keep her upright as she leaned her entire upper body into the window. Her dark hair fell just at her shoulders, and it was styled like a pageboy. With jeans and a striped shirt, she appeared as any other twenty-something. But from the way she hummed and carried herself, you could tell there was a difference.

"Ellie-Bellie-Mellie," Rhys called, his voice vibrating with affection. The moment the words left his lips I thought of Jake's nickname for me. Rhys had always called me the same thing, and although I hated it, I saw now that it meant something to him to call me that.

Slowly, Ellie craned her neck in Rhys's direction. A bright smile lit up her face. With her dark hair and dark eyes, she looked so much like Rhys.

Without a word to Rhys, she hurried over to the other side of the room where a baby grand piano sat. After she eased down on the bench, Rhys grinned. "Must we play now, Ellie? I wanted to introduce you to my friend, Allison."

She didn't reply, nor did she look in my direction. Instead, her posture remained ramrod straight, fingers poised over the keys. "Okay, if you're sure," he said. Still Ellie made no gestures or noises.

I watched in amazement as Rhys crossed the room to Ellie and sat down next to the piano. Out of a case on the floor, he produced a sleek black cello. Easing it between his legs, he took the bow in one hand. Once he had everything adjusted properly, Ellie began to play. Within a few beats, Rhys chimed in with her. "Recognize it?" he questioned over the music.

Closing my eyes, I tried to put a composer or a title with it. "Beethoven?" I asked, as I opened my eyes again.

Rhys nodded. "*Moonlight Sonata*," he called over the music.

"I love Beethoven. He's the perfect classical emo composer."

With a laugh, Rhys replied, "That is true."

Then he focused his attention back on his instrument. He had never mentioned being able to play the cello. I suppose it made sense since in a way the bass guitar was in the same family as the cello. With rapt attention, I watched as he closed his eyes and effortlessly drew the bow across the strings with infinite precision. His left hand moved deftly across the fingerboard, and I couldn't help but shudder a little watching the strength in those fingers.

Although sex should have been the furthest thought from my mind, there was something very erotic about watching him with his eyes closed, biting his lip in extreme concentration as he worked his fingers up and down the neck with the massive cello standing between his legs.

As I fought the urge to fan myself, Trudie came to join me at my side. "They're very talented, aren't they?" she asked.

"It's amazing how well they complement each other."

"Yes, they both were born musically gifted. Ellie learned by listening to Rhys's early music lessons. Then one day I found her repeating what she had heard on the piano."

"So she's pretty much completely self-taught?"

Trudie nodded. "She doesn't read music. She simply hears a piece and commits it to memory."

As the duet came to a close and Trudie and I clapped wildly, Ellie made no move to get up from the piano, but Rhys seemed to anticipate her silent request. "Okay, but just one more. How about instead of the classics, we try *Les Mis* this time?" Rhys said. I sucked in a breath when he jerked his chin up at me and grinned. It meant so much that he had picked a musical he knew was my favorite. We'd just watched the new movie version the other day.

Ellie then began the opening chords of a song I was so familiar with, *Bring Him Home*. As they each played their separate parts that melted into one melody, they complemented each other so well. Tears sprang to my eyes as I watched them execute the music so beautifully. Swiping my cheeks, I realized how precious these moments had to be to Rhys. For a short time, he was wholly connected with Ellie in a world where they were both equals and understood each other so completely. I couldn't help but imagine that from the time they were little, their bond had been tightly woven through the strings of music.

No matter where he had gone in life or what celebrity status had come to him, Rhys had never let his bond break with his sister. It warmed my heart to see him have such a wonderful connection. For someone I had feared didn't know how to love or be loved, he had thankfully proved me wrong.

When they finished, I clapped until my hands were stung red. "That was…" Closing my eyes, I shook my head. "I don't even have words to express how wonderful it was."

Standing up from his chair, Rhys gave me a beaming smile. "I'm so glad you enjoyed the concert. I'll have to play for you again sometime."

"I would love it."

Without a word to any of us, Ellie closed the piano lid and rose off the bench. She then crossed the room to stand in front of the mirror. The humming started up again as she peered at the coming and going guests. Trudie smiled. "I'm afraid I won't be able to get her to bed until the party is over. She wants to take it all in."

"Can't she go?" I asked before I thought better of it. When Rhys stared at me in surprise, I ducked my head. "I'm sorry. I just thought maybe we could take her for a little while. Let her see everything up close and personal, rather than from the window."

"I think that's a fantastic idea," Rhys said.

I jerked my head up. The intensity of his stare caused me to shiver. There were so many emotions radiating in his eyes, but gratitude was one that I could plainly make out. "Really?"

He turned to Trudie. "Can you find her something more appropriate to wear?"

"Yes, I believe she has a few dresses in the closet."

Rhys nodded and then went to Ellie's side. Tenderly, he touched her shoulder. "Ellie, do you want to go with Trudie and find a dress to wear to the party? You'll look so pretty, and you'll get to see all the people you've been watching tonight."

Slowly, she released her hold on the curtains. Turning from the window, she went to Trudie's side. "Let's find you something to wear, shall we?" Trudie asked. She and Ellie left the living room and went into one of the bedrooms.

When the door closed behind them, Rhys exhaled a long breath. With a gracious expression, he said, "Thank you for suggesting that."

I shook my head. "I don't know if it was the right thing. I mean, your mother and father didn't think she should go."

Rhys shook his head. "Don't worry about what they said. They're just trying to save face in front of their stuck-up friends."

I hoped he was right. The door opened, and Ellie appeared in a demure, beaded black dress. Her hair had been swept back with a glittering headband.

"Don't you look beautiful?" Rhys exclaimed, closing the gap between them. He hugged her gently, as if careful not to crowd her. She patted his back with one of her hands. "I'm so lucky to have two beautiful ladies escorting me to the party." Glancing over his shoulder at me, Rhys's wide smile lit up his entire face. It was good seeing him so happy, and I was so grateful that he was letting me share the moment with him and his sister.

As we started to the door, Trudie stopped Rhys. "If you need me, I'll be here." I could tell that although she was thrilled that Ellie was going to the party, Trudie was also worried.

Rhys nodded. "It'll be fine. I'll let her see everyone and listen to the music. I'll make sure to bring her back in an hour so she doesn't get overstimulated by the crowd."

"That sounds good." Trudie patted Ellie's arm. "Have fun, honey."

As we started up the brick pathway, Ellie walked slightly ahead of us, craning her neck to take in the sound of the string quartet coming from the tent off to the side of the house. "She's going to enjoy the hell out of the music," Rhys said, as we walked up the stairs and into the kitchen.

Ellie paid little attention to the people overfilling the main hallway and other rooms. She had a singular focus it seemed, to find the source of the music she was humming. Rhys, on the other hand, was the consummate Southern gentleman. He spoke to everyone he saw— shook hands with the men and kissed a few women's cheeks. Each and every time, he made sure to introduce me. All the while as he socialized, he kept a cautious eye on Ellie.

When she had gotten to the ballroom door that led out onto the veranda, she had stopped. It seemed she had found her perfect spot to listen to the music and watch the dancing partygoers. Those who didn't know her cast frustrated looks when she wouldn't move aside for them.

"Excuse me, Eddie," Rhys said to a bald man in a red and black checked kilt. He then crossed the room to go to Ellie's side. He gently took her by the arm. "Why don't we sit at a table, so you can see and hear better?"

While she didn't appear to acknowledge him, Ellie did let Rhys lead her over to a table in the back of the veranda. I eased down beside Rhys. Glad to be off my feet for a moment, I, too, enjoyed listening to the quartet.

My gaze flickered around the room, taking in the guests. Several were in kilts like Rhys, but most of the men wore tuxes. When a waiter stopped at the table, I gladly took a flute of bubbly. Thankfully another appeared with a tray of hors d' oeuvres. After I greedily devoured the napkin of goodies, I craned my neck to see where another waiter was.

Rhys chuckled beside me. "What?" I asked.

"There is real food in the dining room if you're hungry."

Embarrassment warmed my cheeks. "I guess scarfing that down didn't look too ladylike, huh?"

With a roll of his eyes, Rhys said, "Like I give two shits about anything ladylike." He leaned forward. "What I do care about is if you're hungry."

"I am." *And for more than just food. I'd like to have you as the appetizer, main course, and dessert.* Those were the thoughts derailing my mind in the middle of the party.

He smiled. "Then let me get you a plate." After waving one of the waiters over, Rhys said, "Please bring me three settings of the dinner course."

"Yes, sir."

As the waiter hurried off, I cocked my brows at Rhys. "Wow, that was impressive."

"What do you mean?"

"Having someone at your beck and call like that. No standing in line with the other peasants. Not to mention, you get table side service."

Rhys laughed. "It's basically the same thing as ordering something at a restaurant. The wait-staff always know to keep my parents' guests happy and give them what they ask for."

"So he wasn't falling over himself to give you what you wanted because you were lord of the manor?" I teasingly questioned.

"Maybe." Then he shook his head at me. "I'm not lord of the manor. I told you my branch of the family didn't have a title."

I opened my mouth to tease him more, but the waiter arrived with our plates. "That was fast," I murmured, after he left the table.

"And I'm sure the fast service was because of me being Lord McGowan?" Rhys asked, cocking his brows at me.

"You can't tell me any different."

"Whatever," he replied, with a good-natured chuckle.

While I dug into the deliciously aromatic roast chicken, Rhys coaxed Ellie to eat a little. His efforts went to waste when two bagpipers in full regalia strolled past our table. Ellie dropped her fork and sat up a little straighter, her curiosity piqued.

"You weren't kidding about celebrating Tartan Day, were you?" I asked.

He grinned. "Do you think I'd be rocking this kilt if we weren't hardcore about it?"

"Probably not." Reaching for my purse, I took out my phone. "I should seriously take a pic and send it to Jake."

Before I knew what was happening, Rhys had snatched the phone out of my hand. "No fucking way!"

"Why not?"

"Because he and the others will be ragging my ass for days, if not weeks, if they saw that."

Since I'd often seen firsthand how Jake and AJ loved to tease Rhys, I knew I had to respect his wishes. "Okay, okay. I'll put the phone away." When I held out my hand, Rhys reluctantly slipped it into it. Once I'd put it into my purse, he seemed relieved. We sat back in our chairs to enjoy the rest of the performance by the bagpipers.

Once it had ended and the quartet started up again, Rhys looked over at me and smiled. Motioning out onto the floor filled with swaying couples, he asked, "How about a dance?"

While Ellie seemed content, I wasn't sure about leaving her. I didn't want to upset her by making her feel abandoned. I guess Rhys sensed my apprehension. "It'll be fine, and we can keep an eye on her from the dance floor," he reassured me.

"Okay, I'd love to dance with you."

As Rhys rose out of his chair, he leaned in close to Ellie's ear. "Allison and I are going to dance. We'll be right back, and then I'll take you back to Trudie."

Once again, she didn't acknowledge him. She just kept staring straight ahead with a serene expression on her face. She didn't appear to be upset that we were leaving her. Taking my hand, Rhys led me away from the table. As we weaved in and out of the other couples, the quartet began playing Moon River, the theme song from one of my mom's favorite movies, *Breakfast at Tiffany's*.

We didn't move far into the dance floor. Instead, we stayed on the fringes so that we could see Ellie. Once we had found the perfect place, Rhys pulled me closer to him. Of course, since we were at a society party, we didn't dance like I was accustomed to. It was much more formal. I would have rather wrapped my arms around Rhys's neck than to have had one hand in his and the other on his shoulder. It seemed like there was always something keeping us apart.

When the song ended, Ellie got up from the table. Both Rhys and I froze as we watched her carefully. She went just inside the door to sit at the grand piano. When she began playing along with the quartet, Rhys exhaled a relieved breath.

As we danced to the music, I tried not to think about how frustrated I was with how things were moving along. Then a thought popped into my mind, and I couldn't help giggling. "What is it?" Rhys asked.

"Oh nothing," I muttered, refusing to meet his eye. I couldn't believe I had laughed out loud.

Rhys eyed me with a skeptical look. "Come on. You expect me to buy that? It was obviously something amusing, or you wouldn't have laughed."

At his imploring look, I decided to come clean with him. "Dancing as close as we are, I couldn't help but wonder about Cassie's question from earlier."

Rhys's brows furrowed. "What are you talking about?"

Lowering my voice, I asked, "You know, when she asked you about your kilt?" When he still looked clueless, I sighed. "Are you wearing any underwear under that kilt?"

"My, my, that's awfully intrusive of you. What's gotten into you tonight?"

"Nothing. I was just curious."

He then gave me a sexy little grin that ignited the lacy panties I was wearing. "You really want to know for you or so you can tell Cassie?"

"For me," I whispered.

"Well, you could always be daring and reach under there to see for yourself," he taunted.

I stared at him unblinking and unmoving for a moment. For one, I was shocked that he had even suggested such a thing—it was so uncharacteristic of him. On the other hand, was he actually suggesting that I touch him so very intimately in the middle of a crowded dance floor? "I, uh," I muttered incoherently.

Rhys chuckled. "Too scary of a prospect for you, Allie-Bean?"

His somewhat condescending tone irked me. "No, it's more the fact that I don't think your mother would approve of me groping you in the middle of her fancy fling."

"I really don't give a damn what my mother thinks."

"Yes, well I do. Besides, I have my reputation to contend with. I'm going to have to pass this time."

"Pity then," he replied, his eyes twinkling mischievously. He then ducked his head to where his breath warmed my earlobe. "I'll be nice and put you out of your misery. I'm wearing boxer briefs."

"Oh," I replied, unable to hide the disappointment in my voice. I don't know why it really mattered to me.

Pulling back, Rhys eyed me with an intense expression. "You know, I think we're entering dangerous territory."

I swallowed hard. "W-We are?"

He slowly nodded. "I'm saying things to you tonight that I really shouldn't. It's not right."

"I don't want you to say or do anything different, Rhys," I countered.

"You don't?" he asked, his brows rising in surprise.

"No, I don't. I like you just as you are—the good and the bad."

The sound of a shriek, followed by breaking glass, snatched us out of the moment. Rhys dropped his arms from me and raced back into the house. I followed right on his heels. When I got to the doorway, I froze. In the middle of the room, Ellie was throwing a tantrum, crying, pulling her hair and stomping her feet. Most of the partygoers in the ballroom had scattered to the opposite end of the room and were whispering behind their hands.

Elliot and Margaret made a half circle around Ellie as if they were trying to contain her. They spoke no soothing words of comfort. Instead, they eyed her with contempt. Rhys, however, barreled right past them to try to calm Ellie down. "Ellie-Bellie-Mellie, please don't cry. I'll make it right." His words, coupled with his expression, broke my heart for him. "Shh, it's okay. I'm here. No one is going to hurt you," he said soothingly.

Ellie's crying quieted to whimpers, and she no longer stomped around. Instead, she swayed back and forth, humming the tune that the quartet was playing.

"What did you do?" Rhys demanded, his eyes narrowing at his parents.

Margaret's face was the shade of an eggplant from anger, not embarrassment. "We couldn't hear each other talk over her playing. I simply asked her to stop. When she refused, I closed the lid to force her to stop."

The veins on Rhys's neck bulged in fury. "How could you? She wasn't hurting anyone."

"She was ruining your mother's party. She should have never been here in the first place," Elliot replied.

Ignoring his father, Rhys tentatively put an arm around Ellie's shoulder. "Come on. Let's get you back home. You can play the piano all night if you want to." When Ellie started to resist, Rhys began humming the same music she was. It seemed to calm her, and she willingly let him lead her out of the house. I followed close behind them, unsure of what to say or do. Part of me felt responsible. I'd worried about suggesting she come to the party. Of course, I'd feared some stranger ridiculing her. I never could have imagined her own mother would have treated her so horribly.

When we got to the doorway of the carriage house, Ellie balked and pulled away from Rhys. She started walking across the lawn to the garage. "She wants to go home," Rhys murmured.

"But isn't this her home?"

"Not when she feels hurt and angry. I guess you could say it's her way of running away, putting distance between her and my parents."

Trudie opened the door. The moment she saw Rhys's face she gasped. "What happened?"

"I need to take Ellie back to the Brandewine Institute. Now."

With a nod, Trudie replied, "Let me get my bag."

"You know you don't have to stay with her there," Rhys said.

Trudie smiled and patted his cheek. "I don't have to, but I want to. She needs me tonight." She then disappeared back into the house. Across the yard, Ellie waited patiently at Rhys's car, swaying to the music that floated back from the tent.

Tentatively, I took a step forward. Placing my hand over Rhys's heart, I said the words that were sorely lacking in the moment, but the only ones I could think to even comfort him. "I'm so, so sorry."

He brought his agonized gaze to mine. I could see he was troubled, not at Ellie, or it seemed, not even at me, but, he was too highly strung to form words. Instead, he just nodded his head in acknowledgement at my words.

"Look, I know you need to be with Ellie tonight. Don't worry about me. I'll call a cab and—"

Rhys furiously shook his head. "No, please don't go. Stay here and wait for me to get back." He squeezed my hand that still rested on his chest. "I need you tonight, Allison."

The emotional weight of the moment and his words made it hard to breathe. When I could finally speak again, I didn't realize the irony of my words until after I'd spoken then. "Of course. I'll wait for you, no matter how long it takes."

"Thanks, Allie-Bean." We were interrupted by Trudie coming out the door with a small suitcase. "You can wait for me in the pool house. That's where I've been staying."

I nodded in acknowledgement like I knew what he was talking about. A shadow of a smile played on his lips. "It's right over there." He motioned to the side of the carriage house where a building with a glass roof was connected.

"Okay, I'll wait for you there." I watched as he and Trudie made their way across the yard and got Ellie into the car. I stood in the same spot until the car backed down the driveway and disappeared into the night.

Thankfully the backyard was lit up for the party, and I didn't have any trouble finding the front door. As I pushed it open, I let out a low whistle. The "house" was actually one long, glassed-in room that appeared to have been built over an existing pool. I couldn't help wondering if it had been done as a safety means for Ellie.

On one side of the pool, there was a fully stocked bar that I was tempted to stop at. After the last half hour, I desperately needed a drink to calm my nerves. As I kept on walking, I couldn't help shaking my head. Of course, Rhys's parents didn't have just your average pool. Oh no, it had a partial waterfall in the deep end that led into an alcove with faux rock formations. There was also a large Jacuzzi within the alcove. At the end of the room, my attention was drawn to two wooden doors. With my heels clicking on the tile, I headed to the room. When I opened the door, my nose was assaulted with the smell of Rhys. It must've been where he had been staying. There was a large, four-poster bed along with several pieces of furniture. His suitcases and clothes were strewn all around on the floor.

Several picture frames adorned the nightstand. Most were of Rhys and Ellie while there was some of Runaway Train. With my heart beating wildly, I reached forward and snatched up one of the frames. It was a candid picture from Jake and Abby's wedding with the guys and their families. Instead of the professional one I'd seen in the wedding album, this one captured everyone in a moment of brevity. As my finger traced over the glass, I saw an island paradise in the background as Jake, wearing a teasing smirk, grabbed Abby's boob while she stared wide-eyed with horror out at the camera. Rhys had his head thrown back laughing at something AJ had said about Jake's antics. One of his arms was slung around my waist, drawing me close to him. I stared up at him with an adoring smile. Out of all the pictures, I wondered why he had chosen that one to frame. Surely, he could see by both my eyes and expression that I felt far more for him than friendship.

After I sat it back on the nightstand, I left the bedroom, closing the double doors behind me. With nothing to do but wait for Rhys, I sat down on the edge of the pool. Taking off my naughty heels, I slid up my dress and let my feet drop into the water. I leaned back on my hands, swirling my feet through the cool water.

I don't know how long I had been sitting there lost in thought when Rhys's voice caused me to jump. "Hey," he said softly.

"Hi," I replied.

He dropped down to sit beside me, stretching his legs out on the tiled floor. "Is Ellie okay now?" I asked.

A sad smile formed on his lips. "Yeah, she was just fine when I left. She was listening to music and painting. I suppose I should be grateful for the small mercies of life."

"That she's able to find happiness?" I questioned softly.

He exhaled harshly, his head falling back to gaze up at the moon glowing over the glass roof. "While my heart aches each and every day for Ellie and her situation, sometimes there are days where it aches more for Lucy."

I stared curiously at him. "Why is that?"

"One day when Lucy is older, she'll be cognitive enough to realize that there is something different about her. While I know that Bray and Lily will never do anything to cause it, Lucy will compare herself to Jude and to Melody. Most likely, she'll feel anger and sadness that she isn't the same as them." Rhys glanced over at me. "Ellie never has to do that. She never has to compare herself to me or feel what it's like to not live up to our parents' expectations. She's thankfully oblivious to all of that."

I slowly processed the truth in his words. My chest tightened at the feeling of sweet Lucy ever having to feel bad about herself. Eyeing my painted toenails in the water, I tried to tune out the voice in my head—the one that was nagging me to question Rhys. But then I realized that I had to ask or else I would never be able to look at him the same way. "Rhys?"

"Hmm?" he replied, staring out at the water.

"You've never brought Ellie around the guys much, have you?"

"No, I haven't."

Gnawing on my lip, I finally dared to ask the question that was haunting me. "Is it because you're ashamed of her?"

Rhys jerked his gaze from the water to meet mine. His dark eyes bulged. "How dare you ask me that?"

"It's an honest question. I've only heard you speak of her a few times before tonight. You never mention your family when you're with the guys."

Scowling, he crossed his arms over his chest. "You should know by now that I'm a very private person."

"Private or emotionally shut off?"

Flinching prematurely, I prepared myself for him to yell at me, but he surprised me by murmuring, "A little of both."

"You don't have to be that way with me. I want you to be able to trust me, Rhys."

"I do trust you. If I didn't, I would have never let you meet Ellie." Rhys exhaled an anguished breath. "The truth is I could never be ashamed or embarrassed by Ellie. The reason I don't speak of her or bring her around is I'm more afraid of *my* reactions to the way others treat her."

"What do you mean?"

"I can't respect anyone who finds fault with Ellie. Since I was a kid, I've been defending her. When I was in the fifth grade, I got expelled from a private school because I hit a kid with a golf club after he was telling people my sister was a freaky retard."

"Oh Rhys," I murmured.

He angrily shook his head. "I've ended many friendships, and even a few relationships, with people who expressed disdain and somewhat repulsion being in her presence."

"That's terrible."

"She deserves respect just like anybody else, so why should I give my time to those who have no respect for my blood?" Rhys bellowed.

"No, I mean, it's terrible that anyone would have disdain or repulsion for Ellie," I said, softly.

Rhys's expression softened. "Oh, I'm sorry."

"It's okay."

He shook his head. "I shouldn't have bit your head off like that."

"Stop beating yourself up." When he still appeared unconvinced, I said, "It shows a great depth of character that you care so much about your sister. She's so very lucky that she has you in her life."

"I guess I'm really a bastard for not talking about her, huh?" he questioned. From the look in his eyes, I could tell it was something that really worried him.

"No, I can totally understand your reasons. But at the same time, you're protecting yourself more than you are her. Your motives are better than your parents', but at the same time, you're still hiding her away."

"The more people who know about her, the more ridicule she is going to have," Rhys protested.

"Yes, but at the same time, think of all the good you could do for autistic people if you were to come out and talk about Ellie—if you lent your name to fundraisers and charities. Your celebrity might even change the way some people treat autistic people."

Rhys weighed my words for a few moments. "You're right. I can't believe I didn't see that before." Tears sparkled in his eyes. "Makes me feel like a stupid, selfish prick."

I shook my head. "Sometimes you're just too close to a situation to truly see things the way they should be."

"How could I screw her over like that?"

"Don't you dare say that! You could never, ever do anything to hurt Ellie." Reaching over, I cupped his cheek with my hand. "I'm not going to let you sit here and beat yourself up, okay?"

With a weary smile, he replied, "Okay."

"You've got one of the biggest hearts I know, Rhys. There isn't a malicious bone in your body. You would walk barefoot through a field of glass to make sure Ellie was happy."

"I suppose."

When he stared mournfully out at the water, I clapped my hands together. "You, sir, are in desperate need of a drink." Holding my dress in place with one hand, I rose to my feet. "Come on. Let's be cliché and drink away our troubles."

Rhys stared up at me for a moment before a grin spread across his face. "You're so fucking right. If there was ever a night to get plastered, it's tonight."

While I boosted myself onto one of the stools, Rhys walked around the side of the bar. "What sounds good?" I asked.

"I think the better question is, what is going to get us shitfaced the fastest?"

I giggled. "And if you get shitfaced, how will I get home?"

Rhys shrugged. "Guess you'll just have to stay here."

His reply caused me to gasp. "H-Here?" I stammered.

"Besides the fucking monstrosity main house, I'm pretty sure there's room in the carriage house for you."

"Oh," I murmured, trying not to hide my disappointment.

As Rhys plopped a bottle of tequila down on the bar, he winked. "Of course, my bed is pretty big, and I wouldn't mind sharing it."

My mouth dropped open as I tried processing what he had just said. Like a typical guy, he'd been able to go from emotionally broken to teasing sex-fiend in less than two minutes. I don't know how guys could inflict such whiplash with their feelings. But was Rhys's joke just something to lighten the mood? Or was this really it—a proposition to be with him? Deciding not to let him get one on me, I replied, "I'd be happy to share your bed."

Rhys's dark eyes twinkled. "I think you'd change your mind pretty quick after you heard me snore."

I laughed. "I hog the covers, so we're even."

"Two horrible bedmates, huh?"

"Yep," I replied, although secretly I wouldn't have cared as long as I got to share his bed.

Taking out two shot glasses from under the bar, Rhys sat them in front of me. "Think you've got it in you to do some hardcore shots?"

"I will if you will," I dared.

"Oh, I will," he replied. He unscrewed the lid on a bottle I wasn't familiar with. When he glanced up, he must've noticed my questioning look. "This," he began before waving the bottle, "is pure white tequila from the agave fields outside of Guadalajara."

"Sounds intense."

Rhys grinned. "Trust me, it is. They barely put in a capful of this shit when they make a margarita."

"How did you come to get it?"

"AJ's family has killer connections, so he always brings us back some when he goes to visit."

"I see."

As Rhys picked up his shot glass, I frowned. "No limes or salt?"

Glancing at me over the rim of the glass, Rhys said, "You're not totally hardcore then."

"If you don't have any, that's okay."

Rhys sat down the shot glass. He held up one finger to me before walking to the end of the bar and bending over. Leaning up on my stool, I saw that he was rooting around in a small refrigerator. When he stood up, I saw two limes in his hands. As he started back to me, he started juggling them. "I didn't know you were a man of many talents."

"Oh yeah, I totally wanted to run away with the circus when I was a kid."

I giggled. "Seriously?"

He cocked a brow at me. "You've met my parents. Anything, including the circus, would have been better."

My smile faded as I once again felt the intensity of his pain. When I started to say something to him, Rhys shook his head. "No more of that or we'll have to down the entire bottle. Then I'm pretty sure we'd end up with alcohol poisoning."

After cutting the limes, he brought out a salt shaker. He placed it all before me before he walked around the side of the bar. He took a seat on the stool beside me. "I think we're good to go now."

"Thanks for humoring me with the salt and lime," I said.

"It's nothing. Besides, I owed you."

Furrowing my brows, I asked, "How did you owe me?"

Not meeting my eyes, Rhys ran a finger along the wooden groove in the bar. "You stayed tonight."

"Of course I did."

His gaze flickered from the bar to me. "You didn't have to though. After seeing what happened with Ellie and all the fucked up shit that is my family, you could've bailed. Hell, you probably should have."

I shook my head. "What happened tonight was horrible. My heart aches for Ellie and for you. But it could never make me care about you less."

As his jaw clenched and unclenched, Rhys's eyes remained firmly on mine. "You do care about me, don't you?"

"Very much. I always have and always will," I replied, my voice humming with emotion. I reached across to close my hand over his. "I'll always be here for you, Rhys."

"Take a shot," he commanded, his expression tense, his eyes unreadable.

Goosebumps pebbled my arms at his assertive tone. I wasn't used to him being so forceful. For a moment, I couldn't process his words. It was like the tone of the entire conversation had veered off course. Reluctantly, I followed his orders. When I started to reach for a lime, he stopped me. As I eyed him curiously, he took the shaker of salt in his hand. Tilting his head, he shook the bottle along his neck. Then he leaned over and brought the shaker to my neck. My breathing became erratic at the nearness of him. But most of all, it was the way the tension crackled in the air between us. Nothing really had been spoken out loud, nothing had been done to change things, but in that moment, everything was different.

"Take a shot," he repeated.

With trembling fingers, I reached for the glass. I took it in one hand and the lime in the other. Leaning forward on the stool, I dipped my head down to his neck. My lips hovered over the warmth of his skin. Flicking out my tongue, I brought it against the stubble on his neck. Rhys sucked in a harsh breath at the contact. Slowly, my tongue trailed upward over the faint line of salt, eliciting a small groan from Rhys.

Once I finished, I pulled away. I didn't dare look at Rhys—my skin burned just from the intensity of his stare. Tipping up the glass, I downed it in one fiery gulp. As my eyes pinched shut in pain, I slammed the lime against my lips. My teeth cut through the fruit, as my mouth sucked off the juices. When I swallowed again, a shiver echoed through me.

I opened my eyes to find Rhys still staring at me. His dark eyes shone with such intensity that I would've given anything to know what he was thinking. He reached for his glass and lime. His eyes never left mine as he bent over. I tilted my head to give him better access. At the feel of his warm tongue on my neck, I shuddered, and I remained trembling even after he pulled away. He then downed the tequila without even bothering with the lime.

"Another?"

"Yes."

We repeated the process again. And again. Until we had downed five shots and licked and sucked our way up each other's necks. My skin still tingled from the feel of his tongue. Of course, my entire body was tingling from the strong alcohol pumping through every cell and molecule. It made me feel so alive. While it had just been his tongue on my neck, the feel of his hands drove me crazy as they brushed on my shoulders and whispered across my collarbone. I fantasized that his tongue was following the same path across my chest and down to my breasts.

More than anything in the world, I wanted this man, and tonight I was going to get my wish. From the lust-filled looks he'd been giving me, along with the groans of pleasure when I had licked his skin, I knew what was going to happen. I was finally going to have Rhys.

7: RHYS

It was official—I was fucking wasted. Swaying on the bar stool, I licked the remaining salt off my upper lip as my last shot of tequila burned its way down my stomach. When I glanced over at Allison, my dick jerked in my pants. Damn, she was so fucking sexy. The feel of her tongue on my skin had lit me up like I had never imagined possible. If she could do that just touching my neck, what would it feel like for her to have her hands and mouth on the rest of my body? I shuddered at the pleasurable thought.

Not only had her tongue felt good on me, but her skin had felt satiny smooth under my own tongue. I could have spent days kissing and licking up her neck and face. More than anything, I wanted to kiss those lips that parted each and every time my mouth came close to hers.

Staring at Allison was getting to be too much, so I turned my gaze to the pool. "I think we should swim," I blurted out of nowhere. Considering how we were both looking at each other like we were in heat, it would probably be a good idea to cool the fuck off before things got out of hand.

Allison stared at me in surprise. "Seriously?"

"Mmm, hmm." Without another word to her, I fell off the stool and staggered over to the pool. The water appeared so cool and inviting. Beads of sweat had popped out all over my body from the tequila while itchy warmth had spread its way over my skin. I didn't give it another thought—I just dove right into the deep end.

The coolness of the night made the water chillier than normal. Gliding through the water felt like I had tiny pelts of ice nicking my skin. When I surfaced, Allison stood at the edge of the pool, staring down at me with a worried expression. "What the hell are you doing?"

Treading water, I replied, "Swimming."

"In your tux top and kilt?"

"Fuck the tux. I wanted to swim." I grinned up at her. "Come in. It feels wonderful."

Allison's brows lined as she gazed down at her dress. When I thought she would just jump in and join me, I was wrong. Her hands went around her back, and I soon realized she was unzipping her dress. Mesmerized, I watched as the top slid down her body. Blinking rapidly, I licked my lips as she shimmied the dress off her hips. When it lay in a puddle of satin on the floor, she stepped out of it, standing before me in nothing but a strapless bra and panties. Oh fucking hell, I was in trouble. Allison had the body of goddess—a goddess made for sex.

"Quite a little strip tease you have going on," I said, trying to distract myself for the moment. Although as drunk as I was, I could have been yelling at her to take it all off.

With a shy smile, her arms crisscrossed over her waist. "It's just like a bikini," she protested. Instead of jumping in, she went to the stairs. Slowly, she took them one by one, the water enveloping her body in a teasingly sensual way. I couldn't have kept my eyes off of her even if I wanted to. She was too fucking sexy. And what was totally endearing is she had no idea what kind of effect she had on me.

She swam to me in long strokes, her body causing delicate ripples as it cut through the water. But when she reached me, she kept right on swimming. Eventually, she dipped under the waterfall and disappeared from my view. Weighed down by my clothes, I kicked hard in the water to swim after her. As the waterfall cascaded over my head, I searched for her. She rested back against the man-made rock formation. Her eyes tracked my movements toward her.

Allison seemed so far away. I knew what I had to do once I got to her—I had to fucking devour her. I had spent the last two weeks playing the gentleman by keeping my fucking perverted thoughts at bay. I had also kept reminding myself that she was just a friend, and more importantly, she was Jake's sister. But I'd spent way too much time denying myself someone I truly desired, which was Allison. There was no way I was letting this night end without making her body mine.

When I reached her at the rocks, I tugged her to me. Her slick body fused against mine, causing my cock to twitch with anticipation. "What have you done to me?" I asked, as I stared into her eyes.

Allison's brow lined in confusion. "I haven't done anything."

I shook my head. "You've done something to change me—to make me want you."

"Maybe you wanted me all along and didn't realize it," she challenged softly.

"You mean these past few weeks?"

"I mean for a long, long time. Longer than you would like to admit."

Blinking several times, I tried processing her words in my inebriated state. Through the haze, I wondered if Allison was right. Had there been something between us for a long time? And what the fuck did she mean by longer than I would want to admit? She had been just a kid—a teenager—for most of the years I'd known her, and I sure as hell wasn't some pervy dude who got off on young girls. "I don't know about that. But I do know I want to kiss you again."

"Then kiss me."

For a few seconds, my mouth hovered over hers. I felt her quick pants of breath feather across my cheek. Then without another moment of delay, I pressed my lips to hers. The cold water seemed to have doused the intensity we had before when we were doing the shots. This time Allison was tentative at first, letting me take what I wanted. But then the silk warmth of her tongue flicked across my bottom lip. A groan left my mouth almost instantaneously.

Pulling away, I stared into her face. "Damn, you're so fucking beautiful," I murmured.

She fluttered her eyelashes prettily at me. "Do you really mean that?"

"I would say it was the tequila talking, but I think my wood would prove me wrong."

As her arms came to encircle my neck, she pressed herself against me. "I don't want it to be the tequila talking. I want it to be what you feel deep down inside."

I stared into her eyes, which held such vulnerability. That look caused a feeling of protection to come over me. I didn't want anyone to hurt her, least of all me, and in that moment, I was completely dangerous to her. I knew that she wanted me as much as I wanted her. But, I couldn't see how I could take from her. Through the haze of alcohol and being somewhat tongue-tied, I knew I had to get clarification from her before we went any further. "You *like* me, Allison? You mean, you really like *me*?"

With a solemn expression, she nodded her head. "I always have, and I always will," she whispered.

At the time, I didn't understand the enormity of her statement. All I knew was my dick liked her very, very much, but in my hazy state, I tried to decipher what I felt about her deep down inside. There was so much about her to like—her sweetness, her smile, her sense of humor, her gentle, caring spirit, her artistic talent, and also her friendship. Without even trying, she'd found a way to break down my walls and strip my soul bare. If I was truly honest with myself, I should have been able to see how much I liked her…maybe even was in love with her. But it was impossible to process all of that tonight.

Ignoring the more amorous feelings rocketing through me, I focused instead on the lust that popped and crackled in the air around us. Rolling my hips against hers, I groaned. "I want you, Allison. I want you so fucking bad it hurts."

Her fingers tangled through the wet strands of my hair. "Then take me, Rhys."

My mind screamed at me to man up and do the right thing—to remember Jake, to remember that Allison was drunk, and I was myself. But instead, I did what most guys do in a situation where a soaked and partially naked chick is in front of you. I thought with my dick.

My hands went to grip her around her ass cheeks, hoisting her up to wrap her legs around me. Once she had her legs around my waist, I started walking us out of the pool. "Oh Rhys," Allison murmured, before bringing her lips to mine. Our mouths worked frantically against each other, tasting of a mixture of silver tequila, desperation, and pure lust.

Sloshing through the water, I finally got us over to the pool steps. Allison tightened her arms around my neck as I climbed up the steps, which was no easy feat considering I had both the weight of my wet clothes and Allison to contend with. Our lips and tongues continued working manically against each other. As we went by the bar, I let one of my hands leave her buttocks to grab the bottle of tequila.

After kicking open one of the wooden doors leading to the bedroom, I stalked over to the bed. Just before I lay Allison down, I pulled back to stare into her eyes. "Are you sure about this?"

"Never more certain of anything in my entire life," she replied breathlessly.

Gently, I eased her down on the mattress. As I stood between her legs, she reached behind her back and unfastened her bra, freeing her tits. "Oh fuck me, you're perfect," I muttered.

With a shy smile, Allison then scooted back on the mattress and lay back onto the pillows. She seemed to read my mind when my gaze landed on her lace-clad pussy. She hooked her thumbs in the elastic waistband and then slowly and tediously slid her underwear down her thighs. Either to tease me or because she was feeling shy, she kept her thighs pressed together, so I didn't get a view of the deliciousness between her thighs.

Christ. There was no way I was backing down now that I had her naked and willing in my bed. Sitting the bottle of tequila down on the nightstand, I began to tear the wet clothes from my body. Allison's heated gaze warmed my body as she followed my movements. When I was left in nothing but my boxer briefs, I picked up the tequila and eased down onto the bed.

Allison stared up at me, her skin flushed and her breath coming in anxious pants. Looming over her, I brought the bottle over her body and began pouring out the silver liquid onto her exposed flesh. A stream of tequila ran from her breastbone to pool in her navel while tiny rivulets streaked off her stomach onto the sheets. I dipped my head and swirled my tongue into her belly button, lapping up the tequila. Flattening my tongue, I then licked and sucked the tequila off her abdomen up to her chest. Tiny tremors ran throughout Allison's body as goose-bumps puckered her skin. Pressing her breasts together, I drank up the remaining tequila before sucking and pulling her nipples into my mouth.

Allison's whimper fueled me on to continue my assault. "More, Rhys," she whispered, tugging at the strands of my hair. As I reached her mouth again, my tequila-laced lips met hers in a harsh kiss. My hand dipped between her legs to thrust a finger inside her. Sliding a second finger inside her warm, wet walls, I continued licking and sucking her breasts. She felt and tasted just like heaven. I couldn't wait to get my mouth on her pussy. When Allison started to get close, my thumb began to rub her clit. She came with a shriek, clawing my shoulders with her walls clenching around my fingers. I fought to keep the smirk off my face from the fucking ego trip of having her so responsive to me and coming so quickly.

While our lips and tongues melted together, I removed my fingers. Our bodies then began to move in perfect sync. I rubbed my now painful erection against her core, causing us both to hiss with the delicious friction. I continued thrusting my hips against hers. When I thought I might come just from the minimal contact, I pulled away. "Don't stop!" she cried, grasping for my shoulders.

"I'm just getting started." As I straddled her, I brought the bottle of tequila to my chest. When the liquid started to trickle down my pecs and abs, Allison sat up to catch it with her tongue. As she licked and sucked the tequila off of me, her hand came to rest on my dick. Throwing my head back, I groaned as she worked me over the soaked boxer briefs. When it all began to be too much, I shook my head.

"Lie back," I commanded.

Although she gave me a questioning look, she did lie back to rest her head against the pillow. Bringing my hands to her calves, I spread her legs wide, giving me a view of her glistening pussy. I licked my lips in anticipation before sliding between her thighs. Dipping my head, I buried my mouth in her slickness, lapping up the wetness I'd caused earlier. "Rhys!" Allison cried, her hand finding its way to my hair to tug on the strands. Spreading her folds with my fingers, I then thrust my tongue inside her. As I began to find a rhythm, Allison's hips bucked in time with my tongue, and she mewled with pleasure. I continued to alternate between sucking her clit and tonguing her deep. She jerked my hair hard as she began to come again.

With the walls of Allison's pussy still pulsing, I reluctantly pulled away. I slid off the bed to drop my boxer briefs. Then I reached into the nightstand and pulled out the gold foil package. After tearing open the wrapper, I slid the condom down my length. When I dropped back down onto the bed, Allison opened her thighs for me. Positioning myself between them, the head of my cock nudged against her slick opening. As our lips fused together, I thrust into Allison. She felt like every man's dream—wet, scorching hot, tight, and made for my dick.

Pulling my mouth from hers, I focused on her eyes. "You okay?" I panted.

She smiled. "Oh yes."

God, she was so beautiful. So sexy. So responsive. Even though I knew she was all right, I didn't speed up the pace. Although it was torturous keeping it slow and steady, I knew she was getting more out of it that way. After a few minutes of languid strokes, I sped up the pace of thrusts. Allison wrapped her legs around my buttock ass, drawing me closer and deeper inside her. Our shared breaths and skin slapping together joined the knocking sound. It was a punishing but aching burn that rippled through my body, but I didn't dare stop. It felt too fucking good to stop. She felt too fucking good to stop.

Allison wrapped her arms around my neck, drawing my lips back to hers. My tongue plunged in and out of her mouth, mimicking the actions of my dick below. I never wanted it to end—I wanted to stay deep inside Allison forever. It was a feeling I hadn't experienced many times before. I couldn't help wondering if it was the alcohol or being with Allison.

As I felt her walls begin to tighten around me, I dipped my hand between us to stroke her swollen clit. Allison's mouth jerked away from mine to cry out as her walls clenched and released against my dick. I continued to pump furiously into her until I felt my own release begin. "Allison, oh fuck," I muttered, as I collapsed onto her.

While I worked to catch my breath, Allison's fingers trailed the sweat-stained strands of my hair. As my head lay against her chest, I could hear the beating of her heart. I inhaled of her skin. "You smell like chlorine," I blurted very ineloquently.

Allison giggled. "I think it's because we went swimming."

Raising my head, I grinned at her. "We did. Didn't we?"

She nodded her head. "I wish you could've seen yourself. One minute you were suggesting we go swimming, and then the next, you were jumping in the pool with all your clothes on."

"It was fun though, wasn't it?"

"I promise I'm not complaining. I'm just sorry I smell like chlorine."

"I think we can fix that." With a wink, I rose off of her, even though I wanted to stay close to her warm body. "Let's go shower."

8: ALLISON

Closing my eyes, I let the steam envelop me along with the feel of Rhys's hands on my body. I'd been all for taking a shower, but I hadn't realized that it would mean another round with Rhys. Not that I was complaining. No, I was in the place where my most wonderful dreams and fantasies had come true. I'd finally been with Rhys— he had taken me fully, mind, soul, and now body. I'd always known it would be good. I just hadn't realized exactly how good it would be.

When he brought his wet hand between my thighs and began to stroke me, I moaned and closed my eyes. "God, it's like you're playing my clit just like you would a piece of music."

"I'm awfully good with my fingers."

My eyes snapped open when I realized I had actually voiced the finger playing comment aloud. As mortification rocketed through me, Rhys grinned at me. "Let me oblige the fantasy a little further." He then shifted my hips to where I was in front of him, like I was the cello between his legs. Experiencing the real feel of his fingers was so much more intense than when I had watched him playing his cello earlier. While just the memory sent a tingling over my skin, my body was now alight with exquisite sensation as Rhys moved his fingers with the same glorious precision between my legs.

As I lay my head back on his chest, one of his hands came to cup and knead my breast while the other went back between my thighs. Spreading my legs further apart, I gave him more room to work the magic of his fingers over me. I thrust my hips against his hand, letting his fingers plunge deeper and deeper inside me. Gripping his biceps, I squeezed them tight as the first waves of orgasm overtook me. When I finished and my eyes opened again, I found Rhys staring down at me, watching me absorb the pleasure.

"You're so sexy when you come."

I couldn't help blushing at his response. "I'm not used to coming that hard or so much. At least not with a guy."

Rhys raised his brows at me. "What do you mean?"

With a shy smile, I replied, "You're really going to make me say it, huh?" When he still continued staring at me in confusion, I reached my hands up to cup his face. "You are the only person I've been with who has ever made me come that hard."

His eyes widened. "Seriously?"

"Yeah, seriously." When a smirk curved on his lips, I smacked his chest. "Don't make me regret telling you that."

He laughed. "I'm sorry, but that's too fucking hot not to get stoked about."

Turning around in his arms, I brought my hand between us to stroke his growing erection. "I guess it's your turn now."

"To get clean or get off?"

"A little of both." I sank down on my knees in front of him. His hooded eyes gazed down at me as I flicked my tongue over the head of his erection. He shuddered at the minimal contact. I then alternated between licking it from root to tip and then suctioning the head. Then I took the length into my mouth, bobbing up and down. When I began to hum as I took his length deeper in my mouth, Rhys hissed with what I assumed was pleasure. His hands tangled in the wet strands of my hair, watching as my lips worked up and down his cock.

Sliding my hands between his legs, I gently tugged and massaged his balls. "Oh fuck, Allison," Rhys said, throwing his head back against the tile. I let his erection fall from my mouth to dip my head and take his balls in my mouth. I sucked and nibbled at the sensitive flesh, all the while sliding my hand up and down on his dick.

A tremor ran through his body. He jerked my hair back, but I sucked his cock back into my mouth. I continued sucking hard and fast until I felt his hips buck and the start of his cum spurt into my mouth. Rhys cursed and cried out my name, his head making a loud noise as it banged back against the tile. I licked him dry before I got up off my knees.

As he pulled his head off the wall, he appraised me with a dazed expression that seemed to express total and complete satisfaction. I knew then if he didn't say a word, I had done well. "You're wearing a pleased little smirk there," he said.

When I burst into laughter, I quickly brought my hand over my mouth. "I could say the same for you," I replied, my words somewhat muffled behind my hand.

Rhys grinned. "Come on. Let's get out of here before we turn into prunes."

I nodded. Rhys reached past me to turn off the shower. He opened the glass door and motioned for me to go out first. I stepped out onto the tiled floor and then reached for a towel. Rhys took it from me and then proceeded to dry my arms and shoulders before dropping down to dry my thighs and legs. "Such personal service from my lord," I teased, when he brought himself back up.

"Nothing but the best for you, my little wench."

I smacked him playfully on the arm. Once I wrapped in my towel, I took another off the rack and began to dry off Rhys. The longer my hands stayed on him, rubbing the terry cloth over his body, the more I wanted him buried deep inside me. Again. I wasn't the only one ready for another round. Rhys's growing erection rested against my thigh.

"Let's go to bed." He then led me out of the bathroom and back into the bedroom. "Get on your hands and knees," Rhys commanded, causing me to shiver. Normally, I wasn't in to being told what to do, but the fact that it was him made all the difference.

After I dropped the towel, I climbed onto the bed and crawled toward the center. When I reached it, I gazed back at him over my shoulder. I couldn't resist wiggling my ass at him. "Come on, Rhys. Don't make me wait for it," I urged.

"Do you like it hard?" he asked, as he eased down onto the bed behind me.

"Hmm, yes."

When he smacked my ass cheek, the sound reverberated around the room, causing me to jump out of my skin. "You like that, too?"

"Yes," I hissed. Peering over my shoulder into his lust-filled eyes, I commanded, "Do it again."

This time he smacked my opposite cheek, and I moaned, my fingers gripping the sheets. I knew I couldn't wait any longer to have him. "Please, Rhys." I felt his weight leave the mattress and then he was rustling in the nightstand drawer for a condom. Thankfully, it wasn't too long before I felt him positioning the head of his cock at my entrance.

When he plunged deep into me, we both cried out. There was nothing like the feel of having Rhys inside me. All the nights of fantasizing about him converged on this moment. I tightened my walls around him, causing a groan to rumble through his chest. The sound caused even more moisture to pool between my legs. There was something so erotic about hearing his sounds of pleasure and knowing I had caused them.

As my long hair fanned out over my back, Rhys reached up to tangle his fingers in it. When he jerked my head back, I moaned and bit my lip. Bending over me, Rhys leaned down to where his lips brushed against my face. "You do like it rough and hard, don't you?"

"Just with you. Only with you," I panted, turning my head so that my face could rub against his. And it was the truth.

"That's right. Only I get to take you like this," he replied. I could tell my words had stroked his ego that he was the first one to really be like this with me, just like with the orgasms. But what he still was missing was that I could let myself go and feel so deeply because I truly loved him with every fiber of my being. As he continued pounding into me, our shower soon became a waste as our bodies became coated with the sheen of sweat caused by our exertions.

I gasped when Rhys pulled out of me. Glancing over my shoulder, I watched as he rocked back on his knees, resting his feet under his buttocks. He reached for my hips and eased me up onto my knees as well. When my back was tight against his chest, he reentered me. The sensation was almost overpowering. He and I both groaned at the depth he reached as he entered me.

As Rhys started slowly gliding in and out of me, I started to see the benefit of this position. He was able to reach around me to cup my breasts and pinch my nipples, or he could dip his hand down to stroke me between my legs. As my head fell back against his shoulder, I brought a hand up to tangle through the strands of his dark hair.

My heart melted when Rhys dipped his face down to meet my lips in a frantic kiss. The instant he plunged his tongue into my mouth, I came. "Rhys! Oh God!" I cried, as my walls shuddered. As I was still riding my orgasm, Rhys eased me down onto my stomach and began to pump furiously until he came.

Once he was finished, he eased out of me. I felt so physically wasted that I could barely hold my head up. After Rhys disposed of the condom in the wastebasket beside the bed, he urged me to get back up. "No, no more. I can't now. I'm too tired."

He chuckled. "I was trying to get you up so we could get under the covers."

"Oh," I replied, before I sat up. Rhys tugged the comforter and sheet back, and then I dove underneath them, stretching out on the luxurious cotton. Rhys slipped in beside me and spooned up against my back. His breathing began to grow shallower and shallower, until he was finally asleep. Feeling utterly satisfied, I found myself falling into a deep sleep, enveloped in the warmth of Rhys's strong embrace.

I knew I loved Rhys before tonight. But, after making love with him, I was completely gone. He had always owned my heart. Now he owned my body as well.

9: RHYS

As the morning sunlight streamed across my face, I shifted in the bed. When I started to roll over to get the sun out of my eyes, I found myself entangled in a mass of dark hair. I tried desperately to process where I was and who I was with. And then I realized it was Allison lying beside me. My mind was assaulted with John Milton's phrase, "Hide me from day's garish eye" and its somewhat bastardization of "everything looked different in the garish light of day."

Fucking hell, what had I done? Somewhere between the tequila and what had happened with Ellie, I'd completely let my guard down and allowed myself to give in to the worst temptation. A reel of X-rated images flickered through my mind of doing body shots off

Allison, making out with her in the pool, and then taking her to my bed.

The realization crashed over me, causing me to shudder. I'd fucked Jake's little sister. I'd fucked her in multiple positions and had used way too many condoms. I'd defiled a perfectly sweet and angelic girl who had been the only bright spot in my world, besides Ellie, the last few weeks. Bringing my forearm over my eyes, I groaned. How could she ever forgive me?

"Hey, are you okay?" a small voice asked beside me.

Drawing my arm away, I met Allison's expectant gaze. Even though she should've looked ridden hard and put up wet after all we had done, she was so fucking radiant she glowed. The sunlight hit the back of her hair and shot down her body, illuminating her small curves under the stark white sheet.

With a tentative smile, she placed her hand on my chest over my heart. "Talk to me, Rhys."

At that moment, former coherent thoughts seemed to evaporate instantaneously. Just the sight of Allison stirred something within me. Fucking hell. No! I could not go there again. Groaning once more, I pulled myself up in the bed and leaned back against the headboard. Desperately I searched to find the right words in this moment. "God, Allison, I'm so, so sorry about last night."

Her brows lined in confusion. "Why would you be sorry?"

I furiously rubbed my face. "I took advantage of you when you were just being kind and compassionate. I got you drunk. I—"

She interrupted me by bringing her hand over my mouth. "Stop it. There is nothing to apologize for or to beat yourself up over. Last night was about two consenting adults. And I certainly remember giving my permission."

Vaguely another grainy image flickered in my head of Allison telling me to kiss her again. She certainly seemed to have a good time without coercion last night. But even if she was on board, I knew better than to touch her. "Even if you were okay with it, it wasn't right," I protested.

Rising up in the bed, Allison didn't bother to keep the sheet wrapped around her chest. I pinched my eyes shut to avoid the delicious eyeful of her breasts. "Your head is still too cloudy to process everything. Go get us some coffee, and we'll talk this through."

In the light of morning, Allison appeared so much older. She certainly spoke with such assurance that I was willing to accept or believe anything she said. "Okay?" she prodded.

"All right. I'll throw on some clothes and run up to the main house." As I pulled back the sheet, Allison's eyes stared appreciatively at my dick, and it took everything within me not to flip her onto her back and pound her again. "You should put some clothes on."

"Do you have something I can borrow?"

"Of course."

She gave me a beaming smile, one that lit me afire from the top of my head to the soles of my feet. At the same time, it comforted me. It was like Allison possessed the answers to all the questions and worries I had about my life. I couldn't imagine why the hell I was thinking that about her. She was just a friend…a friend I had now had sex with. Fuuuuck!

Shaking off the weird feelings swimming around in my head, I went to the chest of drawers and took out a T-shirt and some shorts. "Here."

"Thank you." She took them in her hands and then slipped out from under the sheet. I couldn't believe how uninhibited she was in front of me. When she ducked into the bathroom, I headed out the side door to the house.

When I let myself in the backdoor, the kitchen was empty. Knowing my mother, she had asked the cook to bring her a breakfast tray after feigning exhaustion from the party. That or she had insisted on taking her meal outside on the veranda, so she could survey any potential damage done by the partygoers. It was always about her, not what was convenient to others.

I dug a thermos out of the back of the pantry, and then filled it with steaming coffee. Several different types of muffins and fruit were laid out on the island. I grabbed a plate and starting piling up a sampling in case Allison was hungry.

Just as I turned to go, my mother's voice stopped me. "There you are. After I didn't see you again last night after the party, I thought you might have left us again. But when I went for my morning walk, I saw your car was still here."

I drew in a deep breath, trying to temper my response. I turned around. "I went to take Ellie home and make sure she was okay."

My mother's dark eyes narrowed slightly. "This is Eleanor's home."

"This will never be Ellie's home, Mother. You have to be welcome at your home, and we know that will never be the case. Whenever she comes here, she's banished to the carriage house."

"It isn't banishment. It's giving her freedom."

Rolling my eyes, I started backing toward the door. "I don't have the fucking time or energy for this conversation."

Mother crossed her arms over her chest. "Did you take the same care with your date to make sure she made it safely home?"

"Her name is Allison, and from your tone, I'm sure you already know she stayed last night with me in the pool house."

"This is the second time I've seen you with this girl. Are you serious about her?"

I gave a mirthless laugh. "Don't tell me you're actually interested like a real mother is about who her son might be involved with? I'm sure with you it's more of a concern about her social stature and what type of blood runs in her veins."

She narrowed her eyes at me. "Honestly, Rhys, isn't it enough that you have to defy your father's and my wishes by abandoning law school and a future at a prestigious law firm? Must you now bring further shame by dating a girl who is so far removed from our social sphere?"

"Mother, it's far too early in the morning for your snobbery," I retorted sarcastically.

"Don't be a fool, Rhys. This girl is so completely enamored that she's even found a way to get her claws further into you by touring with your band on the pretense of this internship."

Since my mother wasn't the type of woman to confide in about my confused feelings and emotions, I merely shook my head. "Look, I'm hoping this will shut you up on the matter. I'm not dating Allison—not now and not ever. There's absolutely nothing between us but friendship, and there never will be anything else."

At the sound of a gasp behind me, I whirled around. With a horrified expression, Allison stood in the doorway outfitted in the shorts and T-shirt of mine that were way too big for her. Before I could say anything to her, she turned and fled out the door.

"Fuck," I muttered, throwing everything in my hands on the counter. I raced out the door after her. "Allison, wait!" I called.

When Allison turned toward me, tears pooled in her eyes. "What you just said to your mother…is that how you really feel about me?"

I couldn't understand why she was crying, but I knew I needed to get her to calm down. "Look, could we just calm the fuck down for a minute and think about this?"

"What is there to think about exactly?" she pressed.

"Oh, I don't know. Maybe the fact that we made a horrible mistake last night."

Flinching like I had hit her, Allison questioned in a strangled voice, "Is that what it was to you? A mistake?"

"Of course it was. We were both drunk. It had been a hell of a night for me, and you were so sweet to comfort me. I swear to God that I never intended to seduce you."

Allison's eyes widened. "You think you seduced me?"

I grimaced. "I'm sure you would have never done anything like that if I hadn't been coming on to you. I take full responsibility for what happened."

She stared at me like I had grown horns and fangs. It was the oddest expression of agonized disbelief. I could almost see the wheels in her head turning and spinning. And then she shocked the hell out of me by bringing both of her hands to my chest and shoving me hard. "You…you fucking asshole!" she screeched.

My eyes widened at her choice of language along with the fury with which she spoke. She shook her head wildly back and forth at me. "If last night was a mistake and you just seduced me, then what the hell have we been doing the past three weeks?"

I shrugged. "I don't know exactly. Hanging out? Spending time as friends?"

"Just friends? That was all it was to you?"

"What else was it supposed to be?"

"Oh God," she moaned. Allison's eyes then pinched shut. I've known her long enough to know that look, and I feel like utter shit for causing her pain. "I can't believe this. All this time I'd fantasized what it would be like to tell you how I felt about you. But never could I have imagined a nightmare like this."

"I don't understand." And that was certainly an understatement.

Opening her eyes, Allison pinned me with a hard stare. "You've been utterly and completely blind, haven't you? Or I guess it's more like you've been emotionally shut off." She took a tentative step toward me. "Last night meant everything to me because I was with the man

I *loved*. The man I've been in love with since I was thirteen years old."

Her words had the same effect as if a lightning bolt had shot out of the sky to slam me with jolts of electricity. "You're in love with me?" I asked with disbelief.

"I can't believe I ever took you for such a smart man, Rhys," Allison snapped.

Running my hands over my face, I shook my head. How in the hell had this happened? We'd just been hanging out and having fun—I wasn't sure how she had taken it differently. "God, how did I not see it for all those years?" As my mind whirled with thoughts, I wondered if I had just been ignoring all the signs that were already there. I'd never had a girl that was just a friend. All these years, I'd treated Allison as a little sister. Somehow in the last three weeks, our relationship had changed into one of intense friendship. At the same time, I had to wonder if I'd been deluding myself. Was what I was feeling for Allison more than just friendship? Sure, considering how gorgeous and sexy she was, it wasn't hard to be attracted to her physically. But it was the emotional aspect of my attraction that I was worried about.

After exhaling a ragged breath, Allison said, "I've waited and tried to be patient. I thought once I was of age, you would be able to see me differently. And then when that didn't happen, I almost gave up hope that we could ever be together. But no matter who I was with or where you were in the world, that little flicker of love I felt for you never extinguished. Then you came to see me, and we had the most perfect last few weeks together." Tears streaked down her cheeks, causing my chest to clench in anguish. "But all that was for nothing because you're standing before me now saying that you feel nothing for me."

"That's not true. I do care about you very, very much."

"Yeah, as a sister or a friend. But do you care for me as someone different? A girlfriend or a lover?"

Even if I was beginning to feel more for her than I should, there was no way I could ever allow myself to date Allison. Jake would never allow or accept it. The band could implode under the stress and tension. There was also the fact that I didn't do relationships anymore— I wanted my freedom, not to be tied down. Allison wasn't the type of girl who became a fuck buddy. She was the hearts and flowers kind of girl, the hopeless romantic, who was waiting for her Prince Charming. We were at an impasse, and when it came down to it, there was really no future for us. "Allison," I began in an even voice, "what you're feeling for me isn't real."

Sweeping her hands to her hips, she angrily questioned, "It isn't? Then pray tell me exactly what it is."

Never being good at talking about my emotions, I found it hard to try to put into words what I meant. "Infatuation…a crush. All these years you just thought you were in love with me because you had a false sense of who I was. I was the older guy who was off limits. It's romantic wish fulfillment."

There it was—the honest truth. Logical. Intelligent. Allison was still too young to really understand love. Hell, I didn't even understand it. No, this was the right path to take.

"That is the worst bullshit I've ever heard! How dare you tell me how I feel? I know what I've felt for you Rhys, and it's love. Now if you're too chicken shit to admit that you feel something for me, then fine. That's how we'll leave things between us. But don't you ever tell me that I don't know what love is."

"I'm sorry. I didn't mean it like that. I'm just trying to find the right things to say to you."

"The right things to let me down easy? The right way to put the sad, confused little girl out of her misery?"

"Allison, please."

She shook her head. "Why? Why can't you be honest with me? Why can't you be honest with yourself?"

"I am being honest," I argued feebly.

"So in your warped frame of mind, last night was just a mistake? It wasn't an amazing connection between two people who care for each other?"

"We can't get caught up with what happened last night. Yes, the sex was amazing and it was an incredible time, but we were *wasted*. We have to think about Jake and everyone else. Whatever this is between us, it has to stop. Too much is at stake for us just to throw it all away because of a drunken night."

Her hand swept to her throat as a strangled cry escaped her lips. Once again, tears began flowing down her cheeks. "Okay then, I'll put it all behind me. We'll go on like this never happened. If that's what you think is best."

"I'm sorry, but I really do. It'll be fine in the end, you'll see. We'll be able to be friends just like nothing happened."

She gave a quick jerk of her head. "I'll just try not to think each and every time I see you that you're the man who didn't just break my heart—you shattered it."

I didn't anticipate her next move. Wrapping her arms around my neck, she dipped my head down to where she could kiss me. Her lips tasted salty from the tears she'd been shedding. And as the fading thought of her lips left my mind, it was like every molecule in my body jolted, causing me to shudder. The years melted away to another time when I had felt the same way as I kissed Allison. In the moment itself and over the years, I'd denied the feelings I'd experienced with a sixteen-year-old Allison in my arms. But here I was experiencing the exact same reaction again to kissing her.

In that instant, I knew I had been deceiving myself for the past three weeks. I hadn't been just hanging out and having fun with Allison. She had been getting under my skin. I'd slowly been falling for her. But all along, I'd been lying to myself. I'd wanted someone as beautiful, talented, and kind-hearted as she was to care for me on a deeper level. And now that I had it, I was throwing it away. But it really was the only choice I had to keep the peace with Jake. Allison was young—too young to really know what she wanted. When she matured on her, she would realize I was the last person she could truly love.

She would come to believe, as I did now, that she deserved far better. Because I sure as hell knew I didn't deserve her. She was too precious with too much of a bright future ahead of her to be saddled with someone like me. In that moment, I would have given anything to have stayed with my arms around her, with her sweet, soft lips on mine, but it just wasn't meant to be.

Allison's hands slowly fell from around my neck as she pulled away. Without another word to me, she turned and started walking down the path that led to the street. "Wait, let me at least give you a ride."

She shook her head. "I'd rather walk."

"Please don't leave like this."

"There isn't any other way to do this. Goodbye, Rhys." She then continued on down the path before heading out the gate and disappearing from my gaze. Long after she was gone, I continued standing in that same spot, wondering what the fuck had just happened to me. Regardless of the emotions that tightened in my chest, I had to accept the same words I'd given her. Nothing could ever work between Allison and me. There were too many obstacles to overcome.

I would just have to keep telling myself that.

10: ALLISON

It has been ten days and three tour stops since I had talked to Rhys alone on Jake and Abby's bus. Although three months had passed since our time together in Savannah, the pain was just as fresh as the day he had broken my heart. Whoever said time healed all wounds was deluding themselves. Every time I had to see Rhys or be around him, the flimsy gauze I'd placed over my heart was stripped away, leaving the wound to ache and fester.

I'm not sure how I made it through the rest of the semester without completely flunking out. After that agonizing last day when Rhys shattered my world, I found it hard to cope. The first few days I didn't get out of bed. Cassie and my other roommates force-fed me soup and some of my favorite takeout. Then Cassie used tough love on me to get me out of bed. Once I finally came out of that emotional coma, I began a somewhat zombie existence—I went through the motions of school and work, even singing at Saffie's, but my heart wasn't in it. It was too obliterated after the dream I'd harbored since I was just a thirteen-year-old kid had been destroyed.

I didn't hear from Rhys again after he blew out of town that day. While my dress and shoes arrived in a dry-cleaned garment bag, there was no note attached to it. Part of me couldn't believe he didn't at least call to check on me. That would have been the decent thing to do, but I guess I'd been deceived about who he really was all along. At the end of the day, I almost wanted to believe that he was as cold and callous as his parents, but I knew better. Years of watching Jake slowly self-destruct when it came to his relationships with others had made me better able to see Rhys as he truly was. He just couldn't handle what had happened between us. At the end of the day, I truly believed he felt more for me than he could let himself acknowledge.

Thankfully, I hadn't had to see him until Jax and Jules's baptism. I couldn't help wondering if he would try to avoid the ceremony all together. As godmother to Jax, he knew I would be there. Part of me had so desperately wanted him to be there so I could see him again while the other part hoped that he wouldn't so my heart wouldn't be torn in two yet again.

When he had walked into the room where we had all congregated before the ceremony, I found it hard to breathe. I'd clutched Jax tighter in my arms to keep me grounded, so I wouldn't pass out. He'd given me one small smile and a hello—the same kind you would give to someone you were barely acquainted with. It was like I had spent three weeks with an entirely different person— that I'd made love with an entirely different person. And the fissure that had been etched into my heart by his previous behavior grew even wider.

Even without the internship, I would have found myself partaking on a nomadic existence to be Jake and Abby's nanny, and in turn, I would have once again been partaking in Rhys's orbit. While I often could hide away with the kids, the internship forced me to work with the Runaway Train stylist, but more importantly, with the guys of Runaway Train. It was not something I was looking forward to.

Glancing out the bus window, I watched as we pulled into the CenturyLink Center in Omaha for tonight's show. Balancing Jax on my lap, I finished washing off his face from the baby cereal he'd had. Across from me, Jake was doing the same thing to Jules.

While we had been feeding the twins, Abby had been getting ready to go on stage for rehearsals as soon as we got in.

She came out of the bedroom dressed and ready just as the bus eased to a stop. Since Omaha was just a one-night stop, we wouldn't be staying in a hotel room. The twins would be shuttled back and forth between the arena and the bus. It was hard, but somehow we all made it work.

The bus door opened, and Dustin, one of the bodyguards, hopped on. "You guys ready?"

"I think so." When Abby began glancing frantically around, I said, "Everything for the twins is packed. They're all taken care of."

She gave me an appreciative smile. "Thank you, Allison." She then took Jules from Jake. "Can you get their stuff, babe?"

"Sure," Jake replied, a little less than enthusiastically.

We then exited the bus with Jax in my arms, Jules in Abby's, and Jake loaded down with paraphernalia for the twins. "Remind me why there's not a roadie doing this shit?" Jake grumbled, as we made our way into the arena.

"Because in real life, parents with twins don't have roadies to schlep their stuff," Abby replied.

"Blows for them," he replied.

I'm not sure how Abby managed to stay so positive in the face of a grueling tour and raising two infants on a tour bus. I know she didn't have a choice because she was not the type of mom to leave her kids behind, but at the same time, it exhausted me most days, and I was just watching the twins, not giving my heart and soul each night on stage as well.

Because of all of the Runaway Train children, there was always one room designated just for them to be during rehearsals and the shows, especially for the times when we didn't have hotel rooms. When we got inside, we found Mia and Lily already there. Jake happily sat down the baby saucers next to one of the couches. Just as Abby and I got the twins settled in the saucers, a technician appeared in the doorway. "We're ready for Jacob's Ladder."

"I'll be right there," Abby called over her shoulder. She then focused her attention on her son and daughter. "Bye, my angels. I'll be right back. Okay?" Abby said to the twins. They continued bouncing happily in their saucers.

At Abby's hesitation, I tried reassuring her. "They'll be fine."

"I know. I'm such an idiot to get so worked up over leaving them for half an hour."

I smiled. "I think it's more the fact you're a good mom, instead of an idiot."

Abby grinned. "I think I like your way of phrasing things better."

When she hustled out of the room, Jake turned to me. "Hey, where do you want to do the measurements?" he asked. Yesterday when we were on the road, I'd reminded Jake that I needed to get the measurements for Runaway Train and Jacob's Ladder for my internship. I hadn't pressed the matter the first week on the road because I wanted to get settled in. He had taken it very seriously and texted all the guys to make sure they were ready for measurements once we rolled into Omaha.

"How about in the dressing room?"

He bobbed his head. "Sounds good. I'll get the guys together and be there in ten. Okay?"

"Sounds good. I'll just run back to the bus to get my stuff."

"Make sure Dustin or Ed goes with you."

I fought the urge to roll my eyes at his overprotectiveness. "I will. And thanks for being so understanding about my internship."

Leaning over, he ruffled the top of my head. "Anything for you, Allie-Bean."

Bile rose in my throat at the mention of the nickname—the very one Rhys had called me. Of course, I couldn't say anything to Jake about it. Sometimes it was exhausting keeping up a façade around Jake and the others, especially when Rhys was around.

With Mia and Lily keeping an eye on the twins, I headed back to the bus with Ed, the hulking bodyguard, in tow. Once I had all the materials I would need, we made our way back into the arena. I could hear the opening of Jacob's Ladder's rehearsal as we weaved through the chaotic backstage area.

When I got to Runaway Train's dressing room, I found only Jake and Brayden. "Where are the other guys?"

Jake scowled. "Good fucking question. I just texted them where to be."

Up the hall, the sound of Gloria Estefan's *Conga* blared out of the room where the kids were. Jake and I exchanged a look. "I think we know where AJ is," Jake said.

I giggled. "Yeah, that has him written all over it. Of course, it doesn't hurt that all the kids are eighties fans."

Brayden's brows scrunched in confusion. "Since when does he listen to Cuban music?"

Jake grunted. "Since your kids and his are eighties fans and they wear out that Greatest 80s Hits CD."

With a grin, Brayden replied, "Oh yeah, I forgot about that."

Pointing his finger at me, Jake said, "I'll go get AJ, and you can find Rhys."

"No, no, that's all right. I'll grab AJ, and I'm sure Rhys will show up," I quickly replied. The last thing on earth I wanted to do was try to hunt Rhys down. Before Jake could argue with me, I dipped out into the hallway.

When I opened the door to the kids' room, I couldn't help laughing. Jude, Melody, and Bella were all encircling AJ while dancing around. AJ had Gaby in his arms and was putting down some serious moves. Even Jax and Jules were bouncing wildly in their saucers at the music.

At the sight of me, AJ began singing along, "Come on shake your body, baby, do the conga. I know you can't control yourself any longer." With his free hand, he motioned for me to join them.

I held up my hands. "Uh, no, I don't think so."

After handing Gaby off to Jude, he then whisked me into his arms before I could protest anymore and then danced me around the room. "No one can say no to the conga," he replied, when he dipped me.

I giggled. "You're very persuasive."

"Dance wif me, Daddy!" Bella cried behind us.

"Sorry to be a party pooper, but I need to get your measurements."

AJ released me from his arms to smack himself in the forehead. "Shi—I mean, shoot. I totally forgot."

"It's okay."

At Bella's pouty face, AJ leaned down and kissed her on the head. "I'll be right back, mija."

When we got back into the dressing room, I found it was still just Jake and Brayden. "I don't know where the hell he is. I just texted him again."

Waving my hand nonchalantly as if it truly didn't hurt me and piss me off, I replied, "It doesn't matter. I can work on getting all of yours first."

Jake stepped forward. "I'm sure you need to get the most important member first, right?" he asked, wearing a teasing expression.

"Of course," I replied.

Setting down my notepad, I then grabbed my tape measure and pencil and went to work. "Done," I said, once I'd worked my way from his neck all the way down his body.

"You did that just like a professional."

I smiled at his compliment. After I draped the measuring tape back around my neck, I stooped over my notepad to enter Jake's measurements more formally than what I had scribbled on a scratch piece of paper.

When I finished and turned around, AJ was whipping off his "Drummers Bang Harder" T-shirt. I bit down on my lip to keep from laughing. "Um, you don't have to be naked for me to get accurate measurements."

He grinned. "After doing your brother's, I thought you might like to take in an example of a real man's physique."

Jake snorted as he collapsed onto the couch. "Keep dreaming, asshole."

While AJ preened in front of the mirror, flexing his biceps and dancing his pecs, I pulled the tape from around my neck. "Okay, Mr. Hot Stuff, let's do this."

A frown lined AJ's brows as he gazed in the mirror. He ran his hand up and down the washboard abs that drove women wild. "You know, I'm starting to think having kids has turned my six-pack into a keg."

Across the room from us, Brayden howled with laughter. "Last time I checked, it was Mia birthing the kids, not you, so I'm not quite sure how your girlish figure was affected."

After AJ scowled at Brayden, he turned to me. "What do you think, Allison?"

I couldn't help the laughter that tumbled out of my lips at both his question and the seriousness with which he asked it. "I don't think you have anything to worry about, AJ."

With a waggle of his brows, he asked, "So you think I'm a DILF, eh?"

Jake groaned. "Seriously, AJ? Don't ask Allison shit like that."

Ignoring Mr. Overprotective, I nodded. "Totally a DILF. Mia is one lucky woman."

A beaming smile lit up his handsome face. Drawing me into his arms for an appreciative hug, AJ said, "Thank you. I knew you were a woman with very good taste."

That was the moment Rhys chose to appear in the doorway. His gaze momentarily narrowed on at me in AJ's arms. Then as if he realized we weren't alone, his expression softened. "What's going on?"

Taking a step back, AJ peered around me at Rhys. "Where the hell have you been, man? You knew Allison needed to get our measurements before rehearsal."

He shrugged. "Sorry. I didn't know it was such a big deal."

His words had the same effect as if he had driven a dagger deep into my chest. Although I should have looked away, I couldn't help staring into his eyes, desperately trying to find the Rhys I had loved for so long. For the life of me, I couldn't understand why he was being an asshole to me. And while his dissing my internship hurt, the total lack of kindness he was showing me was much worse. Mainly because it was so against Rhys's usual character.

Rising off the couch, Jake eyeballed Rhys, and I could tell the big brother in him was getting rankled. "Allie's fashion internship is a big deal."

Instead of looking at Jake, Rhys looked at me. Deep down, he knew how important it was. He'd been right there with me in Savannah when I'd told him all about it. In fact, he'd believed in me so implicitly then. But now, he was downplaying it like it was nothing at all to him.

"It's fine, Jake. I was busy with you guys anyway," I replied, as I brought the tape measure to AJ's neck.

Undaunted, Jake said, "Why don't you do Allison a favor and go get Eli and Gabe?"

"They're still rehearsing with Abby," Rhys replied, as he grabbed a bottle of water out of the cooler.

"Worthless," Jake muttered under his breath.

Just as I was finishing up with Brayden's measurements, Frank, the head roadie for Runaway Train, came in the door. "Hey, Jake, I need all of you guys to head on up to the stage. One of the set changes is giving us problems in this arena, and I want to make sure you guys think it's working out okay.

"Rhys, once you're done with your measurements, come meet us on the stage," Jake said.

"Okay," Rhys replied.

When the door shut behind them, leaving us all alone, I couldn't help jumping. Loud silence reverberated around the room as if we were locked in a tomb. As I stood in front of Rhys, I slid my measuring tape off my neck. I knew I was going to have to break the silence between us. "You know, I thought we had agreed to be friends."

Rhys's brows shot up in surprise. "Who said we weren't?"

I gave him a sad smile. "This—" I motioned between us, "Doesn't feel much like friendship."

With an apologetic expression, Rhys protested, "I'm trying my best, Allison."

"By blowing off this fitting? You, of all people, know how important this internship is. You were there cheering me on from almost the beginning. Now you act as if you couldn't give a shit."

"Please believe me when I say that I *am* sorry for being late to the fitting. I wasn't intentionally blowing it off to be an asshole. I couldn't say it in front of the others, but I've been trying to give you some space to work through your feelings for me. That's what I was doing this afternoon when I lost track of time. Then I thought by acting like I didn't care in front of Jake, he wouldn't think there had been anything between us."

I couldn't help feeling wounded by the fact he was actually working to avoid me and treating me with kid gloves. But instead of showing my hurt, I plastered a smile onto my face. "I see," I replied. I then brought the tape measure to his neck. The moment my fingers touched his bare skin, he jumped. "Sorry if my fingers are cold."

"It's fine," he replied, as I turned away to scribble down the inches.

"Raise your arms," I requested. As I brought my arms around Rhys, my face brushed against his chest. I couldn't stop the tremor that went through me as I inhaled his cologne. While I fitted the tape against his pecs, I remembered what his bare chest looked like, even what it felt like as his body hovered over mine when we were making love. Even though I hated the way he had been acting, I couldn't deny the attraction I still felt for him. I wanted to rub my body against his, feel his hands on me like they had been once before.

After pushing away my lustful thoughts, I ordered, "Bend your arm at the elbow and place it on your hip."

"Don't I get a 'please'?" he asked, with a teasing lilt in his voice.

"You missed out on 'please' and 'thank you' because you were late," I countered, running the tape measure down his bicep.

He sighed. "I did say I was sorry. I promise the next time you need me for something, I'll be on time. I swear."

Eyeing him, I searched his face and saw true sincerity. I nodded. "Okay then."

After getting his waist and hips, I scribbled down the measurements, all the while dreading what I had to do next. For some reason, it hadn't seemed as mortifying to do Brayden or AJ's inseam. But I already felt my cheeks warming at the mere thought of doing it to Rhys. It also didn't help that we were all alone.

I dropped to my knees in front of him. "What the fuck do you think you're doing?" Rhys demanded, as he jumped back from me like he had been scalded with hot water.

Tilting my head up at him, I blew a few strands of hair out of my face. "I'm sorry. I have to get your inseam, or the pants won't fit right."

Rhys clenched and unclenched his jaw a few moments before he stepped back in front of me. It didn't help matters that my face had to be right on eyelevel with his crotch to get the measurements.

"C-Can you s-spread your legs a little?" With a grunt, Rhys shifted his feet and moved his legs. "Thank you," I replied, as I brought the tape up to the inside of his groin. The moment my hand brushed against his crotch, Rhys's hips jerked forward.

Trying to ignore his reaction, I took the tape and ran it down his leg to the back of his heel. When I started to remove the tape, I sucked in a breath. The front of Rhys's jeans strained with a half-mast bulge.

When I jerked my gaze up to his, he shook his head furiously. "Don't look at me like that!"

"How am I looking at you?" I whispered.

He licked his lips. "Like you want to do something about what you caused."

Heat warmed my cheeks. "I didn't mean to. I was just getting your measurements."

Reaching down, Rhys grabbed me under my arms and hauled me to my feet. My tape measure fell to the floor between us. As Rhys crushed me against his chest, his wild gaze focused on mine. "I guess you're happy about that, huh?"

I didn't like the tone he was using with me—it wasn't him. He had never spoken like this to me before. "No, I—"

"None of the other guys sprung wood while you were touching them, did they?" he demanded. When I shook my head, he said, "I didn't think they did. They're not me—they don't get affected by you like I do."

My heart leapt into my throat at his statement. "Y-You do?"

He slid his hand over my hip to cup my buttocks. When he pressed his bulge against my core, we both gasped at the pleasure. "You tell me. Am I affected by you?"

"Yes. Very much."

Grinding his pelvis into mine again, he asked, "Are you affected by me?"

"Yes. Always," I murmured, staring into his hooded eyes.

With his mouth hovering over mine, Rhys shook his head. "Fuck me, Allison…I thought we were going to be friends."

"We are."

A defeated look crept into his eyes. "This doesn't feel like friendship. It feels like much, much more."

What the hell? He was giving me whiplash from his emotional yo-yoing back and forth. Did he mean that he really wanted me now? Or was he just teasing me for more of his own sadistic fun? I was starting to think Rhys could be one cruel bastard.

"Maybe that's because one of us hasn't been honest about how they truly feel," I countered, jerking my chin up.

As the color drained from his face, Rhys froze his movements against me. Just when he opened his mouth to say something, the door flew open, and Eli burst inside followed by Gabe. "Here we are. Reporting for our fitting," Eli said, giving me a mock salute.

Rhys jerked back from me so fast I was sure he was going to end up with whiplash. He spun around to hide the evidence of his arousal from Eli and Gabe. I turned to face the twins. "Hey guys, I'm ready when you are."

Glancing past me, Gabe's brows furrowed at Rhys. "You okay, man?" he asked.

Instead of replying, Rhys grabbed a shirt off the rack that I was sure he was going to drape in front of his crotch. Plastering on a smile for Gabe, I replied, "It's all my fault. I accidentally stuck him with one of my pins when I was getting his inseam measurement." Thank goodness they bought my lie, considering there was no need for pins at the moment.

Both Eli and Gabe grimaced. Bringing his hand in front of his crotch, Eli said, "You better take extra care around my junk. It's very precious to me."

I laughed. "I'll try hard to remember that." When I bent down to scribble in the last of Rhys's measurements, he finally turned around. The color had returned to his face, and he flashed a smile at the twins.

"If you guys are done rehearsing, guess it means we're up. See you later," Rhys said. He brushed past me without another word.

While I fought to keep my emotions in check, Eli stepped in front of me, blocking my view of Rhys's retreating form. He surveyed me with a dead serious expression. "I'm ready for you, Allison. Are you ready for me?" he said, in a throaty, sexy voice.

I burst out laughing at his teasing. "What?" he questioned, running a hand seductively down his chest to stop right above his belt buckle.

"You're an idiot," Gabe said behind us.

"Don't be jealous of the fact my maleness is overpowering Allison right now," Eli countered.

My hand flew to my mouth to hide my laughter at his antics. Over the last three and a half years, I'd gotten to know Gabe and Eli somewhat well. It wasn't until Eli and I were brought together as Jax's godparents that I got to know him even better. While I'd been trying to avoid Rhys at the baptism, Eli had been more than happy to keep me entertained. We'd spent most of the baptism party together, walking along Jake's property and talking about anything and everything. Eli was fun to be with, and it didn't hurt that he was drop-dead gorgeous either. Part of me couldn't help wishing that I was attracted to Eli on a different level. It might be just the thing to get me to forget about Rhys.

When I finally recovered, I crooked my finger at him to come a little closer. Just to tease him, I whispered in a seductive voice, "Let's get your measurements."

"No pins, right?" he questioned.

"It's fine. I promise."

While Eli stood stock still, I got his upper body measurements. When I dropped down to get his inseam, he snickered like an immature teenage boy. "Seriously?" I questioned.

"Sorry, it's just I usually buy a girl dinner before I expect her on her knees."

"Really?"

He grinned. "Okay, so I rarely have to buy her dinner first."

"You're a real charmer, aren't you, Eli?" I muttered.

Gabe shook his head. "Better be glad Jake wasn't in here to hear you say that. He'd have your dick for sure."

I sighed. "Honestly, Jake has got to get over being so overprotective." When I started to rise off my knees, Eli reached down to help me up. "Thanks."

He gave me a sincere smile. "You're welcome. And don't be giving Jake a hard time. It's only natural for older brothers to feel protective of our sisters. We felt the same way about Abby."

Gabe bobbed his head. "Even though she was totally of age, we all almost shit a brick when she ended up on a bus full of strange rockers."

I laughed. "But that had a happy ending, didn't it?"

"Yes, and that's exactly the only reason why your brother is still breathing and not six feet under," Eli replied, with a wink.

Once I finished with Gabe's measurements, I gathered up my sketch pad. "Thanks again guys for helping me out with this internship."

"We're glad to do it," Gabe replied.

As I started for the door, Eli stopped me. "Where are you going?"

"To my real summer job—watching your niece and nephew."

"Want some help?"

I raised my brows in surprise. "Don't you have better things to be doing before the show?"

He shrugged. "What could be better than spending time with a beautiful girl as well as my flesh and blood?"

My cheeks warmed at his compliment. With everything happening with Rhys, it felt good to have a desirable guy call me beautiful. "I guess not."

Eli grinned as he followed me down the hall to where the kids were corralled. Thankfully, Mia and Lily were watching the twins for me while I was with the guys. But of course, Abby had come straight in from the rehearsal to be with her babies. She had Jules in her arms, rocking her back and forth to quiet her cries.

"Everything okay?" I asked, after I sat my notebook down on the table. I then eased Jax out of his saucer and took him into my arms.

"It's fine. I think she's just ready for a nap." While the room had been booming with noise earlier with AJ playing DJ, it was quiet now. In the far corner at a table away from the others, Lily worked on school work with eight-year-old Jude and five-year-old Melody. Across the room, Mia sat on a pallet full of toys, playing with Bella, Gaby, and Lucy.

Eli swooped over to take Jules into his arms. "What's wrong, baby girl?" he questioned. She immediately quieted and stared wide-eyed up at Eli. He made crazy faces at her until Jules was giggling and kicking her legs and feet. I couldn't help smiling at him along with Jules. Eli certainly had a good heart, and when it came to him and Gabe, he was always much more interested in holding and spending time with the twins.

A roadie appeared in the doorway with a guitar in his hand. "There you are," he said to Eli. He then crossed the room over to us.

"Did you get it fixed?" Eli asked, with an anxious expression.

The roadie nodded. "Try it out and see for yourself."

Eli handed Jules back to Abby. Then he took the guitar in his hand. Easing down on the couch, he propped it on his knee and began strumming some chords. He glanced up and grinned. "Thanks, man. It sounds good as new."

"No problem. Let me know if you have any other problems with it," the roadie replied, before heading out the door.

"Did you break a string during rehearsals?"

"Yeah, the E-string, which totally fu—" Eli glanced around at all the kids within earshot. "Totally messed up the entire set of strings. I didn't know what I was going to do at the show tonight."

"Couldn't you have just borrowed one?" I asked, bouncing Jax on my knee.

At my simple question, Eli sucked in a horrified breath while Abby rolled her eyes. "Did I say something wrong?"

Abby shook her head. "It's just Eli gets a bit OCD about his guitars."

"I'm an artist, and artists are always particular about the palette with which they use," Eli countered.

"When Jacob's Ladder was just starting out, his favored guitar got left behind on a tour stop. When Eli realized what happened, he freaked, and although he had an exact replica to play with, he still barely made it through the show without a ton of mistakes."

"I had no idea you were so particular," I replied.

Strumming the guitar, Eli seemed to tune us out for the moment. Almost instantly I recognized it as Kenny Chesney's *You and Tequila*. For a moment, I was transported away from the dressing room and back to my time in Savannah. Any time the word "tequila" was mentioned, I always thought of Rhys and our night together. It was hard to believe out of all of the songs out there, Eli would choose this one to play.

As I started humming along, I bounced Jax in my arms. When Eli abruptly stopped and the guitar strings made a screeching noise, I jumped. "You," he said, pointing a finger at me.

"Me what?"

"You could totally sing duet with me on this song."

I widened my eyes in horror. "No, I couldn't."

"Oh come on, I'm dying to do this song live, but Abby refuses to sing it with me."

Abby laughed. "Call me crazy, but for some reason, it seems a little odd to be singing a duet with your *brother*. I told you we could totally do it with you as a solo."

When I giggled, Eli scowled at us. "I have one simple request, and I can't make it happen."

Taking pity on him, I eased down on the couch beside him. Once I adjusted Jax on my lap, I smiled at Eli. "I'll sing it with you now, but only so you can practice it to do it alone. I'm not a professional singer, and I'm certainly not going in front of thousands and thousands of people to sing."

"You really will?"

I nodded. "It doesn't hurt that Jax and Jules love to be sung to, and it's almost their nap time."

Eli grinned at me. "I'll take it any way you'll give it to me." Scooting closer to me on the couch, he adjusted the guitar on his knees. After he turned toward me, he then began strumming the opening chords to the song again. It was just pure dumb luck that I even knew the lyrics to the song. I hadn't always been a huge country music fan. It had just grown on me after Jake and Abby got together. I'd tagged along with them to the CMAs, and after meeting Kenny Chesney in person, I started listening to his music.

When Eli started singing the first verse, Jax eased back to lie against my chest. Just like Abby, Eli had an amazing voice. It almost wasn't fair that he was so good-looking and so talented. Not to mention he had such an endearing personality. He really was a triple threat who was going to make some woman very happy someday—I just hated that it most likely wasn't going to be me.

As we got to the chorus, he winked at me. And then I chimed in with him. "You and tequila make me crazy— run like poison in my blood. One more night could kill me, baby…"

Pausing in his singing, Eli closed his eyes in mock ecstasy. "We sound amazing!" he cried, enthusiastically over the music.

Abby and I laughed at his over-the-top comment. In my arms, Jax craned his tiny neck up to watch me as I sang. I smiled down at him, and when I finished my part, I kissed the strands of his dark hair. When we started the second verse, I came in whenever the original singer, Grace Potter, usually sang.

Halfway through, I glanced up to see Rhys framed in the doorway. One hand was braced on the doorframe and his knee was bent as if he froze in mid-walk. His eyes bore into mine, and I felt a rush of warmth singe my cheeks at the intensity of his stare. For a moment, I didn't bother tearing my eyes away from his. Instead, I was too interested in surveying the range of emotions playing out on his face. Curiosity at why I was singing with Eli was there along with actual interest and enjoyment in hearing me sing again. My heartbeat ratcheted up a few notches at what I hoped was the sight of jealousy seething below the surface as he watched Eli directing his singing to me. There was also acknowledgement of the importance of the subject matter of the song.

In his mind, tequila had been our undoing back in Savannah. While it had somewhat attributed to my uninhibited behavior with him, it certainly didn't make me do anything I hadn't dreamed of doing for many years. Regardless of what warped ideas he had in his mind about why we couldn't be together, I knew what the truth was. He was just too damn scared to admit that he cared for me. He feared Jake, but more than anything else, he feared giving himself to someone else. He'd been burned by those who were supposed to love him, so he had no idea how to actually love someone else without getting hurt.

Rhys's brows shot far into his hairline when Eli sang the line, "When it comes to you, oh the damage I could do. It's always your favorite sins that do you in." His free hand came up to rub along his jawline before moving back to grip the strands of his hair at the base of his neck.

I could only imagine why the line was bothering him so much. It was the epitome of the impasse we found ourselves at. And so far, he had managed to do a lot of damage to my heart and to the relationship we'd once had.

Part of me ached to go to Rhys. I wanted to wrap my arms around his neck and tell him that it could all be all right if he would just let go with his preconceived worries. But the other part of me ached to go over and throttle him for being such a stubborn bastard.

At the end of the song, I brought Jax's hands together to clap. He giggled and bounced in my lap. "You liked that, huh?"

As Jax squealed his approval, Eli said, "I think he's giving his seal of approval that a duet needs to happen between the two of us."

"A duet?" Jake's voice bellowed from the doorway. His eyes narrowed at the sight of Eli and I so close together on the couch. "What are you guys doing?"

"Just messing around," I replied.

Knocking Rhys out of the way, Jake then crossed the room in two long strides to stand in front of Eli and me. At the sight of his dad, Jax went crazy lifting his arms and reaching for Jake, so Jake picked him up. He then appeared almost comical with a menacing look on his face directed at Eli as he bounced his baby boy in his arms.

"You've been holding out on us, Jake," Eli said.

"What do you mean?" he asked, glancing between me and Eli.

"Allison can seriously sing."

Jake glowered at him. "Yeah, she's got a good voice. What about it?"

Eli rolled his eyes. "You should be maximizing her talent by putting her out on the stage."

I opened my mouth to argue with him when Rhys piped up behind Jake. "Allison wouldn't want that. While she might like to sing at low-key places, she would never, ever want to perform to thousands of people. Besides, her talents are far better served with fashion design."

Even if I had been forced to, I couldn't have taken my eyes off of Rhys in that moment for anything in the world. He was constantly throwing me emotional curve balls, and this was yet another one. With everyone peering at him in surprise, Rhys shrugged. "It's the truth."

Patting Eli on the leg, I said, "Rhys is right. I'm not a performer."

"Except at Saffie's," Rhys replied, a smile playing at the corners of his lips.

Jake's dark brows furrowed. "What the hell is Saffie's?"

Rhys's wide-eyed, horrified look told me he hadn't meant to out me. I'm sure after all these months, he figured I had told Jake. Exhaling a long breath, I said, "Just a lesbian night club I was singing at once a week back in Savannah."

Shifting Jax to his other hip, Jake then appeared almost comical with a questioning expression on his face. "Allie-Bean, is there something you need to tell me?"

"Huh?"

Jake grimaced. "It doesn't matter to me one way or the other." When I continued giving him a blank look, he said, "Do you need to tell me about you being…" He leaned in and lowered his voice. "Gay," he said, in a whisper.

I busted out laughing. Both Eli and Rhys started laughing along with me. "Jake, I'm not gay. I was just singing at a gay club."

"Oh," Jake replied. For a moment, he didn't appear relieved. In a warped way, I guess it would have been easier for him for me to be gay when we were out on tour with a bunch of horny males. Then his expression changed over to one that was serious big brother protector. "You were underage and singing at a nightclub? I'm pretty sure that Dad and Nancy don't know about this."

"They do now. I didn't tell them at first because I figured they would freak out just like you're starting to do."

"You should have seen her Jake. She was amazing," Rhys said.

Jake's gaze snapped from mine to Rhys's. "What the hell, dude? You knew about this?"

Rhys nodded. "I went to one of her shows."

"And you never thought that maybe I needed to know?"

With a shrug, Rhys replied, "It wasn't for me to tell." He glanced over at me. "She's good. Really good."

My heartbeat accelerated at his words. I was momentarily distracted by Abby's hand on my shoulder. "Oh, Allison, I wish we could have seen you."

"I have it on video," Rhys said, digging his phone out of his pocket.

"You do?" I asked, my voice choking off with emotion.

"I thought Jake might want to see it one day," Rhys replied.

"Oh," I murmured.

Abby squealed with glee and slid in beside Eli on the couch. Jake reluctantly squeezed in beside her. Leaning over the back of the couch, Rhys started playing the video. It was hard processing him being so open about me and my singing. When it came down to it, I couldn't believe he was sharing anything that connected us and our infamous time in Savannah.

"You sound amazing!" Abby exclaimed.

Warmth filled my cheeks at her compliments. "Thanks."

Nudging Jake, Abby said, "Doesn't she sound amazing, babe?"

Jake bobbed his head. "I can't get over how grown up she looks and sounds." He glanced over his shoulder at me. "You're absolutely phenomenal, Allie-Bean."

Tears stung my eyes at the sincerity of his words. "Thank you."

"That's one sexy dress you're rockin' there. You look beautiful in red. Love the boots, too," Eli said, winking at me.

Jake smacked the back of his head. "Ow!" Eli cried.

"Watch what you say to my sister," Jake muttered through gritted teeth.

"Honestly, Jake, I'm almost twenty-one, not twelve," I countered.

"You'll always be my baby sister, even when you're eighty."

"And you're ninety and dead?" Eli questioned.

"Shut up," Jake replied, which caused me to giggle. Jake then jerked his gaze over his shoulder to Rhys. "Anything else I need to know about that happened when you two were together in Savannah?"

His question caused a shudder to run through me. Rhys threw a quick glance at me before fixing his gaze on Jake. A nervous laugh escaped his lips. "Nothing else besides some touristy stuff I dragged Allison to."

Jake snickered. "Guess you're still a history nerd, huh?"

"Yeah, he is," I quickly replied.

After Jake seemed appeased with our responses, he, Abby, and Eli began to run through the merits of my performance. But I tuned them out. All I could do was stare at Rhys. Even when he met my gaze and held it, I couldn't look away. I didn't care what he thought about me staring at him—I enjoyed even the smallest of connections with him. And while my chest clenched with the agony of how I should abandon my feelings for him, I once again wished that somehow or some way things could be different between us.

11: ALLISON

After leaving Omaha in the night, we pulled into Cheyenne, Wyoming just as the sun had begun to rise outside my window. After grabbing a quick shower, I headed into the kitchen. Outfitted in only his boxer shorts, Jake stood in front of the counter mixing up baby cereal while Abby sat at the table holding the wailing twins. "Morning," I said, over Jax and Jules's cries.

"Morning," Jake mumbled.

Nudging him out of the way with my hip, I said, "Here. I'll finish this. You get their bottles."

Jake nodded and then pivoted over to the fridge. I'd prepared their bottles for several feedings the night before. He popped them in the microwave, and when it dinged off, he sprinkled formula on his arm to test it. As I was sucking up the cereal into one of the feeders, Jake was taking Jules into his arms and handing Abby a bottle. Once the twins had their formula, they quieted instantly.

I brought the feeders over to the table. "Can you take her, Allie-Bean? I've got to get the musical arrangement for the new song from Brayden."

"Sure." Jake passed Jules over to me before I eased down at the table. He then hurried back to the bedroom to throw on some clothes. When he returned, he kissed Abby and then each of the twins. After he was gone, Abby and I made small talk as the twins finished their bottles.

As I started bringing the feeder of cereal to Jules's open and waiting mouth, the faint sound of a strumming guitar drew my attention to the window. I glanced across the table at Abby. "Do you hear that?"

She nodded. "Eli must be practicing pretty loud for it to come through the bus like that."

Once Jules was sucking heartily, the music continued growing louder and louder. I rose up and peered out the glass. Balancing Jules on one hip, I used my other hand to pull up the blinds and open the window. I gasped at the sight of Eli strolling down the alley between the buses, playing the melody to James Blunt's *You're Beautiful*.

When he got in front of the window, he grinned up at me and began to sing. "I saw an angel, of that I'm sure."

Warmth spread through my cheeks. Just the night before after Jacob's Ladder's show, he'd caught me in the dressing room singing along to the song on the radio while giving Jax and Jules their bedtime bottles. Shaking his head in mock disgust, he'd questioned, "Don't tell me you actually like that shit?"

"Yes, as a matter of fact I do. I like all of his songs. *Same Mistake and Goodbye My Lover* are some of my favorites, too."

Eli had rolled his eyes as he plopped down on the sofa next to me. After taking Jax into his arms to help me out, he said, "Blunt's a mediocre songwriter at best, not to mention a dick who cheats on women."

Cocking my head, I had countered, "You know an awfully lot about a guy whose music you hate."

He had shrugged. "I know my music."

"Whatever," I had muttered.

"Regardless of the shitty song, I didn't realize you could sing."

"A little."

Eli grinned. "Don't be modest."

"Modesty is something your egocentric self might find beneficial," I teased.

With his free hand, he scratched his chin. "Hmm, I'll give it some thought."

Abby had then appeared, and we had started to the bus to get Jax and Jules down to sleep. Now I couldn't believe Eli was standing before me singing. Pausing in the song, he threw up his arms and cried, "There she is! The beautiful angel who haunts my waking thoughts!" Wagging his eyebrows, he added, "Mmm and maybe some of my naughty dreams."

I burst out laughing at his declaration. "The only angel I know is your sister and the dog, and I'm not sure why you're out here singing to her…or having naughty dreams about her. Wait, is it furry Angel you're hot for because I could get her for you?" At the mention of her name, Angel barked and wagged her tail.

"You're breaking my heart," he said.

Abby joined me at the window. "Eli, what in the world are you doing? It's barely eight a.m."

Rolling his eyes, Eli replied, "Duh, I'm serenading a beautiful woman."

I shook my head. "You've made your point and made fun of my choice of music. Again. So go on."

With his shoulders drooping in defeat, Eli started to walk away. Just as I was about to turn away from the window, he started strumming again. "Yes, she caught my eye as we walked on by. She could see from my face that I was flying high." On the flying high bit, he made a loopy looking face.

Jules kicked her legs and giggled. "Your Uncle Eli is pretty funny, huh?"

Her tiny palm patted against my shoulder almost in time with the music, and even though it was probably way too early, I could already tell she had inherited her parents' musical genes.

At that moment, the bus door opened, and Jake and Rhys came bounding up the stairs. Jake shot me and Abby a disgusted look. "Would someone mind telling me why my brother-in-law is singing some douche song outside my bus?"

I giggled. "It's just a joke between us."

"Us?" Jake repeated, cocking his brows at me.

"What?" I questioned innocently.

Crossing his tattooed arms over his chest, he asked, "Is there an 'us' you'd like to tell me about?"

"Get real, Jake," I muttered, as I swung a now fussy Jules back and forth in my arms.

"What the hell is that supposed to mean?" Jake demanded.

I narrowed my eyes at him. "It means even if there was something between Eli and me, it's none of your business."

"Oh really?"

When I nodded, I caught Rhys's intense gaze over Jake's shoulder. He seemed just as interested as Jake was in what was going on between me and Eli. It infuriated me that he acted like he even cared considering the way he had been treating me lately. One minute he completely ignored me, and then the very next he hovered around as if I was his. It was so damn confusing.

As Eli continued with the second verse, Jake groaned. "Enough is enough."

Choosing to ignore his tirade, I went back to the window and grinned down at Eli. Just as he was about to finish, he started up again. "Eli," I giggled.

Before I realized what was happening, I saw a flicker of Jake's black T-shirt out of the corner of my eyes. Then in a flash, he was beside me with a bucket of water. He then proceeded to dump it out the window, sending water crashing all over Eli. "W-What the f-fuck?" Eli sputtered.

"That'll teach you to sing douche songs to my sister outside my bus window!" Jake replied, through this laughter. Leaning against the kitchen counter, Rhys snickered as well, and it took everything within me not to go over and slap his arrogant face.

Sweeping my free hand to my hip, I demanded, "You two think this is funny?"

Rhys shrugged. "He obviously needed cooling off to stop torturing us with singing."

Jake nodded. "My man speaks the truth. The two of you should be glad he wasn't plugged up to an amp."

I glared at both of them. "You…assholes!" Kissing Jules on the cheek, I then thrust her into Jake's arms. Without another word to them, I grabbed a towel out of the closet. Then I hustled down the aisle and pounded down the bus steps. After throwing open the door, I jumped off the steps onto the pavement.

Eli had propped his guitar against the side of the bus and was wringing out the bottom of his soaking T-shirt. "I'm sorry about Jake. That was a real asshole thing to do."

"It's okay," Eli replied, with a good-natured grin.

"That wasn't your favorite guitar, was it?" I asked, already cringing at the thought.

"No, thankfully it wasn't."

"Oh, I'm so glad to hear that." When I offered him the towel, he shook his head. Then in a flash, he had his sopping wet T-shirt over his head, leaving me to stare at his broad, tattooed, and very naked chest. He dropped the shirt, and then he reached for the towel. Since I was still staring at his chest, he had to whistle at me to get me to hand over the towel.

"Sorry," I mumbled.

As he wiped off his chest, Eli grinned. "It's all good. I like the fact you were ogling me."

Crossing my arms over my chest, I huffed, "I wasn't ogling you. I was admiring your ink."

"Riiiight," he replied with a smirk.

I shook my head at him. "Well, for what it's worth, thanks for the songs."

Eli draped the towel over his neck. "You're welcome. The performance was actually a lead-in for a question I wanted to ask you."

My heartbeat kicked up a notch. "You wanted to ask me something?"

He bobbed his head. "Tomorrow night, Jake's taking Abby to visit some of his mother's family outside Boise, and they're taking the twins with them."

"Yes, Abby had mentioned something about it."

"Since you had the night off, I thought you might like to come out with me and Gabe."

"Out?" I questioned lamely.

"I'm sure Boise doesn't have a whole lot of happening sites, but we're going to try to find a club or two to hang out in." Leaning closer to me, he asked, "You game?"

I blinked my eyes in disbelief. Was Eli asking me out, like out-out? Or was he just being nice and giving me something to do besides staying in my hotel room on my off night. And if he was asking me out, did I want him to? Was I ready to try dating someone new? My head spun so hard with all the crazy questions swimming in it that I brought my hand to my forehead to calm it.

"So, what do you think?" Eli asked.

"I think it sounds like fun," I answered honestly.

He grinned. "Good, I'm glad to hear you think so."

"Just drinks and some dancing, huh?"

"Yep. Unless the mood strikes for more," he replied, wagging his eyebrows.

I couldn't help laughing. "I'll be sure to keep my mood under control then."

"What a pity. We could have some real fun together."

Cocking my head at him, I countered, "Oh yeah, I'm sure I know exactly what kind of fun you're talking about, and I'll have you know I'm not that kind of girl to hop from one guy to another for—" I paused to make air quotes with my fingers, "*Fun.*"

He winked at me. "That's good to know, Allison. You can keep me an honest man."

"Sounds like a challenging job," I replied, with a smile.

"It is. It might even be a full-time one."

"We'll just have to see about that."

"Look, since it's freezing out here, I gotta go get out of these wet clothes. But we're on for tomorrow night, right?"

"Yes, we are."

"Good." He grabbed his wet shirt off the pavement and then picked up his guitar. "Bye, Allison."

"Bye, Eli," I said, waving my fingers at him.

Once he was out of sight, I walked back to the bus. When I came back up the stairs, I found Jake and Rhys had left, and it was just Abby and the twins. "It seems that Eli has a crush."

I shook my head. "It's not like that. We just like to joke around with each other."

Abby gave me a pointed stare. "I know my brother, Allison. Deep down, he isn't kidding."

"Oh," I murmured softly.

"He asked you out tomorrow night, huh?"

My brows shot up in surprise. "How did you know?"

Motioning to the window, Abby replied, "As much as I wanted to give you privacy, I was kind of held hostage with the twins."

"I see."

"So do you think you could like Eli?"

"I already like him."

"You know what I mean."

With a sigh, I flopped down on the couch. "Of course I could like him. He's good-looking, talented and funny."

"But he's not Rhys," she said, with a knowing expression.

I vaulted off the couch. "There's nothing going on with me and Rhys," I protested.

Abby shook her head at me. "Do you really think I'm that stupid?"

Panic sliced its way through me. If Abby knew, then that meant she could tell Jake. Everything Rhys and I feared would come to fruition. "Please don't tell Jake," I whispered.

"Of course I won't tell Jake. What you two feel for each other is not my place to tell."

"How long have you known?"

"Since the twins' baptism. You needed a chainsaw to cut through the unresolved sexual tension between you two."

My cheeks warmed at her words. "We'd already resolved the tension by then. That was part of the problem."

Abby gasped. "You slept with Rhys?"

"Shh!" I cried. Since we were alone on the bus, I wasn't sure why I was trying to quiet her. It wasn't like the twins were going to spill anything.

"When did it happen?"

I realized it was time to unburden myself of everything that happened in Savannah. So I took a seat across from Abby and filled her in. When I finished, she sighed. "I had no idea that had happened. No wonder you two practically combust when you're in the same room together."

"It doesn't matter what happened then. Rhys made it perfectly clear then that he doesn't feel the same way I feel about him, and that's that."

"Well, he's deluding himself if that's what he thinks. He doesn't look at you the way AJ or Brayden looks at you."

Images flashed in my mind of Rhys during his fitting. "But that's just lust. I want him to look at me with more in his eyes." Feeling tears pricking my eyes, I said, "I want him to love me."

"He does look at you with more than lust, Allison. He's guarded with his feelings for you, but it's there."

Swiping the tears away from my eyes, I shook my head. "Even if he did realize how he felt, he's never going to go against Jake by pursuing me."

"You don't know that."

"It's hopeless," I murmured.

We were interrupted by Jax and Jules beginning to fuss at being held captive in their high chairs. As we picked them up and took them to their pallet, Abby said, "There's something else I need to say."

"What is it?" I asked, putting Jax's favorite stuffed animal within his grasp.

Her expression had saddened since we left the table. "You know that more than anything, I want you to be happy."

"Yes."

"Regardless of what happens between you and Rhys, I don't want to see Eli get hurt."

"Me either."

"I know that everything between you two is just fun and games right now. But Eli's already putting himself out there for you far more than he has for a girl in a long, long time. I know it would be easy to use him to get back at Rhys—"

"I would never do that to him."

Abby sighed. "Deep down, I know you wouldn't knowingly do anything to hurt Eli. But just be careful how far you let this go with him. If you go out with him and see that there's nothing really there but friendship, let him know. Just don't lead him on."

"I promise I won't. I know the agony of caring about someone who doesn't feel the same way about you."

Satisfied with my response, Abby nodded. "Good. Now what exactly are you going to wear tomorrow night?"

I laughed at the complete change of conversation. "I have no idea. I'm not even sure I have anything with me that is club worthy. I didn't exactly pack that kind of thing for this summer."

"You and I are pretty much the same size. I'm sure you could borrow one of my show dresses off the rack that I haven't worn." Her eyes widened excitedly. "There are several really sexy dresses from my pre-twins days." When I opened my mouth to protest that she looked like she had lost all her baby weight, she shook her head. "I've gone up a dress size." Then with a devious little grin, she said, "I'll refrain from telling you what Jake had to say about why he liked the weight gain."

Holding up a hand, I said, "Knowing him as well as I do, I really don't want to know."

Abby's girlish giggle sent a longing ache ricocheting through my chest. More than anything in the world, I wanted what she and Jake had—a great romance, a deep love, and lots of fun and heat in the bedroom. As much as I wanted that with Rhys, maybe it was time for me to try to move on. He obviously wasn't going to suddenly become emotionally available or decide that all the reasons not to be together didn't really matter.

Maybe it was meant for me to truly give Eli a chance. I mean, it didn't hurt that he seemed to really like being with me, either as a friend or romantically. He had so many admirable qualities like being kind, thoughtful, and good with the twins. Not to mention the fact he was funny as hell. I could see us getting along really well. So there was really no reason for me to hesitate about giving him a real chance. After all, Rhys had made it very clear that we should forget about Savannah and move on. Maybe this was how I was supposed to do it.

Clinging to that thought, I decided that tomorrow night I was going to be wearing the sexiest dress imaginable, even if I had to make some alterations to it myself. Yes, I was about to change my destiny for the better.

12: RHYS

With my bass guitar strapped to me, my fingers worked to produce the notes that flowed alongside the melodies of Runaway Train's music. Today's rehearsal with the guys found us working on some of the new material we were planning on integrating into the show. Usually we only rehearsed the day of the show, but even though we had tonight off, we were making the most of our time.

While I might have been on stage, my mind could barely focus on anything but Allison. Things had been flowing along so easily between us after our talk on Jake's bus. That was until yesterday. Fuck, being that close to her for the measurements and then reacting the way I did. I'd wanted nothing more than to bury myself deep inside her or have her luscious lips wrapped around my dick.

But it wasn't just the thoughts of screwing that had invaded my mind. No, it had to do with my heart as well, and how Allison had called me out on not being honest about the feelings I had for her. She'd always been a smart girl, and she was smart enough to see I had been lying to her.

"Okay, I think that's good for today. Let's get the hell out of here," Jake said.

After I handed off my guitar to a roadie, I started out of the arena to the car that was waiting to take us back to the hotel. "Rhys!" Jake called behind me.

Pausing, I waited for him to catch up. "Hey man, I need to ask you a favor," Jake said.

"Sure. What is it?"

Jake glanced behind us before he spoke. "You got plans tonight?"

I grinned. "Besides ordering in room service and crashing? Hell no."

"Trust me, that sounds like pure heaven to me too, but I'm taking Abby and the twins out to visit my mom's brother."

"That sounds cool. But where does this favor come in? Don't tell me you have some cousin you want to fix me up with."

With a grimace, Jake replied, "Actually, I need you to go out with Allison tonight."

I skidded on the pavement and almost pitched face first into the limo waiting to take us to the hotel. "Excuse me?"

"She's going out to some club with Gabe and Eli. Normally, I would be stoked to have her chaperoned with two guys, but the way Eli has been looking at her and treating her lately has me fucking wigged out."

My mind instantly went to Eli's serenading Allison yesterday morning. Ugh, the douchebag. Maybe his actions weren't just teasing, and he was really going to pursue something with Allison. When I really thought about it, it did seem he had been spending a lot of time with her after the rehearsals and shows. Fucking hell. I knew I had to drive her away, but the thoughts of driving her straight into Eli's open arms pissed me off. Not that he wasn't a decent guy—she could've sure as hell done worse for herself. While he was known for partying pretty hard and enjoying the company of ladies, Eli wasn't such a bastard that he would pull that shit with

Allison. While he might have to fear Jake's wrath if he mistreated Allison, Eli wasn't a total asshole to play on Allison's emotions. Deep down, I knew his intentions were decent and honest, and he would be good to Allison.

In the end, it was just the principle of it all that pissed me off so much. Although Eli didn't know, Allison was my girl, and I didn't want to think of her with anyone else. The irony that I was having these feelings wasn't lost on me.

"So what's it gonna be, man?" Jake asked, bringing me out of my thoughts.

"Oh, uh, yeah, I can go with them."

He grinned. "Good. I know he won't try any bullshit if you're there."

Inwardly, I groaned. So far, Eli had been an absolute gentleman, while I'd been the vile motherfucker who had defiled his sister. Not to mention the fact that I had been lying to him about my feelings for Allison for the last month, if not longer.

As I slid inside the limo, I had the feeling that tonight was going to be a living hell of epic proportions.

At just before nine, Allison came out of her suite and into Jake and Abby's where I was waiting to meet her. My low whistle interrupted her stuffing her room key in her purse. She jerked her head up and gasped. I'm sure she had been hoping for Eli or Gabe, but instead she had found me. Her pained expression illustrated the fact that I was the last person on the face of the earth that she wanted to see at the moment. "W-What are y-you doing here?" she stammered.

I motioned down to my dress pants and button-down shirt. "Joining you for a night out on the town."

Her brows shot up in surprise. "I thought it was just me and the twins."

Running a hand through my hair, I replied, "Yeah, well, Jake asked me to tag along. I don't think he liked the thought of you out alone with Gabe and Eli. Well, I guess more precisely being alone with Eli." I couldn't help letting my gaze dip down to hungrily take in her appearance. Her long, dark hair fell in loose waves over her shoulders and back. But that wasn't what had me practically stupefied with lust.

It was the fact she was wearing one hell of a red dress. Unlike the one she'd had on at Saffie's, this one molded against her body like a second skin, showing every curve in delicious detail. With its one strap and tight bodice, her cleavage was cinched up again, causing my dick to jerk in my pants. "Of course, I don't think he would have let you out of the suite in that dress."

"This is utter bullshit!"

"Tell me how you really feel about me going," I teased.

Throwing one of her hands up in frustration, Allison challenged, "I'm an adult. It's none of Jake's business what I do." She closed the distance between us in two angry strides. "And I sure as hell don't need *you* tagging along."

"Is that right?"

"Yeah it is. I desperately need to have some fun tonight. Not be constantly reminded of the past."

Her words had a greater effect on me than she could have imagined. While I had to get her to fall out of love with me, I didn't want to hurt her now or ever. The thoughts that what she had experienced with me in Savannah caused her pain caused an ache in my chest. I drew in a deep breath. "Look, Allison, I can never express how truly sorry I am about what happened between us. More than anything, I just want you to be happy."

Narrowing her eyes at me, Allison drew her shoulders back. "Yeah, well, fuck you and your bullshit apologies!" She then proceeded to stomp past me. I stared open-mouthed at her retreating form. When she flung open the door, she turned back to me. "Ready, Mr. McGowan?"

"What the hell is this 'Mr. McGowan' business?" I demanded, as I joined her at the door.

She shrugged. "I figured since you were my chaperone, I should address you formerly. And since you've made it very clear that you want nothing to do with me on a romantic level, I figured calling you that kept the distance you so desired."

I blinked at her several times. This was a side of Allison I was not used to. Immediately, the expression "Hell hath no fury like a woman scorned" flashed in my mind. "Um, okay," I finally managed.

When we got out into the hallway, Gabe and Eli were waiting for us down by the elevators. The sight of Allison in her dress caused both of their eyes to bulge, but Eli stepped forward to draw Allison against him. "Damn, you look mighty fine tonight," he said.

Allison gave him a girlish giggle. "Thank you. It's one of Abby's old dresses. I just made some alterations to it."

Eli pulled away to grimace at Allison. "Ugh, you just totally killed all the naughty fantasies I had running through my head about you by telling me that dress was my sister's!"

As Allison smacked Eli playfully on the arm, I rolled my eyes. At the rate it was going, it was going to be a long, fucking night, and Jake was going to seriously owe me. That was if I managed not to get arrested for throttling Eli.

After taking the elevator downstairs, we hopped into the limo waiting for us. Eli was a quick bastard. After he allowed Allison to get in first, he then slid in behind her. I was left to sit across from them, giving me a fucking eyeful of Allison's legs. I wasn't sure just how happening a nightlife Boise had, but I sure as hell hoped I could get a few good beers in me to numb my mind.

It wasn't too long before the limo pulled up outside a club. Once we got out, we bypassed the others in line and headed straight inside. Not that there was a massive line like it was the old Studio 54 or something, but it was enough to show we were VIPs.

As we made our way through the crowd, multicolored strobe lights lit up the darkened dance floor. Couples, of different sexes and different arrays of dress, gyrated to the beat. "This place is amazing!" Allison called over the thumping bass of the music.

When Eli's hand came to rest on the small of her back, I momentarily saw red. Quickly I tried getting a hold of my raging testosterone-fueled emotions before I went into full-on Hulk mode and ripped Eli's arm from its socket. "Come on. We've got a table reserved in the VIP section," Eli said.

I snorted. "You mean this place actually has a VIP section?"

Ignoring my comment, Allison tilted her head up at Eli. "Oh, so am I a VIP tonight since I'm hanging out with you?"

He flashed her a cocky grin that made me want to punch him. "Maybe."

After we took the stairs to the second floor, the hostess motioned to our table. From our seats, we could see all the action on the dance floor, but at the same time, we were hidden from view. Considering how dark and foggy it was from the smoke machine, I hoped we wouldn't be recognized.

"What can I get you all to drink?" a waitress in tight, black spandex shorts, and a halter top asked.

Rubbing his hands together, Eli said, "Mmm, I'm in the mood for shots tonight. Who else is in for a bottle of 1800 Silver?"

"Me," Allison replied, which caused Eli to grin. He then glanced from her over to me.

"What about you, man?"

With my eyes fixed on Allison's, I replied, "No thanks. Tequila really isn't my thing."

She sucked in a harsh breath as she took in my words. I knew it was a real fucking asshole thing to say considering our history with tequila. But I had to keep pushing her away and get her to forget about me. Once Allison had recovered, she gave me a sickeningly sweet smile. "I'll take Rhys's shot then. I *adore* tequila."

Eli chuckled. "Ooh, I like your way of thinking tonight."

"So a bottle of 1800 and what else?" the waitress asked.

"A Bud on tap," Gabe replied, while giving the waitress his best sexy grin.

"Bud in a bottle," I replied.

The waitress bobbed her head. "Be right back." As she walked away, she gave Gabe a lingering look over her shoulder to which he winked at her.

"Dude, out of all the chicks here, you're macking on the waitress?" Eli questioned.

Gabe shrugged. "She's hot."

It was then that a drunken brunette, with cinched-up cleavage and her ass hanging out of her skirt, staggered up to our table. Her gaze honed straight on me. "Hey baby, wanna dance?"

Ordinarily, I might've been tempted, but there was no way in hell that I was going to hook-up with a chick tonight. I'd promised Jake to keep an eye on Allison, and it would be pretty hard to do if I was banging some chick in the bathroom. Besides, regardless of how I was trying to push Allison away, I refused to be a douchebag and dance with the chick to get at her. The tequila line had been shitty enough. "No thanks."

Her glassy-eyed stare fixed on Gabe next. "What about you?"

He shrugged. "Sure, why not."

"What about the waitress?" Eli asked.

Gabe winked. "The night is still young."

"Ugh, you're disgusting," Allison said, wrinkling her nose.

I got up so Gabe could slide out of the booth. With one hand on the chick's ass, Gabe led her off to the dance floor.

When I sat back down, Eli was eyeing me with a curious expression. "Why did you pass that one up, man? She looked like a sure thing."

"Brunettes aren't my type," I lied.

Allison's eyes bulged at my low dig. Cocking her head at me, she demanded, "And just what *is* your type?"

"I like petite blondes with big tits." The moment the words left my lips, I felt like a total bastard.

Eli chuckled. "Whatever floats your boat, man. I would think after you hadn't been getting any action for a while, you'd jump on the chick, regardless of her positives or negatives."

Once again, I wanted to punch Eli. The last thing I wanted Allison to know was that since Savannah, I hadn't been able to seal the deal with another girl. Desire for anyone else had been completely obliterated by her. Since we'd been on tour, I hadn't once taken one of the girls on Jacob's Ladder's bus to bed. Now it had been so obvious that Eli had noticed.

When I dared to look at Allison, she was staring at me with wide eyes. It was almost as if she was daring herself to believe that I hadn't been with any other girls because of her. With the wheels turning in her head, I could tell I was screwed on many levels.

With a shrug, I replied, "Call me picky in my old age."

Eli laughed. "Whatever, man. We're the same age, and I don't think I could have gone as long as you have without getting any." At Allison's little squeak, Eli's face reddened. "Sorry, I keep forgetting that I'm not just out with the guys, and I need to be more of a gentleman."

Allison gave him a shy smile. "It's okay."

The waitress then returned with our drinks. An ache reverberated through my chest as she sat down the bottle of tequila along with the salt and limes. Instantly, I was transported back to that night in Savannah—the night everything had gone so wrong…or in some ways so right.

Eli poured two shot glasses full for him and Allison. After handing a glass to Allison, he held his up. "To us," he said, with a grin. At Allison's hesitation, Eli quickly added, "To all of us Runaway Train and Jacob's Ladder family."

At his correction, Allison lifted her glass. "To us," she replied, before clinking it against Eli's. She then took the glass and tipped it back, sucking down the contents in one gulp. As she grabbed the lime and hastily brought it to her lips, I remembered almost too painfully what her lips had tasted like after she did her shots in Savannah. The way the salt from my neck had clung to them—the way she tasted. Quickly, I looked away and tried to erase the memories from my mind, but they continued to flash in front of my eyes just like the changing strobe lights.

"Another?" Eli asked.

When Allison nodded, I snorted. "What?" she demanded.

"I was just thinking that maybe multiple tequila shots aren't such a good idea for you." My gaze left hers and went to Eli's. "She's not one for holding her liquor well."

Allison seethed at me from across the table. I'm pretty sure if given the chance, she would have thrown herself across the table to beat the shit out of me for my smart-ass comment. Tossing her hair over her shoulder, she got her composure back. Her eyes narrowed in on mine. "As much as I hate to admit it, Rhys is right. Although I love tequila, I usually make stupid as hell decisions that fuck up my life when I drink it."

Once again, this was a side of Allison I wasn't used to seeing—the bitch with claws. But at the same time, I knew I deserved it. I'd pushed her into making the comments.

After glancing between us, Eli slid the bottle of tequila away from Allison, which caused her to giggle. "Does that mean I don't get another shot?" she asked, batting her eyelashes at him.

"Um, I think it's a pretty good idea for you not to do something that fucks up your life when you're out with me. I have a feeling it would be like a domino effect where Jake would then fuck up my life," Eli replied, with a grin.

"Just one more," Allison pleaded.

Eli rolled his eyes. "Fine, fine. I can never tell beautiful girls no."

"And here I thought it was beautiful girls who couldn't tell you no," I countered, as he poured Allison's shot glass to the brim.

He wagged his eyebrows. "Oh yeah, man, that too."

Allison shot me a disgusted look before she took her shot glass and downed it. Once again, a shudder went over her fabulous body from the alcohol. She then slammed the glass down onto the table. "Let's dance," she suggested to Eli.

"Sounds good to me."

Watching Allison head off to the dance floor with Eli was like a punch in the gut. It took a few seconds to catch my breath. I reached over and grabbed the tequila bottle. Taking Allison's glass, I poured it full before downing it in one fiery gulp. I repeated the process twice to try to numb myself better.

Gabe arrived back at the table sans the girl he had been dancing with earlier. "What happened to your sure thing?"

He chuckled. "My sure thing ended up passing out on the dance floor. I got her to a table and then came back here."

I laughed. "That's classy."

"Tell me about it."

We sat in silence for a few minutes, just drinking our beers. It was a good thing Gabe wasn't feeling talkative because I don't think I could have focused on a fucking thing he was saying. My gaze remained firmly on Eli and Allison dancing. Each time his hands started to wander on her body, I tensed. It took everything within me not to get up and go drag her back to the booth.

After ordering another round of beers, Gabe nudged me. "Why don't you go cut in on the happy couple?"

"Why the hell would I want to do that?" I questioned lamely. I refused to meet Gabe's eyes for fear that they would betray the emotions I was feeling. There was nothing in the world I wanted to do more than go break up Allison and Eli.

Rolling his eyes, Gabe countered, "Come on, man. You've been shooting fucking daggers at my brother the entire time he's been out there with Allison, not to mention the rest of the night. It's pretty obvious how you feel about her."

I shook my head while I played with the label on my beer bottle. "I don't know what you're talking about."

Gabe rested his arms on the back of the booth and eyed me with a shit-eating grin. "Don't try to act like you're not totally hot for her. It's written all over your face when you look at her. I can't say I blame you." He closed his eyes in exaggerated bliss. "If Jake wouldn't have my dick, mmm, I'd love to fuck her brains out."

Slamming my beer bottle down on the table, I thrust my finger in his face. "Watch your fucking mouth!"

Instead of fear, Gabe chuckled. "Oh yeah, you've got it bad."

I ran a hand nervously through my hair. "It doesn't matter what I may or may not feel about Allison. I'm here tonight because Jake wanted me to keep an eye on Allison with Eli."

With a wink, Gabe said, "And all the while, the wolf was guarding the chicken coop."

"Whatever," I mumbled.

"She's hot for you, too, you know."

"Is that right?" I snapped, after taking another long swig of beer.

"Oh yeah, it is. Allison's too sweet a woman to be using Eli just to get at you. If I had to put money on it, I'd imagine that she's trying to transfer what she's feeling for you onto him. Most likely, you were a fucking dick who broke her heart by not being emotionally available to her, so she's ready to move on."

Cocking my head at Gabe, I said, "Well, thank you for that lovely psychoanalysis, Dr. Fucking Phil!"

Gabe laughed heartily. "It doesn't have to end badly, man. Just go out there, ask her to dance, and tell her how you really feel about her." When I opened my mouth to protest, he shook his head. "Yeah, Jake is going to be pissed. But so fucking what? This is your life and happiness we're talking about, not to mention hers. Do you think we were all really happy that some man-whore douchebag like Jake was putting the moves on our virginal baby sister?" Gabe snorted contemptuously. "Hell no, we weren't. But it wasn't up to us—it was up to Jake and Abby."

With a ragged sigh, I weighed Gabe's words. Deep down, I knew he was right. All the reasons I tried to tell myself why Allison and I couldn't be together were really just bullshit and bogus. I was just too much of a fucking pussy to want to risk getting hurt or having Allison realize that I wasn't the man she thought I was.

"Oh fuck," Gabe muttered beside me. I didn't have to wonder what he was talking about when I glanced back out onto the dance floor. Immediately, red flashed before my eyes, and I gripped the booth until my knuckles turned while. I was precariously close to hulking out.

Not only did Eli have his lips on Allison's, but his hands were practically on her ass. "Oh, hell fucking no!" I shouted, as I flung myself out of the booth for battle.

"Rhys, don't!" Gabe shouted behind me, but I ignored him. Instead, I barreled on ahead, straight for Allison and Eli.

13: ALLISON

With Beyoncé's *Drunk in Love* playing sultrily in the background, Eli's head dipped to nuzzle my neck. "Mmm, Allison, you're really starting to get to me," he murmured into my ear, his breath singeing the sensitive flesh of my earlobe. Our lower halves were working in perfect sync to the music.

Craning my neck, I tilted my chin up to look into his eyes. "Am I?"

He nodded. "Although I shouldn't, I'm really starting to like you."

I grinned. "Aw, I like you, too, Eli."

With a snort, he replied, "No, I mean, I *really* like you."

An icy feeling rippled through my veins, causing me to shiver. Having a handsome guy say he liked you romantically should cause your heart to beat faster or a stirring below your waist. But that wasn't the case for me when Eli said the words. I felt nothing.

Dammit, it wasn't supposed to be like this. He was not supposed to be a means to make Rhys jealous. He was supposed to be an opportunity for me to have fun and forget about Rhys. But no matter how hard I tried, I didn't feel the same intensity for Eli as I did for Rhys. It wasn't even a drop in the bucket to what I felt for Rhys.

We'd both just been harmlessly flirting over the last few weeks on tour. Besides yesterday's serenade, there hadn't been anything overly romantic on his part. How was it possible that Eli was starting to have real feelings for me? I guess Abby had been right about the depth of what Eli was feeling.

After my lengthy silence, Eli took one of my arms and spun me away from him. When I came whirling back, I faced him this time. He winked at me before giving me a sexy grin. "Don't get your thong in a twist, Allison. I just said I liked you—not that I wanted to marry you and make babies."

I giggled in relief. "Okay, I can take that."

Eli's arms snaked around my waist, jerking me flush against him. With his lips hovering precariously close to mine, he said, "More than anything, I'd really like to go back to the hotel and screw you so fucking hard that you would scream my name over and over again."

When I jerked back and widened my eyes in shock, he laughed. "Sadly, it's the truth. But since I'm working on being more of a gentleman, I'll refrain from thinking that about you. Instead, why don't you let me take you out?"

"On a date?"

"Yep, a real date, just the two of us. Dinner and a movie or dinner and a club—whatever you want."

I stared into his twinkling blue eyes. He really was a decent guy, not to mention the fact he was so handsome. If given the chance, he would really be good for me. Even though I wasn't feeling as much as I should for him, it was time for me to give someone else a real shot and try to forget about whatever it was that Rhys and I once had. Even if I had to fake it for a little while.

With a groan, Eli mused, "You're killing me here. I don't think I've ever had to work so hard for a date."

I grinned. "I'm sorry for bruising your gigantic ego by playing a little hard to get."

"You've more than bruised my ego—I think you dented it."

"The answer is yes. I would love to go on a date with you."

Eli's blue eyes lit up. "I'm glad to hear it."

"I'm glad you asked me."

"You're welcome." Before I realized what was happening, Eli's hands dipped down to rest above my ass, pressing me harder against him. And then in the next moment, Eli's lips were on mine. He seemed to have completely misinterpreted my agreeing to go on a date with him. While I was in total shock that he had kissed me, I also didn't feel a single zap of electricity like I had with Rhys.

I jerked back. "Eli, I thought we were taking this slow," I protested.

He gave me a pouty, puppy-dog look. "You mean I don't even get a kiss? I thought it was pretty tame after telling you I wanted to screw your brains out."

His expression and comment caused me to laugh in spite of myself. "It's a little too soon for a kiss."

"I'm sorry, Allison," he said, genuinely.

I opened my mouth to tell him it was okay when a commotion behind me interrupted us. With an expression of pure fury, Rhys appeared beside us.

"Get your damn hands off of her!" Rhys growled. All at once, his hand was around my arm, and he was pulling me away from Eli.

"What the fuck, dude?" Eli questioned.

Rhys shook his head. "What the hell do you think you're doing groping her and kissing her?"

Eli narrowed his eyes at Rhys. "I'm sorry. I didn't realize she answered to you."

"I don't," I countered.

Ignoring Eli, Rhys turned his wrath-filled gaze on me. He closed the gap between us. "What the hell do you think you're doing, letting him run his hands all over you?"

Standing toe to toe with him, I snapped, "You're not Jake, or my father, so you can't even begin to try to tell me what I can or can't do!"

"No, but I'm pretty sure Jake would be appalled that you're acting like a cheap whore!"

"Fuck you, Rhys!" I spat, planting my hands on his hard pecs and shoving him away from me. I stalked past him and Eli off the dance floor. When I stomped up to our table, Gabe stared wide-eyed at me. "Give me my purse," I demanded.

He didn't bothering arguing with me or calling me out for my attitude. He just thrust my purse at me. "Thank you."

It was only after I escaped into the VIP bathroom that my adrenaline began to fade. Gripping the sides of the marble sink, I let Rhys's words pierce further and further into me until it felt like a jagged hole had been cut through my heart. He hadn't fought for me because he wanted me—he'd fought because he believed I was acting like a whore. He continued seeing me as only a little sister—not someone he wanted to date or be with.

The bathroom door flew open, and Rhys stormed in. Glancing at his reflection in the mirror, I shook my head. "I have nothing left to say to you, so leave me alone."

"No."

Whirling around, I narrowed my eyes at him. "Excuse me?"

"I said no."

I threw up my hands. "Fine, I concede; you win. Does that make you happy?" When he started to open his mouth, I shook my head furiously from side to side. "Don't you fucking dare say 'no' again!"

"I didn't come in here to gloat."

"Then what did you come for?" When he cocked his brows at me, I demanded, "What do you want from me, Rhys?"

"Everything." He strode across the room to me. "I want to take everything you'll give me and more." Grabbing my arm, he jerked me into the handicapped stall. My body slammed back against the metal wall. My whimper of pain died on my lips as Rhys pressed his body against mine. The hardness of his erection burned into my thigh. Gripping my hips, he tugged me closer against him. His fingers closed over one of my thighs before bringing it up over his. It gave him the perfect angle to rub his erection against my core. I moaned, clawing desperately at him to get more friction.

"Why are you doing this now?" I demanded.

Rhys shook his head. "I don't fucking know. I just know that I couldn't bear sitting in that booth one more minute and letting Eli have everything I wanted."

"You want everything with me or just everything with my body?" I asked.

As he stared into my eyes, his hands slid over my waist to cup my buttocks. "I know I want my hands on this fine ass that you've been shaking all night at everyone but me." One hand left my butt to come and cup my breast. "I want my hands and mouth on these gorgeous tits that you've rubbed all over Eli."

I widened my eyes when his hand left my ass to cup between my legs. "But most of all, I want to bury my dick so far in this pussy that no man here will doubt who it belongs to, especially Eli."

Although I wanted nothing more than to be with Rhys again, this all felt wrong—the anger and jealousy fueling our actions were not healthy. "But it doesn't belong to you," I countered weakly.

"It doesn't?" His fingers tore away my thong before they plunged deep inside me, causing me to gasp with pleasure. "Tell me, Allison, did he make you this wet?" Rhys demanded.

Panting, I shook my head. "No, he didn't."

Rhys rewarded me for my response by speeding up the pace of his fingers. Throwing my head back, I moaned. My hips took on a rhythm of their own. I was getting so deliciously close that my toes were curling in my heels when Rhys suddenly withdrew his fingers. "No, please. Please don't stop," I begged.

"Who is the only man to have made you come so hard you've screamed?"

"You. Only you, Rhys," I replied, breathlessly.

With a lazy smile, he thrust his fingers back inside me while his thumb clamped down on my clit. Gripping his shoulders, I desperately rode his hand to find my orgasm. It had been three long months since a man had made me come—since Rhys had made me come.

"Rhys! Yes, oh, yes!" I cried out, my eyes fluttering closed in bliss. At that moment, I didn't care if there was a bathroom full of women hearing me come. I just wanted the pleasure to never end. I'd barely come back to myself when Rhys's blunt head nudged at my entrance. Somehow he'd managed to unbutton his pants and slip on a condom while I blissed out with my head on his shoulder.

With a grunt, he thrust deep inside me. "Oh fuck, Allison," he groaned, his breath warm against my neck. "No one feels as good as you." His dirty compliment made my heart beat faster. He gripped my other thigh and brought my leg up to wrap around him. As I clung to his shoulders, I was completely impaled on him.

But then a hard revelation crashed upon me, causing me to shudder. I wasn't having sex again with Rhys because he had told me he loved me or that he had feelings for me. No, I was fucking him in a club bathroom because he was jealous over Eli. He wanted to have his cake and eat it too—he wouldn't have me, and he would make sure no one else did either.

Deep down, I knew I deserved to be treated a hell of a lot better by Rhys. I should have pushed him away right then and there for daring to use me like he was. But when it came to him, I was an utter and complete masochist. I seemed utterly incapable of ever denying him. He owned my heart, despite the fact he had refused it. He owned my traitorous body that always responded whenever he was near. In the end, my head and my heart continued to wage a war between each other that would render no winner.

When Rhys dipped his head down to kiss me, I jerked back. For some reason, I felt I could give him my body, but I couldn't kiss him. It was too intimate, and it meant too much.

His brows lined in confusion. "Give me your mouth," he demanded.

"No."

A roll of his hips caused us both to moan. "Give me your mouth," he growled. When I shook my head, he grasped my chin in his fingers as his movements inside me stilled. "Why not?" *Because you don't really want me. You just want to use me, and it hurts too much.*

I narrowed my eyes at him. "What's it to you? You don't care about me. You just came in here to fuck me, so keep fucking me."

Rhys's brows rose in confusion. "I can fuck you but not kiss you? What the hell does that mean?"

"Kissing is personal, so I won't do it with you—not until I know with absolute certainty that I'm not just an easy lay to you, Rhys. Not until you acknowledge you have feelings for me, not just lust."

At my declaration, he stared at me, unblinking and unmoving. As his expression began to lighten, I brought one of my hands up to cup his cheek. Closing his eyes, he leaned his cheek into my palm as if he were savoring the gentle touch. "Don't you really want me, Rhys?"

"I can't," he murmured, his voice laced with agony.

"Please," I whispered.

"You deserve to be loved." He grimaced as if he were in pain. "And we both know I don't know how to love anyone."

Shaking my head furiously back and forth, I countered, "That's not true. You love Ellie, and you love the guys. You have a lot to give me if you would just open up. You could love me as much as I love you."

"Dammit, Allison, we've been over this. It can't work between us—it *won't* work."

His refusal caused white-hot anger to pulse through my veins. Dropping my hand from his face, I stared at him in disbelief for a moment before bringing my hand back up again. But this time it wasn't for comfort. It was to slap the hell out of him. Hard. "Fine then. Finish fucking me since that's all you seem to be good at. Fucking me and fucking me over."

Rhys stared at me in utter disbelief. His mouth opened, but no words came out. And then he surprised the hell out of me by pulling out. He eased me down to where my feet were touching the floor. After sliding off the half used condom, Rhys tucked his slackened dick back into his pants. When he finally met my gaze, he shook his head forlornly. "Jesus, Allison, what have I done to you? What *am* I doing to you?" When I didn't respond, he muttered, "I'm so fucking sorry."

He then exited the stall. When I heard the bathroom door close, I staggered over to the toilet seat and collapsed down onto it. As my body shook with sobs, I tried desperately to get a hold of my emotions. Wrapping my arms around myself, I finally just let go and cried until there wasn't anything left within me. When I finished, I wiped my eyes and left the stall. Standing in front of the mirror, I looked like the hell I felt like. Mascara and eyeliner streaked down my cheeks while my lipstick was smudged from Eli's kiss.

Once I had cleaned up as best I could, I made my way out of the bathroom. I skidded to a stop at the sight of Eli waiting on me. His eyebrows shot up in surprise at the sight of me. "Jesus, Allison. Are you all right?"

I shook my head. "No, I'm not. I'm so sorry, Eli, but I need to go back to the hotel."

"Of course. Whatever you need," he said. He took a tentative step forward to wrap an arm around my shoulder. "Lean on me. I'll get you out of here."

His kindness caused the waterworks to start up again. Turning my head, I buried my face into Eli's chest and let him lead me out of the club. When I got to the limo, Eli helped me inside. Even though I shouldn't have, I snuggled up to him when he opened his arms to me.

"Do you want to talk about it?" he questioned softly, as we began to make our way along the quiet streets.

"No, not really."

Eli sighed. "I knew trying to start something up with you was going to be difficult, but I sure as hell didn't know I'd have competition."

I twisted out of his arms to stare at him in shock. "W-What do you mean?"

"Come on, Allison. I may act like a fool sometimes, but I'm not really one. I know there's something between you and Rhys. Hell, any idiot could see that."

Wincing, I said, "I'm sorry to have put you in the middle of all this. What's happened between Rhys and me is such a mess. I don't even know if it is still possible to even be friends with each other."

"That bad, huh?"

"Yeah, it's pretty abysmal." I shook my head sadly at him. "I'm sure after all this you aren't still interested in our date, huh?"

Eli held up one of his hands. "Whoa, wait a minute. I never said that I didn't want to be with you."

"But you deserve better than a girl who is hung up on some asshole who will never feel the same way about her," I protested.

"Why don't you let me be the judge of that?"

"You're just too good to be true, aren't you?"

He chuckled. "I wouldn't get too carried away singing my praises. Part of me is hanging on because girls with broken hearts or girls with something to prove to asshole ex-boyfriends are easy lays."

My eyes widened in horror at his statement. "Eli Renard, how could you think that about me?"

With a wink, he replied, "I'm just being honest with you, Allison. I don't want you losing sleep worrying about breaking my heart when my motives aren't exactly pure." He cocked his head at me. "Just like I said on the dance floor, I want to have a good time with you, see where it leads us, but I'm sure as hell nowhere near ready to go ask Jake for your hand in marriage."

Even though I should have been appalled at him, I couldn't help but laugh. "You are so bad."

"I know. I'm a bad boy with a somewhat heart of gold who just wants to have some fun with you." Staring intently at me, he asked, "Think you can handle that?"

"I think I can try."

Eli then leaned in and kissed my cheek. "Good. And the date is still on tomorrow night?"

I gave him a tentative smile. "Yes, it is."

14: RHYS

Rolling over in bed, I thumped my pillow for the millionth time. I guess it was more like punching the hell out of it instead of thumping it. After my hellish evening with Allison, I'd found it hard to sleep. I guess it was a combination of a guilty conscience and my mind racing with thoughts. As sleep continued to evade me, I kept tossing and turning while reliving each and every painful detail in my head.

Jesus, how had things gone so wrong between us? I was such a fucking selfish bastard. I'd become the epitome of the douchebags I hated—the men from my parents' world. Every time I tried to do the right thing by pushing Allison away, I just pulled her back to me, hurting her even more. I'd become barely recognizable to who I once was. The old me would have never used Allison like I did in the skeezy club bathroom. I'd been an enraged bastard because she was kissing Eli and telling me I had no control over her. So I'd gone in to prove to her that she did belong to me, even though I had no plans to emotionally claim her. God, I was such an unimaginable bastard. For the life of me, I couldn't fathom why I kept treating Allison the way I did. The old law school part of me started making a case against my own self in my head.

Just when I finally started to doze off around seven a.m., screaming babies jolted me awake. I waited a few minutes for Jake and Abby to get things under control. But when fifteen minutes went by and the twins were still crying, I lost my temper. With a growl, I got out of bed and threw on a T-shirt and a pair of jeans.

I stumbled out of my suite and staggered next door. Raising my fist, I pounded on the door. The crying grew closer and closer until the door flew open. A red-faced and screaming Jax greeted me first. Instead of Abby or Jake, it was Allison standing in the doorway. Motherfucking hell. I couldn't catch a break. Instantly, I regretted my decision to come over. Things were still way too awkward between us after what had happened last night.

"Oh, um, hey," I said.

"Hi," she called over Jax's wailing. Behind her, I could hear Jules crying as well.

"I came over to see what all the commotion was about."

Allison grimaced. "Jake and Abby just left for the doctor—food poisoning or something. They were sick and feverish all night. I think Jake might be pretty dehydrated."

"Are the spawns sick, too?" I asked, gesturing to Jax. That would certainly explain the fucking scream-fest.

"No, they're fine. Well, except for the fact they seem to be going through some early separation anxiety when it comes to their parents. The moment Jake and Abby left the suite, they freaked out. Nothing I do seems to help."

As I glanced from Jax to Allison, I noticed how frazzled she looked. Loose stands of dark hair had escaped from her ponytail, and her face was almost as red as Jax's. "They're not wet or hungry or sleepy—they just want to cry," she said, her voice wavering as if she might cry at any minute as well.

At that moment, I had two options: I could have pulled an utterly douche move by telling her good luck with the screaming hellions and then escaped to my suite. Or I could offer to try to help her calm the twins down.

"Here, let me have him," I said, reaching for Jax.

Allison's dark eyes widened. "Seriously?"

I snorted contemptuously. "Like I'm going to leave you all alone with two screaming babies."

Somehow I imagined that in her head, she was thinking that was exactly what an asshole like me would do, especially after the way we had left things last night. "Thanks," she said softly.

As I took Jax into my arms, he eyeballed me for a moment. When Allison started across the room for Jules, Jax picked up his wailing. "Okay, mama's boy, you certainly have a fine pair of lungs."

Allison jerked her head over her shoulder and scowled at me. "Don't call him that."

"It's the truth, isn't it?"

"Maybe. But he can't help it."

Jax's lip quivered as I stared at him. A smile tugged at my lips. "Come to think of it, you're just like your daddy. He was a pansy-ass mama's boy back in the day, too."

"Rhys!" Allison admonished, as Jax stopped snubbing to momentarily grin at me.

I laughed at both of their reactions. Staring into Jax's face was like looking at a mirror image of Abby except he had Jake's dark hair. "I guess I should give you some slack. I would've been a mama's boy too if I'd been blessed with a mama as sweet as yours."

Allison laughed while bouncing a fussy Jules on her hip. "Abby is a sweetheart and the best mom."

A thought popped into my mind, and before I could stop myself, I blurted it out. "You want that someday?"

With her dark brows lining in confusion, Allison asked, "Do I want to have kids someday?"

"Yeah."

"Yes, of course I do." Allison stared into Jules's face, a slight smile on her lips. "I can't imagine going through life without kids, but at the same time, I don't want them anytime soon."

Her response surprised me. For some reason, I thought she would be just like Abby with wanting to have a family right away. "Really?"

She nodded. "There's a lot I want to do and see before I settle down to get married, and even after, I'd like my husband and I to have some time just to ourselves."

"I see."

As Jules started to ratchet up her fussing into full-fledged crying, Allison asked, "What about you? Do you want kids?"

I exhaled a long sigh. "Yeah, sure, I wouldn't mind having a kid someday. Like you, I sure as hell don't want it to be anytime soon."

It seemed that Jax took my comment about not wanting kids soon a little too personally because he started wailing again. My ears rang as he and Jules seemed determined to outdo each other with their screams. "Guys, please, don't cry. Mommy and Daddy will be back very soon," Allison said, over the noise.

Both of us started walking around the room, bouncing a twin in our arms. But nothing that we did seemed to work. We swapped off babies for a few minutes to see if daddy's girl, Jules, might benefit from being with me. It didn't work. Finally, it was like a light bulb went off in my head. I walked over to Allison. "Here. I have an idea. Take her for a sec."

Allison reluctantly took Jules into her free arm. "What are you going to do?"

"I need to run next door."

Her eyes widened. "You aren't bailing on me, are you?"

I scowled at her for even thinking something so shitty of me. "Of course not. Just trust me. I think I know what will get them to quiet down."

"Okay," she replied, reluctantly.

After I hustled back to my suite, I grabbed my phone off the nightstand. When I returned to Allison, she was walking around the bedroom with both twins in her arms as they continued crying. After scrolling through a few playlists, I picked one. Then I placed my phone on the docking station beside the bed. As I reached out for Jax, the sounds of Abby and Jake singing, *I'll Take You with Me* echoed through the room. At the sounds of their parents' blending voices, Jax and Jules's cries started to quiet. The longer the song played, the more content they grew.

As Allison shifted Jules in her arms, Jules gave a contented coo as she lay her head on Allison's chest. Glancing down at Jax, I asked, "How's that, Jaxy boy? You like hearing your old man and your mama making music?" I asked. He stopped gumming his fist to smile up at me. "I thought you would. They sound good together, don't they? They make a good team."

When I glanced up, Allison appeared almost teary as she watched me with Jax. Once again, the familiar ache burned in my chest. It always happened whenever I tried to ignore the feelings I had for Allison. Under her intense stare, it was almost hard to breathe. Part of me wanted to stop the pain by just admitting to her about how much I cared. But the stubborn ass in me overrode those thoughts and clung to the notion that we simply couldn't be together.

Deciding to change the subject, I jerked my chin at Jules. "She's asleep."

Allison's eyes lit up. "Really?" she whispered. When I nodded, she eyed Jax. "He's almost there."

"Think we could lay them down?"

"We could try." She then stepped over to the Pack 'N Play next to Jake and Abby's massive king-sized bed. She eased Jules down onto the mattress as if she was a ticking time bomb that could go off at any minute. Once she pulled her hands away, she waited a moment to see if Jules would start crying. When she didn't, Allison eased a pacifier into Jules's mouth, and then stepped back.

With a wave of her hand, I stepped forward to bring Jax over. His eyelids were fluttering like he was desperately fighting sleep. After I lay him down, his eyes popped open, and he stared up at me as if daring me to try to walk away. "Easy buddy," I whispered, as I patted his tummy. Allison squeezed in beside me to slide a pacifier between Jax's lips. Once he was sucking voraciously, his eyes started to droop, and then he was finally asleep.

When I stepped back from the bed, Allison and I both exhaled a ragged sigh in unison. "That was intense," I murmured in a low voice.

"Yeah, it was."

Standing side by side with her across from an extreme cuteness overload of two sleeping babies was just a little too much for me. In a weird way, it was like we had been parenting together, and that was far too much of a commitment than I could ever allow myself with Allison. We were not meant to be, regardless of whatever I continued to feel. "Well, I guess now that everything is under control, I'll head back to my room."

After grabbing the baby monitor off the nightstand, she gave me a sincere smile. "I owe you a big thank you. I don't think I could have survived without your help."

"No need to thank me. I was glad to help," I replied. After I grabbed my phone, I started out of the bedroom. Allison followed me out and then closed the door of Jake and Abby's bedroom.

We stood there, staring at each other, both silently daring the other one to mention the white elephant in the room. After what felt like an eternity, neither one of us spoke up to acknowledge it. "Yeah, well, I'll see you later," I muttered before starting for the door.

When I reached for the doorknob, Allison's voice caused me to freeze. "Rhys, wait."

I whirled around. "What is it?"

Nibbling her lip, she appeared to be trying to find the right way to tell me something. Finally, she just blurted, "Eli has asked me out on a date. Alone."

That motherfucker. It wasn't enough he had dry-humped and kissed her last night on the dance floor, but now he was upping the ante by wanting to take her out to wine and dine her. Alone. Jake was going to love the hell out of that. At her expectant look, I knew I needed to get out of there before I betrayed any of my emotions. "Good for him. I hope you have a great time," I replied, unable to contain my sarcasm.

"That's all you have to say?" she asked, her expression one of betrayal.

I shrugged. "Were you looking for my permission or something? You told me last night I'm not Jake, so what does it matter to me what you do?"

Tears pooled in her eyes, causing me to feel like the biggest asshole on the face of the earth. But of course, it didn't make me man up and tell her how I felt about her. No, I was still letting myself be deluded into the notion that I was doing what was best for the both of us. While Jake wasn't keen on the idea of Eli dating Allison, he would feel a hell of a lot different if it were me—his bandmate and brother.

"I just thought…" She shook her head. "Never mind."

"You thought what?" I urged.

Her dark eyes took on a pleading expression as they bore into mine. "Regardless of how badly it ended last night, I don't believe you could be so callous as to use me the way you did," she replied, in a hushed whisper.

Seeing her trembling body, coupled with the haunted look in her eyes, broke me. I almost barreled right through the wall that I had so carefully constructed between us by ensuring her that she wasn't wrong about last night. It had almost been my undoing.

And then at the most inopportune moment, a scene from my childhood flashed in my mind. It reiterated to me once and for all where my horrible sense of self-worth and self-esteem come from. I was sick and home from school—a seven-year-old boy who desperately wanted some of his mother's love and attention. Peeking through the banister, I watched as her heels clicked along the marble floor as she headed out the door to some charity function. Just as she reached the door, I raced down the stairs to grab hold of her waist. "Stay with me, Mommy."

Her venomous voice rang in my ears as if she were standing right in front of me. "Rhys, I told you earlier that I do not have time for you today! Go back to Trudie." Desperately, I clung to her, but she shook me off as she always did. After all, I was always too much of a bother for her to pay any attention to. She stared down at my frail form. "Why can't you do as you're told? God, you're almost as worthless as your sister!"

I had barely been able to make out her face through the blur of my tears. "Don't you love me, Mommy?" I had asked in a soft voice.

"I could love you more if you weren't such a nuisance."

That day my mother had once again broke my already fragile heart into even more unfixable pieces. I toughened up after that, but the hurt was always there. With such a loveless past, how was it possible that I could ever give Allison all that she needed? No, I had to stay strong. I had to keep my true feelings concealed. As much as I wanted to, I could not give in. I had to drive her away once and for all.

Crossing my arms over my shoulder, I asked, "So you were thinking that having angry sex in a club bathroom was supposed to have some underlying meaning besides *just* fucking?"

A lone tear streaked down her cheek. When she raised her hand, I thought she might slap me—I sure as hell deserved it—but instead, she used it to swipe the tear away. "You can say what you want to save face, Rhys, but I know you better than that. It may have started out as ownership, or just sex, but you *wanted* to kiss me. You wanted me just as much as you had three months ago."

"Keep telling yourself that, little girl."

Her face crumpled, and she turned and fled to her bedroom. When the door slammed behind her, I jumped. Her sobs filled the air around me, piercing through my chest like knives. I wished for the moment that she was more like Abby and Mia—that she had verbally berated me for the bastard I was. But no, tears were worse, especially for a girl…or woman like Allison.

Unable to stand the sound of her cries any longer, I fled from Jake and Abby's suite. I bypassed my room and kept stalking down the hallway. When I got to the elevator, I hit the button for the lobby. Once I got downstairs, I headed straight for the revolving doors that took me out into the city.

Then I began to walk aimlessly up and down the streets. I stopped for coffee and something to eat at a small diner. But no matter how long or how far I walked, one thing was still true. Once again, I'd behaved like an utter asshole to Allison—a far cry from the gentleman I'd been raised to be. After all, it was only the best for Mommy and Daddy Dearest. But worse than the despicable things I'd said was the fact I'd lied to her. Again. Why the fuck did I keep doing that?

Last night had meant something. Somehow being inside Allison for that short amount of time had once again made me feel complete. But it had fucking broken me when she wouldn't let me kiss her. In the end, she had been right. I sure as hell didn't deserve her sweet lips. Because of my jealousy, I'd gone off half-cocked to prove that she belonged to no other man. Then I had been a bastard by refusing emotionally to claim her.

Taking out my phone, I Googled a location that I knew would provide some relief to my suffering. Two blocks over, I slipped inside the darkened room of a strip club. Coming here sure as hell wasn't one of my finest moments, but I needed to break my three-month sexual fast, even if it was just a small release. I desperately needed something simple and no-strings attached. If I could free myself of Allison, then in turn, I could set her free from me as well.

With a fifty, I motioned over one of the three girls dancing. She was also the only blonde. I sure as hell didn't want a brunette. With a welcoming smile, she swiveled her hips as she came over to me. "Hey, sugar, you want a private dance?"

"Yeah, I do," I mumbled.

"I'm Sierra," she said.

"Rhys," I replied, not even bothering to give a fake name.

Hopping down from the stage, she took me by the hand and led me back to a private room. A stacked bouncer eyed us before we dipped inside the room. She eased me down on the couch. When her hands went up to undo the strings on her flimsy top, bile lurched in my throat, and I felt like I would throw up. "Wait. Stop," I croaked.

Her hands left her top. One came to rest on my cheek. "What's the matter, sugar? Is this your first time? You don't have to be afraid. I'll take real good care of you."

I shook my head. "That's not it. This was a mistake." When I started to rise off the sofa, she pushed me back down. Instead of slithering across my lap, she sat down next to me.

"Having girlfriend or wife troubles?" When I didn't respond, she asked, "Boyfriend troubles?"

A nervous laugh escaped my lips. "I'm not gay."

She shrugged. "Some guys come here when they're trying to sort out who they are. If you want, I have the name of a club that might have more of what you need."

I held up my hand. "Trust me, a dude is not the problem."

Her hand came to rest on my thigh. "Then what is?"

Closing my eyes, I couldn't believe I was not only sitting in a strip club, but I was about to unburden my troubles on a stripper. She was hardly a therapist. But for some strange fucking reason her open objectivity loosened my usually stubborn tongue. I sure as hell wasn't one to share my feelings with just anybody, but Sierra's willingness to listen compelled me to open up. "So you really want to know?"

She nodded. "I'm on your dime, or your fifty, right now. I'll do whatever you want to do, including listening."

After drawing in a deep breath, I told Sierra the whole story. Her eyes widened in a few places, and she gasped in horror. When I finished, she smacked my chest. "What the hell is your problem?"

"I'd love to know."

"You march your ass back to that hotel room right now and beg for that girl's forgiveness."

"It's not that simple."

"Yes, it is. Do you want to spend the rest of your life feeling like this?"

"Hell no."

"Then it's that simple." Taking my hand in hers, she squeezed it. "Do you know how lucky you are to have someone so wonderful to love you? People search their entire lives to find it, and most end up desperately alone during the pursuit. You just have to stop being afraid of the 'what-ifs'. The 'what-ifs' of this Jake guy being pissed at you or the 'what-ifs' of you being afraid you can't love Allison like you should. It'll all come together because it's meant to be."

As I sat there on the leather sofa with my sage stripper, I couldn't believe how everything had fallen together. Not to mention that the catalyst for my self-discovery had been in a strip club. "You're really wise, you know that?"

Sierra smiled. "Years of hearing people's troubles, sugar."

Digging into the pocket of my jeans, I coupled a hundred with the fifty I originally had. "Here. But it isn't really enough to show you my gratitude."

Shaking her head, Sierra took the bills from me. "While the money is nice, you're only going to show me your gratitude by not fucking things up with this girl." She eyed me pointedly. "Are you going to go beg her forgiveness now and tell her how much you care about her?"

I nodded my head. "Today. I swear."

"Good. I'm glad to hear it." Rising off the couch, she held out her hand for me. "Now get the hell out of here."

With a laugh, I let her help me up. "Yes, ma'am."

Leaning over, Sierra planted a kiss on my cheek. "This Allison is a lucky woman to have you."

"I hope after everything I've done, she will believe that."

"Keep the faith, sugar."

I nodded, and then hurried out of the strip club. One glance at my phone told me I needed to haul ass back to the hotel. The car would be leaving to take us to the auditorium soon. Unfortunately, I'd given all my cash to Sierra, and my debit card was in my wallet back in the hotel room. I'd have to run to make it back on time.

After drawing in a deep breath, I started sprinting back to the hotel, but more importantly back to Allison. Now I knew I was ready. I was ready for all that would come with loving Allison. I sure as hell didn't deserve her, but I wanted—no I had—to make her mine. As for Jake, well, he'd just have to accept that fact. After all, he was just her brother, not her father.

No, I wasn't going to fuck up my life any longer. I needed Allison in my life, and I was going to prove to her that I could love. She had faith in me, and I would die trying to prove her right.

15: ALLISON

After crying myself to sleep, I woke up to Jake and Abby returning from the doctor. The diagnosis was food poisoning, which was terrible considering they had eaten with Jake's family the night before. Even after getting fluids, they were still a little weak and collapsed into a deep sleep. After Jax and Jules woke up again, I moved their Pack 'N Play into my room to let Jake and Abby get some more rest before their rehearsal at two.

Playing with the twins was a welcome relief to get my mind off Rhys. I truly felt like I was at a breaking point with his emotional whiplash. With the way things were at the moment, I couldn't imagine making it through the rest of the tour. Although I would hate to let Jake and Abby down, I didn't see how I could stay on as their nanny. I just wanted to go home. I didn't give a shit about the internship. I just cared about my crumbling sanity that had been wrecked by Rhys. The man that I had loved for seven years and the man I'd spent time with in Savannah was not the man I saw now. He didn't want to change, and I had to accept that.

At one, Jake and Abby reluctantly pulled themselves from their bed, so we could all head to the arena for rehearsal. We took the tour bus since the twins were in tow. Abby never liked for them to be far from her, so we didn't stay back at the hotel until show time.

After we arrived at the arena, Abby and I worked to get the twins to sleep in one of the empty dressing rooms. But unfortunately, they were fussy and didn't want to lie down. They were enjoying their time with Abby too much to sleep.

Finally, they started to calm a little when Abby took them both in her arms and began rocking them in the antique rocking chair they carried with them on tour. With their eyes beginning to droop, Abby glanced at the clock. "Shit, it's almost time for me to be out there. Can you go tell Jake it's just going to be a little while longer?"

"I can put them down for you," I said.

She shook her head. "No, they want me, so I want to do it."

I nodded. "Okay, I'll go tell him."

When I got out to the stage, Runaway Train was just finishing up, and it was time for Jake and Abby to run through their duets with Jacob's Ladder playing the musical accompaniment.

At the sight of me, Jake's brow lined with worry. "Where's Abby?"

"The twins are taking a little longer to go down for their nap today, so she said to give her just a few minutes more."

Groaning, Gabe stopped twirling one of his drumsticks between his fingers. "Can't she let you put them down? You're the nanny after all."

Jake whirled around and pinned Gabe with a hard stare. "The most important thing in Abby's life is being a mother. She worked hard to get those babies, so if she wants to delay rehearsal by thirty minutes so she can be a mom, then she'll fucking do it."

"Okay, okay," Gabe mumbled.

Motioning me with his hand, Jake said, "Help us out a minute, Allie-Bean."

"What do you want me to do?"

"Well, the fucking suits at the label want me and Abby to do an emo duet. Apparently, we sing too many happy love songs. Abby picked one out, and I've got to learn it. I have no clue about the song because I don't listen to emo love songs."

I giggled. "No, I don't imagine you do."

"While we're waiting on Abby, could you play the piano and sing her part?"

"Sure, I guess so. What's the song?"

"*Say Something.*"

My heart clenched so tight I found it hard to breathe. Out of all the songs in the world, why would Jake have to pick that one? The very one I had listened to on repeat last night as I cried myself to sleep. For me, that song represented everything that was mine and Rhys's screwed-up relationship. Anytime it came on the radio, it was agony hearing it. I couldn't even imagine singing it. I didn't know if I could.

As Jake thrust the sheet of music in front of me, my shaking hands could barely grasp it. "Jake, I don't know if this is a good idea."

"You sing and play the piano, don't you?" When I nodded, he added, "Then I don't know why it would be a bad idea."

Staring at the sheet music, I could barely make out the chords. "I should go back and check on Abby and the twins. I'm sure Eli could do it with you."

Eli snorted. "Oh yeah, it'd be a dream come true to duet with Jake."

Jake shook his head. "That's so not happening." Taking me by the shoulders, Jake led me over to the piano and urged me down onto the bench. "Come on, Allie-Bean. Help your big brother out."

A resigned and painful sigh rushed from my lips. Even though I wanted to run away, I was stuck in this nightmare. At the sound of a voice behind me, my eyes snapped shut in pain.

"Uh, how much longer until our rehearsal?" Rhys asked.

"It's gonna be awhile. Abby's putting the twins down for a nap. But I'm going to make the most of the time by working on that fucking duet the label wants us to do."

"With Allison?" Rhys asked.

Jake chuckled. "Yeah, why not?"

Glancing at him over my shoulder, I watched him shrug while giving me a shy smile. "Just surprised, that's all."

Focusing my eyes on the sheet music, I then reached out my shaky fingers to the piano keys. I began playing the melancholy chords. They echoed loudly through the practically silent auditorium. Jake came in with his part, "Say something, I'm giving up on you. I'll be the one, if you want me to…" The deep bravado of his voice echoed through my mind, momentarily making me forget about Rhys. I never tired of hearing Jake sing. As a child, it was a source of comfort to me when I was sick or hurt. But there was no comfort now—this wasn't a wound or an ailment he could fix by singing.

Just as it came time for me to sing, I felt Rhys's presence looming over me. He began to walk slowly around to the front of the piano. With my voice harmonizing with Jake's, I refused to look up at Rhys even though I could feel his heated gaze singeing my cheeks. Instead, I focused on the black and white keys, noting the irony that there was nothing black and white about what had happened between us. It was the gray area that kept causing us so much grief and pain.

After singing a few more lines, I glanced up from the piano to meet Rhys's intense gaze. I knew what line was coming, and since it meant something for me, I wanted it to mean something for him, too. As I held his stare, I sang the line directly to him because in so many ways it was the ugly truth. "You're the one that I love, and I'm saying goodbye." And I was saying goodbye. There was no way around it—no other way to claw myself out of the suffocating pain that overwhelmed me than to say goodbye.

An expression of pure agony stretched across his face. It caused an ache in my chest so harsh that I had to look away from him. With my tears blurring the music to where I could no longer read it, I shot up off the piano bench. It clattered noisily to the floor. When I turned around, Jake stared at me in surprise. "I'm sorry. I can't," I whispered, before running past him into the wings.

I could hear both Jake and Rhys calling my name, but I ignored them. Instead, I just kept running until I got to the Runaway Train dressing room. After slamming myself inside, I stumbled over to the makeup table. The pain cut through me again, causing me to cry out. I doubled over at the waist. I would've collapsed onto the floor if I hadn't gripped onto the sides of the table.

As I glanced up to gaze at my broken self in the mirror, I knew I had no other choice. I had to escape the torment. I had to get away from Rhys.

I was leaving.

16: RHYS

When I had finally gotten back to the hotel, Allison had already left for the arena with Jake and Abby. I didn't wait for the car to take me. After hailing a cab, I headed for the arena. When I got there, I searched everywhere inside for her, but I couldn't find her. With a 'Do Not Disturb' sign on the Runaway Train dressing room, I imagined she was inside with the twins.

With a defeated sigh, I made my way to the stage. I found Gabe and Eli sitting around on the stage while Jake stood at the piano. Then my stomach did a pansy little flip-flop at the sight of Allison seated at the piano bench. Trying not to let my emotions show in front of everyone, I quickly asked about when we were rehearsing. It wasn't too surprising that rehearsal had been delayed for the twins' naptime. But instead of having the opportunity to talk to Allison like I wanted, it was fucking frustrating that Jake had her working with him on some duet.

From the moment her fingers started floating over the black and white keys, her talent once again transfixed me. But once I realized what the song was, I felt an ache burning itself through my chest. I wasn't too emotionally dense to realize the significance of the lyrics. If there was one song that epitomized our relationship, it was this song.

When Allison began to sing with Jake, the wildfire raged stronger in my chest. I desperately needed to see her face, so I began to slowly walk around the edges of the baby grand piano. When her face came into my line of sight, I closed my eyes in pain. Her expression read the agony she was feeling. It appeared she was trying to keep her emotions in check with every fiber of her being. Silently, I willed her to look up from the keys—to look into my eyes and see that all was not lost between us.

But when she did, it drove the knife even deeper into my chest. Staring straight at me, she sang, "You're the one that I love, and I'm saying goodbye."

When I started around the piano for her, the keys banged as she bolted from the bench, sending it crashing onto the stage floor. The next thing I knew she was sprinting away into the wings.

"Allison, wait!" Jake called, at the same time I shouted, "Allison!" When she continued running, he whirled around and pinned Eli with a death glare. "What the fuck have you done?" he demanded, his fists clenched at his sides.

Eli's eyes widened as his face paled considerably. "Nothing, Jake. I swear."

"Then why the hell did she just run out of here like that?"

Glancing from Jake to me, Eli shrugged. "I sure as hell don't know, but I do know everything is good between us."

With a gutted feeling, I turned and ran off stage. I started peeking in each and every one of the empty rooms. All the doors were open except two. I paused only momentarily at the Runaway Train dressing room before I flung open the door. Allison was bent over the makeup table across the room from me.

At the sound of someone behind her, Allison jerked her head up. An odd sense of déjà vu came over me as I met her gaze in the mirror, like a sickening repeat of last night. "Please leave me alone."

I remained standing exactly where I was, my chest rising and falling with heavy breaths. Allison smacked her hands on the table. "If you have any decency left, you'll walk out of here right now."

My head jerked back like she had slapped me. I don't think I had ever seen her so visibly angry. While extremely passionate, she was usually able to keep her emotions in check. Fuck, I had so screwed up. Unable to form the right words, I mumbled a weak, "I'm sorry."

She gave a mirthless laugh. "I'm so fucking tired of you saying that." Shaking her head at me, she said, "I can't do this anymore. Tonight after the show, I'm leaving on the first flight out of here."

Her words had the same effect as if she had punched me in the gut. Gut-wrenching pain caused me momentarily to double at the waist. I struggled to breathe so that I could find the words necessary to make her stay. "No, you can't do that," I argued. I closed my eyes as the agony washed over me. "Please."

"If I stay here one minute longer with you with the way things are between us, I'm going to go crazy."

Extreme panic crept along my spine. This was sure as hell not what I had envisioned happening when it came time to beg for Allison's forgiveness. I started grasping at straws—anything to earn Allison's forgiveness. "What about the internship? You can't just walk away from the opportunity—it means too much."

"I've completed most of the field work, and I can finish the designs and clothes at home. I'm sure Miriam would work with me over Skype."

I felt myself drowning even more in the quicksand of panic about her leaving. "But what about the twins? As much as you love them, you're just going to leave?"

Tears streaked down Allison's face. "I love them more than anything in the world, but right now, I have to love myself more."

I shook my head back and forth. "No, you *can't* do this. I *won't* let you."

Her dark eyes narrowed at me. "Here's a newsflash, Rhys. You don't get to tell me what to do. Since you're not my boyfriend, let alone a true friend, you don't even get to suggest anything for me to do. In the vast scheme of things, you don't matter at all. You're just the heartless bastard who broke my heart."

Her words cut through my chest to pierce my soul. "Allison, please believe me when I say that I'm so fucking sorry. If I could take it all back, I would."

"No, you're not. You say those words because they're easy, but your actions? They'll just keep on torturing me."

When she started to brush past me to make it to the door, I reached out for her. "Please, Allison, let me make it right," I said.

"Don't touch me!" she cried, slapping my hands away.

I hung my head in shame. "I did this to you. I caused you this pain, and I have to make it right. I'm sorry. Please, please, let me make it up to you. Please...don't go."

Burying her face in her hands, Allison said, "Rhys, I meant it. Leave. Now!"

"I can't. Not until you hear me out. I owe you at least that much."

Allison jerked her head up and glared icily at me. "Here, let me help you then." With all the strength she had in her, she shoved me toward the door. "Get out!"

"Why won't you listen to me? I can't leave you right now because I need you too much. And I can't let you leave me."

Her eyelids fluttered as she blinked rapidly. "What?"

"I'm sorry for pushing you away. I'm sorry that I lied when I said I didn't care about you. Most of all, I'm sorry for ever causing you so much pain." I ran my hand nervously through my hair. "This afternoon after I left you in Jake and Abby's suite, I did some serious soul-searching." I thought it was best to leave out the part with Sierra at the moment. "Finally, it hit me like a fucking epiphany, and it was like I saw everything clearly for the first time." Reaching for her hand, I took it in mine and squeezed. "I've been lying to you about my feelings, but most of all, I've been lying to myself."

"Rhys, I—" she began.

I shook my head. "Please. Just listen." I brought her hand to my lips and kissed it gently. "Hear me when I say that I've fallen for you, Allison Slater—heart, soul, and body. That I probably first felt something for you when you were just sixteen—the night I kissed you for the first time. Something changed within me that night—like fate was giving me a preview of things to come. But like everything else with you, I chose to ignore it. Then I came to see you in Savannah, and while I just wanted to believe we were having fun like friends would, the truth was there all along, just waiting beneath the surface to be revealed. And then when the truth was revealed, I got scared, and like a fucking coward, I drove you away and then I ran. That was an asshole move, and I'm sorry. All the while I knew that I cared very deeply for you. I always have. When it came time to see you again for the tour, I, again, convinced myself it would be better off to be friends, to forget that wonderful night of mind blowing sex had ever happened."

I couldn't help smiling when red tinged her cheeks from my mentioning the sex. "But it wasn't just the pleasure of being buried deep inside you or the way your soft skin felt like velvet against mine or the sweet as honey way you tasted on my lips. It was the fact I was making love for the first time—to someone I deeply cared about who was a best friend. A soul mate even. There was no better feeling in the world for me than when I held you in my arms and finally allowed myself to let go. "

While Allison's eyes bulged at my profession, I wasn't finished yet. "During those two weeks in Savannah, I grew to love you more and more. You made me feel important…like I really mattered. And despite all my bullshit hang-ups, you wanted to be with me. I know that after the way I've treated you, I don't deserve a second chance. I callously pushed you too far and for too long, and I regret my fucking abhorrent behavior. But I would give anything in the world if you would let me prove that I'm worthy of you. That I'm not worthless and that I can do right by you."

Allison's dark eyes widened at my words. "You really mean that? No more just being friends or ignoring how good we can be together?"

I shook my head. "No, never again."

"What about Jake?"

With a shrug, I replied, "Well, he'll just have to deal with it."

"Really?" she asked, incredulously.

"Yes, really."

"I can't believe it. I can't believe you're standing in front of me right now, telling me this."

"Believe it, Allison, because every word I say is the truth. I'll spend the rest of my life trying to make you happy and trying to make up for hurting you so much."

Her lip trembled. "I want to believe you—I really do—it's just I'm scared." She hiccupped a sob. "You gutted me, Rhys. You shattered my heart so deeply that I don't know if I can love you again. I ache, Rhys. I ache inside so bad."

Desperation filled me. I hadn't planned for this. I thought I could just apologize and everything would be all right. I'd been a damned fool. "What can I do to change your mind?"

"Give me time." She wiped her eyes. "Let's take things slow. As much as I want to, I can't just run back into your arms today because you said some nice things. I need actions this time. Changed and consistent behavior—no more whiplash from your emotions."

"Then I'll give you actions—I'll give you anything in the world. Somehow and someway I'll prove to you that I'm the right man for you."

"Oh Rhys," she murmured before she threw her arms around my neck. Closing my eyes, I reveled in the feel of her pressed against me. She felt so warm, so soft, and so comforting. Her body was like home—the first one I'd ever truly had. God, this felt so right. This felt so complete—*I* felt so complete.

Tears stung my eyes when I realized how stupid I'd been and how close I'd come to losing her. "I'm sorry. I'm sorry. I'm sorry," I murmured over and over in her ear.

When her hand came to rub wide circles across my back, I lost it. The fact that she could still show me compassion and care after all I'd done to hurt her was too much. I sank to my knees under the strain of the emotions. Although I was mortified at my behavior, I couldn't help it.

"Rhys?" Allison questioned, her voice ringing with concern.

"Fucking hell, I've been so stupid for so long," I moaned, my head pitching forward onto the floor. The harsh carpet fibers scratched along my cheeks, and I welcomed the pain.

I felt Allison kneel down beside me. "Oh Rhys, it's okay…it's going to be okay."

Raising my head up, I stared into her beautiful face. When it came down to it, I couldn't believe such a sweet spirit like Allison actually cared for me…loved me even. "I think about how much I hurt you…" My eyes closed in agony. "You shouldn't forgive me, Allison."

Her tender hands cupped my face. "You let me decide about that one."

"You're too good to me," I argued.

"I know," she said, a teasing grin lighting up her features.

I couldn't help laughing at her comment. "You are going to make me work for your love, right?"

Smiling, she said, "Oh yes, very much so. Don't think you're getting any make-up sex either."

Groaning, I replied, "You are cruel." But then I gave her a small smile. "But I understand, and I'll take whatever you give me.

Allison smiled as she leaned in to bring her lips to mine. It was a soft, almost chaste, kiss. When she started to pull away, I felt desperate to have her close—to feel her skin beneath my fingers, to taste her soft, warm lips. My hand came to the back of her head, keeping her locked firmly in place. My tongue ran across her lips, urging her to open for me, and when she graciously did, I shuddered at the contact. I'd needed to taste her more than anything. The hand that once held Allison's head in place came around to cup her face. My fingers ran over her soft cheeks as our tongues slowly swirled with each other. Although I would had given anything to run my hands all over Allison's body, I reined myself in to respect her and acknowledge the fact we were rebuilding our relationship.

The door flew open, causing me to jerk away from Allison. Eli arched his brows at us from his spot in the doorway. "Just thought you'd like to know that Jake is looking for you."

"T-Thanks," Allison replied, as she pulled herself off the floor. I followed close behind her.

"No problem."

When Eli turned to go, I said, "Wait."

He stared expectantly at me. "I'm sorry, man. I never meant for this to happen. I didn't—"

Eli held up one of his hands to silence me. "After the other night, I knew exactly what I was up against when it came to Allison. I simply wasn't the guy for her."

"That's awfully fucking noble of you. Are you going to bludgeon me in my sleep?"

"Rhys!" Allison shrieked, while Eli only chuckled.

"No, man, we're all good." Glancing from me to Allison, he gave her a warm smile. "It's not like you stole my woman or something because she was never mine to begin with. She was always yours."

Tears pooled in Allison's eyes, and she rushed past me to throw her arms around Eli's neck. I had to fight the caveman urge to go over and yank her away, but I knew this was just part of her kind, compassionate side. "I'm so sorry, Eli. I never meant for you to get put in the middle of all this. You've always been such a good friend to me. I don't want to lose that," she said.

"Don't be sorry, and of course, I'll always be your friend. I'm just glad you're going to be happy now," Eli replied. After Allison pulled away, Eli then gave me a pointed look. "She is going to be happy, right?"

I nodded enthusiastically. "Yes, she is."

"Good. Because I don't want to have to kick your ass for hurting her."

"You won't have to, I swear."

"What about Jake?" Eli asked.

When I opened my mouth to tell him I was planning on telling Jake immediately, Allison shook her head. "He doesn't need to know quite yet."

"He doesn't?" both Eli and I said in unison.

Allison cocked her head at me. "After the last few months of hell, call me crazy, but I'd like to have a little while of happiness with you without things being crazy with Jake."

"She makes a good point," Eli mused.

"Whatever," I grumbled. Before I could argue with her that it probably was a horrible idea not to tell Jake, the man in question came barreling through the door, knocking Eli out of the way.

"There you are. I've been looking everywhere for you. Are you okay, Allie-Bean?" he asked.

"I'm fine," Allison replied.

Jake narrowed his eyes at Eli before pulling Allison into his arms. "Are you sure you're not just saying that because he's here?" Jake questioned in a low voice.

"I'm positive. I just had a little meltdown, okay?"

When Jake pulled away, he gave her a skeptical look. "Look, if taking care of the twins is too hard on top of your internship, we'll hire someone else. I don't want you to be unhappy."

Although I felt like a sappy chick, I couldn't help it when my heart warmed at Jake's suggestion. As much as I cared about Allison, I was glad that she had a big brother who loved her so much. I hoped that intense love also meant that Jake would take the news of us being together a little easier. I mean, he did claim that he didn't want her to be unhappy, right? Deep down, I knew I was grasping at fucking straws on that one.

"No, no, it's fine. I love taking care of the twins," Allison protested.

"But you—"

"I'm just having a really hormonal, PMS day, okay?"

All three of us males groaned in unison at the mention of the dreaded PMS. "And singing that song just made me think of Mitchell," Allison added.

It was completely wrong of me, but I couldn't help being a little impressed by how well she was able to lie so convincingly on her feet. Jake seemed to buy the story. He gave Eli a sheepish look. "Sorry for busting your chops, man."

Eli shrugged. "It's all good. But you might want to start chilling the fuck out when it comes to who Allison is dating."

"Is that right?" Jake challenged, jerking his chin up defiantly.

"If you don't, you're going to have a stroke before it's time for Jules to date."

Jake winced. "Don't even say the words 'Jules' and 'date' in the same sentence." He rubbed his chest. "My heart can't bear the thought of some douche trying to take advantage of my baby girl."

A roadie appeared in the doorway. "Excuse me, Jake, but Abby's onstage and ready to rehearse."

Jake nodded his head in acknowledgement. "I'll be right there."

When the roadie left us all alone again, Jake eyed Allison. "You'll be all right?"

Allison smiled. "I'll be fine. I better go relieve Mia and Lily of twin duty."

Jake and Eli then headed out the door, leaving Allison and me alone again. "Walk with me?" she suggested. I nodded and then followed her down the hall to the Runaway Train dressing room. Allison eased open the door. The darkened room was quiet. Jax and Jules were snoozing away in their portable Pack 'N Play. Mia sat on the couch across from them, feeding Gaby a bottle. At the sight of us, she rose off the couch. "I better go make sure Bella isn't wreaking havoc down the hall…or I should say that *AJ* and Bella aren't wreaking havoc," she said with a smile.

Allison giggled. "Thanks for watching them for me."

Mia glanced between the two of us and then winked. "No problem."

Once she was gone, I slid my arm around Allison's waist, and we stood there together, staring down at the sleeping babies. At Allison's sigh of contentment, I whispered in her ear, "I'm so glad you don't have to leave them."

She bobbed her head in agreement. Then she glanced up at me and smiled. "But I'm also glad I don't have to leave you," she replied, which caused my heart to thrum wildly in my chest.

"So am I."

And we stayed just like that until I heard my name being called in the hallway for rehearsal. Then, and only then, did I tear myself away.

17: ALLISON

After Rhys poured out his heart to me and begged for my forgiveness, I wanted nothing more than to hole up somewhere alone with him for weeks and weeks. But nothing in our lives seemed to want to go the way I fantasized. After Eli found us in the dressing room, we didn't have another moment to ourselves that night. We were constantly with Jake and Abby and the other members of Runaway Train.

When it came time to pull out of Portland for Seattle, I couldn't hide my surprise when Rhys bypassed the Jacob's Ladder bus and started for Jake and Abby's with me. "What are you doing?"

He rolled his eyes playfully. "Staying with you. What does it look like I'm doing?"

As we climbed up the bus stairs, I replied, "While I'm touched by the thought, I would think we wouldn't want to be doing anything to call attention to ourselves."

"Yeah, well, I was thinking that although Eli seemed all right with the two of us, it might be a good idea to give him some space tonight."

"What are you going to tell Jake and Abby?"

Rhys shrugged. "I'll think of something."

He didn't have long to think up a story because Jake and Abby came up the stairs then with the twins in tow. Jake raised his brows at the sight of Rhys. "What's up, man? You lost?"

With a chuckle, Rhys replied, "No, I just thought I might crash here tonight." He looked pointedly at Abby. "Your brothers fucking snore like bears."

Abby giggled. "Yeah, they do. I had to wear Beats headphones when I was on the bus with them just to get a good night's sleep.

And just like that we were off the hook. I helped Abby give Jax and Jules their bottles and then we put them to bed in their crib. While Jake and Rhys sat in the living room drinking beers and shooting the shit, I slipped into the bathroom and changed into a T-shirt and pajama pants. When I came out, I found Abby had joined the guys and was lounging on Jake's lap. When she leaned over and whispered something in his ear, his eyes bulged. "Yeah, we should all get to bed. Abby and I are still kinda weak from recovering."

"Riiiigght. That's why you're going to bed now," Rhys murmured around the mouth of his beer bottle. Abby playfully smacked his leg before she rose off of Jake's lap.

"Night guys," I said.

"Night, Allie-Bean," Jake said, stopping on the way to the bedroom to give me a kiss on the cheek. Abby grinned at me before she disappeared into the bedroom with Jake.

I turned back to look at Rhys. "Guess we better go to bed." Realizing my mistake, I lowered my voice and quickly added, "I mean, we should go to our different roosts to go to bed."

Rhys grinned as he remained on the couch, scratching Angel's ears. "I'm going to stay out here for a while. Unwind a little."

More than anything in the world, I wanted a good night kiss from him. But even though I was pretty sure that Jake and Abby were *busy* and not coming out any time soon, I didn't risk it. "Good night, Rhys," I said, softly.

"Good night, Allison."

I then turned and hightailed it down the aisle to my roost. By the time I settled down, I couldn't go to sleep. Not with the thought that Rhys was so close but so far away. So I grabbed my sketch pad and pencils out of the cubby above the bed and started working on my designs. I don't know how long I'd been working when I thought I heard movement outside my roost.

When I determined it was footsteps in the aisle, I stilled my pencil on my pad. Suddenly, the curtain to my roost jerked open. Before I had a chance to react, Rhys ducked inside, covering my body with his very *naked* one. I widened my eyes in horror. "What are—"

He silenced me by bringing his lips to mine. I immediately moaned. It felt like forever since I had been able to kiss him. Our mouths moved desperately against each other, as if we were trying to feel every single sensation all at once. His tongue lightly swept against my bottom lip, and I thrust my tongue out to meet his. As our tongues began to twirl together, moisture began pooling between my legs. Of course, it didn't hurt that his hips were pumping against mine, a perfect friction that was driving me wild.

When Rhys pulled away from my mouth, I whined in frustration. Ignoring me, he kissed and nibbled a trail across my jawline over to my ear. His sweet, warm breath tickled my earlobe before he began speaking in a soft voice. "Don't be mad at me for coming to you like this. I know you said you were going to make me work for the make-up sex. But I thought if I lay there one more minute so close to you but so far away I would explode."

"You really missed me that much?" I whispered.

Rhys nodded his head against my shoulder. I couldn't help but wonder if he missed me or just desperately needed sex after being celibate for so long. I didn't have to wonder long. I must've tensed because he brought his lips to my ear again. "Whenever I'm not with you, I miss you. I miss your smile, your laugh, the way you nibble on your bottom lip when you're nervous or thinking really hard. Most of all, it's the way you see the best in me when I don't deserve it." He shifted his hips before thrusting them back against me, and I gasped at the feel of his erection rubbing against my core through my pajama pants. "But I'd be lying if I didn't admit that I missed being inside you, too."

My tongue darted out to lick my bottom lip that was already swollen from his kisses. "But Jake and Abby are just down the hall. We could get caught," I whispered.

"We won't. We'll be quiet," he replied.

Although I wanted him buried deep inside, my greatest fear was Jake discovering our secret relationship by busting in on us having sex. Rhys cupped my cheek. "Relax, sweetheart." His hands went to the waistband on my pajama pants. I don't know how he managed to get them down so fast in the confined space, but the next thing I knew cool air was hitting my thighs. I was just about to protest that once again it wasn't a good idea for us to be screwing in the roost when Rhys's deliciously talented mouth was between my legs, licking and sucking my clit.

Forgetting where I was, I shrieked in pleasure, causing Rhys to jerk his head up and bang it on roost's roof. "Shh," he hissed.

A warm flush of embarrassment filled my cheeks. "I'm sorry. It just feels so good," I whispered.

He grinned. "Normally, I would be all about hearing you, but not right now."

After I mimed zipping my lips, he rolled his eyes, smiled, and dipped his head. With one hand, I raked my fingers through the strands of his hair while I clapped the other over my mouth to keep my moans and whimpers as quiet as I could. By the time his tongue darted inside me, I had covered the back of my hand in bite marks to keep silent. Just when I was about to come, he pulled away.

"Rhys," I murmured, my legs scissoring to get both the friction I needed and to keep him locked in place.

"I want to be inside you when you come," he whispered.

Nodding, I widened my legs for him to ease between them. As the head of his naked cock nudged my entrance, I sucked in a breath. Rhys dipped his head to whisper in my ear. "I haven't been with anyone but you…and I've been tested, and I'm clean. I thought with you on the pill…" When I didn't respond at first, he pulled back to survey me. "Allison, is this okay?"

"Yes, of course it is."

At his harsh thrust, we both groaned a little too loudly. After he stretched and filled me so completely, he remained stock still for a few seconds. I think we were both silently hoping that Jake didn't come barging out of the bedroom after our loud groans. When it appeared as though we were in the clear, Rhys slowly pulled out of me. Just the head of his dick remained before he thrust back in. After doing that several more times, he then found his rhythm. My chest began to rise and fall in time with his movements.

Rhys's warm breath once again hovered over my ear. "Mmm, Allison, you feel so good…so good to be back inside you," he murmured in my ear as he sped up his pace.

Cupping his face in my hands, I rubbed my thumbs over the stubble dusting his jawline. Tilting my chin, I stared into his eyes. At first, pure lust burned in them. Then the longer I held his gaze, I noticed the change in them. Intensity, not just lust. Intensity shone bright in them. For a moment, I imagined they were illustrating all the things that he wanted to say but couldn't…or wouldn't. Wishing for a deeper connection with him caused my chest to tighten in agony. Needing a distraction from my out-of-control emotions, I pulled his mouth down to mine. If I was kissing him, I wouldn't have to look into his eyes anymore—I wouldn't have to see the feelings he had for me that he was unable to share.

But Rhys pulled away from my kiss. His hips slowed their frantic pace of thrusting. Instead, his intense gaze once again held mine. "I love you, Allison," he whispered.

My heart shuddered to a stop, causing a slow ache to burn through my chest. Had he really said the words I'd waited so long to hear? As if he sensed my disbelief, Rhys smiled and brushed his hand over my cheek. Then he dipped his head to speak into my ear. "I love you with all my heart and soul. I'm sorry that I waited so long to say it. I know that crammed into this roost isn't the most romantic place to say it, but I hope you can forgive and believe me."

Tears stung my eyes. I had to fight not to go off the emotional cliff and begin sobbing so loud I would wake up Jake and Abby. Instead, I bit down on my lip until I could taste a metallic rush on my tongue. Rhys had finally told me he loved me. Of course, in later years, I would have to fudge the details a little for anyone else. It just wouldn't be the right story to share with our future children about how their father was buried deep inside me during a middle-of-the-night roost sexathon when he finally found the words I'd been longing to hear.

When he pulled back, Rhys's expression was one of curious concern. "Are you okay?"

Since I didn't dare trust myself to speak without sobbing, I nodded my head. I cupped his face with my hands and then pulled his head down to mine for a deep kiss. Rhys once again began moving inside me. Instead of speeding up the pace, he kept it slow and steady. It meant more to me than anything in the world because he was truly making love to me.

Although it wouldn't have mattered to me if I came or not because of what I was feeling emotionally, Rhys helped matters along by dipping his hand between us to rub my clit. His magic, musical fingers once again worked me to an orgasm. He followed soon after me.

Rhys collapsed against me in a tangle of arms and legs. As his chest rose and fell with harsh breaths, I kissed the top of his head and cheeks. He pulled up to smile at me. "I love you," he said again.

I returned his smile. "You know I love you. I never stopped. I'll love you until the day I die," I whispered.

He brought his lips to mine for a passionate kiss. After he pulled away, he eased out of my body and rolled over.

When I started shifting away from him, Rhys grabbed my arm. "Where are you going?" he whispered.

"Bathroom."

He nodded and lay back against the pillow. Peeling back one side of the curtain, I peered down at Jake and Abby's bedroom. The door was still closed, and everything seemed to be quiet. Thank God the twins had started sleeping through the night a few weeks back. Pulling on the hem of my T-shirt, I padded bare-assed across the aisle. After using the bathroom and getting cleaned up from my exertions, I tiptoed back to my roost.

My heartbeat began thrumming wildly in my chest when I pulled back the curtain to find Rhys still there. He held out the covers so I could slide inside. Once I was tucked by his side, I felt like my heart would explode right out of my chest. After lying there a few moments, I propped my head up to look at him. "Should you go back to your roost?" I finally whispered.

"Are you trying to get rid of me?"

I smiled up at him. "Never."

He grinned. "I thought for a minute you'd had your way with me, and now you didn't need me anymore."

"I'm pretty sure it was you having your way with me."

"Whatever. I didn't take you for a 'wham, bam, thank you ma'am' kinda gal."

"I'm not. I'd love for you to stay the night with me." Thinking about Jake, I asked, "You think it'll be okay?"

"Do you have your phone?" When I nodded, he said, "Just set your alarm about thirty minutes before the twins usually get up. We should be fine."

"Good idea."

"I'm always a man with a plan."

I elbowed him playfully as I fumbled around on the shelf over my head. Once I'd grabbed my phone, I set it for five. The twins usually liked to get up around six, and I didn't want to push it with just a half hour window.

After I put the phone back on the shelf, I snuggled back against Rhys and fell into a deep, contented sleep.

18: ALLISON

As per my usual morning routine on the bus, Jax and Jules's hearty morning cries woke me up. Shifting in my roost, I bumped against something warm and hard. My eyes snapped open. Rhys's body was spooned against mine with one arm snaked around my waist, cupping my breast through my T-shirt. "Shit!" I cried.

He slowly roused next to me. "What's wrong?" he asked, forgetting to whisper.

Elbowing him, I hissed, "Shh!"

When he tensed beside me, I knew he realized we were in deep shit. It was morning, and he hadn't gone back to his roost like he was supposed to. Now Jake and Abby were awake along with the twins.

"What happened to the alarm?" he asked.

"I don't know." I shook my head. "God, we are so screwed."

"Look, I'll just duck into the shower. They'll never know the difference."

"I hope you're right."

"Trust me," he murmured, before bestowing a chaste kiss on my lips.

While I would have loved to have stayed there making out with him longer, I knew he had to get going. When his arm reached up to pull back the curtain, Jake's voice caused Rhys to freeze. "Okay, I'll heat their bottles." Rhys and I exchanged a panicked look before the bedroom door flung open. As Jake's feet padded down the hallway, I sucked in a breath. Just when I thought I was in the clear, Jake's hand tapped on my curtain.

"Allie-bean?"

Oh shit. Oh shit. Oh shit. "Uh, yeah?"

"Your sketch pad is out here on the floor."

"Oops, I must've knocked it out when I was sleeping," I replied.

When Jake started to pull back the curtain, I screeched and blocked his hands. "No, no, I'm not dressed yet!"

"Jeez, I'm sorry. I didn't realize you were so modest."

"Yeah, it's a bad character trait of mine," I replied.

"Want me to leave it on the table for you?"

"Yes, please."

Once he was safely down the hall, I exhaled noisily. "That was a close one," I whispered.

Rhys nodded. Drawing in a deep breath, he eased back the curtain and peeked outside. He then swung his legs out of the roost and hopped out. Just as I was about to sigh with relief, Jake's voice once again scared the hell out of me.

"Dude, what the fuck?" he demanded.

Peeking through the curtain, I got a great view of Rhys's bare ass as he stood outside his roost. Peering around him, I watched as Jake stared at Rhys in horror. "What's the problem?" Rhys asked nonchalantly.

Waving one of the twins' bottles around, Jake replied, "Oh, I don't know. Maybe the fact you're buck ass *naked* in the middle of the hallway?"

Rhys shrugged. "You know I sleep in the buff—I always have. Can I help it if you caught me as I was about to get in the shower?"

"Have you forgotten Allison's on this bus? I don't even want her having to see your naked ass this early in the morning."

"Oh shit, man, I forgot. I guess I've gotten used to letting it all hang out with Eli and Gabe."

Jake grimaced. "Try not to forget again. I don't want Abby having to see you, either."

Sweeping his hands to his naked hips, Rhys asked, "Are you afraid of what might happen if she saw a *real* man naked?"

"Trust me, fucker, she's seen a real man naked. She's had a real one between her legs, too."

"JAKE!" Abby shouted from inside the bedroom. I don't know if it was because of his comment about their sex life or the fact the twins had started up crying again.

"Just get your ass in the shower," Jake mumbled, as he bypassed Rhys to get the bottles to Abby and the twins.

"Aye, aye, captain," Rhys teased before ducking into the bathroom. Once Rhys was in the shower and Jake was back in the bedroom, I finally felt like I could breathe again. Reaching down to the foot of my mattress, I unrolled my wadded pajama pants and slid them on. After I hopped out of my roost, I slid my hair into a high ponytail on my way to the kitchen. Once I got there, I turned on the coffee pot. By the time the water had shut off in the bathroom, I'd put in a pan of frozen biscuits and microwaved a plate full of sausage and bacon.

The bathroom door opened, and Rhys poked his head out. When he saw me, he smiled. "Coast clear?"

"For the moment."

With just a towel wrapped around his waist, Rhys strode over to me. Damn, he looked totally delectable with the water drops glistening on his chest and abs. The towel hung especially low on his hips giving me an eyeful of his cut V and the dusting of hair of his happy trail.

Before I could protest, he pulled me into his arms and brought his lips to mine. I'm sure I had horrible morning breath, but Rhys didn't seem to mind. When he pulled away, he grinned. "I enjoyed last night."

"The secret sex?"

He shook his head. "Sleeping with you."

I smiled. "Oh, I enjoyed that, too, along with the orgasms."

He responded to my sassiness with a low chuckle. The sound of Jules's happy squeal down the hall caused us to break apart. "I should go shower."

"You do that." When I turned to go to the bathroom, Rhys popped my ass playfully, causing me to let loose with a shriek.

The bedroom door flung open. "Allison, are you okay?" Jake asked with Jules on his hip.

"I'm fine."

Jake eyed Rhys and me. "But why did you scream?"

Waving my hand dismissively, I replied, "Oh, I saw a spider, but thankfully, Rhys killed it for me."

Rhys nodded his head to go along with my lie. Jake brows lined with confusion, but before he questioned me any further, he sniffed the air appreciatively. "Do I smell bacon?"

I laughed. Leave it to Jake to have food sidetrack him from potentially busting Rhys and me. "Yeah, I have some biscuits baking, too."

"Oh, you are good to your big brother, aren't you?"

"You act like I just whipped up a feast from scratch. I'd hardly call microwaving breakfast meat impressive."

Slinging an arm across my shoulder, Jake pulled me to his side. "It's still sweet of you to take care of me and Abby so well."

"I'm happy to do it."

Jake bestowed a kiss on my cheek. "Aw, I love you, Allie-bean."

"I love you, too." Always the cutest little attention whore ever, Jules squealed and kicked her legs. "And I love you, Miss Jules." She rewarded me with a giant grin. I then disappeared into the bathroom to grab a quick shower. Under the hot stream of water, muscles I had overworked the night before screamed in agony. With my stomach rumbling, I decided to forgo drying my hair. Instead, I left my wet hair down to air-dry.

When I came out of the bathroom, I found everyone seated at the table. "I hope you saved me some," I said, as I slid into the vacant seat next to Rhys.

Abby grinned. "It was hard with these two and their never ending stomachs."

Under the table, Rhys's hand came to rest on my thigh before gently squeezing. As I took a bite of my bacon, I peeked through the shroud of hair to give him a shy smile. He winked at me before turning back to his plate.

As Jake brought his plate filled to the brim with seconds back to the table, he gave me the once over. "You feelin' all right this morning?" he asked.

Tossing my hair over my shoulder, I nodded. "Sure. Why?"

"You don't look like you slept very well, and I thought I heard you moaning several times, like you were having a nightmare."

Beside me, Rhys spewed out the sip of orange juice he'd just taken before succumbing to a coughing fit. "Are you okay?" I asked, after thumping his back a few times.

"Yeah, peachy," he replied, in a strangled voice.

For some reason, the twins thought Rhys's choking fit was the funniest thing in a long time, and they began cackling in their high chairs. Their laughter was infectious and pretty soon we were all laughing. It was a welcomed distraction from Jake's question and Rhys's reaction.

After Rhys sopped up the orange juice he had spewed over the table, he cleared his throat. "So, uh, you're going to see Micah today, right?" he said, conveniently changing the subject.

A wide grin stretched across Abby's face at the mention of seeing her oldest brother—the one whose place she had taken in Jacob's Ladder. "Yes, he and his wife, Valerie, are coming to see us before the show."

"What's he doing in Portland?" I asked.

"He got assigned as a youth minister at a church there. He's really happy." Cocking her head thoughtfully, she added, "Sometimes I think he misses the music business a little. We've convinced him to play with us tonight."

"That's awesome," I said.

Jake grinned. "You'll be off the hook with the twins today, Allie-Bean. Micah and Valerie haven't gotten to see the twins in person yet."

"Ah, I see." I couldn't help feeling a little giddy at the thought of having most of the day free. That meant more time that I could spend with Rhys. Of course, most of it would have to be in secret. Although Rhys was all for telling Jake about us, I wasn't ready yet. I knew how horrible it was going to be after hearing from Rhys how Jake went off on Eli when he thought he had hurt me. I knew that was a slight drop in the bucket to what he would be feeling about us dating.

Rhys must've shared my excitement of getting to be together because he squeezed my thigh again under the table. A shiver of anticipation ran through me, but considering I was sitting across from Jake and Abby I had to curb it. Now it was just managing to make it to where we could be alone again.

Three hours later, the bus rolled into the parking lot of Rose Quarter—the arena in Portland. Jake hadn't been exaggerating about Micah, Valerie, and the twins. The moment we stepped off the bus, they were waiting to each take a twin into their eager arms. After a lot of hugging and some tears on Abby's part, we were hustled inside to prepare for rehearsals.

With slight disappointment, I watched Rhys and Runaway Train take the stage first to rehearse. I hung back to watch them since I rarely got to see their shows now that I was watching the twins. Just the sight of Rhys playing the bass made me flush. It took me back to his shower in Savannah when he had played me just like his cello. The man had some masterful fingers, for damn sure.

Once Runaway Train finished, Rhys came to join me below the stage. I gave him a beaming smile. "You guys sounded amazing, as always."

"It's just a rehearsal."

Nudging him with my hip, I said, "Don't be bashful. You should be proud of your talents."

"Thanks for loving our crappy rehearsal renditions," Rhys replied, with a teasing grin.

"Ass," I muttered, under my breath.

"Hmm, what I'd like to do what that mouth of yours," he murmured.

As Rhys leaned a little closer to me, two roadies interrupted by hustling past us. Rhys gave a frustrated grunt. "Never a fucking moment alone."

Our attention was drawn to the stage where Jake and Abby were starting up their duet rehearsals. Whenever they were in a city that had a song named after it, they liked to use it during their duet time. With us being in Portland, they were aptly singing Jack White and Loretta Lynn's *Portland, Oregon*.

When Micah joined Jacob's Ladder out onstage, I wondered how Valerie was doing with Jax and Jules. "I should go backstage and check on the twins."

"I'm sure they're fine with Micah and Valerie fawning over them." Rhys gave me a slightly pleading look. "Stay here with me."

With his expression and request, it was a no-brainer what I was going to do. As the strong beat of the guitars started up, I stayed rooted to the spot next to Rhys. Turning my attention to the stage, I watched Jake and

Abby begin to perform. After wagging his brows suggestively, Jake closed the gap between him and Abby in a determined swagger. With a cocky grin, he brought the microphone to his lips. "In a booth in the corner with the lights down low, I was movin' in fast; she was takin' it slow. Uh-huh."

Abby gave Jake a teasing grin while sashaying slightly away from him. I couldn't help smiling at their stage antics. Of course, it just went to show how very much in love they still were. "Well, I looked at him and caught him lookin' at me. I knew right then we were playin' free in Oregon."

The moment after Abby finished her lines I could feel Rhys's white-hot stare burning through me. When I turned my head, his lust-filled eyes narrowed on mine. With a slight jerk of his head that no one else would have noticed, he signaled that he wanted us to be alone. And right then.

With my heartbeat thrumming wildly in my chest, I turned and started out of the auditorium to the dressing rooms. I didn't even have to look back to know that Rhys was right on my heels. Thankfully for us, the hallway was clear. His body pressed up against mine only momentarily before he shoved me inside Runaway Train's dressing suite. As one of his arms snaked around my waist, drawing me flush against him, the other went behind us to lock the door. With our tongues battling each other and our hands running over each other's bodies, I could barely catch my breath.

As he started backing me across the room to either the table or the chair, Rhys pulled his mouth from mine to start kissing a hot trail down my chin. His breath scorched against my neck. "Fuck, Allison. You drive me wild," he mumbled, as I fumbled with the button and zipper on his jeans. "I think I could have you every fucking day and never get enough."

I giggled. "That's good to hear."

Pushing my dress up over my hips, his hand then brushed against the front of my panties. A smirk stretched across his face. "Hmm, already soaked for me?"

"Yes," I panted, as he began working his fingers over my mound.

"I must drive you pretty wild too, huh?"

I grinned. "Oh, yes."

After tugging my panties down my thighs and off my legs, Rhys grabbed me by the waist and hoisted me onto the makeup table. The table-top felt cool under my buttocks as Rhys's fingers teased along my thighs, causing me to shiver. I leaned forward and pushed his jeans and boxers farther down his hips. "I want you inside me. Right now," I ordered.

He chuckled. "Your wish is my command." With one hand, he reached between us and took hold of his erection while his other hand slid around my waist, flattening against my back. He then pulled me closer to the edge of the table where I was rewarded with feeling his dick rub against my slick slit. As his mouth met mine, he continued to tease me with rubbing his erection up and down my clit. The friction began to drive me mad. Tearing my lips away from his, I panted, "Now, Rhys."

He obliged me by thrusting hard into me until he buried himself balls deep inside my walls. I moaned in pleasure, grabbing the strands of hair at the back of his neck and tugging hard. This caused Rhys to hiss as he pulled out to slam back into me. He did that delicious torture several more times, causing me to shriek. "Shh, babe, you gotta keep a lid on it or someone is going to come in here."

As he sped up his pace, my back banged into the mirror. Slick skin slapping together meshed with the sound of the bottles on the table crashing and clanking together. Reaching behind him, I grabbed his ass and pressed him tighter to me. As he sank deeper, Rhys moaned and bit down on my shoulder, causing me to shudder. "Harder, oh fuck me harder, Rhys," I cried, clutching at him.

At that moment, the dressing room door flew open. I screamed before ducking my head into Rhys's chest. His hips froze in mid-thrust. When his eyes met mine, I could see him secretly wondering how the hell someone had gotten in with the door locked.

At the sound of the voice that came from behind Rhys, I shuddered violently. "Oh, fuck, man, I'm sorry," Jake said. Rhys didn't respond. Instead, his chest rose and fell in heavy pants.

Clearing his throat, Jake said, "Look, I hate like hell to interrupt you, but my throat is still giving me hell. I had a roadie unlock the door, so I could get my spray."

Pulling his hips back, Rhys's already deflated erection slipped from my body. As he fumbled for his pants while still concealing my identity, a low chuckle rumbled through Jake's chest. "Don't let me stop you, man. I'll grab this and be out of your hair in no time. I mean, it sure as hell ain't the first time I've caught you banging before."

A chill went through me at Jake's words, and under any other circumstances, I might've jerked away from

Rhys. But I couldn't. I had to rely on him to keep both of us out of trouble. "Whatever," Rhys muttered.

To continue hiding me, Rhys twisted around when Jake appeared at the counter. Just the thought that Jake was close enough to touch me sent the shakes through my body. I heard the shuffling of items on the table before Jake said, "Got it."

"Fabulous. Now will you get the hell out of here?" Rhys growled.

"I'm going, I'm going. My apologies to you and your lady friend. By the looks of it, she's mortified by my presence at the moment."

Rhys didn't reply. Instead, his chest kept rising and falling in harsh, heavy breaths. When I finally dared to peek over Rhys's shoulder, I thankfully saw Jake's retreating form. As he strode across the dressing room, he tossed the bottle of spray up and down in his right hand. After shifting the bottle to his left hand, he reached out for the doorknob. Relief flooded me, and I started to exhale the breath I'd been holding. But then fear gripped me again when Jake's hand froze over the doorknob. A tremor shuddered through his body.

"No. Fuck no," he muttered.

19: ALLISON

Rhys's shoulders tensed beneath my hands. We exchanged a panicked glance. Almost in slow motion, Jake turned around. When I dared to look at him, his expression was a mixture of agony and fury.

"This is NOT fucking happening!" he growled.

Rhys spun around, holding up his hands. "Look, it's not what you think."

Jake's eyes widened. "Not what I think? How the fuck could I possibly misinterpret the situation? I caught you with your fucking pants around your fucking ankles screwing my…" He winced in agony. "My baby sister."

"I'm sorry, Jake. I never meant for you to find out this way," I said, as I slid off the table and straightened my dress. With extreme mortification, I reached to grab my discarded panties off the floor. I didn't dare try to slide them back on—instead, I eased them into the pocket on my dress.

Jake pinched his eyes shut at my actions. Then in a strangled voice he said, "Don't talk to me right now. I can't even bear to hear your voice right now after seeing you being used like a...whore."

I sucked in a pained breath at his harsh words. Rhys took a step toward Jake. "What the fuck? Don't you talk that way about Allison."

"And don't you tell me how to talk to my sister!" Jake bellowed.

"You know what, fuck you, if you're going to act like a moron," Rhys retorted.

Out of nowhere, Jake lunged for Rhys, causing me to scream. The crack of Jake's fist along Rhys's jaw echoed through the room, and I covered my ears to try to block out the noise. Rhys staggered back momentarily. He winced as his hand came up to rub his jaw. "Jake, I don't want to fight you. Please, let's just talk about this," Rhys said diplomatically.

"The time to talk is over, you motherfucking cradle robber. You should've had the fucking decency to talk to me before about this, but no, you had to be a coward and sneak around, screwing my sister behind my back."

"I'm sorry. I truly am. But kicking each other's asses isn't going to make a difference."

Jake narrowed his blue eyes. "No, but I'm pretty damn sure that leaving you broken and bloody will make me feel a fucking lot better!" And then he launched one punch to Rhys's gut and then another to his chin. This time Rhys didn't refuse to fight, and he threw two punches back at Jake, nailing him in the face and chest.

With a frustrated growl, Jake started pummeling Rhys's face and chest. "No, Jake! Stop!" I cried. Grabbing onto his back, I tried pulling Jake away from Rhys. But with his adrenaline pumping, Jake slung me off with such a force I slammed back into the wall and collapsed onto the floor.

"You hurt her!" Rhys bellowed.

I shook my head as I tried catching my breath. "Didn't…mean…to," I tried arguing, but Rhys wouldn't listen. He charged at Jake, sending them both careening back. When Jake's legs hit the edge of the table, he went over, taking Rhys with him in a tangle of arms of legs. The table cracked under the combined weight of both men and then splintered into pieces. Jake and Rhys were momentarily disengaged as they crashed to the floor, but then they started punching and kicking again on the floor amid the rubble of the table.

The dressing room door banged open, almost flying off its hinges. AJ and Brayden stood wide-eyed and open-mouthed at the scene before them. "Please! Stop them!" I begged.

In one fluid moment, they rushed forward. "Stop it, guys!" AJ bellowed, as he reached out to try and grab Rhys off Jake. All he managed to do was be elbowed in the gut by Rhys. "Motherfucker!" AJ shouted, his face crumpled in pain.

After surveying the scuffling, Brayden stalked over to the dressing room table, reached in a drawer, rifled through its contents, and then proceeded to take out a small, locked box. As he worked the combination, I couldn't imagine what might be inside—Mace or a Taser maybe? The truth was crazier than what I had imagined. My eyes widened in horror as he raised a sleek, silver pistol into the air. He fired once, causing me to scream and jump out of my skin.

Thankfully, the pistol fire was enough to stop the fighting. Rhys rolled off Jake onto his back. "Nice work with the gun," AJ mused, as he rubbed his stomach.

"Yeah, the last thing I was about to do was risk breaking my playing hand on these fighting fuckers."

AJ snorted. "Tell me about it. I think Rhys broke one of my ribs."

"Pussy," Rhys muttered, which caused AJ to playfully kick Rhys's ass with his foot.

At that moment, two arena security guards along with two Runaway Train bodyguards burst through the doorway. They glanced around, surmising the situation. "Everything okay in here?" one of the security guards asked, his brows cocked questioningly.

Waving the pistol, Brayden replied, "It's fine. I had to use this to get my bandmates attention. We have a permit for the gun, officers. It's carried around in a locked box with our makeup supplies in case things get dicey, and our bodyguards can't get to us."

The bodyguards nodded their heads in agreement with Brayden's explanation. "No problem. Just wanted to check," the security guard replied. The four of them then left us alone.

Crossing his arms over his chest, Brayden asked, "Now you want to tell us what the hell you guys were fighting about?"

Rhys coughed before spitting a stream of blood onto the carpet. "It's none of your fucking business."

AJ's dark eyes narrowed. "Excuse me? We come in to find our two bandmates, our brothers, in a brawl on the floor, and it's none of our fucking business?"

"He's no brother of mine," Jake snapped. With a grunt, he pulled himself into a sitting position. "You should've let me kill him for what he was doing."

AJ and Brayden exchanged a glance. "What do you mean?" AJ asked.

"I came in here to find him disrespecting my little sister like she was some groupie whore."

I gasped while tears stung my eyes at his hurtful declaration. "It was not like that," Rhys protested.

"You were fucking her in our dressing room up against the makeup mirror!"

I shook my head. "Jake, please, just let us explain. I promise it's about more than sex."

Jake snapped his gaze over to me. "There's nothing to explain. You're packing your bags, and you're on the next flight out of here."

My mouth gaped open in shock. "Excuse me?"

"I will *not* stand by and let you be used by him."

"He's not using me, I swear."

"Yeah right," Jake snapped.

The thought of being sent away from Rhys was almost too much to bear. Stepping forward, I grabbed Jake's arm. "Don't you see? I love him!" I blurted, my body beginning to shake from the sobs rolling through me.

Shock and disbelief sliced itself through the room, momentarily cutting off Jake's argument. AJ and Brayden exchanged a look before cutting their gaze over to Jake. As if they expected my outburst to set him off again, they angled themselves protectively in front of Rhys. Brayden's hand remained curled around the pistol in his hand.

Jake didn't move. He didn't charge for Rhys or act like he wanted to strangle him. He barely blinked as he stared at me.

Through my tears, I watched as Rhys took a tentative step forward. "And I love her with all my heart," he said, in a strangled voice.

My hiccupped cry turned in a laugh. "You're *so* stupid, Jake. Don't you realize I've loved him since I was thirteen years old?"

Jake's dark eyes widened in shock as he stared at me. AJ and Brayden once again stepped up to form a protective arc around Rhys. When Jake's glare turned icy, they should have been standing in front of me. After a few seconds of silence, he finally spoke.

"You know what? I call bullshit. You're just a twenty-year-old kid—you don't know anything about love," he snarled.

My tears dried up with my anger at Jake dismissing my feelings. "How dare you stand there and try to tell me what I feel! I know what love is. And I love *him*!" I said pointing at Rhys. "No matter what you do, you can't stop the way I feel about him."

Before Jake could say anything else, Rhys broke past AJ and Brayden to stand by me. Widening my eyes, I stared at him with disbelief as he took my hand in his. After bringing it to his mouth and tenderly kissing it, he said, "You can't deny us being together. Someday I plan on marrying her."

Wheezing out the breath I'd been holding, I struggled to keep my emotions in check at hearing Rhys voice his intense feelings for me in front of everyone.

Cocking his brows, Jake skeptically questioned, "You really do?"

Rhys smiled and squeezed my hand. "Yeah, I really do."

Just when I thought I couldn't get any happier, Jake crushed me. "Yeah, well, fuck that. Allison, you're still out of here on the next plane."

"But I don't want to go."

Jake held up a hand to silence me before closing his eyes in pain. "Don't you get it? Even when it's all said and done, I can barely look at you right now. Seeing you like that with him..." His eyes popped open, and he shook his head. "You broke my heart."

"I'm sorry, Jake. I'm so sorry you feel that way, but as much as you want to, you can't send me away. I'm a grown woman, and I can make my own decisions."

"Then how's this? You're fired as our nanny and from the internship," he seethed.

I hated myself for showing weakness when tears filled my eyes at his venomous words. "You don't mean that," I protested feebly.

"No, he doesn't," a voice came from the doorway. I swiveled around to see Abby standing with Eli and Gabe. With her arms crossed over her chest, she gave Jake a glare that could curl paint off the wall.

"This is not your concern," he snapped.

She cocked her head at him. "Excuse me? While I may not be able to call the shots when it comes to Runaway Train, I sure as hell get to make the choice of who takes care of *my* children."

"Abby—" Jake growled, his jaw clenching and unclenching.

Stalking across the room, she threw a hand up in front of his face. "Oh, hell no. This is *not* how you are going to handle this situation. I'm going to give you time to cool off and get your wits about you, and then you and Allison or you and Rhys are going to sit down and talk about this like a civilized human being would. I will not allow you to kick your baby sister—a sister you love and adore more than life itself—to the curb just because of something you're not happy about." As Jake's chest rose and fell in angry pants, Abby shocked me by reaching up to cup his cheeks in her hand. "Just for a minute, I want you to think about how my brothers could have reacted to us. I was only a year older than Allison when we got together."

"Your brothers were *not* my bandmates. We didn't have a fucking bond and code that went back for years," Jake hissed, cutting his eyes to Rhys.

Rhys exhaled an agonized sigh. "I'm sorry, man. I really am. I never meant to do anything to hurt you or our friendship," Rhys said. He glanced over at me. "I never expected to fall in love with Allison, and when I did, I tried everything I could not to give in to my feelings." Rhys's expression turned apologetic. "In the process of trying to deny what I felt, I hurt Allison pretty badly. At the end of the day, her happiness—our happiness— mattered more than what you would think or do."

"Yeah, well, how fucking long have you been lying to me?" Jake demanded.

Narrowing his eyes, Rhys replied, "Trust me, I've been lying to myself for much longer. If I was to be truthful, I think I first fell for Allison the night of her Sweet Sixteen when she asked me to kiss her."

Jake's mouth flopped open and close like a fish out of water gasping for air. Then he jerked his hands through his hair. "Since she was sixteen?"

"Well, not exactly—" Rhys started, but then Jake lunged at him. Brayden and AJ barreled forward and kept Jake from trying to hit Rhys again.

"Enough!" Abby shrieked. She then took Jake by the bicep and started dragging him from the room.

"Don't shuffle me out of her like some punk-ass kid!" Jake growled.

"Then stop acting like one!" Abby countered.

Jake glared at her for a moment before his expression softened. "Babe, the only reason I'm letting you treat me this way is because I love you more than life itself."

Abby sighed. "I know you do. But I'm just trying not to let you something you'll regret." When they got to the doorway, she glanced at us over her shoulder. "When he's ready to act human again, I'll come for you." Then the door slammed behind her.

"Motherfucking hell," Rhys muttered, before he sank down on the couch. He buried his head in his hands. I eased down beside him, rubbing his back in wide circles. When I glanced up, AJ and Brayden were staring curiously at us.

"Are you angry at us, too?" I asked. My question caused Rhys to jerk his head up and gaze at his bandmates.

"You really care about what we think?" Brayden asked.

"Of course, I do. You two are like brothers to me, too," I replied.

He gave me a genuine smile. "I'm very happy for you both."

"Really?" Rhys asked, his voice vibrating with doubt.

Brayden nodded. "But I can't say that I condone all the secrecy and sneaking around, and I sure as hell think that you guys could have let Jake know in a better way."

While Rhys chuckled at Brayden's comment, my face burned with mortification. It was bad enough that Jake had caught us having sex, but now Brayden and AJ knew as well. I glanced from Brayden to AJ. "What about you?"

AJ eyed us for a few seconds and then pursed his lips. "I gotta agree with Brayden that you two really know how to fuck things up. But at the same time, I didn't ever think I'd hear Rhys say he loved a girl." AJ grinned. "It did my heart good to hear it. So, I think the two of you as a couple is fucking awesome."

I exchanged a look with Rhys who smiled at me. "Thanks, man. That means the world to me to hear you say that."

"I mean, you couldn't have picked a better girl. Besides all of her wonderful attributes of being beautiful, sweet, and talented, Allison is already loved by all the

Runaway Train women, and you know how important that is," AJ said.

Brayden bobbed his head in agreement. "At the same time, she's already loved by all the Runaway Train men, too."

Tears blurred my vision at his sweet words. "Thank you, Bray. That means a lot to me."

With a wink, Brayden then turned his gaze on Rhys. He wagged his finger at him. "But just know, if you hurt her, you're going to be dealing with me."

"And me," AJ chimed in.

Rhys held up his hands defensively. "Trust me, I know that. But I also know that I'd walk through fire before I'd ever hurt Allison again."

My heart beat wildly at his response, and I couldn't resist leaning over and kissing him. When I pulled away, Rhys exhaled a breath in a long whoosh. "Now if we can just get Jake to be okay with us."

AJ waved his hand dismissively. "You know Jake. He's always got to go ape-shit and show his ass. But he always comes around."

Rhys shook his head. "I dunno. Considering the way he feels about Allison, he might hold a pretty long fucking grudge."

It was at that moment that Abby appeared in the doorway. She crooked her finger at me. I shot off the couch and went sprinting toward her. "Jake thinks he can talk to you now."

"Okay." Nervously, I glanced over my shoulder at Rhys. Part of me didn't want to have to face Jake alone, although I was pretty sure that seeing Rhys would only set him off again.

As we started down the hallway to one of the other dressing rooms, Abby took my hand in hers. "While Jake has promised me he won't do it, should he start that macho asshole bullshit, you just get up and walk away. You don't have to listen to that."

"Um, okay," I repeated. This was all new territory for me. Up until the last thirty minutes, Jake had never spoken to me so harshly.

Abby smiled. "What I mean is, if he starts in on you like before, don't take the abuse. Although he's come a long way in handling his emotions, Jake still doesn't know how to navigate a situation by thinking things through first, rather than reacting. Make him see that you will not listen to anything else hurtful—he's said far too much today as it is. If he can't talk to you tenderly and with brotherly love like he always has, then you won't listen to him."

I nodded. "I think that sounds like a good plan."

When we got to a closed door, Abby pulled me into her arms. Into my ear, she whispered, "He loves you so much, Allison."

I sniffled, fighting the urge to cry again. "I know he does."

She patted my back. "Stay strong and stand your ground."

Bobbing my head in agreement, I then pushed open the door. I knew Jake was expecting me, so there was no need in knocking. Glancing around the room, I saw Jake sitting on the couch with his head in his hands.

"Jake," I murmured softly.

After jerking his head up, I could see he was still so visibly angry. "Sit," he ordered, through clenched teeth. At my hesitation, his expression softened slightly. "Please."

On somewhat shaky legs, I stepped forward and eased down in the chair across from him. He stared down at his hands, taking several long breaths before he spoke. It appeared he was still having trouble keeping his emotions in check, and I'm sure he was trying to weigh his words carefully. But of all the things going through his mind, I never imagined what he finally said.

"I hated you when you were born."

I gasped at the harshness of the words. He glanced up and gave me a remorseful smile. "I couldn't help it. In my eyes, you were the reason my parents got divorced. I mean, my mom and dad were trying to work things out after the affair, but then when your mother found out she was pregnant, everything changed. In just a few months, Dad moved out and into a house in Atlanta." Jake drew in a ragged breath, his hands twisting over and over in his lap. "Being a punk ten-year-old kid, I wouldn't acknowledge your existence. After you were born, I refused to visit my dad. I didn't want to be under the same roof as you—the living, breathing symbol of why my mom cried all the time and my life had been turned upside down."

Tears stung my eyes. Never in my life had I ever doubted Jake's love. And now here he was acknowledging that he had once hated me. Part of me could understand—I mean, I probably would have felt the same way toward someone who had caused my parents' divorce. But at the same time, Jake was the big brother I idolized, and I could never, ever accept he had once felt that way about me.

"What changed your mind?" I finally croaked.

"One day my mother sat me down. She told me that regardless of how I felt about my dad and Nancy, you were an innocent in what had happened, and you didn't deserve my hate. She had never wanted me to be an only child, but she'd barely been able to have me, least of all give me a sibling. She explained that you would need a loving big brother, and that I could benefit from the pure, unselfish love of a little sister."

Although I never got to know Susan that well, there wasn't another woman around with such a loving, giving heart. While she had every reason to hate me, Susan had been worried about me enough to try to bridge the gap between her son and me.

"So I finally agreed to visit Dad for the weekend. Mom bought an outfit and some toys for me to give to you." He shook his head with a wry smile. "The whole drive to Atlanta, while I sat with that damn package on my lap, I fantasized the whole time about rolling the window down and chucking it out onto the interstate."

A nervous giggle escaped my lips at both his sentiment and the expression on his face. "After Mom dropped me off, Dad and Nancy gave me my space. They didn't force you on me to start with. Finally after roaming around the house and playing basketball with AJ, curiosity finally got the best of me. I found you in the living room. You were in this frilly bassinet thingy. When I walked over to you, I had a thousand horrible thoughts running through my mind about what harm I'd like to do to you." At my horrified gasp, Jake grimaced. "I said I was a punk kid, didn't I?"

"Yes. But it's just terribly hard for me to imagine that you would ever think such horrible things."

"Ah, that's the unfailing love you have for your big brother speaking. I was a real bastard then."

"What changed your mind about me?"

With a ragged sigh, Jake jerked a hand through his hair. "You."

I furrowed my brows in confusion. "Me?"

"It all changed the moment I bent over the bassinet to look at you. Even though I probably stared down at you with such hate on my face, do you know what you did?"

"What?" I questioned softly.

Tears shimmered in Jake's dark eyes. "You smiled at me."

Witnessing Jake's emotions caused tears to sting my eyes as well. "I did?"

He bobbed his head before dragging his sleeve across his face. "And then just like that—" he paused to snap his fingers, "any hate or anger I had toward you evaporated. The longer I stood there, the longer you kept smiling and cooing like I was the best thing you had ever lay eyes on. Nancy came in the room and asked me if I wanted to hold you. Never would I have imagined saying yes, but I did—I wanted to feel you in my arms, snuggle you against my chest." With tears streaming down his face, Jake smiled. "And from that day on, I've loved you with all my heart, Allie-bean."

I hiccupped a sob at his words. Fumbling out of the chair, I couldn't seem to get to him fast enough. When I threw my arms around his neck, Jake pulled me down beside him on the couch. "Oh Jake, I love you so much," I murmured, as I hugged him tight.

"I know, baby girl. I know. I love you just as much."

Relief flooded me when Jake's arms came around me. They felt safe and comforting just like they always did. I hoped that meant that he had forgiven me for what he had witnessed earlier. Pulling away, I stared up into his handsome face. "Nothing will ever change my love for you or how much I need you as a big brother. Not even my feelings for Rhys."

Jake's expression darkened at the mention of Rhys. "I just can't believe he betrayed me by going behind my back with you."

Shaking my head, I replied, "He didn't betray you. It takes two, and I'm just as guilty as he is."

"Allison, you're just a kid, but Rhys is a man. He knows better. Just the thought that he seduced you for his own selfish, bullshit reasons makes me want to throttle him again."

"He didn't seduce me." When Jake started to protest, I held up my hand. "Didn't you hear me say that I've been in love with Rhys since I was thirteen years old? Trust me, no one wanted this more or consented more than I did."

Jake's brows creased with confusion. "What are you saying?"

"There's never been and never will be any man in the world for me but Rhys."

"But how?" Jake croaked.

I laughed. "Are you asking me to explain why I love him? Because I don't necessarily think I can. Just like I'm sure it would be hard for you to explain why you fell in love with Abby despite your differences and the fact the world was against you guys."

Jake winced as if he knew what I was saying was true but hated to admit it. "I promise you that Rhys never set out to seduce me into his bed and make me one of his conquests. More than anything, he fought against what he felt for me because he didn't want me to get hurt. But Jake most of all, he didn't want to jeopardize your friendship."

"Really?" Jake asked, his brows rising in surprise.

"Yes. Runaway Train is the only true family he has, and he didn't want to do anything to risk it, even if it meant throwing away his own happiness and mine to keep the peace."

Running his hand through his hair, Jake gave a ragged sigh. "I had no idea."

"No, you've been too much of a stubborn ass to see anything past your own feelings," I replied.

Jake's eyes momentarily bulged. "Hey now."

Cocking my head at him, I gave him a tentative smile. "It's the truth on some level, and you know it."

With a sheepish expression, Jake said, "Yeah, I guess it is. You know me too well, Allie-Bean." He then glanced down at his hands and sighed raggedly. "Hell, I knew Rhys's home life was fucked up, but I had no idea how strongly he needed the band. Not only do I feel terrible about hitting him, but I feel like a huge ass for all of the horrible things I said to him. The truth is he's never been like me in the way he treated women. I shouldn't have called him out for behavior that wasn't really his. It's just hard to think any man would ever be fucking good enough for my baby sister, Allie-Bean."

"All you have to do to make it right is apologize." When Jake gave a frustrated grunt, I brought my hand to his cheek. "Rhys isn't the type of guy to hold a grudge. The most important thing in his life is harmony between those he loves. You can make things right because you love him and because you love me."

Jake brought his gaze to mine. "Fine. I'll fucking apologize, okay?" he growled.

"Can you work on your tone a little before you try?" I teasingly asked. He plastered on a hideous fake smile. "Well, that is truly frightening."

He chuckled. "You're really busting my balls, kiddo."

I grinned. "Just go easy on Rhys, okay?"

Jake nodded. "For you, I will."

"Don't just do it for me. Do it because of your love for him. He's your family."

Rolling his eyes, Jake gripped my waist and then set me on my feet. "Fine, fine. I'll get all mushy and sentimental and do it for our—" he paused to make air quotes, "bromance. How's that?"

"Very good."

Motioning to the door, he said, "Go send him in."

Although I felt like everything was good between us, I was still a little scared to have Jake talk with Rhys. "Alone?"

"Yesss," Jake hissed, as if he couldn't believe I doubted his ability to be civil.

"Okay, okay," I replied, heading for the door. Peeking my head out into the hallway, I saw Rhys pacing back and forth. It warmed my heart to see that he had stayed relatively close in case things went bad. "Rhys?" I called.

His head snapped up, and he whirled around to stare expectantly at me. "Is everything okay?"

"It's fine. Jake's ready to talk to you now."

Rhys's brows shot up. "Really?"

I nodded as he exhaled his breath in one long whoosh. As he strode up to me, he gave a shaky smile. His being nervous would have been quite comical if I hadn't been so apprehensive myself. "So should I be worried about more bodily harm?"

With a laugh, I replied, "No, I think you're okay."

"And we're okay?"

"We're great."

He leaned in and gave me a tender kiss. "I'm glad to hear that."

I was almost too overwhelmed with emotions to respond. I felt like pinching myself to make sure this was really happening. It felt too good to be true. With a gentle nudge, I pointed Rhys in the direction of the doorway. "Go on, face the music, and get it over with."

"Yes, ma'am," he replied, before giving me a mock salute.

After he disappeared inside the room and shut the door behind him, I couldn't help saying a prayer that everything would finally be right between us—and that meant all of us.

20: RHYS

While I tried masking my nerves about Jake in front of Allison, I was still a basket case inside. Sure, I had made my argument and stood my ground, but there was still a pansy-ass part of me that dreaded facing Jake. Somehow I couldn't help being a little apprehensive about actually sitting down with him to talk man to man about what I had done. Throwing back my shoulders, I gave Allison a reassuring smile. Then I took in a deep breath, bit the bullet, and headed inside the room.

When I shut the door, Jake raised his brows at me and then winced in pain. "You look like hell," he mumbled, as he rubbed his forehead.

"Yeah, some crazy fucker punched me," I replied, with a wry smile.

The corners of Jake's lips turned up a little. "Guess we're going to give Darla a run for her money in the makeup chair tonight, huh?"

"Yeah, I think she's going be pretty pissed at us."

"Have a seat," he said, motioning to the couch across from him.

After I eased down onto the sofa, I glanced expectantly at him. "Your right hook is pretty intense," I said, trying to ease the tension that hung heavily in the air.

Jake chuckled as he flexed his fingers. "It's been a long time since I've had to throw a punch. I wasn't sure I still had it in me."

"So glad I could help get you back in the ring."

"Yeah, whatever," Jake replied.

We sat in an uncomfortable silence for what felt like a small eternity. Finally, I bit the bullet and went straight to the heart of the matter. "Look man, I'm really fucking sorry you had to find out about Allison and me the way you did."

Jake cringed. "Yeah, me too."

"We really haven't been dating behind your back, Jake. It was only yesterday that we came together as a couple. I had every intention of coming straight to you and openly discussing my intentions toward Allison, but she wanted to wait. She felt certain of how you would react and wanted a little time for us to enjoy some happiness before shit hit the fan."

Jake gave a small smile. "I see." He then leaned forward, resting his elbows on his knees. "So Allison gave me her side of the story. What do you have to say?"

"Just that I'm sorry."

With his brows shooting up in surprise, Jake asked, "That's it?"

I shrugged. "I don't know what else to say, but that I'm so fucking sorry. Our friendship has always been in the forefront of my mind, so I feel like shit for keeping Allison and me a secret from you. I don't want my love for your sister to fuck with our friendship, man. But sometimes you can't help the path your life takes, and when it comes to Allison, mine derailed in the best damn way possible. She's one hell of an amazing woman, and I can't help but love her with all my heart." When Jake remained uncharacteristically silent, I continued on, "Trust me, I fought like hell not to give in to what I was feeling. But I'm sorry if I'm a selfish bastard for finally deciding that *her* happiness and *my* happiness meant more than how you could have felt about us."

Jake weighed my words. "How am I supposed to believe that you're not going to break her heart?" he questioned. Before I could respond, he continued on. "I mean, you've barely had any long-term relationships since I've known you."

Cocking my head at him, I countered, "Yeah, I'm pretty sure I could have said the same thing to you when you decided to date Abby."

Jake grimaced. "Are you and Allison *ever* going to stop throwing Abby's and my relationship in my face?"

"No, because it's the only thing I can think of to get you to see reason. In so many ways, our relationships are similar. I'm hoping that fact will help you to see that you have nothing to be worried about. I'm going to love Allison as completely as you do Abby. I will honor her and protect her all the days of my life."

"That last bit sounded like wedding vows."

I shrugged. "Maybe it did. We're not planning on running off to Vegas anytime soon. We have a lot to work on in our relationship before we get married. Plus, she's still young. I want her to be able to finish her degree and get established in the fashion world before I tie her down."

"I won't lie that it does make me feel better to hear you say that. But at the same time, there's still worry in the pit of my stomach. I just don't want to think that in a couple of months you're going to get tired of Allison and leave her."

I shook my head furiously. "How could I, Jake? Every day I discover something new about her, and I can't wait to get to spend more time discovering every little quirk she has. None of us can predict what the future holds, but I promise you that I will work my ass off to make her happy."

Jake stared at me for a moment. Then he exhaled noisily. "I guess she could have picked a worse guy to fall in love with," he mused.

"Easy there," I countered, with a smile.

"You know I will have to kill you if you ever hurt her again."

I held my hands up. "I'm willing to take that chance."

Jake shook his head. "You're really fucking sincere about this, aren't you?"

"You act surprised?"

"I guess I expected to hear Allison profess her love for you. It just seems surreal that you're really sitting here before me claiming you love my sister."

"It's the truth. Each and every word of it."

Jake pursed his lips before easing forward on the couch. After he rose to his feet, he threw his hand out. I couldn't help staring at it in surprise. "Then welcome to the family."

"You really mean it, man?"

He gave me a genuine smile. "Yeah, I really meant it. Since we formed the band, you've been my brother. One day in the future, you can be my brother-in-law."

I returned his smile. "Fuck, yes." I rose off the couch. Instead of shaking his hand, I reached over to hug him. "I love you, man," I said.

Jake squeezed me tight. "Love ya, too, bro. Still wanna throttle you good but I love ya."

I laughed. "I'm sorry—really fucking sorry."

"Yeah, well, for now, I think it would be best for you to continue riding on Jacob's Ladder's bus."

Pulling away, I stared at him in shock. "And why the hell would I want to do that?"

He scowled at me. "I just can't hack waking up in the middle of the night and hearing you two going at it, okay?"

Oh, hell no. I could not believe after all that had been said and done, Jake was still acting this way. "You've got to be shitting me? We just got together. How would you have liked it if after you and Abby started dating, her brothers demanded she ride Jacob's Ladder's bus, rather than with Runaway Train?"

Crossing his arms over his chest, Jake replied, "I would have told them to fuck off."

I cocked my brows at him. "Oh really?"

His scowl grew even deeper. "Can't you for one second imagine what it's like for me?"

My mind went to Ellie and what it would be like if things were different with her. I guess Jake had a point because I sure as hell wouldn't want to have to see or hear her getting busy with a dude. At the same time, I wasn't ready to give up my intimate time with Allison. We'd had so few chances to really be together. "Maybe we can find a compromise. Like what if Allison came with me some nights on Jacob's Ladder's bus?"

Although his expression told me that he didn't like the thought one fucking bit, he did manage to bob his head. "Yeah, I guess so."

Since I knew how much it pained him, I replied, "Thanks, Jake."

He jerked his chin to the door. "Think we should go out there and put Allie-Bean out of her misery? I'm sure she's pacing the floor all worried that I'm about to kick your ass again."

"Excuse me? Who said you kicked my ass? I thought we were pretty even," I countered.

"Dream on, McGowan," Jake replied, with a grin.

"You're such a smug motherfucker."

"Damn straight." He then opened the door. After stepping outside, we saw Allison and Abby leaning against the wall across from us. Allison gnawed on her fingernails while Abby wrung her hands. At the sight of us, their brows rose in unison.

"Well?" Allison asked tentatively.

Jake glanced at me before he spoke. "Not that my opinion really matters, but I guess you can date this ugly bastard if he makes you happy."

Allison squealed with happiness before throwing her arms around Jake. "Thank you, Jake. Thank you for accepting us!" She kissed his cheek before pulling away to bound over to me. As I wrapped my arms around her, Jake took Abby into his arms. He spoke softly into her ear, and by her changing expression, I knew he was making things right between them.

After they walked on ahead of us, I kept my arms firmly around Allison. She felt too good to let go of yet. "Oh Rhys, I don't think I could ever be happier than in this moment!" Allison exclaimed, the decibel of her voice almost busting my eardrum.

"Me too," I said, closing my eyes to savor the feeling of holding my love—the woman I wanted to spend the rest of my life with. I never imagined that I would know this feeling. Although having been around my bandmates had shown me that marriages could be good, happy, and wonderfully life-altering, I had always felt embittered by my parents' sham of a relationship. But now that I had the right woman by my side, I no longer felt that way. I was truly and completely changed.

Pressing herself tighter against me, Allison leaned up to whisper in my ear. "I'm all for finishing what we started earlier, if you are?"

As she rubbed her pelvis against mine, I groaned. "Oh God, yes." Just as I brought my lips to hers, a roadie cleared his throat in front of us.

"Uh, sorry to interrupt, but Frank said he needed you guys onstage again."

With an extremely frustrated grunt, I pulled my lips from Allison's. "Be right there," I mumbled.

Instead of looking disappointed, Allison only stared at me with a beaming smile. "I better go check on the twins."

"After the show, I'm not taking no for an answer."

She laughed. "And I don't plan on putting up a fight."

"Hmm, you make me so fucking happy," I replied, before bringing my lips to hers again. Just as we were getting hot and heavy, Jake's voice broke up our happy reunion.

"Get your lips off my sister and get your ass up to the stage!"

Still kissing Allison, I raised one hand and flipped Jake off. "Douchebag," he muttered. Frankly, he could call me all the names he wanted to as long as I had Allison. She was my heart, my soul, and my world, and I was one lucky bastard to have her.

21: ALLISON

Two months later

As the sunlight streamed across my face, I woke slowly to the gentle sway of the bus driving down the interstate. Stretching in the bed, I found myself wrapped in a cocoon of sheets, along with the man I loved. For the past two days, Eli and Gabe had taken pity on Rhys and me and given us the bedroom on their bus. Well, I say pity. I think some money might have been exchanged to ensure our privacy. It was glorious getting to sleep with Rhys without having to worry about anyone barging in or Jake freaking out. Not to mention we had room to move as opposed to being cramped into a roost.

Glancing over my shoulder, I saw Rhys was still sound asleep. Wanting to give him a naughty wakeup call, I shifted in the bed before sliding the sheet down to his knees. While he remained dead to the world, his cock strained with its usual morning blood flow. I took it into my hand and stroked it a few times, bringing it to full mast.

After kissing a slow, wet trail down his chest and abdomen, I slid his hardness into my mouth. Rhys's eyes remained closed, but his brows furrowed as if he was trying to decide whether he was enjoying real life or a dream. I continued to bob up and down on his erection, suctioning the tip and giving special attention to the sensitive head. At Rhys's groan, I felt the slickness between my thighs begin to grow. His eyelids popped open. Rising up on his elbows, he stared down at me in surprise. With my eyes, I conveyed the message that there was nothing else in the world I wanted to be doing than sucking him off. "Oh fuck, Allison. You sure know how to wake a man up," he murmured, a pleased smile curving on his lips.

I continued stroking him with my hands and tongue. With my free hand, I cupped his balls, causing Rhys to groan again. His head fell back against the pillow while he thrust up his hips to fill my mouth even farther with his dick. As I continued to suck and lick his straining erection, Rhys's hands came to my waist. When he started lifting me as if I weighed nothing at all, I stilled my movements, letting him fall free of my mouth. After emitting a gasp of surprise, I let Rhys turn and then slide my lower body across his chest. He eased me up on my knees where my pussy was directly over his face, and we were in a delicious 69 position.

Giving him head had already turned me on so much that there were beads of moisture trickling along my inner thighs. Rhys flattened his tongue against my skin and licked me dry. "You taste so fucking good," he said, his voice vibrating against my core.

I moaned when his tongue began to lick and suck my clit. Once again, I took his erection in my hands and stroked it up and down. When my hungry mouth sucked him inside again, Rhys groaned against my clit. The vibration caused me to shiver. His fingers came to spread me open to give his delicious tongue better access. He plunged deeper and deeper until I was moaning and groaning against his dick. Finally, it grew to be too much, and I pulled away, crying out as I came in hard shudders.

Rhys's hands once again came to my waist. He gently turned me around to where I was facing him, my core rubbing against his dick. I rose up on my knees to straddle him better. Once I was in place, I took his erection in my hand and guided him to my ready entrance. As I slid inch by inch down on him, I whimpered as his fullness filled me. Glancing down at

Rhys, I watched as he closed his eyes and bit his lip. "You feel so fucking good around my dick," he murmured.

"You feel good inside of me," I panted, as I rose off him to slowly ease back down. We both groaned at the sensation. Placing my hands on his chest, I began to raise my hips on and off of him. Each time, he almost slid free of my body only to have me slam back down on him. As I began to ride him, Rhys's hands came up to cup my breasts. His fingers tweaked my pebbled nipples, making them harder and more sensitive. When I met his gaze, I showed him with my eyes what I desperately wanted.

Rising up into a position, he brought his arms around my back—his fingers feathered light touches along my spine causing me to shiver. But he gave me what I wanted more than anything when he dipped his head to bring his warm mouth to my breast, sucking my nipple until I gasped with pleasure. Just when I thought I couldn't stand the pleasure anymore, he slid over to my other breast, making me pant and cry out his name.

Cocking his head at me, he twisted his fingers through the strands of my hair, pulling my face down to where our eyes were on level with each other. "Tell me you love me," he commanded.

I slowed down my frantic pace of riding him. Cupping his face in my hands, I smiled. "I love you, Rhys McGowan. I always have and always will."

His hands feathered down my body to grip my hips. "And I love you, Allison Slater. You and only you."

My heart began beating wildly in my chest at his declaration. No matter how many times I heard him say the words, they never got old. I'd waited too long and fought too hard to ever take them for granted.

Rhys began to push me on and off of him. Our mouths fused together as we sped up the soft and sweet rhythm from before into one that was more frantic. Wrapping my arms tight around his neck, I pressed my breasts flush against his chest. I loved the feeling of this position—the closeness and connection. I could feel Rhys tensing up, and I knew he was just as close as me. Pulling my lips from his, I stared into his eyes as we both went over the edge. Together.

We remained in bed late into the morning. After making a bathroom break, I'd thrown on one of Rhys's T-shirts along with my panties. Rhys, however, remained naked under the sheet. As I lay with my cheek pressed to his chest, I could hear the gentle thump, thump of his heart beating. One of my hands was entwined with his. There was a white elephant in the room that neither one of us seemed to want to mention. It was the last day of the summer tour, and I was supposed to be returning to Savannah tomorrow to start classes on Monday. The weeks and months together seemed to have flown by at warp speed. I wanted nothing more than to slow time down to a standstill so I could savor each and every moment with him.

After an eternity of silence, Rhys cleared his throat. "I have something for you."

I rose up to prop my head on my elbow. "You do?"

He nodded. "I hope it's something to make leaving a little easier." With my curiosity piqued, I reluctantly let him untangle himself from me. I got an appreciate eyeful of his ass when he got out of bed and strode over to his suitcase. It didn't take him long to take out a box.

When he returned to the bed, he slipped under the covers again. "After we got together this summer, I kept thinking that I wanted to give you this to show you how much you mean to me."

The size of the box gave me a little concern. It was most definitely a ring box. As much as I loved and cared for Rhys, I was most definitely not ready for an engagement ring. Not just yet. Not after we had been working on building a relationship and a life together.

With trembling fingers, I tore off the pink ribbon. An odd sense of déjà vu filled me. I was no longer in the bedroom on the bus. Instead, I was transported back to my Sweet Sixteen when Rhys had given me another gift with a pink ribbon. When I cracked open the box, I gasped.

Inside was a ring, but not the one I had feared. It was an oval disc with a magnolia just like the one Ellie had painted years before. Taking it in my hand, I saw that it was on a platinum band with diamonds encircling the magnolia. Even the bud of the magnolia was a yellow princess cut diamond. Tears filled my eyes, blurring the beautiful image before me.

"I didn't think we were quite ready for an engagement ring, and even though they're kind of passé, I liked the idea of a promise ring. I'm promised to you and only you for the rest of my life, Allison." Considering my emotions were bubbling over, I could only nod my head. "I didn't want to get just any ring. I wanted it to have meaning for us." Reaching over, his fingers gripped my chin, tipping my head up so that I met his gaze. "And then it hit me—the magnolia. It's the lasting symbol between us—the very string that tied our hearts together all those years ago."

"Oh, Rhys," I murmured, the tears flowing freely down my cheeks.

"I had Ellie paint another one for me, and then I took it to a jeweler I know who does unique pieces."

"It's…the most beautiful thing I've ever seen," I whispered.

He smiled. "Then it belongs on the most beautiful woman I've ever seen."

Unable to hold myself back any longer, I threw my arms around Rhys's neck, holding him tight. When I pulled back, I feathered kisses all over his face. "I love you. I love you. I love you."

Rhys chuckled. "I love you, too, babe." Taking the box from me, he took out the ring. "Give me your hand."

When I happily obliged, he slid it onto my left hand. "This signifies that you belong to me and only to me."

Cocking my brows at him, I couldn't help but counter, "And what about you? Where's my ring to bind you to me?"

He held up his left hand in front of me and wiggled his fingers for a second. I stared blankly at his palm before my eyes honed in on his ring finger. I gasped.

"Oh. My. God." On the back of his ring finger was my name. Tattooed permanently in black ink. "When did you...how did you?"

Rhys laughed. "Yesterday when you and Abby were off shopping with the twins, I snuck into a tattoo parlor. I thought it made sense to do the inside now. Then when we get married, I'll do the outside."

For the life of me, I couldn't think of what to say. I guess Rhys noticed because he asked, "Don't you like it?"

"I love it," I blurted.

He grinned. "I sure as hell hope so."

I shook my head. "I just can't believe you did that. For me."

"For us," he corrected.

Leaning over, I brought my mouth to his. "I love you, Rhys," I murmured against his lips.

"I love you, too."

After we made out for a few minutes, I pulled away, breathless and flushed. "If we don't stop, I don't think I'll be able to walk today."

Rhys chuckled. "I'm sorry. It's just I can't seem to get enough of you. And I guess it's the thought of your departure tomorrow that makes me fucking starved for every bit of you. I don't want to be deprived of one minute of you."

It was now or never time for me to take the white elephant by the trunk, so to speak. "I have a surprise for you, too," I said.

"You do?" Rhys asked, his lips nuzzling my neck

My stomach turned a few nervous flip-flops as I braced myself to give him the news. "We're not going to be separated after all."

Pulling back, Rhys stared questioningly at me. "What are you talking about?"

Over the last few weeks, I'd kept pretty silent about the plans I'd been making and the avenues I'd been exploring. I didn't want to get Rhys's hopes up before I knew with absolute certainty that things would work out. After exhaling a ragged breath, I said, "I'm not going back to Savannah. I'm going on the road with you."

Several emotions ricocheted through Rhys's eyes before he started furiously shaking his head. "No, I'm not letting you do that."

"Excuse me? Since when do I need your permission?"

"You can't just drop out of college, Allison. Not as hard as you have worked."

"Oh really? I know someone else who did, and last time I checked, he's doing pretty well for himself."

Rhys scowled at me. "My situation was totally different, and I did get my Bachelor's degree in pre-law."

"Actually, I think mine is a little better. I'll actually be working on my degree while doing more apprenticeship."

His brows lined in confusion. "What do you mean?"

"I'm going to take some online classes. At the end of the day, I don't have to have a degree to launch my own clothing line. I need real world experience, and I'll be getting that with your stylist, Renee."

"Do your parents know about this?" When I bobbed my head, Rhys groaned. "Great, just another fucking reason for them to hate me."

"Actually, Mr. Negative, they thought it was a great idea."

"You're shitting me?"

"No, I'm not. I'm still fulfilling the requirements of my degree while getting on-the-job training. In another year or two, I may have to go back to Savannah for a semester to finish up, but I *will* finish. I promise." When Rhys remained silent, my lips turned down in a determined pout. "Don't you want me to stay with you?"

He rolled his dark eyes at me. "Of course, I want you with me. I can't imagine anything better. But at the same time, I don't want you doing anything that you're going to regret later on down the road."

As I ran my fingers through his hair, I shook my head. "I could never regret one single thing about you."

Cocking his head, he asked, "So you're really coming out on tour with me?"

I grinned. "Yep, I am."

"Good. 'Cause I think that's a fucking amazing idea," he replied, with a grin.

"I'm glad to hear you say that." As Rhys pulled me back to lie down again, I peered up at him. "Now that we've got all that settled, I want you to buy me something."

Rhys chuckled. "The ring wasn't enough for you?"

Gazing down at my left hand that glittered with his ring, I sighed with contentment. "It's more than enough." I glanced up to stare pointedly at him. "Actually, what I want from you is more for the both of us."

"Hmm, lingerie and sex toys?"

I smacked his arm. "Smart ass. That is NOT what I was talking about it."

With his dark eyes twinkling with amusement, Rhys asked, "Then what is it?"

"A tour bus of our own."

"So we can have privacy to defile every square inch?" he teased.

"Well, that will certainly be a plus, but I wasn't exactly thinking on a sexual level."

"Besides the privacy, what else would it be good for? A tax write-off?"

Brushing my hand across his cheek, I smiled. "I want to give you a home, Rhys."

His expression momentarily darkened. I could tell from the emotions flickering in his eyes that he was reliving some of the painful aspects of his past. More than anything in the world, I wanted to help him move past all that—to give him a future filled with happy memories. "Let me give you a home, Rhys," I repeated.

"You already have." Covering my heart with his hand, he said, "Right here."

Tears filled my eyes as I leaned over to kiss him. I let all the love I had for him pour out in those kisses. When I finally pulled away, Rhys smiled at me. Brushing his thumb across my cheek, he asked, "You won't go crazy decorating it with frilly pillows and lace shit everywhere, will you?"

With a grin, I teased, "I can't make any promises."

He groaned. "Just don't make it so over the top that my man card gets revoked by the guys."

"I won't. I like your man card, and your manhood, too much to do that."

A devilish look twinkled in his eyes. "You do, huh?"

"Mmm, hmm."

In a flash, Rhys rolled us over to where I was on my back. "I think I know how to solve that problem about you not being able to walk today after too much sex."

"Oh, what's that?" I questioned breathlessly, as he ground his growing erection against my core.

"I'll just have to carry you," he replied with a wink.

"My pervy, yet chivalrous, knight in shining armor. You've been looking out for me since I was just a kid."

Rhys's teasing expression turned serious. "And I'll never stop. Ever."

Deep down, I knew he never would. Although times might get tough and the path might be rough, we would somehow have our happily ever after. Our heartstrings were irrevocably intertwined.

ACKNOWLEDGEMENTS

First and foremost thanks goes to **God** for all of his amazing blessing in my life the past year.

To my readers: I cannot thank you enough for your support and your love of my books. You are the most amazing blessing I have had in this business. Big, big hugs and love from me!

To Cris Hadarly: Words can't express my gratitude for all you do for me. You go above and beyond each and every day to promote my books and make my journey through the book world easier. I couldn't make it in the business without your love, support, and prayers. Your friendship means the world for me, and I cherish the fact that I have someone as caring, compassionate, and loving in my corner. I'm truly blessed.

To Marion Archer—editor and plot magician extraordinaire—I couldn't make it without you. You bring so much to my books and make me a better writer and story-teller. You push me to make my stories the best they could possibly be. But I also need to thank you for your friendship, support, and prayers. You may be an ocean away, but I feel your love right here with me.

To Marilyn Medina: Your "eagle eyes" know no bounds, and I'm so thankful for getting to work with you, as well as your friendship. Golden Girls 4-Ever! Thanks for burning the midnight oil for way too many days to make sure my procrastinating ass had edits!! Thanks for always being there to cheer me up, make me laugh, and give me some naughty inspiration. #bananahammocks

To Kim Bias: I can't thank you enough for talking me down from the ledge as well as making my books the best they can be. Thanks for the plot/blurb sessions and for your wiliness to read in chunks and several times. Thank for making it feel like we're in this together and checking in on my progress both book wise and emotionally!

To Shannon Fuhrman, Tamara Debbaut, Jen Gerchick, Jen Oreto, and Brandi Money: Thank you so much for being my "sluts" and working so hard to promote and support me. I can't tell you how much I appreciate it. Thanks also for your support in the difficult times as well as your prayers. They mean so much!

To my street team, Ashley's Angels, thank you so much for your support of me and my books.

To Raine Miller and RK Lilley: SCOLS 4-EVER! Thanks for your unfailing love and support in all areas personally and professionally. I couldn't ask for better friends and travel partners!

To the ladies of the Hot Ones: Karen Lawson, Amy Lineaweaver, Marion Archer, and Merci Arellano, thank you all for the laughter, the friendship, and the support. You're all amazing!!

ABOUT THE AUTHOR

Katie Ashley is the New York Times, USA Today, and Amazon Best-Selling author of The Proposition. She lives outside of Atlanta, Georgia with her two very spoiled dogs and one outnumbered cat. She has a slight obsession with Pinterest, The Golden Girls, Harry Potter, Shakespeare, Supernatural, Designing Women, and Scooby-Doo.

She spent 11 1/2 years educating the Youth of America aka teaching MS and HS English until she left to write full time in December 2012.

She also writes Young Adult fiction under the name Krista Ashe.

Follow Katie Ashley

Website

Facebook

Twitter

Pinterest

Goodreads

Other Works of Katie Ashley

The Proposition | The Proposal | The Party | The Pairing

Music of the Heart | Beat of the Heart | Music of the Soul

Search Me | Don't Hate the Player…Hate the Game

Nets and Lies | Jules, the Bounty Hunter

The Guardians | Testament

3023

CPSIA information can be obtained at www.ICGtesting.com
Printed in the USA
BVOW04s0218220514

353982BV00015B/47/P

9 781497 394339